gifted

JOHN DANIEL

gifted

a novel

John Daniel

COUNTERPOINT | BERKELEY, CALIFORNIA

William Stafford, "A Story That Could be True," "Bi-Focal," and "The Farm on the Great Plains" from *Ask Me: 100 Essential Poems*. Copyright © 2014 by the Estate of William Stafford. Reprinted with the permission of The Permissions Company, Inc. on behalf of Graywolf Press, Minneapolis, Minnesota, www.graywolfpress.org.

Library of Congress Cataloging-in-Publication Data Is Available.

Cover design by Faceout
Interior design by Neuwirth & Associates

ISBN 978-1-61902-920-0

COUNTERPOINT
2560 Ninth Street, Suite 318
Berkeley, CA 94710
www.counterpointpress.com

Printed in the United States of America
Distributed by Publishers Group West

10 9 8 7 6 5 4 3 2 1

Once again,
with love,
for Marilyn

note to the reader

This work of fiction is set in a mythologized version of the Oregon Coast Range foothill country where I live. Many natural features, and some towns, roads, businesses, and public institutions, have been modified or renamed. Many are outright inventions. A few retain their actual names and identities. No character in the book is modeled even partially on any resident of this region, living or dead, with the exception of myself.

The story takes place in the mid-1990s, a period when passions about old-growth forests ran high in the Northwest in what we have come to call the Timber Wars.

And the lion will lay down by the lamb,

that's what he said,

And the host from the wild will be led by a little child . . .

—Traditional (variant)

prologue

You know, he's young and still unproven
And to himself unspoken,
And his roads like thieves appear,
Lead him to think he's left what's near . . .

—Al Strehli, from "Sally"

It's a good city, Portland, especially its humbler neighborhoods. I like the drab corner taverns here and there east of the river that haven't changed a lot over the years   unpretentious, cool as a cavern in summer, cozy in winter as you look out to the rainy street where the neon sign reflects. A pool table, a jukebox, sometimes a hardwood shuffleboard table and the pleasant click and thump of sliding metal pucks and the banter of the players. No fights. A few good beers on tap, and Hamm's or Miller for the older regulars. I drink moderately now. I nurse a pint or two for a long time, maybe write in my notebook a little—I've been dabbling most of my life—or maybe just sit until I feel like walking again.

My friends, all two of them, ask sometimes why I don't move back to the Coast Range foothills I loved so much as a kid. There's no good answer. Maybe too much happened down there. Maybe the city is comfortable, or comfortable enough. I wandered through my twenties into my thirties, and Portland was the place I kept coming back to. Was I happy? I'm asking the question, so I probably wasn't. There's a version of happiness, though, in the agreeable climate of tavern sociability. "Oh the night life, it ain't no good life," sings Willie Nelson, "but it's *my* life. . . ."

I still own the property down there, and over the years I've visited now and then to see the homeplace and tramp the ten acres. I've gone in February to hear the chorus frogs testify in the little marsh. I've gone in the spring to catch the trillium in bloom, or later the camas and wild iris. I've walked and sat still in the fall woods, hoping the animals might trust me again. The foundation of the old house is there, the crucible of my life, overgrown with blackberry brambles, the yard filled in with Scotch broom that glows lurid yellow in May. On my visits I'd go for coffee at Lily's Lift and stop at the library where my mother used to work, the lumber mill where my father made our living, the Sam and Max Saloon where he used to drink. Sometimes I'd drive the gravel roads west into the Coast Range, looking for the route I'd taken when I was fifteen and decided to walk overland to the Pacific.

I tried to write my story back then, when I was a teenager, but it was too fresh and I was too young. "You're writing with oven mitts on," said Lynn, my friend and lover at the time. "You can't write a good book that way. You can't heal, either." I thrashed around with it for a few months and gave it up. In the year 2000 the two of us moved to Portland, and a couple of years later Lynn left for the East Coast to get an MFA in creative writing and I stayed behind. I started driving long trips through the American West, hiking, fishing, working when I had to, wandering after the person I was supposed to become. I wrote stories and poems, but never for long enough or well enough to call myself a writer.

Then one night in a Portland bar where I liked to watch the Seattle Mariners, I found myself staring across the room, from behind, at a head of hair I thought I knew, straight and black, not quite to the shoulders. The shoulders looked right too. No way, I told myself. A half hour later, coming back from the men's room, looking up to check on the ball game, I half-collided with the black-haired one and it was Lynn. We hugged, hard, the spirit surging through me the way it had when we were in love. I cried, which hadn't happened in years. It felt like a good rainstorm.

Lynn was living in Portland again, a writer now, with a book coming out and a job at Portland Community College. We arranged to meet the next day in Waterfront Park. In sunlight I saw gray strands sparsed into that fine black hair, crinkles around the calm, clear, still utterly bewitching eyes. We walked and talked the whole afternoon, then ate supper in a bar getting good and drunk. I knew the question was coming.

"Have you written your story, Henry?"

"What story."

"Have you tried to write it?"

I drained the rest of my pint and set the glass down with a thump. "Will you help me?"

Lynn looked me in the eye with that cute almost-smile. "If you're serious, I'll help you. But you have to *want* to, Henry. Remember what your mother said? You'll have to be fierce."

"Where does it begin?" I asked.

Lynn gave a full smile now. "Doesn't matter. Pick a scene, any scene that seems to belong. Show what happened, what things looked like, felt like. See where it leads you. Once you're inside the story it'll start shaping itself. If you complete a full draft, your beginning won't be the beginning anymore."

part one

So, the world happens twice—
once what we see it as;
second it legends itself
deep, the way it is.

—William Stafford, from "Bi-Focal"

one

I saw the deer and held still. She stepped slowly toward me, picking her way through the young Douglas firs and big-leaf maples, rounding a big rotted ghost stump from the first woods. I'd been crying, but now the old joy came. She kept her eyes on me and kept coming and stopped not six feet away. I saw the whiskers on her muzzle, the line where her white throat blended into brown, the little bumps or scars along her back and right side, her perfect black hooves. Her long ears tilted, swiveled, tuning in sounds I couldn't hear, and through her moist nose she was inhaling a flowing language that I couldn't read. But I felt the movement of it, the constant open knowing of her quiet mind, like a breeze making ripples and sheens of light on a pond.

Every time was different but the same, always like a silent dream but the dream was true, true as the sky and the gray-barked firs and the ground I stood on. Somehow I didn't smell like danger. I was three the first time it happened, playing in the backyard sandbox when a dark-hooded bird with orangey flanks lit on the cedar-plank siding of the box, two feet from my face, and cocked its head and stared at me through one red eye. I reached, laughing, and the bird took two hops away on the plank. I pulled my hand back and the bird hopped closer again. We were one somehow, we were something warm in the sun and glad. I remember laughing. Then my father pushed open the screen door and called me inside, and the bird flew away. I had few words then, but now I see that encounter as the moment I first felt sorrow, right after the moment I first felt joy.

The bird was a towhee, I would learn, a rufous-sided towhee, but knowing its name and what it looks like, if that's all you know, is like knowing the name "apple" when you've never tasted one.

Now the deer looked away a few seconds, maybe because my attention had looked away. She dipped her head to her right, raised her right rear hoof and scratched the side of her neck with quick little strokes, the way a dog does. I slowly lifted my right hand and scratched my neck. She watched, and my heart soared. I started to ease down on hands and knees, but she turned away. No fear, she just turned and took a few delicate steps, paused to sniff something on the ground, and slowly stepped away through the woods.

When I was eight I told my mother about this thing that sometimes happened with wild animals. We were at the kitchen table that morning, she drinking coffee, me spooning stray Cheerios out of my bowl and hoping to miss the school bus. I thought she might not believe me, but she smiled and said, "I've seen you, Henry. I saw that squirrel climb right up your arm. And I saw you with a deer once, it gave me chills. No wild deer would get that close to me."

"Were you gonna tell me that you saw me?"

She smiled. "Mothers spy on their kids. It's part of loving them."

Saint Francis must have been like me, she said, because birds would come unafraid and light on his shoulders. And over the Cascades where she had grown up, in a little town called Chiloquin, her Klamath Indian friends told stories about elders of their people who'd had powers like that. She called it sharing spirit.

"The Holy Spirit?"

"Holy Spirit, Great Spirit, doesn't matter. Somehow you're open to it. It's a gift, Henry. Be grateful for it."

My mother was wearing a thin silver chain that morning, with a turquoise set in silver. I remember the look of her straight black hair, the curl where it touched her shoulders, and her smile—when it was wide enough you could see that one of her front teeth was a tiny bit crooked.

Now, in the woods, my cheeks felt cool and taut where tears had dried, and suddenly I was crying again. I wasn't ready to go home. Everything at home reminded me of her. I wanted to hike across the Coast Range to the Pacific and watch the waves roll in. I wanted to walk into the summer evening and keep walking until I lifted into the fading light, into the breeze just stirring the treetops. But I knew I would go home, and knowing it made me angry. I took my time, picking up one dead branch after another and swinging it against the nearest tree trunk hard as I could, like a baseball bat, until the branch broke.

* * *

My father was where I had left him, in his big easy chair facing the TV, his bourbon glass half-full. He looked a mess. His dark red hair was tusseled every which way, his eyes weepy, cheeks puffy and blotched. He'd been wearing the same khaki work shirt for days, the same jeans. His socks were rumpled around his ankles. I went for the sofa, steering clear of the easy chair because I didn't want him to hug me against the armrest again and tell me what a fine woman my mother had been, and what a fine boy I was, and how he'd never once imagined it would turn out this way. I hadn't either, but what the hell did it matter what we'd imagined?

My father gave me a scattered look. "Where you been?"

"Messin' around in the woods."

He nodded. "Need somethin' to eat?"

"I'm okay," I said. A rerun was on, *Walker, Texas Ranger.* I lay back on the sofa to watch, and we didn't talk anymore.

We'd been eating only when we felt like it, toaster waffles, tuna sandwiches, meat from the freezer. Neighbors and people from church brought food, too, and we ate it and set the empty pans and bowls out on the entryway.

My mother, toward the end, didn't eat anything but marijuana fudge. I sat with her after school while my dad was still on his shift at the mill. If the nurse was there, I told her to kick back with the TV. My mom slept a lot, but when she was awake she liked me to read things I'd written at school and tell her what had happened that day. I read her poems and chapters out of books she liked. She'd been an English major at Oregon State, and she used to work part-time at Fern Ridge Library in the town of Long Tom. I was a quiet baby, she told me, so she usually took me along, in a basket behind the front desk. I breathed library air before I knew who I was, loved the smell of books before I ever read one. Once I could read—it came early— she brought books home and I'd run through the whole batch, skimming some, liking some, blown away by a few. I'd go with her to the library and help her pick out more. Stories, novels, mythology, books about trees and animals, weather, the stars and the universe, how mountains are born and wear down. And Indians. Together we read all we could find about the Chelamela, the band of Kalapuya Indians that used to live where we lived now, in the shallow winding valley of the Long Tom River.

There was a plastic bottle of pills—the painkillers—and there was the fudge. When she wanted some, I just asked how many of which and brought the dose with a glass of water. She had a hard time swallowing, but a few minutes later she would look more peaceful and usually fell asleep, the sweat shining on her face, strands of black hair wetted down on her forehead and hollowed temples. It scared me how thin she was. I wanted to make her well, wanted her to sit at the breakfast table and laugh and talk again, and so I prayed. I closed my eyes and put my hands together and prayed to God who moved on the face of the waters, to Jesus who raised Lazarus from the dead, and I prayed to the Holy Spirit and Great Spirit both, in case they were different after all. Spirit was the name of God I most believed in, because it wasn't a person giving commands like some kind of dictator. Spirit just was. I felt it with me sometimes when I walked the woods behind our house or up Brother Jim Butte or along Evelyn's Run or the Long Tom, watching the slow current move through my own transparent reflection.

Once, maybe two weeks before she died, I opened my eyes after praying and she was looking at me, wide awake.

"Sweetheart?" she said. "I know what you're praying for, but my body won't bear me anymore. It just won't."

She was smiling as she said it, and I saw a light around her head and shoulders, a clear simple light.

"What happens when you die?" I asked her.

"We can't see from here," she said. "But when you're in your gift with the animals? If there's a chance I can touch you, it might be then. You're praying then too, you know. You don't have to be asking for something."

Three days later she said she'd been dreaming about me. She gripped my arm, her dark eyes glittering. "You're gifted," she said, "you're good, but you'll need to be strong, Henry. You'll need to be *fierce.*"

She squeezed my arm and looked fierce as she said it. Her cheekbones and arm bones showed under her skin, as if they were slowly rising to the surface.

"Like Eagle Boy?" I asked.

When I'd worried about being one of the smallest kids in grade school, she told a story she'd learned from the Klamath and Modoc Indians where she grew up. Eagle Boy was the smallest kid in the village and the last one left to fight Thunder, the one-legged bully with a red cane and a quiver of red arrows.

"He drew fierceness from everything around him," my mother said now. "You won't get it from your father, Henry. Pray to be fierce." She gripped my arm even harder.

Soon she fell asleep. She was speaking less and less. The next afternoon, she woke for a moment while I was at her bedside. She smiled as if she barely could and whispered, "You will always know where I am." Two days later they took her to Eugene. Not to the hospital but the other place near it, the place where people went to die. My father visited every day and took me twice, just long enough both times to see her sleeping. I didn't like how it smelled there, and the puke-green walls, and I didn't like the workers who didn't know my mother, but I knew what she would tell me if she could. The workers were doing their best and weren't getting paid a lot, either.

Two days after I last saw her, my father came home with the news. "She's gone, Henry. I wish she hadn't left us, but your mother's gone."

He hugged me so hard I thought my ribs might pop. Then he sat down in his easy chair and stayed there the rest of the day, working on a bottle of George Dickel. That night, as I listened in bed, he walked the creaky hallway floor back and forth from living room to kitchen, one end of the house to the other. I could hear him trying not to cry but sobbing despite himself, and he was raging, too. He smacked the wall and smacked it again. "*Damn it,* Leenie," he said. Eventually he stumbled out the back door. I heard his pickup start, crunch gravel out to the road, then accelerate on the pavement.

I was angry too. I should have been with her. She should have died at home. I should have been there when she took her last breath and let it go.

A week later, a letter came addressed to me. It was from one of the women who ran the home for the dying. She knew my mother a little, from college and then a book group in Eugene. She wrote to tell me that my mother had been awake on her last day and said that leaving me was her one sorrow. The woman thought I'd want to know that. And later, she said, before my mother fell asleep for the last time, she reached her right hand up as if she was trying to touch something, and her eyes were open and clear and focused on whatever she was seeing.

two

The service for Eileen Durham Fielder was held at our church on June 27th. Her mother was there, from Los Angeles, a sweet woman who looked a lot like her daughter, just heavier and with gray in her hair. She couldn't stop crying and I avoided her as much as I could. Her first husband, my mother's dad, was a heavy-equipment operator who had left the family when my mother was three. She remembered her mother crying about him, but not him. My father's mother also came, from Missouri, a tall woman named Zelda who stood straight and wore her white hair back in a bun and didn't talk much. Her I liked to watch—she seemed dignified, like royalty almost, but not full of herself.

I was glad when the service was over. It shouldn't have been in church, because my mother wasn't a churchgoer. I was hot and half-strangled in my jacket and dorky tie and didn't like everybody talking to me in the same sorrowful voice.

I rode my bike that summer, went fishing a few times with my dad. I was used to reading forty or fifty books in a summer, or more, but that summer I started few and finished none. I tramped the woods and fields, as always, but the animals kept their distance. I was angry, impatient, and they felt it. I wasn't really there. My footsteps weren't all the way to the ground.

Even before my mother died, I never cared much for summer. It was always good to be out of school, of course, and the strawberries and raspberries and blueberries and blackberries were always sweet as they came into season, but summer to me was already the season of dying, when leaves got full-grown and started to dry, to get spots and blights and chomped on by bugs. Even the Doug firs near the roads looked dusty and tired. And that summer, more than most, the late afternoon went orange many days from the high smoke of wildfires in the Coast Range or Cascades, and it seemed that every time I went out on my bike I passed through the stink of a road-killed possum or coon or skunk, a buzzard flapping away as I coasted silently toward the kill. "Why did the possum cross the road?" a kid at middle school once joked. "To show his guts, of course."

All of it was natural—wasn't death as natural as life?—but that didn't mean I had to like it.

* * *

The best and worst thing I did that summer came early, while my mother was still alive.

I'd always been pretty much a loner. My only real friend was Abner Truitt, who had long, curly brown hair and blue eyes and was much more social than me, always had a swirl of girls and guys around him. He could be serious, though. We talked about real things. Abner called me Tracker, because I liked being in the woods and had black hair and skin a shade darker than most kids and was obsessed with the Chelamela to the point where I wanted to be one. My mother said the hair and skin came from her father, who she thought had Filipino blood. Maybe so, but I hoped hard that she was mistaken and somewhere along the line there'd been an Indian or two.

I'd been fascinated ever since my mother helped me get it that the Chelamela had lived for more generations than they could remember right where the roads and towns and homes and clearcuts were now, the gas stations, the stores, the noise of roadways and railroad and the mill. For thousands of years the land had been theirs, and now, in the 1990s, kids came up through the grades not knowing they had ever existed. Their place names were gone. The only Indian I saw growing up was a little pot-bellied guy wearing nothing but a bikini bottom and a string of beads, waving hi with a goofy smile on the sign at Big's Hi-Yu-He-He restaurant in the town of Long Tom, just off Highway 126 to the Oregon coast. The place did a good business. My dad took me once for breakfast, and we had to feel our way through the cigarette smoke to a table. The little Indian decorated the menu, too. We ordered bacon and eggs, and they were fine, and the big-as-a-plate biscuit Big's was known for really was that big, but soggy and about as tasty as wood pulp. My clothes stunk of smoke all that day. My dad always enjoyed Big's—"I kind of like that little Indian," he liked to say—but I never went back. My mom never went there once.

I couldn't do anything about my mother dying, but I decided I could do something about that sign. Abner Truitt didn't care about Indians one way or the other, but he was my friend and knew I was hurting, so in crazy generosity he offered two dozen cherry bombs he'd got on the sly from his very cool cousin in Springfield. We tried to rig the bombs together so they'd go off in one big blast, but gave it up—good thing, might have saved us some fingers and maybe our faces—and we were kind of skeptical anyway that the blast would weaken the metal pole enough to bring down the sign.

So we changed plans. Summer vacation had just started, and I stayed over a night at Abner's house in Long Tom. At midnight we snuck out like Tom Sawyer and Huck Finn in black Ninja suits, with a plastic sack of balloons full of red paint. We lurked behind the restaurant, whispering, on edge, till no headlights were in sight.

"Tracker," Abner whispered, a paint bomb in each hand, "requesting permission." *"Attack,"* I croaked. But the sign was high, the balloons were squishy and hard to throw, and half of them fell back intact or bleeding and exploded on the parking lot and on us. We did score two significant splatters, though.

I blinked and rubbed the paint away from my eyes, grabbed the empty garbage sack, and we ran up Territorial Road, ducking into a handy yard or driveway whenever a pair of headlights approached. We were catching our breath when "Shit!" Abner hissed, pointing back where a porch light lit the sidewalk. We were leaving a trail of red paint.

"Oh hell," I said, and just then in a surge of fear I came in my pants—my first orgasm, which only panicked me more. "This way," I whispered, and peeled off onto a side street, not in the direction of Abner's house. We ran to the skate park, which wasn't lit at night, and slipped behind a big oak.

"Strip down," I whispered. "Shoes too."

"I like these shoes," said Abner.

"Look at 'em, Abs. They're *evidence*."

We stuffed everything into the plastic sack. It was too big for the garbage can, so I just crammed it behind a thick hedge along a concrete retaining wall, and we pattered along the side streets in our underwear to Abner's house. Only one bad moment—somebody's security light popped on as we passed. We barely stifled shrieks of fear and ran faster.

Abner's parents never stirred as we tiptoed in and scrubbed the paint off our hands and faces in the basement utility sink. Safely back in his bedroom, we felt like we'd won a war. I thanked Abner for his loyalty, and he praised my Trackerish presence of mind for disguising our trail. We talked all the way to dawn.

Abner said the sheriff would have the Hi-Yu-He-He staked out, since criminals always return to the scene of the crime, but I biked past it anyway on my way home. A couple of men were out front smoking cigarettes, looking up at the sign and talking. The two dripping red splotches were triumphantly bright and bold. One had covered most of "Big's Hi-" and one had taken out a "He" and dripped onto the little Indian.

Back home—about an hour, by bike—I took a chance and told my mother about the raid. She laughed at first, then scolded me and said never do such a dumb thing again. Then she laughed some more and told me to open her top dresser drawer and take a wild turkey feather. I was glad I'd made her laugh.

That night my father walked by where I was reading a book and asked how I'd gotten red in the hair on top of my head. I froze a moment, but recovered.

"Haven't you noticed, Dad? A lot of kids are coloring their hair now."

"Not like that, I haven't. Looks like paint."

I gave a loud sigh. "Okay," I said. "You don't know enough to understand this, Dad, but it's an Indian ritual. Eagle Boy had the top of his head painted red before going to wrestle Thunder, and that's all I can tell you. The rest of it's a secret."

My father scoffed. "You're too damned old to be playin' Indian, you hear? You need to grow up."

I kept reading my book, and he let me be.

Sometimes I got the feeling as a kid that my dad was jealous of the closeness me and my mom had, as if I had jumped into the world just to plug myself smack dab between them. Not that he didn't love me, because he did and I knew he did, and it wasn't anything in particular he said, but he'd shove a drawer shut, hard, as my mom and I laughed together at the kitchen table, or he'd whistle loud—he was a wonderful whistler—as he took his time sharpening his pocketknife on a little stone, leaning against the counter. He was quick at finding chores for me, too, whenever he thought I was wasting too much time reading or talking about books and Nature with my mother.

I know they argued about me, because when they were drinking they were loud, or he was, and I could hear from my room. Sometimes he'd say she was spoiling me rotten. She'd fire back that I was a gifted child and she wanted me to develop my mind and go to college and *finish* college, unlike either of them. "I don't want him to have to work at the mill, George," she said more than once, and he would blow up and holler, "You want him workin' at the *library*, Leenie? The mill's not good enough for him? Makes you and me and him a pretty nice livin', last I checked." And he'd stride away down the hallway to sulk in the kitchen. Just a few times, I heard something worse—him shaking her, it sounded like, maybe shoving her to the floor, and a couple of times I was pretty sure he smacked her across the face.

Usually the drinking led in a better direction. They had some rollicking good times, playing with each other on the sofa, laughing like kids, and dancing to George Strait or Patsy Cline. I loved to be around in that good weather, both of them happy and me happy because they were. I knew they loved in their bedroom, too, because my room was next door and I heard through the wall when they were too loaded to worry about keeping quiet. It scared me when I was little, but I came to like those animal noises, so fierce and tender at the same time.

Once my mother knew she was dying, she told me some things she thought I should know, things my father probably wouldn't. They'd met at Oregon State in 1975. She was two years younger, a sophomore studying English, and he was taking economics and accounting, just a class or two, because he wanted to go into business some way or another. He'd left southwest Missouri for Oregon because he hankered to have some mountains in his life, new country to hunt and fish. His mother had remarried by then, didn't need him anymore to help run the family farm, and he was glad to get away. His father had died when his son was thirteen—Georgie, as his mother called him, found him under the overturned tractor in a ditch—and things changed after that. Georgie had to plow and disc and plant and harvest, sell the hogs when the time came, fix things when they broke down, and, along with all that and school too, he always had a part-time job, right from the month his father died.

They dated for a year, Eileen Durham and George Fielder, went camping in the mountains and on the coast, visited her birth country over in Klamath County, and lived in a van all one summer on the backroads near Duckworth, pretty close to the house where I would grow up. He pulled green chain at the Siuslaw Pacific mill—the entry-level position, green kids hauling green planks and timbers off a conveyor into stacks. Instead of going back to school when summer ended, they got married and moved to Missouri, all excited to try farming. They didn't have any land to do it in Oregon. They lived in a singlewide on the Fielder farm and grew organic vegetables to sell at the farmers' markets, but she was homesick. The climate was steamy and buggy half the year, sloppy and snowy the other half. In the winter he sold tires in a Sears store and she got on part-time at J.C. Penney. They lived right under his mother's and step-dad's noses, and she didn't know a soul.

They almost had a baby back there, but it died before it was born. My mother never said it, but I think I owe my life to that tiny brother or sister who wasn't quite ready to breathe air. Or maybe it was me, and I got cold feet. My mother was down in the dumps for months, she told me. They'd been two years in Missouri and weren't getting anywhere, so they returned to Oregon. My father got back on the green chain at Siuslaw (*sigh-OOS-law*, if you're wondering), and she worked part-time at Tiffany's Drugstore in Long Tom. They borrowed from his mother and put money down on ten acres and a rickety old house on Stamper Road. The place had sat vacant for a couple of years and sold cheap. My father only meant to work long enough to save up and start his business, but he never figured out what business to start. Then they had a baby that was ready to breathe, my father moved up to driving a loader, and mill jobs in those days paid good wages and benefits. "We just kind of settled into a life together," my mother told me. "You made us a family, Henry."

* * *

The second night after the raid on the Hi-Yu-He-He, my father came home from the mill and one look told me I was in trouble. "Follow me," he said, and led me out the back door and into the detached garage. He turned around and stared me down with his hazel eyes.

"Drove by Big's today, Henry. You lied to my face. You got any more lies?"

I shook my head.

"Was your friend Abner with you?"

I nodded.

"Your idea or his?"

"Mine."

He pointed his index finger at me. "The only reason I'm not turnin' you in, Henry, the only reason, is I don't want the stain on our good name. Your mother's on her deathbed in that house, and you're out vandalizin' private property? What the hell got into you?"

I shrugged and looked at my feet.

He reached for the green willow wand he had ready on the tool bench. "If there's one peep out of you and your mother hears it, I'll make it a lot worse. You got that? Take your shirt off."

I did and assumed the position, leaning forward against the tool bench. He laid the licks on hard. I was crying by the third, whimpering by the fifth, but I kept it down. I was hoping—praying—that he'd stop at ten, and he did.

"Drop your pants. Underwear too."

He gave me two thwacks on the butt with his forehand and two more with his backhand. The last one caught the back of my left thigh and I couldn't stop myself from crying out.

"Sshhh," he said, his hand on my shoulder as I blubbered quietly on the tool bench. "You shush now, Henry. And don't make me do this again, you hear? We're"—he got a catch in his voice—"we're gonna be on our own now. I need you to grow up, see?"

And then he was crying himself, fighting off sobs, not that I cared. After a while he pulled himself together, said "Come in for some supper now," and left the garage.

That night he came into my room and gently smeared some kind of salve on my welts.

* * *

Siuslaw told my father to take as much time off as he needed, but he went back right away after the service. I was glad. Not because he'd whipped me, and not because I hated him, because I never hated him for long. He was just totally wrecked that his Leenie had died. She was the only woman he'd ever been with, she told me, and he loved her with everything he had. Now he didn't know what to do with himself but drink, watch TV, and walk the house like a man with an armload of ruined possessions from his flooded home, a load he wasn't sure he could keep up but was very sure he could never put down.

He was a grader at S.P. by then, one of the highest-paid men, a guy who examines high-quality boards going by on a belt and marks each one with a grease pencil for its best use. It required a man's complete attention and a little more, my father liked to say. He took me with him once in a while, and Wendell Truckner, the man who had hired him twice, told me it usually took several years to make a good grader, but my dad had picked it up quick. "He's got libraries of lumber in his head," Mr. Truckner said. "That belt keeps coming. He's got to see, know, mark, just like that." I had a green streak even then, I thought there was too much logging going on in western Oregon, but I was proud of what my father did, too.

After his shift he didn't stop at the Sam and Max Saloon for beers and shots. He came straight home and hugged me first thing. We ate hamburgers or fried chicken he'd brought from Long Tom, or TV dinners or pot pies from the freezer. We didn't talk a lot, but we never had.

Like always, he drove me to my summer league baseball games. I played all right at second base, handled most of the grounders and pop-ups that came my way, and at second my weak throwing arm was strong enough. The shortstop and I even turned a few double plays. At the plate, though, I stunk. I'd been a pretty good singles hitter, but now I was getting over or under everything I swung at, hitting dribblers or duck-snort pop-ups. The harder I tried the worse it got, until my dad—after watching a game in which I went 0 for 4, struck out twice, and got into two arguments with the umpire— pointed out what should have been obvious. I was over-swinging, trying to crush the ball. My balance was breaking down. I needed to wait on the pitch, lead with my hands and throw the barrel of the bat to the ball. It burned me that he was right. "And Henry," he said, "don't be barkin' at the umpire. He's doin' his job. You do yours."

After a game we usually went to Burger King or Dairy Queen for a drive-through hamburger and milk shake. We sat in the truck and talked about the game, laughing at crazy plays or some kid's batting stance or the potbelly on the other team's coach.

The Seattle Mariners were actually in a pennant race, that summer of smoke and dying, and we watched a lot of games. Along with OPB specials on wildlife or stars and the universe, baseball was all I liked about TV. Most kids at school hated the game because it was so slow, but that's exactly what I loved. Baseball told a clear story, moment by moment. Every pitch was a ball or a strike. Every batted ball was fair or foul, a hit, out, or error. Every runner was out or safe, and if he touched home plate he scored a run. And every game, how-ever long it took, was won or lost and it was over, and the next day there was a box score in the newspaper and usually a new game.

My father would lie back in his easy chair, drinking Budweisers, and I would sit or lie on the carpet next to him but a little behind, so I could watch him sometimes without him knowing. His hairline had backed away from his forehead some but he still had plenty of auburn hair, not yet going gray, kind of shaggy around his ears and close to his collar in back. He had a few freckles, and fine crow-lines curved from the corners of his eyes down over his cheekbones. When he smiled, which had used to be a lot, he could light up a forest at midnight. He was not quite forty years old, my father, six feet tall with a body as hard as green hemlock, and he was a handsome man.

He knew it, too. More than once I had peeked at him in the bathroom running a long black comb through his hair, whistling, just eating himself up in the mirror. People sometimes said he resembled Robert Duvall, the movie star, and my dad didn't mind that at all. Now, though, since my mother had died, his eyes weren't lighting anything. When he didn't have a game or something to distract him, they flicked around like they didn't quite know what they were seeing.

His Budweisers settled him some, and baseball usually cheered him up. Ken Griffey, Jr. and Edgar Martinez were belting the ball, Randy Johnson was mowing batters down. They looked good for the playoffs. About once an inning my father would pass his beer down for me to have a sip, a custom we had. When I was little I'd asked for a taste once when my dad's best friend Jonah Rutledge was over, and they thought it was cute. I was surprised by the beer's bite, the way it jumped right up the back of my nose, but it made me feel grown-up. I learned the hard way, though, that sips were the limit. I snuck a bottle out of the reefer once—that's what my parents called the refrigerator—and to my surprise he noticed it missing. I lied the best I could, which just made the whipping worse. I didn't steal any more beer. Now, watching the Mariners with my dad, I satisfied myself taking gulps disguised as sips when he handed down the can.

three

It's strange, writing about myself at fifteen. He seems like somebody else, that kid, more like a son than like me. Everything I've written is just as I remember it—but what does that mean, exactly? My memory has a lot of holes in it, a lot of hazy happenings. I've been putting talk into my mother's and father's mouths, and my own mouth, and I doubt it's exactly what we said. Lynn, when I asked, said not to worry about it, everyone writing from life faces the same problem because memory isn't a tape recording, it's a hodgepodge of raw material, and it blends with imagination. You're not writing journalism or history, Lynn said. Work with what memory gives you and write your way into the haze, aiming at truth the best you can.

So that's what I'm doing. The sentences come, taking their time. I'm trying to write the truest story I can.

* * *

One evening in July my father barbecued venison from last fall's buck and we had a good meal of it, with baked potatoes, at the picnic table in the backyard. Some of my mother's roses were blooming, white and yellow, and the Swainson's thrushes had arrived from Mexico. Two of them were calling up in the trees, my favorite bird music, a flutelike song that seems to spiral upward into silence.

When we were done eating, my father wiped his mouth with a paper towel and said, "I've asked to switch over to swing shift."

"How come?"

"You didn't get good grades last year, Henry. I don't know if it's them or you to blame, but maybe we can do better at home."

"Home *school*, you mean?"

My father nodded.

"No way," I said. "Mom was sick, Dad. I didn't care about grades."

"You sure didn't. Then you went and pulled that stunt at Big's. I'm worried, Henry. You don't seem to give a damn about anything."

"Dad, you can't just do that. There's a really good tenth-grade English teacher."

My father snorted. "Much as you read, you probably already know what he'd teach. You and me can do it at your pace. What's wrong with that?"

"Well, you're not an English teacher, are you."

That stung him, but I didn't care. It pissed me off, changing my life like that. Not that I would miss school all that much. I tended to hang out by himself, and in groups I almost never talked, just laughed when other people did, and wondered if it was somebody else's feet or underarms that smelled bad or if it was mine.

But my dad was right about my grades, and it wasn't just because of my mom. You could say I was a lazy student. I read what I was supposed to read and did the assignments, mostly, but I didn't have my heart in it—and not all of my head, either. I cheated on tests, when I could. Sitting next to a straight-A student is a pretty good cure for multiple-choice and true-false questions. I'd read a lot and liked writing, so the essays I could handle. All I really wanted to do, if I couldn't be outside, was sit at my desk reading a good book. In PE I might play softball or soccer but sometimes snuck off if I could.

When school was out I'd take the bus if it was raining hard, but I preferred to hike the four miles home through the woods on the old out-of-use logging roads. I took my time, found a lot of ways to walk those miles, and sometimes I met up with a critter. Sharing spirit always settled me, left me easy and happy.

My dad had already ordered some kind of homeschooling kit, with textbooks, and by the time it arrived he was working swing shift and we started school together, every weekday morning after breakfast. We agreed to get going in summer so that I could take some time off in the fall, my favorite season. I was sulky at first. I had to do geometry, and just like algebra I stunk at it. I can still see, clear as daylight, my father pointing his freckled finger at a proof on the little dryboard he'd set up on the kitchen table, smiling on one side of his mouth the way he did when he knew something I didn't. American History was interesting, though—my dad knew that pretty well—and so was English once I talked him into letting me read the advanced books. The ones we couldn't get through Fern Ridge Library he bought for me in Eugene. I loved building my little library. I would read a book and write an essay about it, which my dad would correct for spelling and grammar and thought development and give back for rewriting. He had to consult his guides a lot, and a dictionary, which pleased me no end. To get work out of his student, he had to work too. Did more reading in a month than he'd probably done in five years.

For biology, besides the textbook, he let me traipse around the forest looking for bugs and plants and birds—bones, tracks, scat, feathers—that I didn't already know. I brought specimens home (not birds, of course, except the ones that broke their necks on a window or had been left headless by a great horned owl) and tried to identify them in my field guides or on the computer. I was surprised. Home-schooling was turning out better than I'd expected.

* * *

My father didn't like to run the furnace if he didn't have to, with stove oil so pricey, so as summer turned toward fall he took me to cut firewood for the two woodstoves, one at each end of the house. He'd drop a sound Doug fir or hemlock snag and buck it into rounds with the chainsaw, and I'd carry or roll the rounds to the truck and split them with a maul and wedges. I hefted the split halves into the truck, leaving the heaviest for him. I could do more now than a year or two back, but I was still small for my age and a couple of truckloads wore me out. I'd always been pretty lame about doing chores—I was honest about it with myself, just not honest enough to change—but now, getting in the firewood, it felt good to work hard with my father. I threw myself at it.

Every couple of weeks we took a science field trip to Rampage Creek. My assignment was to notice something new, like the color of the water, whether it was up or down since last time, what kinds of bugs there were, how a windfall limb or tree had changed the flow, or where an undercut bank had slumped. Sometimes I found chert or obsidian chips in those eroded places that might have come from Chelamelas knapping arrowheads. Everything but the stone chips had a bearing on where the rainbow or native cutthroat trout were denned up, which happened to be our chief topic of academic inquiry. The fish weren't big, but a mess of them made a nice breakfast or supper.

One day at the creek, my father was studying upstream somewhere as I conducted research with a silver spinner, casting it to the head of a pool, letting it sink a little, retrieving it slow, twitching the rod tip, and a trout hit—that electric jolt up your arms from something alive and wild and determined to stay that way.

"Whoa!" I said, fingering the spool as the trout stripped off line toward a branchy snag—"Not there, dude!" This was a bigger-than-usual fish, and my spinning gear was ultralight. I got him turned and cranked like a meth-head as he sliced right at me and jumped, flailing to shake the hook—"Nice try!"—then dove to the deepest part of the hole, stripping out line again but slowly giving it back, darting weakly as I gentled him closer, murmuring, "Your eyes . . . are get . . . ting heavy. . . ." I saw glints of him but he saw me, too, and took another run. "Forgot," I muttered, "fish eyes don't close." I worked him back and pretty soon a fine-looking trout was in the shallows at my feet. Holding the rod tip high to keep tension on the line, I reached my left hand down for his mouth, but my sneaker slipped on a mossy stone, the line went slack, the trout summoned one last thrash, the spinner popped off his lip and was still in the air as I dropped the pole and lunged, both hands, the trout's tail slipping through my fingers as I plunged headfirst into the creek.

I sputtered to my feet and used my words. "*DIE, you slimy mother- fucker!*" Plus one appropriate gesture.

Then I heard a small noise behind me and there was my father, totally locked up in laughter.

"You were *watchin'* all that?"

He could only nod, shaking all over, his face squinched and red. I tromped past him toward the road. "If there's a key in the truck, I'm drivin' it home."

My father got there close behind me, with our fishing poles and the pan-sized trout we'd caught.

"Well, Henry," he said on the way home, "your story was lively, but your ending was obscene. Completely unacceptable. And you know what?"—he started to laugh again—"I hate to tell you, but landing a nice fish is a pass/fail deal, and I really do *wish* I could pass you. . . ." He was cramping up again, his ribs shaking, so he reached over and gave me a squeeze on the back of my neck, and in a moment I was laughing too, though not like he was.

"You could've helped," I said.

"You were doin' it just right," he said back. "Bad luck, Henry, that's all it was," and he reached over again and ran his fingers through my wet hair.

Just as I was falling asleep that night, I realized why my dad was homeschooling me. He wanted to spend more time with me.

four

It was sundown, a hot September day beginning to cool, and I was biking home from town the long way. I took the turn from Shepherd Creek Road onto Stamper, and as I sped up on the downslope I saw a rider on a bike a quarter-mile ahead, pedaling fast on the flat by the Long Tom River. I took it as my solemn duty to overtake him, and was getting close when it happened. A rabbit shot out of the brush just ahead of the rider, and right behind the rabbit came a bigger critter, and the bike hit that critter and rider and bike went tumbling ass over teakettle into the ditch.

I raced ahead. The bobcat lay stunned on the gravel shoulder, and just past him the stunned rider was lying in the ditch, gray hair sticking out under his helmet. "You okay?" I asked—or I hope I did, because if he answered I didn't hear it. I was kneeling on the road staring at the cat, who was on his side, his spotted flank rising and falling in quick pants. The pointed ears were fat and tufted with cottony hair. I could feel his spirit, clenched and writhing.

The man sat up and turned to look. "Holy socks," he said. "Is that a mountain lion?"

"It's a bobcat, sir. And I think he's gonna be all right."

We watched the cat stir and get itself up to a sit, still loopy. Tawny in front, with black crossbars. I caught his eyes now—keyhole black pupils on yellow—but there was nothing to connect with. The cat was discombobulated, fierce and hurting and afraid in one big snarl.

I was glad to see the man get to his feet, brushing himself off. He was tall, with a noticeable boiler under his t-shirt and a bleeding right knee. "Anything broke?" I asked.

"Just my pride," he said. I gave him my bandanna to stop the bleeding.

The cat found his feet, took a few wobbly steps, and sat back on his haunches. Then he stood, gave us a glance, and my spirit soared with his as he bounded, once, twice—the backs of his legs black as stove soot—and disappeared in the brambles and Scotch broom. It was like a young prince had just remembered who he was.

The man had a touch of awe in his voice. "How could I not have seen him?"

"'Cause you were watchin' the rabbit, like he was. Does that arm hurt bad?"

The man lifted his right forearm, which was scraped and bloody. "Yikes," he said. "I'm too old to fall off a bike."

"Well," I said, "if it makes you feel any better, sir, you did save a rabbit's life today."

He laughed and reached out his hand, which was big and warm. "My name is Carter Stephens," he said. His eyes were blue, heavy sags beneath. I saw that he'd scraped his right cheek too.

"I'm Henry Fielder."

"Looks like you're going my way, Henry Fielder. Will you ride with me?"

"Don't you think I better, Mr. Stephens? In case you hit another bobcat?"

He had a good smile and a warm laugh.

"So, are there a lot of those bobcats around here?" Carter Stephens asked, raising his voice a little as we pedaled side by side.

"Dusk or dawn, you're likeliest to see 'em, but never up close like that. That was one of the biggest honors of my life."

"I plowed a bicycle into a bobcat," Mr. Stephens went on. "What were the chances?"

"Pretty small," I said. "Unless it had to happen."

"Oh?" said Carter Stephens. "Do you think it had to happen?"

"Sometimes I do. I know it *did* happen. I know it, you know it, the cat knows it. I think that's a mighty truth."

"You're pretty young for a philosopher, Mr. Fielder. What are you reading in school?"

"I don't go to school. I'm homeschooled now."

"Ah. Your mother teaches you?"

I shook my head. "My mother died this summer."

"Oh, I'm so sorry," Mr. Stephens said quickly. He'd heard my voice break and now he held silent, just the thin whir of our tires on pavement. I smelled the warm evening sweetness off the fencerows, where yellowjackets were getting after the blackberries. The big-leaf maples near the road showed a touch of yellow in their top leaves. The ditches were full of Queen Anne's lace, occasionally goldenrod. Up on the flank of Noble Dog Ridge, to the north, the bright re-planted forest almost vibrated gold-green in the last sunlight.

I didn't want Carter Stephens to have to feel sorry for me, so I spoke up.

"Those trees up there? They're fifteen, like me, and they're five or six times my height."

Carter Stephens wasn't impressed. "Little green soldiers at attention. Poor excuse for a forest, don't you think?"

"Well, it's a planted forest. This is timber country, you know."

"I've noticed. Seems a new hillside gets scalped every month."

"Yeah," I said. "I wish they'd take it slower, but the cuts do green up pretty quick. If you like old growth, the Methuselah grove is two valleys over. There was a big protest there last spring."

"There was indeed. I was part of it."

"Whoa. Did you get arrested?"

"Oh no," he laughed. "I haven't been arrested since the 1970s. My wife and I had only just moved here. We went to support the kids who sat in the trees and blocked the road. What did you think of all that, Mr. Fielder?"

"Well, I'm glad those trees are safe. But my father works for Siuslaw Pacific, over in Daugherty. The only mill still goin' around here, so I see it from that side too."

Carter Stephens sighed. "I know mills have closed," he said. "But there used to be thousands of steel workers in Pittsburgh, and now there aren't any. The economy changes. People adjust."

The back of my neck bristled, a sure sign that I was about to commit smartassery. "Yes sir," I said, "some folks in western Oregon are having to move away 'cause they can't make a living anymore where they were born, and their parents and some of their grandparents before 'em. How'd you adjust?"

I was afraid I'd pissed him off, but when I peeked over, Carter Stephens was looking my way with a smile. "Touché," he said. "Do you know what that means?"

"Duh. Means I poked you pretty good with my sword."

Twilight was coming on now, Noble Dog and the ridge to the south gone to shadow. Two bats flicked across the road ahead of us, but Carter Stephens didn't notice.

"Henry," he said, "clearly you read. What kinds of books do you like?"

"All kinds. Novels. True books about animals and Nature. The Indians who used to live here. Anything about the universe that I can understand. World religions, mythology. American history. I've always read a lot more than most kids."

"Do you have favorite writers?"

"Oh sure. Mark Twain, Jack London, Robert Louis Stevenson . . . Carl Sagan, the guy who wrote *Cosmos*. Bernard DeVoto, I'm reading him for American history."

"Do you read poetry?"

"Some. Robert Service, Rudyard Kipling. Robert Frost. Walt Whitman, a little. Oh, and William Stafford, who wrote poems here in Oregon till he died."

"A nice list, Mr. Fielder. I salute you. And now, that gray house coming up on the right is mine."

"Yeah, I know."

"You do?"

"Mr. Stephens," I said, "when you move to the country, people notice. I started seeing you on your porch early in the spring. And your wife. Your little Toyota truck with California plates. I'm a neighborhood spy."

We stopped our bikes at the driveway, Carter Stephens laughing.

"And where's your home?" he asked.

"Two miles on, over Boomer Mountain. Can't see it from the road. By the way, do you wear that t-shirt much?"

"Now and then. Why?"

"Well, nobody'll pay it any mind in Eugene, but out here a Sierra Club shirt might get you some looks."

Mr. Stephens smiled. "I've seen those looks. You know what I saw in Duckworth the other day? A Cream of Spotted Owl Soup t-shirt. It turned my stomach."

"Yeah, I don't like that one either. It's not the owl's fault."

"You know," said Mr. Stephens, "there's another protest coming this fall. The Bureau of Land Management wants to sell timber close around the Methuselah Preserve."

"I didn't know that. You going?"

Carter Stephens nodded. "The preserve is much too small. This time I'll be one of the blockaders."

"They could put you in jail," I said.

He smiled and shrugged, then said he'd enjoyed our conversation and invited me to drop by sometime. "And Henry?" he said. His eyes looked right into mine. "I'm very, very sorry about your mother."

I snuffled a little over Boomer Mountain. From the day my mother died, everybody told me how sorry they were, but they always tacked on that she was in a better place now, or it was God's will, or she'd lived a good life and was so very proud of me. Carter Stephens, who didn't even know me, just said he was sorry, and that was the best thing anybody said.

From the driveway I saw Jonah Rutledge's pickup parked next to my father's in front of the house. I blew a snot-rocket out of each nostril and rubbed my eyes dry.

They were in the living room drinking beers, my father in his easy chair, Jonah sprawled on the sofa. "Henry boy!" said Jonah. "Forever and a day since I've seen you."

"You saw me last Sunday at church, Jonah," I reminded him. Jonah had a bright mood only ninety-seven percent of the time. He was wiry and a lot shorter than George Fielder—I could relate—with a graying mustache and goatee. I'd always thought of him as a curly-headed elf. Jonah had been coming by a lot since my mother died.

"Were *you* at church?" Jonah put on a look. "I must've been so deep in God's pocket I missed you."

"Hmm," I said. "Why didn't he put me in there?"

"Did you open your heart to Him?" said Jonah.

"Did he open his heart to me?" I said back. My father looked like they'd been having a serious talk, so I peeled off down the hall to the kitchen. Jonah and I liked scuffling over religion. He drove a log truck, and with the big timber slow-down on federal lands he'd been hustling harder for work. "Good thing I love to drive," he said. Like my parents, Jonah had never graduated from Oregon State, but he started cello lessons as a kid, showed a rare talent for it, and kept studying and practicing right up through the years. Now he played in a country-folk band and also in church sometimes, spirituals and classical pieces. It was beautiful to hear, the tones as rich and deep as the old varnished wood of the cello itself.

In the kitchen I opened a can of sardines and was doing the cross-word puzzle in the *Register-Guard* when I picked up my mother's name from the muffled drift of their talk. I pulled off my sneakers and slid in my socks up the hallway till I could hear. Jonah was say-ing, "Leenie wouldn't want you dragging around like a sick dog, George."

"Is that right, Doctor. What do you prescribe?"

"Less of this, for starters." Jonah must have lifted his beer. "And *do* something, for Pete's sake. Fix that roof, replace those rafters like you've been meaning to since Adam and Eve. Volunteer, I don't know. And if you have to drink, drink at the Sam and Max, where you might meet a woman."

My father scoffed. "Hasn't been a new woman at the Sam and Max for a hundred years."

"Find an old one then. You know what Ben Franklin said, don't you? 'All cats are gray in the dark.'"

My father was a little ticked. "She's only been dead three months, Jonah."

"Well," Jonah sighed, "if you insist on being a miserable wretch, then *make* something of it. Sing the blues. You used to strum a guitar sometimes."

My father gave a little grunt.

"Look," Jonah said, "there's this too. I've said it before, I'll say it again. You go to God's house now and then, but you haven't given yourself. He'll help you, George, but you do have to ask."

"So you want me to hook up with gray cats in the dark and with Jesus too? How does Jesus feel about that?"

It lifted me to hear my father laugh, Jonah too.

"Jesus knows how you cherished your wife, George. Jesus wants you to build a new life. So would Eileen."

I heard Jonah shift on the sofa, maybe to get up, so I slid quickly to my bedroom and very softly closed the door.

five

One afternoon I cranked up my courage and turned my bike into Carter Stephens' driveway. Cart and Josie, as they liked to be called, gave me coffee and cookies and were friendly as could be. It was just them and their gray tabby Catrick, who Cart claimed had been born in Ireland. They had real paintings and art photographs on their walls, and most of the photos Josie Stephens had taken herself. They were scenes from the California coast and deserts and mountain places, but not like the ones you see on calendars and in doctors' waiting rooms that make Nature look like somebody arranged it and prettied it up. Hers were black and white, which Nature isn't, but they looked true. "Color is candy for the eyes," Josie told me.

Cart was an editor—not the magazine kind, though he'd done that, but a freelancer, someone you send your writing to and he helps you shape it into a book. I asked if he was a writer too, and he said he did write some but hadn't written any books. He and Josie had owned a small bookstore in the San Francisco Bay Area for the last thirty years, and it looked like they'd brought all the books in the store with them to Oregon—shelves and shelves of books, hardbacks mostly, in all the rooms. "This is a *library!*" I just about shouted, and Cart said he'd show me through the collection next time and I could borrow books if I wanted. The walls of his workroom at the back of the house were nothing but books from floor to ceiling, just one window that looked out from his desk through a few sizable Douglas firs into Jimmy Hepworth's pasture.

The Stephenses had sold their California house—nothing fancy, they said—for a lot more than they'd paid for it, and they'd settled in Oregon because their money would go farther here, and they liked Eugene, and they'd been to the Oregon Country Fair before, on the Long Tom River just a few miles from their new home—"Three days of old Berkeley, once a year in the country," Josie called it. The new Berkeley had got to feeling too crowded; they loved the quiet of their new home, having deer around, hearing owls and coyotes at night. Neither one had ever heard a coyote before.

Cart was a little taller than average, Josie maybe six inches shorter. Her hair was brown with gray streaks, and she wore it tied back. Her glasses, which she kept on a chain around her neck, usually perched near the tip of her nose. She was from Massachusetts and had a face full of lines, as if she'd been born smiling and never quit. I couldn't guess at the time—old's just old, to a kid—but it turned out they were in their early sixties. Cart's gray hair, slightly curly, kind of rambled around his head like a dry weed patch the wind never got done rearranging. "I can't grow an Afro," he said, "so I grew a Eur-americano." Around the house he wore baggy sweatpants, slippers, and a t-shirt not tucked in. He had a bit of a gut, all right, and was biking to lose it, on the roads when the weather let him and the rest of the time on an exercise stand in the garage, pedaling, as he liked to say, a million miles to nowhere.

I'd never met people like Cart and Josie or been in a home like theirs. It felt like more than I deserved or had any right to, but they were so friendly and casual they put me at ease. Said they'd like to get to know me. Hoped I would visit often and asked if I could show them some good day hikes in the area and help them identify trees and wildflowers and animals.

Sure, I said, and I started going over there. Twenty years later, I still do. I don't know how I'd have made it if I hadn't met those two.

* * *

Even back then, when I could, I kept hours like an owl. It's my natural habit. I was reading in bed one night, around one or two, when the pickup headlights swam across my window and I heard the gravel popping. My father came in the back and stopped in my doorway.

"Up a little late, aren't you?" he said.

"What's late?"

He went back to the kitchen for a beer, popped the top, and came to my doorway again, leaning his shoulder against the frame.

"We had a run of logs full of nails," he said. "The saws were breakin' teeth all shift. Siuslaw lost more money than they made tonight."

He'd stayed late drinking shots and beers at the Sam and Max, I could smell it on him. He didn't usually work Saturday nights; he was filling in for somebody sick.

"Just random nails, or were they spiked?"

"Just nails, looked like," he said. "Some outfits won't buy timber anymore from anywhere near an old house. Always full of metal."

I was trying to read my book—*The Catcher in the Rye*, lent by Cart and Josie—but he sighed and kept talking.

"No tellin' with the environuts, though. I hear they're spikin' trees with super-hard ceramics now, to beat the metal detector."

"They're fighting for what they believe in, Dad."

"Puttin' loggers and millworkers at risk? They believe in that?"

"I know," I said, "you told me about the guy in the redwood mill. . . ."

"Mm-hmm. Got his throat cut half an inch from the jugular when the band saw broke."

"It's just the Earth Firsters who spike trees and sabotage equipment, Dad. And even they aren't *trying* to hurt people."

He snorted. "I heard about those newcomers you met. They move up here and first thing they're helpin' that bunch of hippies at the protest. Been here five minutes, and they know how to manage the woods better than the people who've lived here forever."

I closed my book. "You're not from here either, you know."

"Well, Mr. Oregon Native," he said, his lopsided smile turning a little sneery. "Aren't you special. Tell you what, I'm a damn sight more of an Oregonian than those two. Or any of 'em, pourin' up I-5 in motorcades."

"Whatever, Dad. I'm gonna sleep now."

"Tell you somethin' else, too. If those folks are puttin' wacko ideas in your head, you're not gonna see 'em anymore, you hear? I won't have it, Henry."

"I fill my own head, Dad, and I can't help it if you fill yours with ignorant trash. Would you go to bed?"

"When I'm ready," he said.

I turned off my bedside lamp and pulled the sheet over my head. After a while he sighed. "Your mother was soft on you, Henry, God bless 'er. You and your Indians, your animal friends. . . ."

A long pause.

"Yep. A little soft, Leenie. Half-spoiled this boy."

After a while he said, "Church tomorrow" and walked slowly back to the kitchen.

* * *

As always, George Fielder cut a handsome figure in church. Looked neat and proper in his slacks and blue dress shirt, stood and sat at the right times, sang along or at least moved his lips to the hymns. Didn't seem hung over at all. He was taking better care of himself—he'd had his hair trimmed and was using some kind of gel.

We went to church every two weeks, on average, and I still don't know why he went at all. He never would talk about God and religion at home, and I wanted to. He'd grown up going to church in Missouri—Presbyterian—so maybe now he did it for me. Might have been an insurance policy, too, just in case there really was something to the heaven and hell thing. When I was little I worried about that, but over the years, Pastor Rogers pretty much cured me of it. He read well from the Bible, and sometimes he preached on interesting things, but wherever he went with his sermon, he'd just about always work it around to saying there was only one way to salvation. If you don't have Jesus, you don't have shit. It never made sense to me that one religion could be totally right and all the others totally wrong.

Singing was the best part. Not that I could sing well, but as the organ powered us on, there were moments when I felt just about ready to rise off the floor. It's a wonderful thing when regular people, on key or off, put their voices together in a spirit of praise and wonder or just happy willingness to be there and sing. I had read around a little in the Bible and loved the language, words like *name, spirit, love, father, son, faith, works, light, flesh, word.* There was so much stirring in those words, like the woods at daybreak or a deep pool in the river where you see little swirls rising. One of the first things I learned from Cart Stephens was that the King James Bible was written by English poets just after the time of William Shakespeare, so maybe that was why I liked the language, why so many people did. It was written by great poets. In a Christian bookstore once, I opened one of those newer Bibles, and it read more like a newspaper than a poem.

My mother never went to church with us. She didn't talk much about it, but I got the idea that she was some kind of hippie in the 1970s before she married my dad—ate magic mushrooms, hung out with the Indians, kind of created her own religion. That's what the Indians did, she taught me—grew their own worship right out of the American land, until Europeans barged in with their book about a man and his father-God in some desert halfway to kingdom come.

Our truth is now your truth, they announced. Forced people off their homelands, shipped their kids to boarding schools where they weren't allowed to speak their own languages or dress in their ways or practice their beliefs. I loved books, but I vowed to myself when I was twelve that I would never believe in any book *that* way.

At coffee fellowship that Sunday my father talked with the women, and it lit him up. He was still getting sorrys and long sad looks, and it looked to me like they wanted to give him more than looks. He hadn't gone out with any women—hadn't brought any home, anyway. Maybe he wasn't ready. Maybe he wouldn't ever be ready. Or maybe he knew that I wasn't ready, and was holding back on my account. There's so much about him I'll never know.

As we were about to go, Cloudy Rains snuck up behind me and whispered into my left ear, "Don't you leave here, Henry Fielder, without giving me the time of day!"

Cloudy, the first woman ever elected mayor of Long Tom, was short and pretty and shook every part of her stocky body when she laughed, which was often. Most people come to church because they believe. Cloudy started because she liked the people, and came to believe along the way.

I squirmed in her hug-from-behind, but I liked it, too. Cloudy turned me around, put her hands on my shoulders, and said, "Henry, you are one handsome young man."

My face burned.

"George?" she called over to my father. "The girls are coming."

* * *

"Those people you like," my father said a few days later at the breakfast table. "I drove by their place last night, and you should've seen the party. Old farts spillin' out the door, rock 'n' roll loud as bedlam. They had one of those strobe lights, you know? I can only imagine the drugs. . . ."

"Oh right, Dad. They were probably drinkin' booze, like you. And smokin' some weed, maybe."

He gave me a sharp look. "Whatta you know about pot?"

I smiled at him. "I know you and Mom smoked it sometimes."

"We're adults, you're not. Are those old hippies givin' it to you?"

I kept my smile. "What if they are?"

"Don't mess with me, boy. If you're smokin' pot with them, I'm gonna ground you and report them to the sheriff."

"Cool your jets, Dad. Cart and Josie are really nice people. I'd introduce you if I thought you'd give 'em a chance."

He shook his head. "It was one in the mornin' and you wouldn't believe the racket they were makin'. . . ."

"So what? They don't have near neighbors. Didn't you hear Len Peppers's stereo the other night? Must've had his windows open. George Jones for *hours*. Made me hate a great song, 'He Stopped Loving Her Today.'"

Len was a retired logger from the glory days of old-growth timber and an official community character who lived a half mile up Boomer Mountain. I'd grown up with country music—my dad usually had it on, at home and in the truck—but Len had taught me who the great ones were, who had influenced who, who was the real deal and not just some poser in rhinestones.

"Well, Len *has* to turn it up, 'cause he's hard of hearing," my father said. "I heard he might be sick with somethin', by the way."

"Uh-oh," I said. "I better go see him."

* * *

Later that week my father had errands to do in Eugene, so I had the day off from homeschool. I decided I needed to see my oldest friends.

The morning was clear with just a hint of sharpness in the air. The day before, mowing the yard, I'd seen at the edge of the woods a perfect orb-weaver spider web, a sure sign of fall. The promise of life after summer!

Felt good to be on my bike, air rushing my face. I pedaled hard up Boomer Mountain, working up a sweat, and turned into Len Peppers's short driveway. His truck wasn't there, but I knocked twice just to be sure. A good sign, I figured. If he was well enough to drive, he couldn't be too sick.

I turned north on the gravel BLM road, down into the leafy bottom and then up and over Noble Dog Ridge. I stashed my bike in a planted forest and struck out overland, skirting upslope above a sheep pasture and a small vineyard. I crossed Rampage Creek the usual way, on a fallen buckskin snag, thrashed through an overgrown clearcut on the next little ridge and down through young and middle-aged timber, the trees getting bigger as I went. I saw something new—colored BLM flagging on some of the trees, marking the timber sale Cart Stephens had mentioned. "A forest is a continuum," he'd said—a new word, for me. "You can't simply draw a little square on a map and say, 'Inside this square is a forest we will protect from all harm. Outside this square we will clearcut and replant in a thirty-to-forty-year harvest cycle.'"

My father had been half right. Cart and Josie weren't giving me weed—though my keen public-schooled nose told me they smoked it—but they were broadening my outlook on logging and wilderness. "You have to see it from above to appreciate just how hard this country has been logged," Cart said, and he showed me some aerial photos. The whole central Coast Range was shot through with clearcuts and squiggly logging roads. It looked like a patchwork quilt, I decided, but Grandma'd had a bad day cutting the patches and must have lost her pattern and then got crazy with the sewing machine, running squiggly lines all over the quilt just for the hell of it.

"It's been riddled," Cart said. "And what's the answer to the riddle?" He stared me down with his baggy blue eyes. "Resistance, Henry. Resistance."

It was called the Karen Creek timber sale. Nobody knew when the logging would begin, maybe not till spring, maybe this fall if the weather stayed fair. The people planning the blockade, the Methuselah Forest Collective, weren't taking any chances— they were getting ready, Cart with them. Josie would be on the support team.

I kept on down through the continuum of trees to the bottom where the Methuselahs had been growing in their huge shaggy quiet for centuries.

My mother first took me when I was a month old, and we went there, sometimes my father too, countless times as I grew up. Douglas firs and hemlocks, a few western red cedars, the last sizable remnant in the inland Coast Range of the woods that French trappers and American missionaries and Oregon Trail pioneers knew, and the Kalapuyas for all those seasons going back deep into time. One family had owned the property from Territorial days, farmers down in the valley who could have sold the timber but didn't. Each of their generations wanted their kids to grow up knowing the trees. Everybody else wanted it for their kids too, so the family did a generous thing. They swapped with the government for some other forest lands, and the Bureau of Land Management set aside 36 acres around the biggest trees as an Area of Critical Environmental Concern, which is BLM talk for "no logging for as long as we say so." The demonstration that Cart and Josie had supported was for a bigger set-aside; the timber industry had wanted it smaller. Nobody came out very happy.

I did my usual—walked a little, sat a little, touched the thick, crusted bark. In an old-growth forest there's more light than most people expect, a glareless light filtering through the crowns of the big trees and the understory of big-leaf maples and wild hazelnuts. A winter wren was flitting around among the sword ferns and salal, the fallen trunks and limbs that the mossy ground was claiming for its own. I could see up into the crowns of a few trees—two hundred feet tall, some of them. Each tree showed its history, written in dead stubs and snapped-off green limbs among the living limbs still whole. Lightning had scarred some trees, lightning or storm wind had blasted the tops off a few. The lower trunks, down at my level, showed old char from ground fires that had killed brush and smaller trees, the great ones inside their thick bark not even feeling the flames.

In the library once, I'd found a book of photographs of old people from around the world. Their faces were amazing—*landscapes* of wrinkles, creases, sags, blotches, scars, their eyes hollowed under their brows, sometimes dark, sometimes with a faraway light like the sky. Those faces gave me the same urge to kneel, to bow, that the Methuselahs did. Trees, humans, they had never stopped becoming themselves. The people in the photographs were probably dead now, in the ground, and most of the Methuselahs already tilted a little, starting into their fall, and the fallen ones were there too, melting into ground, mossed-over, growing riots of fungus and seedling trees.

My mother never got the chance to live herself old. Where was she now? *What* was she now? I thought I'd felt her near a few times, just over my shoulder, or in the treetops stirring with a wind I heard but couldn't feel. But just that. Not her black hair, her crooked tooth, the smell of her when we hugged. "How could you just *go*?" I called out loud, then dropped to hands and knees and closed my eyes and stuck my nose into a hump of moss and rot that used to be a tree, breathing it in. There's no richer smell, nothing in Nature I love more, and a kind of vision opened inside me. I felt green life in all its forms rising everywhere out of the ground, leaves and spears and fronds and crowns slowly unfolding through the ages, and in all that green life, mind was opening too, the rising life *was* mind, there was a knowing in seeds and needle buds and blossoms, in the land itself taking form as mountain ranges and rivers, great deserts and deep rocky gorges and windy prairies, whole landscapes opening like leaves or butterfly wings or a baby uncurling from the womb, opening like a waking soul. And in all of it, formed in the great pattern and almost obscured by it, a human face was emerging—not man or woman, not young or old, the color of all colors, the face behind all faces.

I came out of it hearing a car whining and lurching up the pot-holed road from the east, and I was on my way upslope out of the grove by the time I heard doors open and close, the drift of human voices—a pleasant sound, but the problem with making a place a park is that everybody wants to go there. Decent people, mostly, with as much right to be there as I had. The Methuselahs don't judge. But still, should there be any road at all to a place so mighty? To be worthy of that majesty, we should walk. Any who can't walk could be carried on the backs of their friends.

* * *

When I got home, after dark, my father was in the kitchen. He tossed a worn plastic zipper bag onto the table. It looked familiar.

"Look what I found," he said.

"Who said you could search my room?"

"You lied again, Henry. You said those people weren't givin' you—"

"I got it from a friend, Dad. And gosh, it's almost enough to get high on."

"No sass, Henry. You're grounded. Lessons in the morning, chores in the afternoon. You're not to leave this property."

"Why are you such a *dick?*" I yelled. "You drink like a fish, and I can't have a bud or two of weed?"

He came around the table and slapped my cheek with the back of his hand. "This isn't a democracy, Henry. You're fifteen years old, you're headed down the wrong track, and I'm doin' somethin' about it."

I pulled away toward the hall.

"There's a plate of dinner for you," he called after me, but I slammed my bedroom door on his voice.

I flopped down on my bed but was too worked up to just lie there. I got up and sharpened my pocketknife on the small whetstone I kept in my desk drawer. I took off my shirt and looked at the underside of my left forearm. I drew the point of the blade from the wrist three inches up the arm, just hard enough to break skin. The sting of the cut felt good. I drew another line, parallel. I stared at the cuts, the blood welling up and beginning to dribble. I felt calmer. I watched the dribbles stop and begin to harden.

When he'd gone to bed I went to the kitchen and got the plate of pork chops and mashed potatoes from the oven, took it to my room and ate at my desk, cutting the meat with my pocketknife, taking dips of potatoes with my fingers.

six

I was thirsty for the rains.

Once they came and set in—October, usually, back then—the weather would tend gray and wet all around the curve of winter into spring, with a few sun spells along the way that hurt everybody's eyes. Then rain and sun would come all mixed up as Indian plum and swamp lantern and dogwoods came into bloom, and camas and wild iris, right into the daisies and oceanspray of early summer. July and August are a hazy blue kingdom, maybe sixteen raindrops between the two, and by the middle of August only Queen Anne's lace is blooming along the roadways. The flat fronds of bracken, in open areas like clearcuts, dry into dead brown ghosts that break when you wade through them. In the forest, the ground plants—sword fern, salal, Oregon grape, dewberries—don't have deep roots, but they grow in the shade of the trees and they practice patience. They know how to keep through an Oregon summer.

On a gray afternoon at the end of September—my father had left early for work—I hiked around the south side of Brother Jim Butte. The cloud cover was darkening, a promising smell was in the air, so I sat down in oak and pine woods at the edge of a meadow and waited. There was a vine maple a little ways out in the meadow, and after a while one of its leaves shook. Then another, another, and pretty soon sparse rain was pattering the vine maple and worn-out bracken and calling a lively dance in the dry meadow grasses. I heard it in the tree crowns above me, and before too long the first drip-downs were stirring the understory leaves around me and tapping my shoulders and head. The land was waking. The greens got greener, everything a-glisten, the rain came faster and ran together in a gentle liquidy *yesssss*, and I knew from the good smell rising from the moistening ground that once again I'd found my way back home.

I felt my mother near and remembered her delight when we learned that the Chelamela, like the other bands of Kalapuyas up and down the Willamette Valley, considered the new moon of late August or early September the beginning of their year. It marked the reset, the time of renewal. They finished their harvests of camas bulbs, berries, acorns, and tarweed, burned the prairies so that grass and edible plants and deer would come back strong in the spring, and combed the burn for their last feast of fire-toasted grasshoppers, their delicacy. They started fitting out their lodges down on the lower Long Tom and laying in the stores of summer, dried, smoked, pounded, pressed into cakes, and packed away in baskets.

I tried to imagine their dim winter spaces, two or three families in each lodge, rain on the roof and stories in the air like smoke from the fire. Stories were their books, my mother used to say. They carried their library inside, no need to check anything out or return it. The stories reminded them of who they were, and how the land with its life had come to be ordered the way it was, and how they had learned to live in it. Their lives weren't long, they had evils and misfortunes—some held slaves, some were slaves—but they knew the land, they honored it, they gave it names we will never know, and they didn't overrun it. They knew how to keep in this country.

* * *

After the great pot bust I did lessons with my father like before, just more sullen, and in the afternoon he put me to mowing or pruning or pulling weeds in the garden beds or splitting firewood with a maul and wedge. Sweeping, cleaning the bathroom, straightening up the kitchen. He got decent slave labor out of me, but whatever I was grunting at, any weekday around three o'clock, as soon as I heard his foot hit the gas on Stamper Road, I was free. He wouldn't be home till after midnight—way after, nights he stayed out drinking—and I was my own boy. I could play Jimmie Dale Gilmore or Emmy Lou Harris as loud as I liked, I could read in silence, take a ramble outside, watch the Mariners, or check out the latest magazine or romance book my father kept by his bed, which I responded to just like he did, probably. Didn't take long. I could even take a little ride in my mother's white Dodge, which my father kept in the garage because he couldn't bear to see it but couldn't bear to part with it, either. I'd lifted the keys from her purse just long enough to get a copy made at Hamilton & Sons, and I knew well enough how to drive. My dad had taught me, on the back roads when we went fishing or hunting. I had my learner's permit, which made me semi-legal. I didn't drive the car much, though, because I knew the price in pain would be steep if I got caught.

Once in a while I called Abner and biked into Long Tom to mess around with him. We'd breathe a hit or two of smoke—he usually had good bud—and take his BMX bike to the skate park and try tricks on it, or hang out in his room or play foosball in the basement, drinking apricot brandy or whatever he had on hand in his private stash. Abner's cousin kept him well supplied. If his parents invited me to eat dinner with them, I did. They didn't know I was grounded; I don't think they and my father had ever exchanged twelve words. I always got home by midnight just in case.

Abner would tell me what was going on in school, the girls he liked, his latest music fixations. "Tracker," he asked once, "don't you get lonely out there? I miss you, man."

"Nah," I said, "you know I like bein' on my own." Saying it, though, I did feel lonely, especially for him.

Abner shook his head slowly. "Get on email, dude, and at least we could do that."

We'd had a computer—a used one bought from a chiropractor that never seemed to work quite right—for less than a year and got online through dial-up. My mom used it—she knew how from the library— but my dad had never seen any point in emailing and hardly touched the computer. I had learned to click around the internet a little, though half the time I got stopped cold by a full-screen window that said, THIS PROGRAM HAS PERFORMED AN ILLEGAL OPERATION AND WILL BE SHUT DOWN. "What fucking ever," I'd mutter, and so much for grazing the free pastures of the World Wide Web. Email sounded good, though—communicating in silence, in private, in written words—and Abner helped me get going on AOL.

Cart and Josie didn't know I'd been grounded either. Josie asked if I'd show them the few big trees on top of Noble Dog Ridge, and I picked a day when I knew my dad would be leaving early. Turned out to be a rainy afternoon. That first shower had turned into a long stretch of very leaky weather, always raining or about to. They picked me up, we drove the gravel road up to the BLM gate, and from there we hiked the road up through little-tree plantations and stopped at a landing a dozer had scraped out for an old logging show. Josie and I stood on a stump that was five feet across, looking out to the south-west into the heart of the Coast Range, and I felt a mild embarrassment I'd felt before. No peaks or glaciers, nothing dramatic, just a bumpy and ridgey landscape covered in trees and patched with mist, none of it over a thousand feet in elevation. A few of the bumps were big enough to have names and be called mountains.

"The trees are different," Josie said, "but the terrain reminds me of parts of New England. Steep, forested hills."

Rain was dripping off the brim of her hat. A very pretty woman, I thought, despite her age. Game for any ramble, too. A stronger hiker than Cart, who was off catching his wind.

"The Indians you study, did they live out there?" she asked.

"Summer camps, to hunt and fish," I said. "Their winter villages were east, toward the Willamette."

"There doesn't seem to be a reservation. . . ."

I shook my head. "Not in their home country. Most of 'em died from diseases before settlers even got here, and the rest got herded onto reservations upstate with a lot of Indians from other tribes. Now they run the biggest casino in Oregon."

"That's unfortunate," said Josie.

"Really?" I challenged. "They lost their homeland, got just about wiped out, why shouldn't they soak some money from white people?"

Josie met my eyes and smiled, not necessarily in agreement but to say she'd heard and would think about it. She snapped some pictures, and the three of us hoofed on up to the older woods on the ridgetop. I led them off the road to a stand of tall Douglas firs, maybe ten feet around the trunk.

They admired the trees, but Cart was already bent out of shape—I knew he would be—by the view down the far side of Noble Dog Ridge, which was a lot like the near side—replanted clearcuts. The older growth where we stood now was only a topknot on a patchy crewcut ridge.

Cart took off his floppy hat and spoke slowly. "Why . . . are . . . they . . . allowed to *do* this?"

I sighed. "Because they own the land, Cart. And 'cause your house and furniture and books are made of trees. It can't all be locked up like the Methuselahs." I didn't want an argument. Not that he was wrong—Noble Dog had been overcut, all right—but he was leaving things out of the picture as surely as my father was.

Times were changing in the woods, and they probably needed to, but the ones preaching for the change weren't the ones getting hurt by it.

"Come on," I said. "I'll get you *really* pissed off."

"Oh, goodie," said Cart.

They tramped behind me, stumbling on roots and rocks hiding in the ground greenery, as I led them east along the ridge crest.

Josie gasped when she saw it. "Oh, what a shame," she said. Cart just stood gaping. The tree they were looking at was eight feet, seven inches in diameter at its base. I knew that because I'd measured it, and it had been easy to measure because the entire tree was lying along the slope, neatly bucked into thirty-foot lengths.

"Why?" said Cart. "Why cut it down, cut it up, and . . . ?"

"Nobody's been able to tell me," I said. "Maybe the outfit logging below saw this granddaddy and tried to poach it. Thousands of dollars in it. They dropped it, bucked it, and got caught before they could truck it out."

"I hope they went to jail," Cart muttered.

"It's a double waste," I said. "Should still be a tree, but once it was down it should've been sold. Beautiful clear lumber in a tree that size. The mills don't see many like it anymore."

Cart gave a snort. "Its real value is to sink into the ground and nurture the forest."

I bristled, but bit my tongue. "See those seedlings growing on top? It's gonna be a big mama nurse log with lots of kids. Let's check it out in two hundred years."

Josie, meanwhile, was all around and over that tree in pieces, taking close looks and snapping pictures, her pants soaked and smeared, wood rot on her sleeves and lichen in her hair. She smiled when I walked over. "Thanks for bringing us here," she said. "This tree is very compelling."

"It's like a poem I don't understand," I said. "So I keep coming back to it."

* * *

It was twilight by the time we got back to the truck and started home. The rain had quit. Cart set a record for slow driving down the potholed and washboarded road, and still the three of us lurched side to side, Josie in the middle, squished together in the little cab of their Toy truck. It was fun. Felt like family.

On pavement again, Cart sped up. I watched the low-hanging mist on the fields and pastures and Steve Barton's Christmas tree farm, where the harvest would get under way before long. A few oaks stood above the mist, ghostly, and the needle trees in the background showed their pointed tops against the night-blue sky where stars were coming out.

"The land's itself now," I said. "You see it best when it's half-hidden. . . ."

Cart tilted his head my way—"What was that?"—and *bam*, we'd hit her before we saw her. Cart braked and I was out the door to kneel with her as she surged on the pavement, trying to get up and run on her broken left shoulder. I thought her terror would explode my head.

"You got a gun in the truck?" I yelled, but I knew they didn't. Cart had backed and turned his one good headlight on the deer. I took out my pocket knife and cradled her head and cut deep across her throat. The blood came strong and I kept my hand on the back of her neck as it poured out of her.

"You're all right now," I whispered. She eased, the life going out of her eye. "You're all right." I felt tired as all the world. Could barely move, but I reached my fingers into the slit and brought her blood to my mouth. It didn't taste like mine. It was warm and too rich and made me shiver. My fingers went to the slit again and streaked blood down my cheekbones.

Cart was staring, more at me than the deer. The two of us lifted her into the back of the truck. "We'll keep her head out here on the tailgate," I said, "'cause she'll bleed some more. Just drive slow."

"Is this . . . legal?" Cart asked.

"We killed it. Least we can do is put it to use. You'll share in it, if you want."

Driving to my house, Cart couldn't stop saying how sorry he was, he'd hit the brake too late, and I kept telling him the truth, that I'd been talking and she'd jumped right out of the mist and there was nothing he could have done. Josie had her arm around my shoulders the whole way. I couldn't stop shaking.

We got her laid out on a tarp in the garage in front of my mother's white Dodge, and I told Cart and Josie they could go on home. Organ damage can ruin the meat, my dad wouldn't be home for hours, so I fetched his knives. I'd watched him dress his deer every fall, each time letting me do more of it. I cut in deep around the bung and tied it off with a piece of cord. Then I got her on her back and slit the belly down to the pelvis. Cut a little too deep, nicked the stomach and intestine, cussed myself. I rolled her on her side again and got the first whiff of innards as they slumped out, then the full steamy cloud as I held the belly open and leaned in to cut the organ train loose from the skirt on down. I had to stand for a moment or I'd've thrown up. I've got it too, I thought. Everything alive's got this hot breath of guts inside.

I used a small bow saw to split the breast bone, bits of bone and hair flying everywhere including my face. My dad was strong enough to cut it clean with a serrated knife. I pulled out the heart and lungs and cut loose what I could of the gullet and windpipe. Then I worked a piece of rebar through cuts between tendon and bone behind the rear ankles and hoisted the carcass clear of the floor, an inch or two per pull, with my dad's come-along strung over a crossbeam, anchored to a leg of the tool bench. I propped the ribcage open with kindling sticks and cut out the rest of the gullet and windpipe right to the jaw.

Then I stopped and looked at her, gutted, dead-eyed, strung up ass-first in a garage. Just two hours ago she'd been alive and light on her feet in the misted woods. Where was the bounding spirit that went to terror in a broken body and faded as her blood spilled on the pavement? Where was she now? You can tell me she was hanging in front of me, and I'll tell you right back, she was more than that. I and my dad and others would eat her flesh, but her spirit was out there yet, still on the move in the rain and mist.

I got a bucket of water and swabbed out the cavity with a clean rag. Three ribs were broken, besides the left front shoulder, but if I hadn't screwed it up too badly the meat would be okay. I took the heart and liver to the kitchen, put them in zipper bags and into the reefer. Then I gathered the tarp around the guts and toted the load by headlamp out back to a little opening in the woods and dumped it there for the coyotes and vultures. After hosing off the tarp and rinsing and drying my father's knives, I went back to the garage and sat in a corner and looked at the hanging body. Pretty soon I started to cry, and I fell asleep right there. I didn't wake up until my father was standing in the doorway with his arms folded looking at the deer.

"Dog my cats," he said. "You've been busy." I could smell the whiskey on him, but he was fine. My dad could drink buckets of booze and remain a capable man.

"Cart hit it and didn't know what to do with it," I said.

My father grunted, picking loose hair and bone bits from the meat. "What'd you do, take a saw to that breastbone?"

Finally he stepped back and said, "First time on your own, Henry, that's pretty good work."

I smiled and got to my feet.

My father stared at my face. "What the *hell?*"

I'd forgotten. "I wanted her on me," I said. "When Cart hit it, I—"

My father's face set hard. "You were with him, weren't you."

I nodded.

"Get in the house and clean yourself up. I'll deal with you when I come in."

In the morning, in silence, my father made scrambled eggs, drop biscuits, and fried backstrap, the little strips of flesh tucked in along the backbone that pull out with your fingers. My back stung from the whipping, but the meat was so sweet and tender it didn't taste like meat at all. It tasted like grass, like leaves. It tasted like mist in the twilit woods.

* * *

The next time I called on Len Peppers, he opened the door and smiled behind his long white beard. "I'll be go to hell," he said. "Get in here, Henry boy."

We sat at the kitchen table, as always. As Len slowly clumped around bringing the coffee, he seemed short of breath. I spoke loud so he could hear me. "I need some travelin' music, Len."

"You got leavin' on your mind?" He was quoting Patsy Cline.

"Someday," I said. "Soon, maybe."

"I'll play you a great one," Len said, and went to fumbling around in his heaps of CDs and cassette tapes. His beard and mustache were yellowed around his mouth from dipping snoose, maybe coffee too. The gold in his teeth showed when he talked, and his white hair flowed down over his shoulders. Len hadn't been any kind of hippie back in the 1960s, when he ran high-lead logging shows in the old-growth forest near Mount St. Helens, but now, in his seventies, he was the freest spirit I knew.

"*There* you are," he whispered, and put on Hank Williams's "Ramblin' Man." We listened to it three times, Len commanding with his remote. That song just about makes a religion out of riding the freight trains—*I love you, bay-bee*, the guy tells his sweetheart, *but you got to unnnderstand, when the Lord made me, he made a raaamblin' man. . . .*

"Now that guy," Len said, studying my face, "he loves the ramblin', but he don't tell us what he's ramblin' *from*, does he."

"Did you know, Len? What you were ramblin' from?"

He chuckled. "Two things, old son. Kansas was awful flat, and of school I was awful sick. Jumped a Santa Fe freight, knocked around the West, hopped off a boxcar in Longview with my last dollar, and . . ." He paused to take a breath. "Next day I was settin' chokers for Weyerhaeuser, Camp 19, out of Spirit Lake. . . . Wasn't two weeks along," he went on, grinning, "just gettin' my boots broke in, when a turn of logs goin' up the hill kicked up a six-foot chunk . . . knocked me over and broke my shoulder."

He rubbed it. "Still hurts, but I was hooked. I knew where I'd make my life."

"That's what I need," I said. "A life."

Len sipped his coffee with a frown. "Now this-here ain't Kansas," he said, "and I know for a fact you love it here like a dog on a bone. . . . Think you'll find someplace you love better?"

"Probably not. But my dad and I aren't gettin' along."

Len raised the thickets of his eyebrows, which were salt with still some pepper. "Been a rough year for you both. What you fightin' about?"

"Oh, everything," I said, and veered away. "Len, did you ever think those big companies were cuttin' too much timber?"

Len turned the corners of his mouth down and shrugged. "Too much for who? War was over, the U.S.A. buildin' like beavers. Needed the lumber . . . the plywood, the jobs. . . . And all those rail cars haulin' loads?" He gave a sly smile. "Came back empty, every one."

Len used the table to raise himself out of his chair and brought a bottle of Wild Turkey, breathing hard from the effort. I asked if he was sick, and he laughed as he sat down. "Just seventy-five years packin' too much freight," he said, patting his belly. "Don't get old, Henry." He poured whiskey into his coffee, tested it, and leaned back in his chair.

"I'll confess you this," he said. "I did wonder sometimes, lot of us did. . . . They had an *empire*, Weyerhaeuser, them others. They didn't have to run through it like a gaggle of gold rushers. . . . And they *damn* well shouldn't been sellin' logs to Japan, either. . . . The Japs were sinkin' 'em into Tokyo Harbor, so we heard. Preservin' 'em for the future. . . . *Their* future."

Len seemed to brood inside himself a few seconds, then slapped his leg. "Plumb forgot! You came to lift your spirits. Here's the guy who *invented* travelin' music."

I stayed for three hours listening with Len to Jimmie Rodgers, the Singing Brakeman, whose high voice rode his sunny heart right through all the hisses and pops of the old recordings, and then Merle Haggard singing the same songs. Len gave me a little glass with an ice cube and slid the bottle across the table now and then, saying only, "Just a nip, now." When it got dark he roasted hot dogs one at a time on a fork over one of the gas stove burners, and we dipped those dogs into a jar of mustard and a jar of relish and ate as many as Len cooked. It was one of the best meals I've ever had.

"Henry," he said in the doorway as I was leaving. "Jimmie Rodgers got sick, but he kept tourin' and tourin' . . . fell dead, thirty-five years old. Hank Williams, he died in his convertible, all drunk . . . drugged up, not even thirty. Sure, somethin' over the hill they had to see, but Henry . . . all they ever found was that Lost Highway. Look me in the eye, now. . . . You get the itch to vamoose, you see me first."

"I will," I said.

"I'll take it personal if you don't, old son. Promise me."

"I promise, Len."

seven

After their early start, which set a record for September, the rains petered out in October. Cold nights, crisp mornings, afternoons with a fine cool warmth. Sunlight came pale, touched with smoke haze, a lonesome light. In the clearcuts, and along the roadways in open country, the vine maples, humble trees no taller than fifteen feet, were turning orange and scarlet like burning bushes. The Oregon ashes and big-leaf maples were turning their reliable dull yellow with some rusty orange. But the best tree colors, like always, were in the city of Eugene, where all the imported maples and sweet gums and oaks were putting on a show. I'd heard people say it was only a taste of what you see out East, where they've got whole mountains of crazy-beautiful fall foliage, and I vowed to see it someday.

The leaves were starting to fall, the trees drawing back into themselves, their deepest nature. I was trying to read the poems of Emily Dickinson that fall—Josie had given me a book, said I should be reading some women—and mostly the poems were passing around my head or straight through it. But they were short, so I read them all, and once in a while some lines jumped clear off the page—

There's a certain Slant of light,
Winter Afternoons—
That oppresses, like the Heft
Of Cathedral Tunes—

Heavenly Hurt it gives us—
We can find no scar,
But internal difference,
Where the Meanings, are—

"Heavenly Hurt"—those two words put together made no sense, but somehow they did. Those two words and the slanted afternoon light meant something about being alive that I couldn't explain but knew was true. My mother was near, I felt her, and for a moment my sorrow seemed outside me, out in the green, yellow-tinged hills.

* * *

The day after the deer disaster, Josie told me later, my father drove over to the Stephens place, banged on the door, and spent five minutes yelling in their faces that they were not to come anywhere near his son or call him or have any contact with him whatsoever, and if they did he would file charges and personally make their lives very unpleasant. Cart got hot himself and told my father not to threaten them or they would call the police, and my father laughed and told them this wasn't San Francisco, there weren't any police, there was a deputy sheriff and he was a friend and wouldn't take kindly to newcomers meddling with George Fielder's young son against the wishes of George Fielder. Cart shut the door on him. My father yelled through the door a while longer and then drove off, the truck's rear wheels spraying gravel toward the house as he gunned the engine out of the driveway.

As for me, "I'd shut you up in the cellar if it locked," he said. He'd already served me a hard whipping, but one fair thing about my father was that he didn't pile on the punishment. He gave it when he thought he needed to and moved on. In our school sessions now he loaded me up with assignments due the next day, hoping to keep me home with my nose in a book, but we both knew he had no control over me while he was at work. If I didn't do the assignments, and mostly I didn't, what could he do—fail me? Assign the work all over again? His homeschooling scheme was starting to backfire. I volunteered to wear one of those dog collars that give a shock if the dog tries to leave the yard, but he told me to shut up and not be a smartass.

In the sessions we didn't talk much. Mostly he just gave me some geometry problems or history readings and went out back to split firewood—I heard the *whack* of his maul and the split pieces rattling onto the pile as I read about Antietam and Gettysburg. I continued to flub geometry, which continued to annoy him, which I continued to like doing. Math didn't come easy to me, but I can see now that I was more or less intentionally diddling him. Likewise with the papers I turned in—sloppy handwriting, poor grammar and spelling, ridiculous ideas. He wasn't confident enough to call me on some of the ideas, which amused me in a superior sort of way, but he knew I wasn't doing my best because he had seen my best.

Lynn warned me that to tell the story truly I'd have to be fair to my father, to show the good in him along with the bad. I'm trying to do that. At the time I saw his frustration, I saw the inexpressible pain of his loss, but mainly I saw an angry tyrant. I didn't yet see that he was scared to death that he might be losing his son too, who was all he had left of the love of his life, to a pair of outlanders who offered gifts he couldn't match, scarcely understood, and bitterly resented. I did sense it, though. Once in a while I'd glance when he wasn't looking and catch a look in his stubbled face that he might have seen on mine—a wince almost, a certain cast of the eyes, a blunt sadness that morning by morning we were pissing away, in hard words and sullen silence, something precious between us that we had never been able to speak.

* * *

When I went to Cart and Josie's now, I always rode the back way on my mountain bike, around the south side of Boomer Mountain on old logging roads through the second-growth woods. No one would see me back there, not Jonah or anyone else who might report to my father. He might well have asked the deputy sheriff to look out for me. I came out on the south side of Jimmy Hepworth's pasture and had only to climb two fences to be at the Stephens place, directly outside Cart's study window at the back of the house. He'd usually be there at his desk, Catrick the gray tabby by his computer screen. I'd catch his eyes and he'd wave me in.

They were concerned about my father's temper and asked how he treated me. I fudged around, said things weren't so bad. I didn't want them any deeper in my mess than they already were. I did ask them not to talk to anyone about seeing me, and of course that just worried them more. Josie talked a little about grieving, how everyone did it their own way and the loss was still very fresh for both of us. She offered to help find counseling for me or my father or us both, and I think she was taken aback when I laughed out loud. "Can't see my dad doing that," I said. "Me either, really."

With the surprise clear weather, word was out that the Karen Creek logging might get under way soon. Cart had been going to Eugene a lot for final planning with the Methuselah Forest Collective. There would be a human blockade anchored in place along the steel gate across the access road. "They want to gate the public out?" Cart said. "We'll take their gate and keep *them* out." Up behind the gate, in the timber sale on federal land, young people would be camped in some of the bigger trees, on little platforms or hanging in hammocks, attended by helpers on the ground. Cart had yearned to be one of them—he'd bought gear and was practicing tree-climbing and hammock-sleeping in his own trees—but he was the oldest person in the protest by far, and the group wanted him in the blockade, where he'd be visible and could be one of the spokespersons for the collective.

Technically, Karen Creek was a thinning sale, aimed at clearing out the smaller growth in the forest, but Cart told me that this one, like many thinning sales, included a lot of bigger trees too, and it was those that made it valuable. "It's dishonest," he said. "It's a sneaky way of almost clearcutting." All my life I'd heard the industry side of the timber wars; now I was hearing the chants of an environmentalist on the warpath. Once in a while I just had to let some air out of his tires. He was raving against the industry one day, saying the timber companies had no allegiance to their workers and communities.

"Most mill hands are raising families," I told him. "They make a good wage. And by the way, what do you think of our Fern Ridge Library?"

Cart looked puzzled. "For the size of the town," he said cautiously, "I think it's very good."

"Well, not long ago it was a little two-room shack, maybe a quarter the size it is now. They wanted to expand it and went and asked the owner of Siuslaw Pacific how to raise money. He asked how much they needed. Then he wrote out a check for $300,000, said match it with local contributions in six months and they could cash it."

"Hmm," said Cart Stephens, a man rarely at a loss for words.

Josie was supporting his activism but not so worked up. She came from Quaker people and didn't care for confrontations. She hoped that the images she made did some good for the cause. "Celebrating the natural world is as necessary as fighting for it," she told me once. "To celebrate it *is* to fight for it."

On one visit she took me into her darkroom to look at pictures she'd taken on Noble Dog Ridge. She had found a way to shoot the bucked-up mystery tree and get three sections of it into one view, with me crouching near one of the cuts so you could get the size of the thing, lying along the hillside like some giant broken-backed snake, beautiful and ruined. One of her prints was a little grainy, but that was on purpose, she said, and when she told me I could see why. It was like the mist. Sometimes you have to blur a thing, push it out of sure sight, to really see it.

Cart showed me how to climb the rope he'd anchored in the crown of his tallest Doug fir. I loved it up there, a hundred-forty feet off the ground, a breeze stirring the tree so slightly I felt it only in my belly. Up in a tall tree you see the greater home—the pasture with horses taking it easy, young woods on the flat beyond rising into Brother Jim Butte. Turn your head and there's the sloping shoulder of Boomer Mountain, there's the south side of Noble Dog Ridge with its plantations and ludicrous mohawk of real trees, there's the flats of the Long Tom River and a Christmas tree farm and some-body's single-wide with a blue tarp over one end of the roof, Ham-merstone Mountain in the distance.

I spent so long up there, Cart hollered up asking if I was okay.

"I'm great," I yelled back. "I found the fountain of youth!"

"Bring it down, I need it," his voice came up.

"Too bad, old-timer, it's all mine!"

And it was, right there in my sticky hands. In a tree maybe a cen-tury and a half old, I couldn't climb the last few feet to the very top because the tree was too young. It was a Christmas tree, a limber sapling dripping with pitch and studded with clenched green cones.

On the ground again, I was giddy. "Can I be a tree-sitter?" I asked. "I wanna do my part."

Cart smiled, his Euramericano doing showy poses in the breeze. "We'd love it," he said, "but think of your father, Henry. He's angry enough already, at you *and* us."

"Right," I said. "My father."

When Pap Finn got just too terrible, Huck had to leave. I day-dreamed about it. I wasn't up to staging my own murder, like Huck did, and a raft wouldn't get me very far down the majestic Long Tom, but I could see myself in a cabin in the hills somewhere—eastern

Oregon, Alaska, Wyoming—a small cabin, nothing fancy. Maybe I'd build it myself. I'd grow green beans and tomatoes and potatoes, I'd fish the streams for trout, only what I needed. I'd shoot rabbits and squirrels with my slingshot or the .22 I'd steal from my dad, I'd read books from a library and mind my own business. Only Abner would know where I was. Maybe there'd be a girl and we'd like each other. Maybe I'd coach a summer-league baseball team. Maybe I'd learn how to make beautiful photographs or write books.

I knew I'd never do any of it, but I also knew I had to do *something*. I was over-amped, my moods crazy. At any time—at home, in the woods, on my bike—an anger would rush me like a hot draft up a chimney. I hated my dad, myself, luck, God, whatever. Even my mother, for leaving the two of us to mess up our life together. I had to kick things or take a stick and whip down some weeds and grasses, bash twigs off bushes. I'd always believed that the things that happened to me were good things, because they made me what I was and so they *had* to have happened. My mother dying of cancer demolished that belief, but recently I'd felt it starting to trickle back, like a little stream. Maybe losing her was my Heavenly Hurt, I thought one day, maybe you had to get wounded to become what you're supposed to be. But then the anger flared up and I cussed myself for such a pathetic idea.

And the angrier I got, the farther I got from my gift. The deer, they heard me and ran. Bluejays screeched, flew off. A coyote eyed me across a clearcut as he took a dump, then turned and loped off into the trees. The songbirds wouldn't come to my hand for seed, and they didn't come to me in the woods. The gift had come rising out of the ground like a spring, surprising me all over again each time. I longed for the stillness it gave, the fullness of more than me. There was one flicker who stopped in his spotted suit on a close-by limb and gave me the eye. It was a chance, a real chance, but the spirit didn't flow. I was trying, and when you have to try, it doesn't work. After a few seconds the flicker took off and left me feeling like a fire-killed snag.

* * *

One Saturday morning my father actually smiled at breakfast.

The Mariners had made a run into the playoffs, and we'd watched a few games together. Only about the ball game, but we talked. He even handed his beer down. Then Seattle got knocked out by the Cleveland Indians, whose grinning mascot, an Indian they called Chief Wahoo, I wanted to shoot every time I saw it. (Imagine a cartoon of a *black* guy showing his teeth like that. There'd be riots.) My dad and I were both bummed out for a few days, but at least we were bummed about the same thing.

Then he smiled over his pancakes and said, "I hear there's steelhead in the Nesqualla. Wanna go see?"

We made the two-hour drive and without too much looking found a hole to ourselves. It was a sweet stretch, moving about as fast as a man walks. I had a good feeling about my fifth cast—five is the Kalapuya sacred number—and sure enough, something slammed my spinner. A steelhead is a muscled-up rainbow trout with recent experience of the great Pacific—instant panic, in other words, and so of course I tried to crank him in. "Don't horse him!" my dad yelled, and I fumbled the drag loose enough for the steelhead to pull line off but get tired doing it. "Let me win this one," I prayed softly to the river, and gradually I gained line, gave it back, gained a little more, and the worn-down fish came glinting into the shallows to my left. My dad was there in hip boots to reach down and grab it by the mouth and gill. "All right, Henry! I bet he goes twenty-six inches!"

No monster, but the biggest I'd ever caught. I admired his colors—shades of red and green, a touch of gold—then conked him out of his misery with a hefty driftwood stick. I was too jangled to fish after that, so I walked the bank and fidgeted, trembling all over, and watched my dad fish and drank a little coffee from his steel thermos. I strongly suspected that whiskey had gotten into the coffee somehow, but I poured another cup anyway and came to like it pretty well. My father caught a fish too, not as big as mine, and I was right there to grapple it onshore, but the steelhead was slick and threshing around and my hands were shaking and I wasn't getting it done, so finally my father had to reach down himself and hoist it out of the river. I stood there watching, quivering like the fish.

On the highway home, I fed Willie Nelson's greatest hits into the tape deck and cranked him up loud—"Whiskey River," "My Heroes Have Always Been Cowboys," and the others right up to "Angel Flying Too Close to the Ground." My dad had been singing along, but now he turned the volume way down. "We used to dance to this," he said to the windshield. "Slow dance."

I had never been in love but still I felt the power of it, the guy just pouring it out about a girl who fell his way, and he helped her heal and now she's about to fly on, like he knew she would. *"Leave me if you need to. . . ,"* he sings, *"I'd rather see you up than see you down. . . ."* And you believe him—kind of—but still, he's standing there watching her go and he knows she's not coming back.

"She flew away, Dad. She didn't have a choice."

"But she didn't fly up, did she."

"She did too fly up, her spirit did. Don't you believe that?"

"The woman I knew is ashes in the ground."

"Well, I feel her close sometimes. Like a breath of wind, kind of."

He blew air through his lips. "You feel her close. You don't know jack about holdin' a woman close."

"Not the way you mean, but she's not far away."

"Don't tell me about far away, damn it! She died, Henry. She flat died. In *this* world, not your make-believe dreams."

* * *

At home he filleted the two fish, cutting close to the spine and ribs and wasting nothing, and then barbecued two of the slabs the usual way, skin down on the grill with butter, sesame oil, powdered ginger, and some splashes of Lea & Perrins sauce, cutting diagonal slashes in the meat to let the flavors in.

I tore some lettuce and cut a red bell pepper for a salad. My mom hadn't left me a lot of instructions, but she did say to put something green on my father's plate every now and again, because she knew he would buy the stuff for me but wouldn't eat it himself. It was a fine meal. The steelhead, the salad, even the Tater Tots tasted better than usual. My dad surprised me when he brought two cans of Bud to the table and set one at my place. I took it in little sips as I ate, and pretty soon I was feeling a nice warm glow. I burped once, loud, not knowing I was going to, and broke out in giggles.

"Watch your manners," he said, "or I'll cut you off."

I wagged a finger at him. "Yes sir," I said. "And you eat your salad."

He flashed a quick grin. "She told you to do that, didn't she."

"Yup. And I guess she told you to let me drink beer."

"The hell she did. What else'd she say?"

"She said to give me her white Dodge and let me drive it."

He started to laugh but stopped short, his eyes glistening. "I drove that car from Missouri. Gave it to her on our first anniversary." He stared at his plate. "We had it just right," he said. "Just right, goddamn it. . . ."

We finished the meal in silence.

"How can anybody drink more than one of these?" I asked, sticking my belly out and patting it like a drum.

"You don't need to know that," my father said.

I read for a while in bed, the last twenty pages of *Catcher in the Rye*. I liked that book pretty well, even though the whole story, just about, takes place in New York City and all the kid telling it does is smoke cigarettes and drink and call up girls he used to date and old teachers. He's pretty lame, really, but I ended up liking him because he looks out for his little sister, and even though he's a fuckup he's fair-minded and tries to do the right thing. He takes taxis and asks the drivers if they know where the ducks in the big park go when the ponds freeze over. Nobody can tell him. The snow and the rain and those ducks are the only natural things in the story. I liked that he worried about the ducks, but still, it seemed kind of pathetic that nobody in that whole city knew what ducks do in the winter. Maybe that was the point, I wasn't sure.

eight

Abner Truitt came out the next afternoon, after church, with a surprise. I was still grounded and not supposed to see him, so I'd asked my father if I could take a bike ride. He said sure, and I waited up the road as Abner and I had planned. Instead of him on his bike, though, a green Subaru slowed down and stopped. A girl was driving, Abner riding shotgun, another girl in the back seat.

"Change of plans, Tracker!" Abner hollered as his window went down, shaking his long curly locks, and the door in back of him opened. I stashed my bike in the woods and got in the car.

"Tracker, this is Julie," said Abner, his hand on Julie's shoulder playing with her blond hair. She smiled up at the rearview mirror. "She's sixteen and legal to drive, dude, in case you care. And I think you know Tess Bailey. . . ."

"Hey," I said. I'd seen her—she was part of the social swirl around Abner—but couldn't remember a thing about her. Also, I'd forgotten how to talk. All I could think of was my dirty jeans and ratty sneakers.

"Hi, Henry," she said. She had short hair, three or four inches long, just the brown color of a chestnut chickadee's shoulders, and dark brown eyes. She was wearing jeans and a blue blouse and was way pretty.

"I was in English class with you," she said. "With Mr. Stacey?"

"Oh yeah, right. . . ."

"You know what I remember? You didn't talk much, but when you did, you always said something interesting. You seemed like two grades ahead of the rest of us."

This gave me hope—a girl who liked me for my mind—but didn't solve my immediate problem of being dumbstruck.

We limped along with many silences as Julie and Abner—he had his arm around her now, so close he was almost steering—drove us to our destination, which was a picnic on Hammerstone Mountain, south of Daugherty. It was a sunny day, no clouds.

"Catered by Burger King," announced Abner as he brought the food in white bags to the blanket Tess and Julie had spread out. We had a nice view up the Coast Range to the north, and east across the Willamette Valley to the Cascades. The Three Sisters were showing fresh snow, the two who like to talk to each other and the one who keeps to herself. "And," Abner went on, brandishing a cooler, "from our exclusive Long Tom cellars, a new release of Mickey's Malt Liquor."

When we were done eating, Abner and Julie disappeared. Tess and I were on our own, but the Mickey's had loosened me up and I didn't fret so much. I learned that Tess was an only child and lived in Long Tom with her mother. They'd moved down from Portland two years before, when her parents divorced, and Tess really missed the city and her friends. We talked about that for a while.

Then, after a silence, Tess asked, "What do you see out there?" gesturing north.

"I see one of the richest river valleys anywhere on Earth and a good green hill country that wants to be trees," I said.

"*Wants to be trees. . . ,*" I heard her whisper. "But all the clearcuts," she said.

I nodded—wisely, I hoped. "People've been living out there twelve thousand years, probably, and never once made it look like that. Took us just a hundred."

"It's sad," said Tess.

"But you know what?" I said. "The wildness is still there. In the soil, the weather, the critters. In the long run, the land'll stay true to itself."

She slid closer and put her hand on my shoulder. "Hello, critter."

I started to speak but she pulled my face to hers and whatever I'd meant to say she smothered in a long easy kiss, her lips moving on mine, the tip of her tongue touching against my teeth until they opened and my tongue tip came out to meet hers like some shy animal in its cave.

"I don't know much . . . about this," I whispered, but Tess just laughed. "Trust your wildness, Henry," and she kissed me again.

When Abner and Julie came back, glowing like they'd won the lottery, we all talked a while and drank up the Mickey's and loaded up for home. Abner drove the gravel roads, then Julie on the pavement.

Three hours after they'd picked me up, there I was again on Stamper Road, watching Tess wave through the back window of Julie's car.

* * *

Early one frosty morning a week later, I rode shotgun as Josie Stephens drove the Toy truck up the gravel road leading to the Karen Creek timber sale. The protesters had heard—they had an informer, Cart hinted—that this was the day the timber company would bring in their machines and get set up for logging. I knew I was begging for trouble, and Josie tried to talk me out of it, but I'd decided I had to be there. I'd left a note telling my dad I'd gone on an all-day hike, then met Josie out on the road before sunup. Cart had spent the night in Eugene with his fellow greeniacs and would already be on-site.

Josie parked and we hiked up the road in growing dawnlight, carrying two backpacks of supplies, and there they were. People were milling around in a quiet hubbub of voices, men's and women's, an occasional hoot or trill. There was a high banner strung across the road between two trees:

THE METHUSELAH FOREST COLLECTIVE
NO CHAINSAWS   WOLVES PLEASE ENTER

Under the banner, four women and three men sat across the road, their backs to the yellow-painted steel gate, each one wearing a harness of heavy steel strap that looked like armor. The harnesses were hitched together by heavy-gauge log chain that was locked—and maybe welded too—to the gate and gateposts. And smack dab in the middle of the chain-gang, three young persons to each side of him, sat Carter Stephens, a generous length of gray hair sticking out from under his bicycle helmet like a raggedy halo.

Josie had tears in her eyes as we walked up to him and knelt down. She hugged his unchained head and neck. I didn't feel worthy to even be there, but Cart said, "Sometime you might want to try this, Henry. It's exhilarating." And it was true—his blue eyes catching early sunlight through the trees, he looked mighty happy.

"When are they coming?" I asked.

"We don't know, and we don't even know who 'they' will be. Probably a crew with a bulldozer to cut spur roads. And law enforcement, state and BLM. They know we're here. We've told them everything."

"Why the state?" I asked.

"Because we're on private property here. Federal land begins a hundred feet above the gate."

"You're brave, Cart."

He smiled. "The worst we expect is handcuffs and a night or two in jail. Pepper spray, maybe. I'll probably survive."

"I should have brought you a piss bottle," I said.

"Got it," Cart grinned. "Strapped to my thigh. I've installed plumbing."

A woman next to him, with brown hair and dimples, smiled and said, "We admire your grandfather very much."

"I do too, Granddaddy," I laughed, then left to give him and Josie some space.

People were moving gear around and taking pictures and talking, laughing a lot. One woman in a long loose skirt was dancing by herself out in the trees. A few small kids were playing soccer, squealing and shouting, with a ponderosa pine cone. There didn't seem to be any leaders. I asked one guy about the tree-sitters, and he said they were in some of the big trees that had been flagged for "thinning" along with the runts and pecker poles. "How long can they stay in the trees?" I asked.

"As long as it takes," he answered. He had a narrow face with a wispy blond beard.

"Did you guys spike trees too?"

He gave me a sharp look.

"I'm on your side," I said. "That's my grandfather hitched to the gate. I don't know anything about this stuff."

"In this group we've pledged no monkeywrenching," he said. "The movement is split. I haven't quite resolved it myself."

"What's wrong with monkeywrenching?" I asked.

"Some believe all violence is wrong, even against property, and it hurts our cause because the public reacts against it. Others say that protests and lawsuits and peaceful disobedience haven't worked. Maybe direct action will."

He and the others seemed to be doing what they believed in and willing to go to jail for it. I wished I was one of them. "Good luck," I said to the guy. "I hope we win."

Everybody was waiting and nothing was going on, so I caught a nap on the needle duff in a sunny spot of forest. Josie woke me to say she was leaving to do errands, the main one being to gather cash from the bank to bail people out. I decided to stay put.

By noon a few people had showed up just down the road to protest the protest. Their signs said, "This Community Supported by Timber Dollars" and "Hug a Logger—You'll Never Go Back to Trees." "Hey," one guy hollered our way, "Earth First!" Some in our bunch answered with surprised cheers.

"Right," the guy yelled back, pumping his fist in the air. "We'll log the other planets later!" We jeered, they jeered and heckled back, more mocking than angry. The vibe was loose and tense, like a ballpark where fans from both teams are sitting close together, and the game matters. I didn't see anybody I knew but hung back in the trees anyway.

It was maybe one o'clock when we heard the clank and rumble of heavy machinery coming up the road. A D-8 Caterpillar bulldozer came in the lead, making a colossal racket, with a State Police van, a couple of pickups, and a BLM rig trained up behind. Our group gathered by the gate on both sides of the road. As the Cat trundled up past the protest-protesters and got within fifty feet of the gate, it didn't let up at all. The noise was insane. People started shouting *"Stop!"* Thirty feet, twenty feet, the dozer kept coming, people screaming now, till finally it clanked to an idle maybe eight feet shy of the blockaders, giving them the full effect of the dust it'd kicked up. A state trooper in sunglasses and a blue uniform came running up and yelled at the smirking operator, maybe for driving the Cat so close. Then he turned to talk to the blockaders, but nobody could hear him. He angrily waved at the operator to cut the engine.

The trooper held up his arms for quiet. People were yelling at him, and I heard some crying, too. He told the chain-gang they had picked a nice day to spend in the woods but they couldn't spend it in the roadway. They were committing criminal trespass and would be cut out of their chains if necessary. He'd give them some time to think it over. One blockader said they had thought it over and weren't going anywhere. "We're in the trees too," somebody called. "We're in your head," somebody else piped up. Then Cart said that he and some of the others might not be there if the plan had truly been just thinning. A BLM guy in a brown-and-green uniform said that the timber company wasn't real excited either, they'd wanted more board footage. "Our agency is as responsible to them, and to those folks down the road, as it is to you," he said.

Then the state trooper said that he believed in the rule of law and hoped Cart did too. Cart said he did, and he hoped the officer believed in breaking the law when a higher good was at stake, because the American revolutionaries had believed that, and the movement to abolish slavery, and the American labor movement and civil rights movement, and they had changed history.

The trooper smiled and said, "Nice speech, old-timer, but you can't make history in this road. Think it through, all of you. Make the right choice." Then he and the Cat operator and the rest of them went back to their rigs, which turned around and drove away. They left the big Cat staring the blockaders in the face.

The protesters of the protest had moved closer to see the bust come down and were disappointed it hadn't. They heckled a little but didn't have their hearts in it. Somebody invited them for beer and a joint, but they lost interest and went away.

Our people seemed let down too, not sure what to do. Many were upset about the reckless bulldozer and wanted to disable it, but the nonviolent wing of the party won out, and two or three of the angry ones hiked off down the road in disgust. The seven blockaders were freed from their chains—the harnesses were hinged in back and swung open—and seven more took their places for the afternoon. Cart walked my way, stiff and grimy in the face but triumphant. "We repelled their charge!" he said.

"They just about ran you over, Cart. Weren't you scared?"

"Oh no," he said with a smile, "I knew they wouldn't damage this nice gate." Then he sighed. "Hell yes, I was scared, Henry. I'm glad Josie didn't have to see it."

We noticed a few people bringing armfuls of Doug fir boughs and laying them on the blade and tread and cab of the dozer. Pretty soon most of us—Josie too, when she came back—were gathering boughs, salal, fern fronds (only one or two from each fern), big yellow maple leaves, mossy branches, and any other pretty things we could find. We built a cairn of rocks on the cab. We decked out that yellow metal monster like a hulking coffin.

* * *

I made sure to come home sweaty and dirty that afternoon wearing my daypack. My father was still home and oh, just a little ticked off that I'd bailed on our homeschool session. He pushed me against the living room wall by my shoulders and shouted at me, his red face inches from mine, delivering spittle with his tirade. "*What's it gonna take, Henry? Do I have to lock you up to get you to obey me? I'm doin' this teachin' for you, and you just waltz off on one of your nature walks. . . .*" He thumped my shoulders against the wall a few times, shouted some more, and let me go. I was grounded, I'd have extra school-work, I was not to leave the property, he'd be calling home from work and if even once I didn't answer the phone he was gonna give me a whipping I'd never forget.

The good news was that he believed I'd gone for a hike. It was completely in character, after all. Nature, to him, didn't mean much more than hunting and fishing and the nuisance of bad weather, but he knew that I cared about it and he'd always allowed me that—except for sharing spirit with animals. He and Jonah Rutledge thought that was just me having imaginary friends. Once, when my mother and I were talking about it in the kitchen, my dad had just smiled, looked out the window, and said, "Growin' up in Missouri I got pretty close to lots of wild animals. Half the time they ended up cooked on the dinner table, the other half *I* ended up bit, clawed, or in need of a vinegar bath."

My father called home from work that evening, true to his word, and I was there to answer in my sullenest voice. When the phone rang again later, I picked up and said, "Yeah, *what?*" But it was Tess Bailey, and the conversation went as awkwardly as it began. I didn't know what to say, and when I did start to speak it was just when *she* started, and we kept tripping each other up like that. I was sweating within seconds. I did get it that she was inviting me to visit her in town sometime, so I wrote down her phone number and told her I'd call.

* * *

The rains came back at the start of November, and they meant business—easy, hard, straight, slanting, pouring, splashing, drizzling, mizzling, easing off then starting again with a new light tap dance on the roof. The fronts rolled in off the Pacific like waves on the beach, drenching the Coast Range and Willamette Valley and dumping snow on the Cascades if the front was cold enough. Rain soaked into the ground and swelled the streams, filled the roadside ditches, and even the little, peace-loving Long Tom River rose up fast and brown and went over its banks three times, flooding a few houses on the flats and making a lake on the lowest stretch of Stamper Road. We heard about floods all over western Oregon. The reservoirs on the Willamette and McKenzie rivers and their tributaries were rising close to capacity, forcing the dam operators to release water through the spillways, getting just enough breaks between fronts to stay out of the worst trouble. The dam downstream of us on the lower Long Tom was made out of earth, just a big levee. Fern Ridge Lake, behind it, was almost full, with most of the rainy season still to go.

Me, I loved the weather, every gust and drop of it. My father let me walk after homeschool and getting my house chores done, as long as I came back before he left for work. There was really only one break in his shift when he could call, between eight and eight-thirty, so as soon as he left I went back out till nightfall. Sometimes when the wind drove rain into my face I hollered out of sheer pleasure. Once I saw a tree go down, a leaner, an Oregon ash. Its roots lost their grip in the soggy ground just as the wind picked up and I happened by. What were the chances? I howled my happiness.

After rummaging for supper I stayed home reading, not just for school. I hadn't gone near my mother's books, but now I felt I could. They stood on shelves in their bedroom and on other shelves in the living room. Some had "Eileen Durham" signed in cursive inside the front cover, and in some she had made small notes on the pages. I spent hours leafing through just to find her words. There were doodles, too, mostly in books from her time at Oregon State—little designs or faces, and under one of the faces she'd written, "Really? A man named George?" I could see where the face *might* have looked like my dad, if you didn't count the long hair and droopy mustache, which he ditched before I ever saw him.

My father didn't care for the rain. He was restless and tense. Most nights he came home buzzed from the Sam and Max—if I was awake in bed I'd hear him walk to the bathroom, the floorboards creaking, and back to the kitchen, then the little clink of the whiskey bottle touching another bottle as he took it from the cupboard and a squeak as he twisted the cork out. He drank through the weekends, too, though never till evening. Sometimes he talked about moving—Colorado maybe, New Mexico. Montana, he announced one day. "I wouldn't mind a little more sun," he said, looking out the dripping window. "And trade this goddamn rain for *snow*. Get a new start, you know?"

"This is reading weather," I said. "Read about Montana."

"If I wanted to read I'd go back to school," he came back.

"You read," I said. I'd seen him time to time with a Zane Grey western, *Huckleberry Finn, Tom Sawyer*, or a Jack London novel. He started *A River Runs Through It* but quit because he considered fly fishermen snobs. My mother had tried to get him into Ernest Hemingway and John Steinbeck. He'd pick up a book, read a story, a chapter or two, then set it aside. He had read some American history and taught it well when he tried.

"Dad," I said, "just in case you're serious, my home's right here."

"Is that right?" he snapped. "How 'bout you take better care of it then? You got your chores done today?"

"Not all of 'em," I mumbled.

"Well, get your sorry ass off the sofa then," he barked. Then suddenly he changed. "Henry," he said, real pain in his voice. "Your mother's gone. It's you and me, and we've got to work together here. Yesterday I patched a leak in the roof, split a quarter-cord of wood, straightened up the house, made you breakfast and lunch, and put in an eight-hour shift at the mill. You could do your chores, couldn't you?"

"Okay," I whispered, my face burning, and closed my book.

It's not like he was asking a lot. Bring in firewood, feed the stoves, mow the yard, help keep the kitchen and bathrooms more or less clean, keep my bedroom straight, take out the garbage—the work wasn't even hard, I just preferred to be walking the woods or fishing or climbing a tree. As Mr. Walt Whitman wrote of himself, I liked to lean and loafe at my ease, observing a spear of summer grass—or observing anything else outdoors, and indoors I liked to loafe at my ease reading books. My dad was probably right about my mother spoiling me, or indulging me anyway. She'd never gotten on my case about chores, so that had left him the only cop on duty.

* * *

There were books on myth and religion in my mother's collection and books on science right next to them. I opened one about cosmology by a physicist writing for people who aren't physicists, and I found I could understand the main ideas. He said the universe began fourteen billion years ago from a single point of being that exploded into super-hot gases that cooled and pressed together in the spell of gravity and formed stars, and those stars were nuclear furnaces that created the elements we know today and blasted them into space when the stars went nova, and gravity whirled that dust and gas in eddies that formed new stars, like our sun, and the little worlds that circle them. The writer said we couldn't know where that seed of space and time came from—that was for religion—but he was positive that sun and Earth and life all came from it, all one evolving story. I had never imagined that much time, all those thousands of millions of years, and as I read I felt time stretching out slowly inside me like a plant just barely growing, second by second by second. . . .

Out in the woods one misty night that wasn't too cold, I took off my clothes and watched zillions of tiny droplets glide and swirl in my flashlight's beam, a slow aimless tide riding breezes I couldn't feel. I breathed into the beam and made a tiny hurricane, but almost right away the specks went back to their natural dance, drifting, lifting and falling, just big enough to be seen, too light and next-to-nothing to ever hold still. I clicked off the light. The droplets were touching my bare body every moment, and they were touching everything around me—each needle of every Douglas fir and hemlock from the granddaddies right down to the skinny saplings, all the hazelnuts and big-leaf maples, every sword fern and lady fern and licorice fern, all the salal and Oregon grape, and the mushrooms, and the cushiony moss on the ground under my bare feet just drinking the droplets in. On my body it felt like the clothing I was born for.

When I used my hand on myself it felt right, like it never quite did in bed or the bathroom. By then I was shivering, and I pulled my clothes back on.

Those bitty drops of mist, more than the stars even, showed me something of God. I had some high moments in church, but on my own I wouldn't look for God under a roof. The stars, I knew that they in their multitudes were moving too, hurtling through space, and if I could see with the eyes of God they might look just like the mist, tiny droplets of fire. But I see with the eyes I have. It's something fierce and lonesome to look at the stars, to really look, but their light is far away and cold as ice. The mist is *alive*, right here, right now, and we have just the right eyes to see it when it hangs low on the fields at evening, and drapes itself, soft as smoke, in wisps and streaks along the far hills, and gathers in the clefts and stream valleys, and moves like spirit through a beam of light in the dark.

When I was seven I asked my mother, "Would you like to see what mist is made of?" and took her outside with the flashlight. It delighted her, and after that we went out a few times every fall and winter. Now she was gone, but the mist eased me. She was gone but was not lost to me. I still cried, but I didn't whack trees with sticks anymore. She'd known I was angry that she was dying. She told me, "Be sad, Henry. Let sadness take you down the river. Anger just pounds you against the rocks. Remember the Kalapuya word?"

"*Hal-ba*," I answered. "Downstream."

"*Hal-ba*," she said. "And remember this. Sadness rhymes with gladness, like twin sisters."

nine

On November 10th, as I rode with my father up to the cemetery, it was only drizzling. We'd decided we would celebrate my mother's birthday, not mourn her death day, and this was the first, the day she would have turned thirty-eight. She had chosen to be cremated and buried here, she told me, not over the mountains in Chiloquin, so she'd be near me in my home country.

The headstone glistened, bright with rain, the ground pretty well healed over with grass from the summer burial. My father took a knee and laid a beautiful bouquet, which he must have bought in Eugene, against the headstone. I left him to be alone with her and wandered downhill into the woods to find my own offering. Most leaves were gone from the Oregon white oaks and their winter dress was showing. Patches of moss on the trunks and bigger limbs glowed green as green can be, rejoicing in rain, and the branches and boughs were tufted with gray-green lichen, and still more lichen draped from some of the branches like robes on a minister. Those garments grow with the rain as the leaves loosen, and all winter, the leaves long gone, they take in the rainwater and drip it down, ever so slowly, from the tufts and the tips of their long strands. I call it ghost foliage.

As I poked around, not sure what I wanted, suddenly something knew I was there, something at home in the woods and the small sounds of rain and the mist hanging in little pockets where the woods opened up. I'd felt it often, in different ways. Sometimes it came slow and still and vague, as if the forest itself had a way of knowing. I'd also felt it in flashes—on and off, here, now there— like the spirit of a songbird or squirrel. And a very few times it came so concentrated, so clear and kingly, that I knew exactly what it was, though I'd never been blessed to see one. I could almost feel its broad paws on wet needle duff, could almost see its tawny body crouched, its eyes on me, listening, its dark tail-tip twitching, its mind a field of invisible light that knew me truer than I knew myself.

But this time the knowing was dark and kind of confused and made me chilly. I walked a little faster, stopped and bent down for a nice lichen beard on a fallen oak twig, and just as I turned to start up the hill my eyes locked with the black eyes of a raven, on a branch three feet from my face. Fear shocked me like nothing ever, pouring from the raven's wild eyes into mine and from me back into him. The bird was jabbering, croaking, whistling. I screamed, I must have, because my father came plowing down through the brushy trees calling my name, and the raven gave a half-strangled cry and flew.

"Henry! You all right, Henry?"

He put his hand on my shoulder, worry in his eyes. "What was it?"

"I don't know," I said. "I don't know what it was."

"You sounded awful scared," he said, pulling me to him. I broke away and started up the hill.

I placed my twig of lichen on top of the headstone, weighted with a small rock, the beard draping down and touching my mother's name.

* * *

The rain broke for a couple of days, and good thing. For that point in the season, mid-November, the rainfall total was a crazy ten inches above average. We heard of floods and mudslides all around western Oregon. I stopped in to ask Len Peppers if he'd ever seen anything like it.

"God yes," he said. "Flood of sixty-four. Roads washin' out, big ol' gullies. . . . A landin' gave way, I watched a hunnerd-ten-foot Skagit tower slidin' . . . down a mountainside, slowwwwly tippin' over. Sorry sight to a logger. . . . No work, no pay. Came right at Christmastime."

Len chuckled. "Damn sight better sittin' this side of the window."

"I love gettin' out in it," I said.

"Well do you now, nature boy." Len grinned, showing the gold in his yellow teeth. "I'd love to get you just once draggin' a thirty-foot choker in a drivin' rain and . . . scrabblin' down in the mud to jam the knob under a big log. . . . Make a man of you, that will. My first year I set one like that, come back all soaked . . . muddied up, and the riggin' slinger says . . . "Shit oh dear, kid. I couldn't tell, were you chokin' that log . . . or tryin' to *screw* it?" Len punched me in the shoulder and fell into a wheezy laugh.

I was visiting Len because my father had told me to mow the yard that afternoon, before the rain came back. Grass grows a little right through the fall and winter here, and he liked to get a jump on it while it was dry enough. Myself, I never saw the point of mowing. In summer all it did was train ten-inch daisies and buttercups to become, over time, two-inch daisies and buttercups. I thought those flowers were evolving all right on their own. Didn't like killing garter snakes, either. By the time I saw the snake, it was usually in two pieces and I felt sick in my stomach and my luck was poisoned for days.

I told my dad that burning the grass, like the Chelamela and other Kalapuyas did, made a lot more sense. Right, he said, let's burn the house down.

I started the mowing, but halfway through I declared an Air Pollution Alert—I was tired of breathing exhaust—and tromped out into the woods.

I was feeling perky because I'd been getting ready to run. I kept my hiking boots greased, and in my backpack in my bedroom closet were my sleeping bag, tube tent, extra pocketknife, headlamp and batteries, butane lighter, and other possibles. I'd been lifting cash from my father's wallet whenever I could, not enough that he would notice. When the time came I'd take his debit card, too. I'd watched him punch in his PIN at the ATM—it was LEEN, for Leenie. I had no idea where I'd go or how to get there, or if I'd go at all, but preparing for it was a comfort.

I always liked checking out the trees. The biggest on our ten acres were the ones close by the south side of the house, Douglas firs ten or twelve feet around the trunk that probably got started in Lewis and Clark's days. The flats out behind the house had been old growth once, the big trees felled by crosscut saws long before Len Peppers set his first choker, the logs hauled out by teams of mules or horses, later by steam donkeys. Their stumps were rotted away, not even ghosts anymore. Most of the woods had been clearcut twice since then, probably, and hadn't been replanted. The new growth came in crowds of spindly trees with puny green crowns, some already shaded to death by their taller kin. One part of our woods, though, maybe three acres, had been logged selectively, so the trees they spared had some size now and some room between them, with a few younger ones coming up. I liked the openness of that woods—plenty of dappled light and shade in fair weather, a healthy ground cover of sword fern and salal and evergreen huckleberry. A woods that invited you to walk.

It would be logged again, of course—my dad had talked about the two of us doing it ourselves when I got older—and afterward it would look pretty ragged. But the younger trees would get more sun and grow faster, and the ground would heal over, and the woods would look pretty nice again in a couple of years. Cart Stephens was right that growing trees like a field of corn made a poor excuse for a forest, and even those same-age plantations would be clearcut again in thirty or forty years, when the trees were just pecker poles still in grade school. That made no sense to me, but it must have paid because the owners kept doing it. Afterward, they usually sprayed the cut with herbicides to eliminate competition against another regiment of Doug fir soldier boys. When they sprayed larger areas, from helicopters, the poison sometimes drifted to homes and schools and showed up in the groundwater. Selectively cut woodlots weren't sprayed, and every time I saw one I admired it.

Walking the woods, looking and thinking, or just walking and looking, felt free and easy and comfortable to me, like Huck Finn said about life on a raft on the Mississippi. You're bound to fetch up somewhere and get caught in human complications, but you're not there now. If you're Huck you're on the river, and if you're me you're walking in the light of late autumn in a humble green kingdom, with juncos around you, siskins and kinglets, a towhee scratching the forest floor, and far off somewhere a flicker or pileated woodpecker hammering a snag.

* * *

What's a bad climate good for if you can't have fun with it? Cart and Josie, who I visited every few days—going the back way, of course—were only partway into their first full rainy season, and it just happened to be a doozy. They didn't regret where they'd settled, but Cart did grouse a little. "Is there an Oregon law against the sun shining in autumn?" he grumped once. "Yes there is," I answered. "Sunshine is too damn much like California for us."

He and Josie had been trying to think up a good name for their soggy little piece of heaven, and now it came to them. Their estate would be known forevermore, Cart announced with what might have been a smile, as "Dismal Acre."

They kept me up to date on what was going on at Karen Creek, where the bust still hadn't come down. State troopers had come back a few times but just sat in their rigs and watched. BLM law enforcers had been spotted eyeing the tree-sitters. One day an operator came, started the Cat, and drove it away, shedding fir boughs and mossy branches behind it, and parked it a quarter-mile down the road. The logging had almost certainly been put off till spring, but the Methuselans were taking no chances. A group of younger ones put up tents in the woods above the gate and settled in, and others, Cart and Josie included, were delivering supplies and news. They called the new community Chelamela Village. The tree-sitters were down from their trees and no one was inhabiting the irons at the gate, but scouts kept a lookout during daylight hours.

Cart stayed busy with the goings-on, writing press releases for the occupiers and keeping up with the other field of battle, in the courts. "I may have to re-retire to Berkeley to get some rest," he quipped. A delay till spring would give the legal team more time to mount another challenge to the Karen Creek sale, and maybe this time they'd win. "It's a damn good thing we kept them out of there," Cart said, a touch of pride in his voice.

I still marvel at how easy I was with Cart and Josie from the beginning. They were like instant grandparents who were also good friends. They never mentioned kids of their own, so I assumed—correctly, it turned out—that they'd wanted children but couldn't have any. They'd been missing me before they even met me. And maybe I'd been missing them.

One afternoon Josie peered over her half-frame glasses with her soft gray eyes and said, "Henry, I sense there's something troubling you. I don't mean to pry, but is your father mistreating you?"

I didn't answer for a few seconds. "Not really," I said. "He's just angry so much."

"Ah," she said. "Grief denied sometimes comes out that way. Would you say he's depressed?"

I shrugged. "I don't know what that is, really. I know he totally misses my mom. And he's drinking a lot. . . ."

"Counseling or a twelve-step program would be *so* good for him, and I bet his health insurance would cover it. Does he know that?"

"I don't know, but Josie, he doesn't think like you do. . . ."

"Then maybe speaking with Pastor Rogers could help?"

I gave a little snort. "My dad doesn't even like Pastor Rogers. He only goes to church for show."

"Well, how about you? Would you be comfortable speaking with the pastor?"

I shook my head. "I don't really know him like that."

"I understand," said Josie. "But Henry"—she reached out and touched my shoulder, a saucepan in her other hand—"please know that we are here to listen, any time. Sometimes talking out a problem really helps."

I couldn't meet her eyes. "Okay," I mumbled. "Thanks."

Hiking home by headlamp, I wondered what would've happened if I'd told her about my father whipping me and roughing me up. But at the time I thought other fathers probably did the same thing—my dad's father had whipped him hard, my mother told me—and to tell on him would have felt like betraying him. He was my only parent, and our little mess was just ours. So I didn't regret holding back, but I've regretted it ever since. Things might have turned out differently.

* * *

Jonah Rutledge came over with Cloudy Rains and her new dog one Saturday night for a roadkill venison dinner. The two of them had been an item for years, off and on, and now they were on. When they broke up Jonah always said they knew each other too well, but they couldn't quite get cured of each other, either. Cloudy, who was in her late thirties, was born in Duckworth and grew up all over the West in communes and Rainbow Gatherings and small towns; then she lived in Portland for a time, on her own, and resettled in Long Tom when I was a little kid. "I got dizzy growing up," she liked to say. "I was everywhere and wasn't anywhere, so I came home." I liked her for that. A lot of kids at school talked about leaving Duckworth and Long Tom as quick as they could to make a life somewhere else, but I wasn't one of them.

Cloudy—her given name was Claudia—made jewelry and jazzy quilts and sold enough to get by. When nobody else wanted to be mayor—it's not a whole lot of money or power—she ran for it and won.

I groaned to myself when I saw her dog, a yappy white cockapoo with hair over its eyes, but Cloudy was obviously in love with her. After dinner we were sitting in the living room. "You are just the sweetest *thing*," she said, and the little dog shook all over and wagged its stubby tail and sat up and gave Cloudy her front paws, at which Cloudy shook all over her short body and leaned down and kissed the dog on her nose.

"Jonah," said my father, "I'm afraid you can't compete with this rival."

Jonah smiled and said, "Looks about right for cougar bait to me."

My dad played along. "That's illegal, idn'it?"

"It is," said Jonah, "but only in the case of a real dog."

Cloudy leaned over and swatted his arm.

"I can't believe you rude men," she said. "Henry, surely *you* appreciate Miss Clover?"

"I really do," I said. "I'll give you a dollar if you let me stuff her and keep her for a pillow."

Cloudy threw up her arms and howled in misery. It was nice having company in the house, and laughter.

While they talked about other things, I played with Miss Clover. I got her good and amped up in the living room, then tore down the hall with her right on my heels and grabbed the molding at the kitchen doorway and swung to the side as Miss Clover shot skittering sideways across the kitchen linoleum as if it was ice, her poor little paws scrabbling fast as they could. I felt bad about it, though, so I lay down with her on my bed and looked into her eyes to see what we could share. I had tried with dogs and it hadn't worked, probably because dogs are so tuned in to humans they're just about human themselves. They key on our eyes and movements and tone of voice, always *readyready* to chase the ball or nip a cow's hocks or *EAT! PLEASE! NOW!*—or do anything else that might end with a scratch between the ears or a biscuit. Except for the mistreated ones, of course, who have nothing but yelps and snarls all twisted together inside, just like the humans who made them that way.

Humans, of course, are the hardest. I learned early on to tune people out the best I could, because if I didn't it was like loud staticky radio stations playing at once—anywhere, everywhere, in the past, in the future, only moments in the here and now. People were talking about "multitasking" back then; to me it sounded like a curse. A wild animal, if it isn't threatened, or hurt and half-looped like the bobcat Cart Stephens hit, is clearer, quieter, its mind right there in its body and senses. When I was in my gift, I didn't see the world through the animal's eyes or know what the animal knew, but I touched the stillness where the knowing lived. It was the stillness that gave me joy, and the one person I could share it with was my mother. We talked easily, but we could also just sit there, silent, and be together. Maybe that was why my father felt left out.

All I found in Miss Clover's eyes was a glow of tired eagerness.

I brought her back to the living room when I heard the conversation shift to the Karen Creek blockaders. "They'll wash out of there by Christmas," my father was saying.

"Ha!" said Jonah. "You said they'd wash out by Thanksgiving."

"I bet you five dollars," I piped up, "they'll still be there come spring, unless they win in court sooner."

"Why's that, Henry?" Cloudy asked.

"'Cause they believe in what they're doing, that's why. They're committed. They've got a whole little tent city in there."

My father was staring at me. "How the hell do you know so much?"

"I read the newspaper, duh."

Cloudy said, "I think Henry's right, you two. They're sincere, and in my humble opinion they're not all wrong."

"They're all wrong for my work," Jonah shot back. "His too."

"Sweetie pie," said Cloudy, "there's other places they can log. They don't have to cut so close to the big trees."

My father was shaking his head. "If you don't thin that forest, Cloudy, it's one big fire trap. And why the hell *shouldn't* they log there? The enviros got their park, didn't they? Where's it end, what they want?"

I tried to keep quiet but couldn't. "A forest is a continuum, Dad, did you know that? It's all one forest. There's a lot of mature trees in that sale, not just pecker poles."

He nailed me with a glare. "Mature means ready to mill. Why is it you sound just like they do?"

I shrugged. "'Cause I agree with 'em. And with Cloudy."

"Oh you do, do you?" He bit his lip and looked away.

Cloudy and Jonah steered the conversation to Thanksgiving, which was the coming Thursday. We were all going to Cloudy's place in Long Tom, where Jonah would barbecue a big turkey like he always did. But the mood had gone sour, and pretty soon they took off.

My father didn't waste any time. "You've been seein' those people again, haven't you."

"What if I have?"

"I'll show you what," he said.

"Stay away, Dad. I'm done with you whippin' me. . . ."

He swung the back of his hand and caught my face hard enough to knock me back on the sofa. I tasted blood in my mouth. I had tears in my eyes, but I stood up smiling.

"Guess what, Dad. I've been out there to Karen Creek, to help out. I might just go live with them."

He raised the back of his hand to swat me again but just held it there, his auburn hair all rumpled, his greenish-brown eyes wild, but he spoke slow and clear. "What do I have to do, Henry?"

"Hit me again, I guess. See if you can knock some teeth out this time. Big guy like you, shouldn't be a problem."

He lowered his hand.

"You know what, Dad? I like Cart and Josie because they're nice to me and fun to be with and they know more than you do. All you know how to do is read lumber and drink and get mad at everything. They're better than you, that's what they are."

His face kind of fell apart, as if he wasn't sure what he'd heard.

I went to my room and sat on my bed. I was trembling all over, but I felt cool fire inside. As if I had knocked *him* down. As if I'd hit a home run and my teammates were mobbing me at the plate.

When I'd calmed down a little, I went to the kitchen, found a bag of peas in the freezer, and went out the back door to the garage. My father was still in the living room. I sat in my mother's white Dodge, holding the bag of peas to my cheek. Her dreamcatcher, a hoop of woven willow strung with beaded silver-thread netting, hung from the rearview mirror.

"Is this what you meant?" I whispered.

In grade school I was a shrimp, my nose always in a book. I got picked on, called a pussy, so my mother told me a story from the Indians where she grew up. Thunder, the one-legged, red-painted bully whose Indian name was Yahya'haas, wrestled Eagle Boy's five uncles, the strongest men in the village, and threw each of them off a cliff into Klamath Lake. Their bones rose to the surface and clattered against the rocks.

Other villagers went to fight Thunder the next day, and Eagle Boy tagged along, though everyone told him he was too little. His mother said, "Let the boy go. Maybe he can teach us things." The boy said, "I want to die with my uncles." He asked to be painted red on the crown of his head, where his thoughts came in and taught him.

This time Yahya'haas was painted yellow and wearing a yellow coat that rattled as he hopped along on his yellow cane and one leg. As he wrestled the men and threw each into the lake, Eagle Boy watched at the cliff edge. He saw his five uncles and the others swimming under the surface of the lake, and he felt strong and glad. When all the men had been thrown—one of them almost broke Thunder's leg—Thunder taunted the boy: "I wonder if such a little fellow can wrestle. Come and try." He laughed at Eagle Boy and picked him up and juggled him in the air.

"You shouldn't laugh," said the boy, and being small he slipped through Thunder's hands, twisted off his leg, and pushed him into the lake.

"Come out, my people!" Eagle Boy then called, and all the defeated men rose out of the water.

As Eagle Boy led them away, the spirit of Yahya'haas screamed from the lake: "The boy lies, he didn't throw me! Look back and see!" Don't, the boy said, or the spirit would regain his power. The boy didn't look back as he called to the Thunder spirit: "You will never threaten my people again, but you will always live, on the mountains and by the lakes and rivers. You will mutter, you will grumble, but you will never harm me or my people again."

I remembered my mother telling me the story, and I remembered her before she died, bones showing under her skin as she gripped my arm, her dark eyes glinting.

"What am I supposed to do?" I whispered to the dreamcatcher.

After a while I got the blanket my mother always kept in the trunk, lay down across the back seat, and fell asleep to rain drumming lively on the garage roof.

ten

When I came into the kitchen in the morning, there was a plate of pancakes and bacon on the table. The shower was running in the bathroom. I took the plate to my bedroom and ate in there. He knocked on the door, said to get ready for church, and I said I couldn't worship today on account of injury. He opened the door and stared at me. "You don't look so bad," he said. "Don't make me do it again, Henry. Get dressed."

"Okay," I said. "Be right there."

I dressed, grabbed my slicker, slipped out the front door, circled around the house, caught his eye through the kitchen window above the sink, waved with a grin, and trotted into the woods.

The rain had slackened, and pretty soon it quit.

On an old logging road, a motion on the puddly track caught my eye. Three garter snakes, the little kind, were swimming and slithering overland when they should have been asleep in the ground. I'd never seen a snake so late in the year. Flushed out by the rains, I figured. Then I heard a familiar shrill call from the winter marsh, and another, and one more. Usually I didn't hear the first few chorus frogs till December, the full congregation not till February. "Good luck, boys!" I hollered.

I walked all day, rambling, knowing where I was because I knew the turns and connections of the overgrown roads. I saw garter snakes again, and newts crawling overland in a slow hurry. A red-tailed hawk was flapping in place on a high snag, something I'd never seen a hawk do. I saw an oak full of crows—not unusual— holding completely still and silent—very weird, in daylight. I felt weird myself, all worked up in a giddy confusion, my mind blowing around like a nervous wind. Was it me? Was *I* making the animals crazy?

When it got toward dark I put on my headlamp and headed home. My father's pickup was gone. I stoked the woodstoves and rummaged through the freezer and found a package of fish sticks. While they were cooking in the oven, I put ice in a glass and took my father's bottle of George Dickel out of its cabinet and poured some. Just a nip now, I said to myself.

I dipped the fish sticks in ranch dressing and ate every one, leafing through the Sunday *Register-Guard*. I remembered my mother then and cut up some lettuce and a carrot and celery and ate it with ranch dressing. For dessert I found vanilla ice cream and ate all of it with a sauce of raspberry jam and George Dickel. Tasty. George Dickel was made in Tullahoma, Tennessee, the label said—"Glad to see you if you can find us."

"I'll find you," I said. "Tennessee, Kentucky, Mississippi," I chanted in a whisper. "Oklahoma, Arkansas, Kansas, Nebraska. . . ."

* * *

I called Abner Truitt that evening and talked him into ditching school the next day. In my bed I heard my father come home late in the night and walk the hall to the kitchen and stop and swear to himself. He had to be looking at the dirty dishes and the George

Dickel bottle I'd left on the table. No pretending, I'd decided. I'll do what I do.

I slipped out before he woke up and did bike slaloms on the broken yellow line on Stamper Road until Abner showed up. We pumped up Boomer Mountain and down the far side to Cart and Josie's house. They were in the Bay Area till Wednesday and had hired me to check on Catrick every other day.

I liked showing Abner around the house, bragging on Josie's photos and Cart's books and their nice furniture.

"There's no TV," Abner said.

"They don't watch TV," I informed him. "They listen to public radio and they read. They drink martinis."

Abner raised his eyebrows. "What's in a martini?"

I groaned at my friend's ignorance. "Gin is, duh. But some people prefer whiskey in theirs."

Abner cracked a smile, gave his long brown curls a shake. "Do you know where they keep it?"

"'Course I do. They told me to help myself if I felt like it."

I knew the liquor cupboard because I'd seen Cart go to it. I pulled out a few bottles and a couple of glasses and we started tasting at the kitchen table. Gin finished last in the rankings. Canadian whiskey came in third, Mexican brandy placed second, and rum, we agreed, black rum with a palm tree on the label, took the blue ribbon.

"Too bad they don't have tequila," Abner mused. "Tequila is the *numero uno* of all hard liquor."

"They probably ran out," I speculated, then jumped up. "I'll tell you something they *do* have." I'd smelled it the first time I was in Cart's study, that unmistakable tang, the universal fragrance of public schools.

I found it in plain sight, a small wooden box tucked between books on a shelf. We sat on the living-room sofa and checked it out.

"Isn't much weed," I said.

"Come on, Tracker, we have to make smoke."

I took a hit and passed Cart's pipe.

"Whoa," said Abner, exhaling. "This is decent."

"Of course," I said. "Cart always keeps quality bud in the house."

Abner reached and shook me by my shoulders, his laugh rolling up in fluid waves. "Dude, you are so totally full of *shit!*" His touch felt good.

We had another hit. Lying back, my eyes closed, I felt made of light. A familiar thought opened. "Does it ever seem strange to you," I said, "that we're here in this world, and we're exactly who we are? And it's exactly this world?"

"It is what it is, man. We're here."

"But why, Abs? Why are you you? Why do Doug fir limbs curve up like outstretched arms? Why are things just this way?"

Abner shrugged. "This way's a good way."

"We're here and we *know* we're here," I pondered on. "Why do we know we're here?"

"Yeaaaah," Abner whispered in a long sigh. "Who can know that shit, Tracker? You remember Morgan Smith, from ninth grade? That girl has *developed*, man. She's what I'd like to know. . . ."

He chuckled, I snorted, we dissolved in laughter again. "Have you called Tess yet?" he asked.

"She called me. I didn't know what to say."

"Tracker, she is totally hot for you. But you have to respond, you know?"

"I will, I will. . . . But we're not 'just here,' Abs. Fourteen billion years of stars and planets aren't 'just here.' It *means* something that they're here, and we're here, and we know we're here, and. . . ."

But Abner had slipped into his dream of Morgan Smith, so I slipped away too, into the river just under my daylight mind where other meanings moved. But the river went still, and suddenly there in sharp focus was the bobcat on his haunches by the road, not stunned or hurt, but face-on with his full spirit—dark barring across the gray-tawny front, the ears needle-pointed, the eyes clear and sure. And then it wasn't him anymore. It was the big cat, not the prince but the king. Fear rippled through me . . . but there was no hunger in those great yellow eyes, no love or hatred, nothing but his clear, deep-as-drinkwater knowing. He was looking at me, and he knew me.

Surfacing through his fading face, I was myself again. I put the pipe and pot back in the box and the box back on Cart's shelf, then checked the cat's kibble and water and cleaned his litter box. "Caaat-rick," I called softly, "where are you, gray ghost?" Usually he wasn't shy, he'd come out and be sociable. Even the tame animal was acting strange.

Abner came into the kitchen shaking his head. "Is it still today?"

"It's happy hour. One for the road?"

We had one, and two more. I put the bottles back and rinsed the glasses and we stumbled out into the afternoon. For some reason it was hard to pedal in a straight line on the mile-long grade up Boomer Mountain. We swerved and wobbled all over the road, giggly and hollering. Abner lost it, dumped flat down on the pavement and lay there laughing. "Dude, it's the Special Olympics, and I just won!"

I laughed so hard I had to brake and stick a foot to the pavement to keep upright.

We heard a pickup coming up the grade half a mile behind us. "Better walk the bikes," I said. The truck slowed, pulled alongside, and the elfish face of Jonah Rutledge smiled out the open window. "Just a wild guess," he said, "but do you boys need a ride?"

"Angel!" I cried. "Sent by Heaven!"

"He cares where sparrows fall," said Jonah. "Throw the bikes in back."

"So where was the party, boys?" he asked with a goateed grin as we got going.

"Oh," I said. "Well, we found a bottle of whiskey, up on Pribble Hill. You know, where the older kids go to make out?"

"Hope the bottle wasn't full," Jonah said, "'cause I'm sure it's empty now. Smells like you found something to smoke too."

Abner snickered.

"Jonah, you won't tell my dad, will you? Please?"

"I'll tell you this, Henry. You're fifteen years old and you shouldn't be getting stoned and plastered. You do this a lot?"

"Almost never. We found the bottle, and . . . I don't mean to say it was divine providence, but. . . ."

"Don't saddle God with your behavior, Henry. Your dad tells me you're getting rebellious. Acting up."

"Not really," I said.

"Not really? You're all he's got now, Henry. You mean everything to him. Can't you just try to get along?"

"Yeah. I could do better."

"I won't tell him. But if I see you like this again. . . . Enough said?"

"Loud and clear, Jonah. Thank you."

He gave me a pat on the knee.

Jonah dropped me at the driveway mouth and drove on to take Abner home, going out of his way to do it.

My father should have been at work, but his pickup was right there. I walked my bike past the house, kind of wobbly, and leaned it against the far side of the garage. I slipped inside to the white Dodge, my home away from home. Everything was spinning. I thought I might puke and wished I would, but didn't. Then suddenly the light came on and he was yanking me out of the car by the arm. He half-dragged me across the yard into the kitchen.

"Look at you," he said. "Full of liquor, and I smell pot, too. Get in that room." He shoved me into my bedroom and slammed the door shut.

I flopped on the bed, the room spinning around me. I wanted to cut myself, but the desk was too far. After a while I fumbled out of my pants and shirt and got in under the covers. I lay on my belly, and the spinning eased off a little.

*　*　*

Hands, a commotion. Ripe whiskey breath. My underwear was down and his knees between my legs before I was even awake. *"Stop it!"* I hollered, but I was groggy and heavy and he pulled my rear end up and fumbled and pushed it into me. I screamed.

"Shut up and take your medicine," he said, his voice tight. I could only squirm—he had my arms pinned, my feet had nothing to kick up against. He grunted as he thrusted.

"Makin' me train you like a dog," he whispered.

"Dad, it *hurts.* . . ."

"Gonna mind me now?"

"*Yes*, all right?"

"Am I good enough for you?"

"Yes!"

Then he groaned as if he'd been stabbed and it got all slick in there. He kept driving it, but at least it didn't hurt as much. He groaned again.

As he climbed off I twisted myself face up and swung blindly, hitting his shoulder, and swung again. "Get out of here!" I screamed.

He grabbed my wrists. "Settle down, Henry. You know damn well you had this comin'."

I tried to spit in his face, but my mouth was dry as sand. "Just get out," I said, my voice rasping in my throat. I felt electric-shocked.

This is really happening, was all I could think. I knew everything had changed, but it was more than I could think about, and so—I know it sounds crazy, but it's true—I just fell back to sleep.

part two

There is a road, no simple highway,
Between the dawn and the dark of night.
And if you go no one may follow,
That path is for your steps alone.

—Grateful Dead, from "Ripple"

eleven

In the early sun I went out back with the black sunflower seeds. I held out my hand but the chickadees hung back, hopping in the wild hazelnuts and the big rhododendron, singing their scold. Three of them. Four.

Skriiitch a-dee. . . a-dee dee . . .

They didn't like what I was.

I'd have to get quieter. I breathed in and let it out, then again not so deep, and again. The hazelnut leaves were turning a little in a slight breeze, the light blinking through. I closed my eyes and felt cool sun and shadow moving on my face, showing pink through my eyelids. I tried to let the breeze breathe through me.

I heard their talk, their flutters—but they wouldn't come.

I held out the seeds in my other hand. *Please,* I prayed.

Skriiitch a-dee . . .

Then at last the touch, tiny claws on my first finger. I'd flinched and scared them off the first times I tried it. Now I knew that dry, ticklish grip. The chickadee hopped once, twice, toward the seeds. Then the quick poke, the seeds shifting as the bird took one, then a quick flit of wings and gone.

Songbirds have a spirit like tiny puffs of air. All in motion, all now. What they know they don't know for long, but they never don't know.

I changed arms, got quiet again, and another one came. I watched through the slit under one eyelid its black cap and brown shoulders, its little head cocked, the quick take, one seed only. Tickled my palm as it flew off. I heard it in the hazelnuts, tapping the seed it held against a branch with its feet.

A nuthatch sounded, that mournful one-note call. A flat dart of a bird with a black-and-white striped head, dark gray wings, orange underneath. I tried to breathe myself still again, but the nuthatch wouldn't come. I waited. I waited. I scattered the rest of the seed. Usually none was left. But two had come, at least.

The day was chilly but I had dressed for it, long underwear, gloves, and a knit cap under my helmet. As I got on my bike, I heard the front door open. "Come in and have some breakfast, Henry."

"Touch me and I'll call the sheriff," I said.

It helped to be on the move, pumping hard over Brautigan Ridge, then coasting the curves down the far side toward town. My bottom was in bad shape for riding, so I stood up on the pedals all I could.

Hamilton & Sons wouldn't open for half an hour, so I pedaled north along a side street to Duckworth High. It's nothing special to look at, a few small buildings connected by covered walkways to keep the weather off. Everyone was in class. Two hours ago there'd been cars and pickups pulling in, shouts and laughs, yellow buses. Now it was a sleeping city, wind clanking the flag-rope hardware against the pole.

I rode slowly south on Territorial Road through Duckworth, taking comfort in the familiar buildings. Mac Johnson's barber shop, where my father and I got our six-dollar haircuts. Hood's Have-it Sell-it Collectibles and Used Books, in a rundown yellow house. Across the road was Lily's Lift, an old gas station turned into a coffee shop. Lily had painted the little building purple, grew rambling roses up the gas pumps, hung chains of sparkly beads and mirror glass around the interior, baked great cinnamon buns, made good espresso, and the business caught on. Coffee turned out to sell better than gas, though it cost a lot more per gallon.

Then the post office, and Hamilton & Sons Hardware just across the road.

The elder Hamilton, Roger, had retired to paint pictures. I asked Sangg, the son on duty that day, what the strongest door lock was.

"For security," he said, "there is no substitute for a deadbolt. Is it for a front door?"

"An inside door."

Sangg folded his arms and took a troubled look on his face. He was a few years older than me, and it pained him how ignorant people could be about hardware. "Usually, Henry, for an interior door, the lock in the knob set is considered sufficient."

"It's an old house," I told him. "Old knobs, no locks. Could I just get one of those slide locks you work by hand?"

"Well," said Sangg, "I can sell you one of those, Henry, but you'll have to cut out a section of the molding on the door frame to get the receiving bracket flush with the sliding part on the door, and I'd hate to see you ruin your molding. How about installing a new locking knob set?"

"I don't know how to do that," I said.

"Well, your dad could help you, couldn't he?"

"Just a slide lock, please. I don't care about the molding. Two slide locks."

Heading on south, I crossed over the Long Tom River—a mighty thirty feet broad at that point, running high and muddy from the rains—and veered into the parking lot of Big's Hi-Yu-He-He in Long Tom. The sign had been repainted, but the red splats on the rubbly asphalt were holding up pretty well after five months of tires and weather. I stared for a while, remembering, and suddenly an idea burst open in my head with a rush of cool anger, breaking the dead sadness I'd been packing around all morning. It was not a good idea. It was a very bad idea, but in the moment it felt very good. I knew what to do.

I kept on south down Territorial Road with new energy, past the library where my mother had worked and I began my life smelling books, then turned west up Heather Hill and down along the beautiful shady bottoms of Evelyn's Run to the town of Daugherty, which is mainly the plant and log yards of the Siuslaw Pacific Timber Company, plus Tom and Vic's gas and convenience store, a post office the size of a closet, and the Sam and Max Saloon, an old roadhouse on the way to the coast named for its twin-brother founders. Today the signboard read: Beer Drinkers Wanted. Inquire Within.

The S.P. log decks, which included many hefty ones, loomed by the road like a dark mountain range. All my life I had loved the smell of the place—the pitchy tang of fresh-sliced green Doug fir, and the mellower homey scent of dry lumber stacked around the yard. It had always smelled like a new beginning, but now I remembered my father catcalling three hippies sitting cross-legged by the fence during the Oregon Country Fair, chanting a lament for the fallen trees. I'd laughed with my father at the time, but now those enormous stacks of tree trunks, and the roaring, clanking, shrieking din of saws, beltlines, and forklifts, and even the smells I loved seemed evil pure and simple, as wrong and ugly as anything could be. My dander rose and my bad idea got much bigger. *This'll be for the three hippies*, I said to myself.

I was all revved up but couldn't go home, not yet, so I pumped up Hammerstone Mountain for the view, then down to the little cemetery where a lot of Free Souls motorcyclists were buried, with cool painted headstones and rock gardens marking the graves. When the sun got low enough, I biked home on roads where my father wouldn't see me as he drove to work.

In the garage I found what I wanted, a sack almost full, under the workbench where we ran a tumbler sometimes to polish agates from the coast. I put the sack in the white Dodge and went in to spend some time on the computer as I waited for full darkness. Since that day at the blockade, I'd been doing some reading on environmental protests, all kinds. I knew my father had no clue how to track where I went on the computer. I didn't either, so I'd written down some step-by-step notes that got me now where I wanted to go. Computers were just getting big back then, and people were saying the Information Superhighway would lead us to some kind of heaven on Earth, and all for free! They might come to regret the whole thing, I remember thinking as I clicked and keyed my way into the details of my very bad idea.

* * *

The white Dodge was an automatic, easy to drive. Even in daylight those country roads had little traffic, almost none at night. Two cars passed me going the other way, and as each came up I didn't know if I should sit up straight to look more like an adult or slump down to look less like anybody. I knew you don't get a good look at other drivers at night, but still, in the glare of those headlights I felt totally exposed. It was a relief to turn onto the gravel road. On the spur road up to the site I went parking lights-only and very, very slow. They'd probably moved it again, I told myself—halfway hopefully—but very soon there it was, that huge hulk, off the road on the left.

I pulled over, got out, stood still. A stiff wind was blowing in the treetops. The gate was a quarter-mile up the road, Chelamela Village farther yet. I took a deep breath, turned my headlamp on, got the diagrams I'd printed from the computer, and circled the machine three times. Not everything matched up with the diagrams, but the oil-fill cap with a pull handle did, on the front right side of the dozer. The cap, with a built-in dipstick, had no lock. I went for the sack and the funnel I'd grabbed in the kitchen, and that fine-grade silicon carbide rock-polishing grit flowed nicely into the oil intake. The instructions said a pocketful would be plenty, but it was a big machine so I poured in several pocketfuls. After that I looked for other intakes and opened one with a big screw-off cap. One sniff told me I'd found the diesel tank, so I poured some grit into that too, saving a couple of handfuls. Then I went back and checked the oil-fill dipstick, wiping and rechecking it until no grit showed. I took my weapons to the Dodge and drove it out of there by parking lights, feeling as high as Eagle Boy must have when he'd thrown Big Thunder over the cliff.

Back home, I took the grit sack and funnel from the seat beside me and started out of the garage, then froze. Where were the diagrams? Oh shit shit shit. I ran back and opened all the car doors, checked the floors and under the seats and the papers weren't anywhere. Like other things I'd printed from the computer, they had time and date printed at the bottom and numbers at the top that for all I knew were the serial number of our computer. I'd have to go back. I reached for the keys in my jacket pocket and something crinkled. Ahhh. . . . The papers, right where I'd folded and tucked them away.

In the house I burned the diagrams in the kitchen woodstove. The other job, my first bad idea, could only be done later. My father would be home in two hours and I needed to secure my room.

I fetched the tools, but when I looked at the locks I knew they wouldn't do the job. So I measured my window, went out with a bow saw and found a stout Doug-fir pole where we kept some behind the shed. It was raining now, the wind rising. On the back steps I sawed off two lengths, each a tiny bit long, then came in and jammed them into the window frame on top of the lower sash so it couldn't be raised. I went to the kitchen and loaded a couple of shopping bags from the reefer and pantry, whatever looked good, and carried the bags to my room. I pulled and shoved my bed from its place in the far corner by the window, and butted the head of it against the door to the hall. I sized up all the large objects in the room—my dresser, my desk, a big wooden chair, a trunk from the closet—and lined them up to brace the foot of the bed against the outside wall I'd moved it from. There was still a gap, so I filled it in with my mother's library-size dictionary and some other hardbacks, then squeezed in a few thin paperbacks for the final tightening. The power of books.

I climbed out the window and came in the back and rammed the bedroom door hard as I could with my shoulder. Not a shiver. Then I went down the cellar stairs for one last thing and found it in its usual place. The wind was howling now, rain lashing the house in sheets.

Back in my fort, the window stops in place and the shade down, I tore into a couple of bananas and some crackers and cheese. Hadn't eaten a thing all day, I realized. I was on the bed, propped up on pillows against the door, when I heard my father come in the back and walk to my doorway. He knocked hard twice, right behind my head.

"Henry?" he said. "This storm's a big one. There's trees goin' down all over." He was trying to be conversational.

"Thanks for the weather report," I said.

"Did you get some dinner?"

"Yup, sure did."

"Well, I expect you to be up and ready for lessons tomorrow. I'll wake you if I need to."

"Okeydokey."

I snoozed for a while, half listening to the wind hurling its rain. It was an old house, kind of loose-jointed, and it groaned along with the storm. My reading lamp flickered, went off for a second, and came back on.

When I thought I heard my father snoring, I pressed my ear to the wall to be sure. I put on my headlamp, quietly opened the window and slipped out into the wet rhododendrons. The rain had slackened some, but the wind was sounding a steady swell in the tree crowns, with a *crack* now and then when a limb or small tree went down. I fetched my weapons and went to my father's truck, parked by the garage. The wind muffled my noises, and the operation didn't take long. Pop the hood, screw off the oil-fill cap, insert the funnel, pour in the rest of the grit. Replace the cap, gently latch down the hood. Piece of cake, for an experienced terrorist. I felt a pang for the truck, which I'd always liked, but I had justice to do.

As I hurried around back of the house, I heard a good-sized tree go down in the woods with a crackle and a thudding crash.

Inside, I toweled my head with a dirty t-shirt, pissed out the window and secured it. Threw my wet clothes in a corner and put on fresh jeans and shirt.

In bed I felt zingy, light-headed as if with a low fever, my thoughts rattling like an engine running with busted parts. I was excited to the brink of fear, the way I'd felt in a raft floating toward Rainie Falls on the Rogue River, excitement that stirs your belly and makes your dick a little hard. I slowed my breathing, intentionally relaxed my muscles, and I must have slept because I woke with a jolt of panic when my father knocked like two gunshots and told me to get up.

"I'm takin' the day off," I hollered through the door.

He turned the knob and tried to open the door, then put his shoulder to it a few times, hard. The bed shook but the barricade only creaked. I heard him swear.

"Open it!" he shouted.

"That's okay," I shouted back. "I've got my breakfast, don't need room service."

As he clumped out the back door, I sat up at the head of the bed, facing the blinded window across the room. I heard him claw at the window, but he had no purchase.

"Henry," he said, his voice hoarse. "Don't do this. Just come on out."

"I'm not comin' out," I told him. "Don't recommend you comin' in, either."

In the silence, rain pattering the rhododendrons, I could just about hear him think. I held the deer rifle against my knees, tilted up to the left. My thumb was on the safety. I'd chambered a cartridge before going to bed.

I heard him push out of the rhodies, come in the back door, clomp down the cellar stairs and back up.

"You don't need that gun, Henry," he said through the bedroom door. "Just come out when you're ready. I won't hurt you, I promise." And that was the last I heard from him till midafternoon, when he said through the door that he was going to work and he'd be home about the usual time. I heard the pickup start and drive out.

My plan's fatal flaw was that I didn't have a plan, but it didn't matter. Things were just happening. I liked being in control, but I was definitely *out* of control, all worked up and fidgety. I paced the room, jumped up and down for a few minutes, took a pillow and whapped its stuffing out on the furniture bracing the bed. I stood on my head for as long as I could, then did it again. I got paper and a pencil out of the desk and started writing random stuff that came into my head, raging on the page, wrote two pages and quit. I took off my clothes and sat in the closet, put my clothes back on and a hoodie and crawled out the window.

It was dark now, and still. The rain had quit and stars were out, sharp and glinting. Orion the Hunter, his sword dangling, was framed by the black treetops. What could he be hunting up there? Only stars, and he was made of stars himself. . . . I skipped and danced around the backyard, arms folded across my chest, my body warming. The earth all full of rain smelled rich and good, but the night air seemed to vibrate. Light flashed at the edges of my vision.

Suddenly, in the trees, a flap and thrash—a black shadow flew out just over my head with a screech as I fell backward to the grass. A great horned owl—I saw his pointed tufts against the stars—but an owl out of its head, doing nothing like an owl ever did.

"What?" I said aloud. "What's wrong?"

In the near woods other birds, little ones, were flitting with a familiar scold. *Skriiitch a dee . . . a dee dee . . . .*

"At *night?* Tell me why," I pleaded.

I stood up, stopped short. Closed my eyes, looked again. Through the break in the woods to the south, a blue light, whitish blue, was wavering faintly around the dark rise of Brother Jim Butte. It wasn't my eyes. The light was there, going almost dark and returning, a shimmering aura. I thought of the movie, *Close Encounters*. I was shaking all over.

Kyew, kyew, went a bird I didn't know.

I ran for the house and grabbed a half-rack of my father's Bud from the reefer. In my fortress again, I twisted the top off a beer and drank it fast, sitting on my bed. Settle down, I told myself. Drank another beer. Settle down. Drank another beer and relaxed a little. Got up and pissed out the window. My bedside clock said midnight, so after that I kept the window braced and the blind down and pissed into empty beer bottles. Recycling. Maybe I'd drink all twelve, piss the empties full, twist the tops back on and put the half-rack back in the reefer.

When my dad came home he tried the bedroom door, not hard, and went out the back. "Henry?" his voice came, outside the window.

"Still here."

"Henry, I don't want you to hurt yourself."

"Okay, I won't."

"Will you open the window, please?"

I left the rifle on the bed, crawled to the window so my silhouette wouldn't show, tugged on the shade and let it roll up with a loud snap. Heard a quick thrash in the bushes. Scared him! I scampered back to bed, leaned against the pillows, the deer rifle angled up against my knees.

"You don't get to say," I told him. "You lost that right."

Through the window, in the light of the ceiling lamp, his face looked ghostly. I wondered what I looked like to him.

"Henry, could we just talk?"

"You. Don't. Get. To. Say. Is there part of that you don't understand?"

"I'll have to break the window then."

"Bad idea, Dad."

I put the rifle to my shoulder, resting it on my knees tilted to-gether. Through the scope his face was a pale watery pool. I set the crosshairs between the hollows of his eyes. Thumbed the safety off. I'd only fired this gun a couple of times. My finger didn't know its trigger the way it knew the .22's.

I couldn't believe my father was standing there, a thirty-ought-six trained on his face, and him just staring back. He wasn't afraid, and he should have been.

"Stand away from the window," I ordered.

He didn't move.

"*Stand away!*" I yelled, and my finger squeezed before I meant it to.

For an instant I saw a hole in the middle of a crazy-crack pattern, then glass falling with a tinkle and clatter inside and out. I worked the bolt to eject the shell, breathed the powder smoke, chambered a new cartridge, and closed the bolt as loud as I could.

"That's better," I said. "It was stuffy in here." But it came out qua-very, not the way I wanted.

"Want a beer, Dad?" I pulled one from the half-case and tossed it through the empty window frame into the rhodies, then twisted the top off one for myself. "Don't be shy, you paid for it."

Just the sound of wind in the big trees by the house.

"Dad?"

I'd gulped about half my beer when he finally spoke. "I'm here," he said, and I let out a long breath. He sounded uncertain, like a little boy.

"Dad, go to bed. I'm not gonna hurt myself, and if you stay out I'm not gonna hurt you."

After a while I heard the front door open and close, and a few min-utes later I heard him in the bathroom and then in his bedroom.

I got an extra blanket from the closet and went to bed myself, the rifle beside me on top of the covers, the safety on. I turned off the ceiling light and my lamp. It was nice having the outside in. Wind was surging in the trees, singing its old, happy, and mournful song, from a thousand years and a thousand miles away. It sang strong and true, rising and falling in slow swells, it sang in the trees and under the eaves of the house and flowed in through the blown-out window and touched my face.

twelve

The rifle hit the floor with a clunk. The bed was shaking, the room was shaking, pans were clattering in the kitchen, dishes falling. I saw 4:46 on my bedside clock just as the red numbers went dark. Limbs were banging the roof like somebody angry to get in. Then the shaking settled to a queasy liquidy roll. The wind whistling, the house creaking.

Now came a loud, ripping groan and the room exploded.

Next thing I knew, I was crouched by the right side of the bed, choking on dust and wondering what smelled so strong. Felt the nightstand for my headlamp, found it on the floor, fumbled it on. The left half of my room was smashed in almost to my bed, a ridiculous mess of splintered lumber, lath and plaster, and cardboard boxes spilling out Christmas decorations and phonograph records. A huge limb with broken boughs was thrust down into the mess with strips of bark hanging off it, showing the white sapwood. That was it. The green sap-smell of Douglas fir. The corner of the room where I had slept since I was three, almost every night of my life until the day before yesterday, was crushed and buried.

"Dad?" I called.

I wondered how I'd gotten dressed, then remembered I'd slept in my clothes to be ready for anything. Found my sneakers—I'd been crouching on them—and went to the part of the window I could still see. The jumble was loose there, mostly lath and plaster. I cleared it, then used a piece of plank to knock the jagged edging of glass out of the frame and clambered out. Best I could tell in the dark, the tree wasn't the one I had guessed, the leaner, but a bigger one next to it, and that one had brought down a smaller one with it, and together they'd stove in half of my father's bedroom and half of mine. I scrambled around back and in through the kitchen, where broken dishes were scattered all over the floor. The hallway ceiling was sagging, the walls bowed and cracked. My father's door was jammed shut.

"Dad!" I yelled.

I tried the door with my shoulder but just bounced off, so I ran to the shed for a maul and axe and went at the door with sideways swings of the maul. It was solid wood, not hollow, and I had to stop when I was gasping and my arms wouldn't move. For a moment the house was shaking and rolling again. I went back to bashing, the battered door scraped open an inch, and I kept hitting it till I could squeeze through.

There wasn't much to see. My father's bed, its head against the outside wall, was totally buried.

"Dad!"

A few seconds later: "Henry . . . get me out of here, Henry." His voice was weak.

"I will, Dad. Are you hurt, or just stuck?"

He didn't answer. On my way out through the kitchen I lifted the phone, but of course it was dead. In the shed I rounded up a pry bar, come-along, both chainsaws, the fuel can, and carried everything into the hallway in two trips. Then in the bedroom I started yanking away loose rubble toward where the bed was buried.

"Are you hurt?" I hollered.

"I'm pinned," he said. "Son of a bitch, Henry, I got joists and crap all over me. My ribs are broke. . . ." I heard his wheezy breathing.

"Hang on, Dad. Which side of the bed are you on?"

"What? Right side . . . east side."

"Good, that helps." I cleared a way to the near bedpost, felt the quilt as far up as I could and touched something. "You feel my hand on your foot?" I heard the wind keening through the torn roof.

"I feel it."

Alongside the bed the debris was heavier, under more pressure, a series of two-by-twelve joists and punky rafters jammed against the bed and floor. My father was groaning. I cranked up the smaller chainsaw and cut through a joist, careful not to get the bar bound up. I worried the load would sag down harder, but it didn't seem to, so I sawed through the next joist and some particleboard flooring, shoving away the loose pieces, some magazines, a lamp.

"Talk to me, Dad."

"I can't move," he whispered. "I can move my right arm . . . my head a little."

Piece by piece I opened a tunnel along the bedside, scared to death I'd make it worse, breathing in plaster dust, saw chips, exhaust. One joist jammed against the floor seemed to be bearing an extra lot of weight, so I left it and worked around it. On the next one I hit big nails and broke the chain in a spew of yellow sparks, the loose chain just about raking my face. I cleared debris and backed out for the other saw.

"Dad. You there?"

"Hurry," he said. He sounded faint.

The big saw was harder to work with in that tight space. I just laid the bar to whatever was next, the chips flying into my face—goggles, forgot goggles—the exhaust choking me, until finally I had to kill the saw and back away to clear my head and not pass out. When I'd blinked and watered my eyes clear and could breathe again, I crawled in, pulled away more rubble, everything I could reach that would move, and there in the headlamp beam was an opening swimming with plaster dust but I could see the side of my father's head.

"Dad!"

His eyes opened. He turned his head toward me a couple of inches. I heard his rumbly breath.

"I'm fadin' out," he whispered. "I love you, Henry. . . . And I'm sorry."

"I love you too," I said, just as his eyes closed. "You'll see Mom. I know you don't believe it, but you will." I reached through the gap but couldn't touch him.

I watched and listened. His breath stirred the dust floating over his face, came slower, then quit. I stayed a few minutes to be sure, kneeling, full of everything but thoughts. There was nothing I could do. I heard the wind whistling, felt the draft. The ruined house was breathing, but not my father.

* * *

I suppose I was in shock, or denial, but my one thought was: I belong to the State of Oregon now. They'll stick me in some orphanage or foster home. They'll send me to one of my grandmothers.

I decided to bolt. I needed to hide out a while, get myself together, let things settle and see where I stood.

My gear was packed. My dad's wallet was on his dresser by the door. I took the cash and his credit card and ATM card and his truck keys, then went to my bedroom and crammed my backpack with food, the house rolling and groaning with another shake. Crammed in a little more in the kitchen. I didn't hang around wondering did I have this or would I need that.

I'd thought to start out on my bike, but I had to climb out the driveway, it was so choked with blowdowns and shakedowns, and Stamper Road wasn't much better. The wind was easing now. Voices floated out of the woods here and there as I started up Boomer

Mountain, clambering over tree after tree. The pack weighed a ton. A woman was sobbing, a man's voice trying to comfort her. Somebody had a radio going, broadcasters breaking in on each other with news I heard in pieces . . . *An overpass down . . . no word from the coast . . . Ya-Po-Ah Terrace . . . mudslides, the South Hills . . . unconfirmed deaths.* . . . Plenty of misery, but I had my own. Two or three homes— smart people—had generators going. A chainsaw started, revved, then whined steady as it bit into wood. Somebody hollered, maybe to me. I didn't look. I kept going.

The pavement had cracked, and some of the cracks yawned. Len Peppers' little house looked fine, just a couple of small ones leaning on it as if they'd needed to rest. He could be hurt, though. I started into his drive, then stopped. If I talked to Len, talked to anyone, I'd have to explain myself. I'd lose my purpose. The house looked okay. "Len," I murmured, "you're a tough old logger, you'll be all right."

I worried about Cart and Josie, too, but I'd have to go clear down the far side of Boomer Mountain to check. The bigger trees at Dismal Acre were away from the house, and the house was newer than ours and well built. If it had taken a hit, probably not much harm. I hoped Josie's photos were okay, but I needed to light out, to get gone. Turning north on the gravel road felt like shutting a door behind me, a big heavy door. Down across the little stream bottom, where there weren't many blowdowns, up Noble Dog Ridge, and I was starting to get some spirit. I was even happy, maybe. Jimmie Dale Gilmore was singing in my head, so I started singing myself: *Laid around and stayed around this old town too long, summer's almost gone, winter's comin' on.* . . .

In the plantations on Noble Dog there'd been a lot of little earthslides, each taking a clump of little trees with it, but hardly any blowdown—the soldier trees weren't tall enough, it would take a tornado or a bomb. I stopped once, queasy in my gut, and realized the ground was swimming again. This solid earth is just a different kind of liquid, and the wind that stirs it blows underground. I wondered about the coast, how big the tsunami had been, what it had done to old-town Florence on the river mouth, and to Yachats, Waldport, all the towns and homes. Some were up on cliffs and headlands, they'd be fine. The coast itself would be fine, just rearranged a little, but a lot of buildings and a lot of people would be gone.

I remembered traveling 101 with my mom and dad, the absurd blue "Tsunami Zone" signs. My dad would say, "Oh hell, look out to sea, Henry, is it comin'?" And I'd say back, "Be a lot less trouble if it wasn't," and we all wondered where exactly they expected people to go with a fifty-foot wave rearing up the beach. Higher ground was scarce, and if the quake came in summer, the towns would be packed with traffic. People on the beach would have ten or fifteen minutes, if they even heard the siren. It would all be very natural, of course. A good rainstorm can drown whole cities of ants. We think we're smarter, but I doubted our smarts had impressed the tsunami much.

Rampage Creek was living up to its name, but I crawled just above the angry brown torrent on a new-fallen Douglas fir, my pack wobbling me side to side. Farther on, I heard sheep bawling, patches of human voice downslope to the east. Smoke was rising from the vineyard, not just stove smoke. As I neared the Methuselahs I thought I heard a drift of voices from Chelamela Village. They'd be fine, unless someone had pitched a tent under the wrong limb.

The ancient ones had shed a lot of litter, but only one tree had gone down that I could see. The oldest of them had known earthquakes before, three hundred years ago. I sat on my pack, resting my back against a mossy trunk, drinking water. My arms were rubber. I'd wrenched my right shoulder. My left elbow was swelling where I'd banged it, my knees were rubbed raw, and my hands were grubby and full of splinters from grabbing debris. Work gloves, I'd forgotten them too. My eyes felt caked with dust.

There was daylight left, but the longer I sat the clearer it got that I was done for the day. Wherever I was going, it wasn't a race. Nobody would be driving in to bother me, either. The Methuselah Grove was wilderness again. The sign on the road down below told visitors no fires, no overnight camping, no this and no that, but like the sign Woody Guthrie saw in "This Land Is Your Land," on the back side, my side, it didn't say a goddamn thing.

Stiff, shivering, I cleared a few fallen limbs and strung my tube-tent on a mossy patch between two small trees. Gathered twigs off shrubs and dry tinder from inside a rotting log, some bigger sticks that weren't too wet, and lit a fire with my handy Bic lighter—the white man's fire drill, my father liked to call it. Ate a can of tuna fish and a candy bar and took a couple of swallows off my father's last bottle of George Dickel. Then I remembered what day it was. I had just eaten Thanksgiving dinner. Just like that I was crying, and I cried for a long time, and to get myself to quit crying I finished the whiskey. With my gut burning I lurched over to a little mossy rock, held the bottle by its neck and smashed it. In the firelight I looked at the jagged neck. I rolled up my right sleeve and watched as I opened a long line winding like a river down the inside of my forearm. I stared for a moment, the blood gathering, then dropped the bottle neck into the fire and stumbled to the tube-tent. My father was on my mind, but I shut the door on him, a door of thick heavy planks. In my sleeping bag I licked the blood from my arm and felt the ground gently roll as I fell asleep.

* * *

In the morning I was stiff and hurt all over, and I got going right away. The moment I woke, I knew my course had been set. I would hike to the Pacific, overland. I'd see what it looked like over there. Maybe I could help somehow, then I'd decide what was next. Maybe hitchhike 101, north or south, whichever way was open. I knew it would be a hard ramble. The Coast Range isn't much for elevation, but the little mountains are steep, the stream bottoms full of thickets and logjams. The lay of the land is all up and all down, and most of it's a nasty thrash to bushwhack. The logging roads would help, though, and I was in no hurry, and I needed a challenge. I had plenty to think about and no desire to think about it. I wanted to be finding my way, climbing the next hill, sleeping good sleeps.

I'd been hiking less than an hour when I topped a little ridge and looked to my left—and there he was at last, in a shallow ravine, crouched by the deer carcass he'd just looked up from. Not fifty feet away, his long tawny tail twitching like a mind of its own. He was enormous. I froze on shaky knees, which is probably the right thing to do in the presence of a god. For a sliver of a second, looking into those yellow eyes, I felt the big cat's bright, ranging spirit. I recognized him the way it happens in a dream, when someone's with you and it's no one from your regular life, but you know this companion and always have. You know him in your soul.

I kept expecting him to run, but he never left his crouch, never shifted his eyes, the dark tip of his tail twirling. I feared and I felt flooded with glory. Finally I had to look away, and when I did I realized that I was the one who needed to leave. I started to bow to him from the waist, but I owed him more than that. I slipped out of my pack, went to my knees, put my hands together and lowered my forehead clear to the needle duff. The back of the neck is where they kill deer, shearing the spine with jaws like a steel trap. I was his if he wanted, and I halfway longed for it. The lunge, the raking claws, the last split second of letting go. . . . My life was pretty well screwed up, and this would be a good death.

The cat was sitting, a little more relaxed, when I stood to go. "Thank you for the honor," I said. "I know you have watched me many times."

As I walked away, on rubber knees, I couldn't help taking quick looks back. They can jump thirty feet from a standstill, so maybe looking is right too, when you're not a god yourself.

I hiked on in a glow. I was walking the truest ground of my life. By noon, more or less—I've never worn a watch—I was farther west than I'd ever day-hiked in that direction. My backpack felt full of bricks. I had a compass and was just trying to go mostly west, north or south in little jags where it would help. The land was a jumble, the forest was thick, clearcuts were brushy and stumbly but occasionally gave a glimpse to the west. The logging roads were good walking but mostly tended north or south. To stay on course I had to keep plunging down off a road through brushy woods, slipping all the way on rocks and moss and wet salal and sword fern, and at the bottom use my walking stick—one of my father's—to hack down the devil's club, which is a big angry plant armed with daggers, and then clumsy my way through the strew of deadfalls covering the stream and up the other side of the canyon, using bushes and saplings for handholds and thanking them for the favor. I'd take a breather on the ridge top, where usually all I could see was trees.

There was snow on some of the ridges. I'd been seeing signs of the quake and windstorm, but nothing huge—slumps of earth and a lot of fresh-fallen trees, the sopped yellowy clay clinging to their broken, upthrust roots, which looked totally shocked to be caught out in daylight. Then, later in the afternoon, I topped out on a ridge and the other side of the ridge was gone. There'd been a logging road across the slope, clearcuts above and below it, and the middle stretch of the road had slid down the hill on a huge raft of soil. The slide had plowed through the buffer strip of woods at the bottom into the stream, which was ponded up behind the earth dam and working its way through. The water was clear coming in, the meager outflow thick and yellow-muddy. Flowing water is an honest witness, it tells truth about everything it touches. Nobody intended that slide—wet soil had loaded it, a big shake had set it off—but if someone *had* wanted to destroy a mountainside, nothing would have done it better than the road and clearcuts had.

I took that road, north of the slide where it still was where they'd built it, and it curled me mostly west for a good mile before it ended at a landing. I threshed westward downslope into a replanted cut, tripping on the old slash, the springy boughs of the little trees slapping my face.

The sky grayed up and got thicker and rain was falling, not heavy but steady. I put on my slicker and pushed ahead. I wanted to be so committed to my trek that I couldn't turn back. I felt like a soldier under orders. I kept that heavy plank door shut tight behind. I saw no life but a couple of crows, a Douglas squirrel, a few turkey vultures. Critters were still laying low, a sensible plan when the foundation of the world has thrown a fit and isn't done throwing it. I'd felt two more lazy aftershocks. Now I knew why the birds and snakes had been acting crazy, why *I* had been zinged out of my mind, at least partly why. All that monster force building and building, those lumbering rock plates locked up against each other like sumo wrestlers, the pressure building, building. . . . I knew nothing about it, but there *had* to be some influence on the surface, on creatures who'd evolved on the land with earthquakes for hundreds of millions of years, from all that colossal energy bound up and about to break. I bet it turns out that ants and fish and even amoebas act strangely in the buildup to a quake. Might look like confusion to us, but maybe they're doing something sensible for themselves. Or maybe they're just scared half to death, but whatever it is, they *know*. How come it takes the big jolt itself for the self-proclaimed smartest animal on Earth to get what's going on?

Late in the afternoon, down in a stream bottom, I came across a really big tree, a western hemlock and a serious leaner. Looked like it could go any time, but it also looked like it had looked that way for a good long time and might go on looking that way for another long time. Most old-growth trees have a tilt. Maybe in the quake a root or two broke underground, maybe the trunk leaned an inch or two more. In any case, the trees know where they will lie in state, no arrangements needed.

As I hiked on, my mood darkened like the day. Trees rise, die, and rise again in new trees, but my mother wouldn't. I felt lost from her, and I needed her. Maybe she was all in the ground, like my father had said. Maybe this is all we are, we live our years and then we're gone, we're bones or ashes and then not even that, just a little nutrition for the grass. We never lived, we never will. Maybe I'd only imagined feeling my mother's spirit near because I missed her, maybe sharing spirit was nothing but my own vivid delusion, having a dream and calling it real. Scientists would say that. Maybe life on Earth is just a parade of bodies, born for a moment of daylight and dying into endless night.

The rain kept falling like it meant to spend the night as I climbed out of a bottom and topped out in trees on a broad ridge. Fat snowflakes were coming down with the rain. I put on my headlamp and stumbled around looking for a spot not too bumpy with roots and rocks, feeling crummier by the minute, and finally just threw the tube tent down in a bunch of ferns and didn't even try to string it up, just crawled into it with my backpack and tried to fold the ends down under so they wouldn't collect water. I got out of most of my clothes and into my sleeping bag, which was still mostly dry. I ate some peanut butter, gobbing it out of the jar with my fingers, and a few crushed doughnuts, then lay there listening to rain whapping the plastic next to my ear and wishing I'd stayed in the Methuselahs. Some Chelamela I would make. No Indian in his right mind, not even a shaman or a kid on a vision quest, would be alone in almost-winter on a rainy and snowy ridgetop. They'd all be in their winter lodges, stocked up with firewood and camas cake and acorn meal and dried venison, taking sweats and smoking tobacco they'd grown or traded for and telling their kids stories about Indians who did dumb things and made trouble for themselves and the whole tribe, *and don't be that Indian, you hear?*

The door was closed behind me. I couldn't see anything to look for ahead. I felt heavier than death and about as happy.

thirteen

I kept waking up shivering all through the night. Water was getting in, soaking my goose-feather bag, but there was nothing to do but curl up tighter. When I woke up for good, the rain had quit and it was light out, gray and still. I warmed up quickly once I got moving. I wrung out the sleeping bag, then rounded up dry twigs and tinder. With a granola-bar wrapper and the label off a can of peaches, I got a fire going and draped the wet bag on sticks and rocks where it could get some of the heat from the fire. Goose feathers keep you warm when they're dry, but when they're wet they're pretty much worthless.

I ate the peaches and set the can halfway into the fire with water from my canteen and a good spill of Seattle's Best coffee and let it simmer. I was starting to feel perkier, like I was on an expedition again. I folded my bandanna for a hot pad and carried my can of coffee to a rocky perch that gave me a short view to the west. What I could see was bumpy, ridgey, workaday Coast Range standard— clearcuts, replant forest, patches of older woods, a few fresh puke-outs and one big slide. Those little mountains had been worked hard, all right. The slope just below me had been clearcut, and the exposed edge of second-growth woods looked the way clearcut borders always did, those pale-barked trees like a line of spindly boys embarrassed to be caught naked out in the light.

The coffee was peachy. You'd pay big money for it at Starbucks. I guessed I might be on Christopher Divide, which would mean I had left the Long Tom and was looking at the drainage of the Siuslaw, a sea-going river. That was good news—I'd come pretty far in a day—and bad news too. I had read about a guy in the early 1800s who scouted every coastal drainage from the Columbia down to the Rogue. The only one that gave him trouble was the Siuslaw, which was so choked with fallen trees he gave up on it. Looked like I could stay high on the divide, though, as it curled to the southwest, then drop off due west, and with some ups and downs and a little luck I might get to the farthest ridge I could see, a bald-top that ran west of northwest into higher country. So I finished the fruity coffee and packed up. The sleeping bag hadn't dried much. I stuffed it into its sack, wrapped the tube tent around it, and lashed it to my pack.

A wind came up as I hiked, the gray sky thinning to blue haze, then clear. The sun felt good but didn't give much warmth. I didn't care—I was under way, greeting a new day like I hadn't in a long time, working up my own heat. An old Jeep road took me downward along the spine of the divide. Soon I couldn't see the lay of the land anymore and didn't know where to strike out overland, so I made my best guess and plunged into the woods. Got through a bottom that wasn't too bad a thrash—there was an old car body down in the log jam—and was climbing the next ridge when I came to a small rocky overhang. I was thinking Indian shelter, maybe some points or tools, but it wasn't that. It was a church—a shallow cave of dripping gray rock pillowed with green moss and sprouting the loveliest scarfs of maidenhair ferns, their fine, pale green fronds with ink-black stems draping down out of cracks and ledges, cascades of ferns and moss seeping drops of water into a shallow pool. It was so beautiful I went to my knees. I didn't have words, then I did. *This is the world we are given, that we may give ourselves to it.*

I rested there, took a long cool drink from the pool, and filled my canteen.

Over that ridge, keeping west, the next canyon was different, dry and rocky-bottomed. Its far side was cliffs broken up with gullies, the rock all falling apart with moss and wet dirt. I tried a gully, but it was full of the nastiest devil's club and briars, so I retreated. Tried another, further down-canyon, that was easier climbing but ended at a cliff. The canyon itself was easy going and tended south, so I sat down in the rocky bottom and thought. I could follow the canyon south and eventually I'd come to gravel roads that would feed me to Highway 126. The highway, even shut down with blowdown and mudslides, would make leveler hiking than I'd been finding. But I didn't want the highway. Not east—my door of planks and iron bracing was shut on that—and not west either. I wanted to stay loyal to my mission.

So I rested, ate some cheese and raisins, daydreaming about the coast. I pictured it wet and scoured clean, the surf rolling in as it had at the beginning of the world. It was cruel to think that—there would be hundreds or thousands dead, millions of creatures dead, a mess to end all messes—but I couldn't get those waves out of my mind, combing in off the face of the deep as they must have done before anything was alive to see.

My canyon bottom was out of the wind, and the sun made me drowsy. I lay down for a nap and woke up shivering. I hurried into my long underwear, got my clothes back on, and retraced my steps north, on past where I'd first dropped into the canyon. I'd come out of my nap with a question—*Who are you really, wanderer?* It was a line, the only one I could remember, from a poem by William Stafford called "A Story That Could Be True." A poet came to my fourth-grade class to teach us creative writing and read it out loud— you should have heard the spellbound silence—and when I asked, he made a copy for me. For a while I'd had the poem memorized. Now it had gone to air.

As I hiked, I started whispering like a chant: "Who are you really, wanderer?" I knew it came from near the end of the poem.

Pretty soon I found a gully I could bushwhack up and finally escaped the canyon to the west. When I saw the sun I realized I'd lost most of the afternoon—but there was a halo around it, and a bright spot on the left of the halo, a sundog. The land had swallowed me up, along with the bald-top ridge I'd spied that morning. The day was cooling fast. I almost turned back to the canyon, but instead I aimed myself at the sun with its dog and forged down into the next little canyon, and scrambling out of that to higher ground, using all fours, suddenly my spirit poured upward. A raven croaked overhead, once, twice, and for an instant I saw him above the treetops, blue-black in a golden haze, quartering off to my left. I followed, climbing, then dropped into a draw and climbed again through mature timber up what I hoped was the bald-top. Woods gave way to thick brush and big gray stumps, then grass and more stumps. It was the ridge, all right, and as I broke out on top, the wind hit me like a riptide and taught me how cold it really was.

The sun had just sunk in a pale glow and the twilit sky was clear, the first stars showing. I put on everything I had—jacket, wool cap, gloves—and hiked ahead, but my armor felt pretty thin. The bitter wind was rushing from the west, into my face, steady and sure of itself. I walked fast as I could, shivering, stumbling. I banged my shin on a stump and went sprawling down on its hard table, which was as wide as I was tall. There was no cover from the wind, nothing but grass and ghost stumps and a few scraggly trees. I hated to give up the high ground I'd won, but the only way out of the wind was to angle down the north side of the ridge into a forest of small trees. There was old snow on the slope, freezing into ice. I kicked steps into it, traversing down, imagining myself by a fire in a nice sheltered camp.

But there was no level ground. I was out of the big wind, but currents came whistling down through the trees and I was shivering hard. The slope would bottom out, I hoped, and kept angling down till my right boot slipped on an icy patch and I slid straight downhill and stopped hard against a tree. Lay there dazed a few seconds— *Who are you really, wanderer?*—then got my pack off and found my headlamp, cussing myself for not having it on. Good way to get killed. But the light had nothing encouraging to show me, either. The slope below me steepened, maybe dropped off at a cliff. My toes and fingers were stinging. Shivering now was shaking.

Okay, I said to myself. It's crazy cold and I've got a wet sleeping bag. Can't go down any farther. Best I can do is contour along the side of this ridge, get to the head of this ravine to my right and hope for a shelf. I don't need much, just a halfway-level place with firewood.

It was slow going. Sidehill hiking is the worst anyway, unless one of your legs is a foot longer than the other, and I was dead weary and not feeling my feet real well and the frozen slope was slick. There were lots of little trees, though, so I stepped and half-pulled myself from one to the next, grabbing branches and trunks, resting every few trees. My little lamp didn't shine very far, but it always showed the next tree. My breath was clouding in my face. My ears were stinging, even under the wool cap, and my face felt hard with cold.

However long I did that—an hour, maybe?—eventually the pitch of the side-slope eased a little, eased some more, and the trees got bigger and farther apart, and then I was walking—staggering, more like it—on hummocky but campable ground, with patches free of snow. Looked like the Promised Land. I dropped the pack and broke dead branches off the firs, then knelt down and broke twigs off the branches. I rummaged in the pack, but the only paper I could find was a photograph of my mother I kept in a deerskin purse. I'd used up my cans and candy bars. Then I remembered the money I'd lifted from my father's wallet and dug the roll out of a zip pocket. I picked Abe Lincoln, a crisp fiver, and crumpled and tore it a little. Didn't look like enough, so I crumpled a few singles to go with it and laid twigs overtop with fumbling fingers and struck the lighter. The flame looked small and cold. The money burned, but slow, sleepy. *Come on.* I blew on it. A burning edge of red and black advanced across Abe's face, but with hardly a flame. I struck the lighter and set the flame on one of the unburned edges and blew on it. *Come on, come on.*

I pushed the unburned parts together and added more crumpled dollars and held the flame right under the heart of that money—and watched the flame pull slowly back into the lighter, smaller, smaller, gone. I struck the lighter. And struck it. And dropped it and cradled my hands around the pile of twigs and money and blew gently, blew like a prayer, but those worthless notes just slowly shriveled into black ash. I shook the lighter, tried it sideways and upside down, tried it again and again and then threw it far as I could. *Good idea to carry an extra*, I remembered my father saying. *They're cheap and they don't weigh nothin'. . . .*

So. I stood and jumped up and down and walked in place and flapped my wings and wiggled my toes and fingers until I got some feeling back, and told myself I could do it all night if I had to, but I didn't believe it. I pulled my sleeping bag out of its sack. It laid out stiff and thin and creased, frozen, no loft at all. Frozen feathers equal no feathers equal no warmth. It was as useless as the money. If I fell asleep I'd die, like the guy Jack London wrote his story about. I crammed the bag into the sack, shouldered the pack, and was turning to see where I could go when my headlamp beam crossed my dad's roll, splayed open on the ground. I felt like leaving it, but if I ever made it out of the mountains I'd need it. It was my inheritance.

I walked the only way I could, westward, up the narrow, gently sloping stream course I'd side-hilled into, just above where it dropped off in a falls. The stream was only a few shallow puddles, skinned with new ice. The bunchgrasses were frosted stiff, like me. I didn't hurry. Long as I was putting one foot in front of the other, I was okay. I stumbled ahead, clubfooted, hoping.

Who are you really, wanderer?

A fool. An ignorant, lame-ass fool.

Maybe it's the final act, I said to myself. Well I don't want to die, myself said back. I vowed to keep moving until something showed me how to survive.

The bottom rose in little steps, then it pinched and steepened into a narrow rocky channel with water trickling down. I climbed to the left of the trickle, hands and feet, watching out for the wet and mossy patches, which reminded me of the church where I'd worshiped a long time ago. *That we may give ourselves to it.* . . . At least there was no ice in this skinnier passage. A deeper cleft in the mountainside.

Finally the skinny canyon headed up in a near-vertical rock wall about thirty feet high, with a little fall of water splashing from the top. I thought I saw a way to climb, left of the waterfall, and studying that I caught sight of the thin sliver of a new moon. I turned and stepped back to a level spot, turned off my headlamp, and spoke what some of the Kalapuya used to speak when the new moon came, and maybe some still do. "I am still alive here," I said. "Now you have come out again, and I am here to see you."

The rock was typical Coast Range, rotten and unreliable. I clapped my hands, hard, until the fingers stung. I reached up to test a handhold and it pulled out in my hand. I let it clatter down behind me and reached for another. Climb, I told myself. This is Eagle Boy and Thunder. If he throws you, well, no worries about keeping warm. About halfway up, the holds took me closer to the little waterfall, and then a small ledge I'd used as a handhold gave way under my right foot. My right hand had a good grip, but my body swung into the mossy cleft where water was splashing, so cold it scalded my face and down my neck. A voice cried out that didn't seem mine. My boots found footing, I made a move up, and another, and hoisted myself over the lip of the cliff, my breath coming in heaves. I didn't rest. Down below I'd been sleepwalking. The climb, the burn of that water, had wakened me.

I pressed on along the tiny stream through brush and little trees, and the passageway opened out. Couldn't see much, but it felt like I'd entered a flat-bottomed bowl with a few big trees. I walked toward the center and came out on grassy ground sloping into a marsh. But I wasn't looking at that. Partway around the bowl, tucked up in front of a huge fallen tree, a fire was glowing.

Couldn't be. But there it was, a quiet fire. And somebody sitting by it.

"Hello!" I called.

"Hello" echoed back.

I started left, around the bowl, at a ragged trot, my boots crunching frosted grass. Bushes and trees blocked my view, but glimpses showed me the fire was there, pale and very still—but what else could it be? I tripped, sprawled on my face, surged to my feet and kept going, a heavy machine powered by gasping.

"*Hello!*" I called again, and the echo came back twice as I broke into the clear and shook off the pack and ran. The sitting man was only a big broken limb, but the pale fire was right there, spilling in embers from the side of the huge butt end of a trunk fallen into the marsh. I slid to my knees, reached out my hands and scooped up a double handful of glowing coals—alive, beautiful, giving no heat at all, just a cold greenish-white light pulsing faintly in my numb fingers.

Didn't look like a fire at all—but oh, it had. And it was a sign, if anything ever was. I was meant to trust my life to it.

I retrieved my pack and got out the plastic trowel I carried to bury my deposits, and with that and my jackknife and my wooden fingers I dug into the luminous rotted innards of the tree. The rot was dry and came out easily. Deeper into the log it didn't glow much. *St. Elmo's fire*, was that the name? It was lighting my way. . . . *Foxfire!* Huck and Tom used hunks of it from a swamp when they tunneled into the shed where Nigger Jim was held captive. . . . It wasn't so common in the wet Northwest, but I'd heard reports of it.

I burrowed like a cold bear into that tree until I had a small cave, a curve of roof above and wall behind and floor beneath. Then I bored into the length of the trunk until I hit hard pitchwood on the butt end and wet rot on the marsh end, and I had a tight shelter I could just curl into. It was a good time to be Eagle Boy and not Goliath.

The cave would keep the wind off and give some insulation, but it had two big flaws. The only source of heat was me, and the front entryway gaped wide open.

I pulled my frozen sleeping bag from the stuff sack, stiff as wrinkled cardboard, and laid it near the entryway, where I could reach a corner of it from inside. I took off my jacket long enough to put on an extra shirt I found in my pack, pulled a pair of clean underwear over my cap and a pair of socks over my gloves. Then I tossed the nearly empty pack into the cave, heaped all the foxfire embers right up to the door, and squirmed over the heap into my chamber. I worked my feet into the empty pack and scooped the embers in, half-burying myself and filling some of the entryway. I reached out for the stiff sleeping bag and pulled it toward me to plug the rest of the doorway in a half-assed way. I wanted to go out and tack it securely to the trunk, but I was done going out, and I'd forgotten the hammer and the tacks.

My chamber glowed with faint green light that didn't cheer me. My gosh, I was cold. I wrapped myself in my own arms, hands in armpits, and wriggled down into the embers best I could. I rocked a little to raise some warmth but then just lay there shuddering, the embers jiggling around me. "Who are you really, wanderer?" I heard myself ask out loud, my voice quavering like a fool with a fever. And then I spoke the answer, the final lines, which had come to me when I'd pulled myself over the top of the waterfall cliff:

And the answer you have to give
no matter how dark and cold
the world around you is:
"Maybe I'm a king."

fourteen

When I tell you what happened the rest of that night, there's a fair chance you won't believe me. You may think I'm lying, or you may think it was all a delusion from nearly freezing to death. I asked Lynn how I could write it to make it believable, but for an answer I got only a shrug, a smile, and: "Just write it, Henry. I believe you."

I was sure I'd die in that tree trunk. I was scared, but being very cold, it turns out, walks all over being scared. After a while—how long I have no idea—I stopped shaking, and nothing else really mattered. I felt calm. Somewhere I'd read that hypothermia gets really serious when you pass beyond the shaking. Sometimes you even feel warm and start taking off clothes. I remembered that, but it seemed like information about another world. I was easy and glad not to be cold, and a big black bird was gliding and soaring above me in a sky of white light. Any bird looks black in a bright sky, but you can tell from its silhouette if it's a red-tail or an osprey or an eagle, they look different enough. This wasn't any of those, it was a great black bird and its long black feathers trailed behind it, spreading and waving in the wind, as it soared and banked and circled. The most beautiful bird I'd ever seen. It reminded me of something, I wasn't sure what. I loved watching it, the strands of black stretching out longer and longer behind, and then it slowly swooped down low and passed directly above and I saw my mother's face, her long black hair shimmering behind her.

She smiled, and I was rising toward her out of my heavy body, rising on a wind of love and gratitude, but just like that her smile stabbed me with a deep pain, and I was falling from that sky of white light and she was gliding off, higher and smaller, her black hair streaming behind her, where I couldn't go. I sank back into myself, a cry stuck in my chest like an icicle.

Could have been minutes, could have been hours, but the next thing I knew I was awake in the cave again, the sleeping bag was off the doorway, and the stars were out. I was warm, too warm, fumbling with my jacket, but I quit that and watched the stars—swashes of stars, flaring, shimmering, a living dance of stars. I knew I was dying. I was sad but not afraid. Words thought themselves in something bigger than my own mind: *This is the light of worlds. In this light I will never be lost.* And as the words were hanging there, a big shooting star streaked across the sky trailing a wavery tail.

When I woke the next time there were no stars, the air was close, and I was shivering hard, but shivering the way you do when you're getting warmer. I could see nothing in the puny light of the embers. I felt softly muffled in some loose blanket made of darkness and the body and spirit of a great animal. Not deer, not bird, not anything that flitted or scurried or swam or burrowed. This spirit was lordly and deeply calm. And the lordly spirit was warm in its body, and its body was right there, tucked up in the entryway, a few inches from my face. I could smell its clean fur. I could feel on my face its animal warmth.

I pulled my left hand out of my right armpit, slowly, with the creakiness an old man must feel. In the close darkness I started to reach. But I stopped. I brought my hand back. Sometimes I wish I had gone ahead, so I could say to people, to you, "I touched it. I touched its warm, breathing body." But always I come to see again that I chose right. I didn't want the visitant to move, for one thing. It was saving my life. But I also knew it wasn't for me to take that liberty. I remembered the Bible story of the sick woman in the time of Jesus who said, "If I may but touch the hem of his garment, I shall be whole." And she was made whole, and the warmth of my visitant's garment was already touching me and making me whole. It was for me to marvel, to shiver in its presence and the open, untellable secret of its spirit, where winds moved that I had never heard across distances I would never know, where an awareness lived that did me a mercy not to share itself completely, because it would have swallowed me alive. It was for me to accept the gift and give thanks.

I did mean to stay awake, because I wanted to be consciously in the visitant's spirit and the warmth of its body as long as I could, and to thank it and bow to it when it took its leave. But that was beyond me. I had hiked and climbed, the Earth had shaken and the wind had surged and the trees had come down, I had been cold to the border of death, and I was still here. It's only a little, what we can know, and the little I knew in that moment was treasure enough. I was tired, I was shivering with life, and I slept.

* * *

I woke to daylight, as if returned from a long journey, and I wondered if my body could move at all. I started with my head, lifting it an inch, and right away I saw that the rot-wood pieces outside the opening were pressed down smooth. Nothing I remembered during the night would have caused that. I could have done things I didn't recall, and don't recall now, but everything I do remember I'm telling you.

I uncreaked myself, joint by joint, then squirmed and wriggled painfully out of the cave. I did it carefully as I could but couldn't help disturbing the rot-wood. I've never been so stiff. Every part of me hurt. If that's what it's like being old, I'll be ready to go. I lay on the frozen ground rocking side to side, moving my arms and legs, then got myself to my knees, and finally stood and staggered in circles until my legs halfway loosened. I stomped my feet and shook my arms, clumsy as a scarecrow trying to come alive. Then I did jumping jacks, as I'd done in school PE, and as my father had made me do when he'd felt like being a homeschool gym teacher.

Right away I regretted reminding myself of my father, but I knew I'd be thinking of him now. That heavy plank door had swung open during the night.

The morning sky had clouded with low overcast, taking the edge off the cold. I was in a bowl, all right, maybe seventy yards across, a rocky rim around most of it and a marsh in the middle. A few big Douglas firs stood in the dryer ground around the marsh. My tree was one of several, and the biggest, that had toppled. Most of the trunk was swallowed up in the marsh, a few barkless gray limbs sticking up among the reeds and cattails. The gigantic root wad, maybe fifteen feet high, still held its shape, the soil long weathered off the roots—a clutch of gray snakes like Medusa's hair if Medusa had been a Northwesterner.

The tracks, I knew, should be at least three inches long and three inches wide, but the ground was rocky and grassy away from the marsh, and nearer the marsh it was frozen mud. Nothing that would show a track, but I looked. Then I rummaged for something to eat and found some hazelnuts loose in the pack and a small zip-bag of raisins. I chomped it all down and got my things together. My sleeping bag was softer but still part-frozen and withered. As I crammed it into the stuff-sack, I looked at my shallow cave and wished I had a camera. I went over and looked closer. The embers of night looked like simple rot-wood by day. I'd messed up the heap with my clumsy exit, but not all of it. One part was still pressed down, the way it would be from bearing weight. I looked closely for fur but found none. I backed away, knelt, put my hands together and bowed to the frozen ground.

Scrambling out of the bowl to the south, I dropped through a shallow draw, then angled up in old snow to the open ridgetop I'd been hiking the evening before. It felt a whole lot better today. I walked west on easy ground, passing big ghost stumps, and soon came to a pretty good lookout where the ridge sloped away. The steep little hills were cut and roaded. A few fresh earthslides, patches of wind-thrown trees lying in the same direction. Somewhere in the distance I heard chainsaws whining like hornets. Clearing a road, probably. The downed trees would keep salvage loggers busy for quite a while.

Down off the ridge, the first stream I came to was just a trickle. An hour later there was a bigger stream, its water running muddy. I turned south to follow it, going with the watershed. The decision had been made during the night, when my mother sent me back. I wasn't hiking to the coast anymore. My mother had opened the door, my mother. . . . Suddenly I remembered the first few lines of "A Story That Could Be True":

> *If you were exchanged in the cradle*
> *and your real mother died*
> *without ever telling the story*
> *then no one knows your name . . .*

The next lines were close, just over the horizon. . . .

I stayed above the stream, mostly, keeping out of the worst brush and log jumbles. Where the banks were thickety and the water open, I rock-hopped in the muddy stream. Now and then one of the side-slopes leveled into a flat, with alder trees and brush. It was slow going. By noon I'd officially rewarmed myself from the cold of night. I stopped to take off my jacket and cap and realized I'd been wearing underwear on my head.

Further down, on one of the flats, I came to a patch of alders with three dead ones that looked like they'd been girdled by a beaver. Then I saw some sheep-wire fencing coming off its tree-trunk posts, and right then my left boot came down on something and stuck. I had to pull my foot back to get it loose, and there, angling out of the ground, was a sharp wooden spike that had stabbed my vibram sole. I stepped ahead, watching the ground, and a hornet stung the side of my head. I slapped at it and another one stung my hand, then again, and my hand was stuck—on hooks, fishhooks on invisible monofilament line strung between trees. "Son of a *bitch!*" I yelled. "What else has to happen?"

With my free hand, my left, I got the fishhook out of my scalp and my knife out of my pocket, then used the fingers of both hands to open the knife and cut the monofilament. One hook came out of my pinkie finger easily, but the jerking around had sunk the barb of the other one deep into the ham of my thumb. I cut the loose fishing line off the hook and looked around. The bamboo spikes and hooked line were all over the place, along with a tipped-over black plastic tank, some plastic piping that looked like a bear had tried his teeth on it, and a few dead and dry pot plants still standing. Picking my way carefully, I walked to the plants, broke off a few buds to put in my pocket—I'd earned a reward—and hiked on downstream, my hand with the fishhook starting to throb.

I remembered my father telling me what to do if I ever got hooked like that, and just like that the next few lines of the poem stopped me cold:

> *. . . and somewhere in the world*
> *your father is lost and needs you*
> *but you are far away.*
> *He can never find*
> *how true you are, how ready . . .*

I stood there crying a while, then hiked on. "I'm coming," I said.

The going was slow, brushy, a clutter of deadfalls. The stream joined another one, the water clearer now, and by late afternoon the land settled down to a rolling flat of trees and little meadows. Made sense there'd be a homeplace soon, and there was. On a broad flat I came out of alders, fought through a blackberry bramble covering an old, beat-down fence, and stumbled out into a pasture as a few terrified sheep ran off. I headed for a little house and shed, both painted white. A guy had heard the sheep bolt and was out on the small covered porch. Didn't seem to have a gun. As I got closer I saw he was smiling.

"Nobody's ever come to us from that direction before," he said.

He had long black hair tied behind his head and a friendly, intelligent face, maybe in his twenties. I must have looked like a little Bigfoot. At least I'd shed the underwear.

"Hard traveling?" he asked.

"Too hard for me," I said. I held out my hand with the fishhook. "Do you have a pair of pliers and some metal snips?"

"Come in," he said.

He helped me out of my pack and had me sit in an office chair at a little desk while he fetched a tool bag and first-aid kit. He found pliers and wire cutters, then crouched and looked me in the eyes. His eyes were deep green and very clear. He asked my name and I told him.

"Henry," he said, "one person here has EMT training. I can get him. . . ."

"He'd only do what I aim to. My dad told me how."

He handed me the pliers, then held up his index finger, went to the kitchen and came back with a small glass of black rum. "I don't have a bullet you can bite, but this should help," he said. "Be ready with the cutters," I said, then shot down the rum and gripped the shaft of the hook with the pliers. In the flush of liquor with a scream I couldn't stifle, I twisted the pliers to drive the point of the hook on and up and out through the skin till the barb was exposed. As I held the hook stable with the pliers, my host squeezed hard with the cutters till the barb snapped off, and I backed the barbless hook out of my thumb. He gave me a gauze pad to stop the bleeding.

I cocked my head toward the shot glass. The guy smiled and held up his finger again, then fetched the bottle and another glass. "Henry Fielder," he said, raising his, "you're a brave boy."

"Not near as brave as I need to be," I answered, but we clinked glasses and drank.

I let him work some iodine into all the hook-pricks and put a couple of big band-aids on the thumb.

"What's your name?" I asked.

"Call me Raven," he said. "This is a community, the Sweet Grass Confederacy. Nineteen of us live here."

I wanted to know more, but that door in my mind was wide open, and I blurted, loud, "Can you take me back home?"

"Where's home?" Raven asked.

"East from here, near Duckworth. Could you take me?"

Raven put a hand on my knee. "Henry, we'll get you there," he said, looking right at me. His clear green eyes seemed to radiate calm. "But 126 is shut down at least till tomorrow. And Highway 36 will have mudslides all over it for weeks."

"Oh shit," I said, crumpling with shame, "I forgot all about the earthquake. How's Florence? How bad was the tsunami?"

Raven smiled. "Not bad at all. There wasn't any."

I just stared at him.

"This wasn't the big one," he said. "Wasn't a subduction quake. We felt it here but it was centered over your way, the southern Willamette Valley. We've heard on the radio that a few buildings went down in Eugene. There was a warming center where the homeless sleep—an old church, full for the night, it collapsed and four people died. There were earthslides in the South Hills. One of the bridges might have collapsed. . . ."

"Did you hear anything about Long Tom or Duckworth? Daugherty?"

"Only that Fern Ridge Dam may have been weakened and they've evacuated downstream," he said. "They're releasing all the water they can." Raven paused a moment. "Henry? Have you been walking the woods since the earthquake?"

I nodded.

"You walked here from Duckworth, overland?"

I nodded again and felt tears start. His face showed everything he wanted to ask me, had every reason to, but had the kindness not to. He said, "We've got a four-wheel-drive truck, Henry, and tomorrow if the highway's open I will drive you home. We can't do it tonight."

He paused, and I felt myself nodding.

"What we can do," Raven started up again, "is get you a bath, and some supper, and a bed to sleep in. Does that sound all right?"

"Yes it does," I said.

"Good. I'll start a fire to get the bathwater hot. Takes only ten minutes. In the meantime I'll go for some food. Unless"—he raised his eyebrows and smiled—"you'd like to meet eighteen people at Commons tonight?"

He picked up my pack and led me to a small bedroom, the only one. I started to say something, but Raven cut me off. "It's yours tonight. I like the sofa, and you know what? I didn't just walk here from Duckworth with a fishhook in my hand."

"Which reminds me." He raised his finger again. "I know where those hooks caught you, and I want to apologize, for all of us. I'll tell you the story later."

He went to start the fire, however that worked, and after that he left the cottage, calling out, "Eight minutes to hot water! Don't get the band-aids wet."

I knew if I lay down I'd fall asleep, so I just sat on the bed. After a while I ran the bathwater, which was hot enough that it needed some cold, dropped my clothes on the floor and got in the tub. My father was all I could think about. Maybe he's all right, I thought. Jonah would've found him. Somebody would've. I cleaned myself with soap and lay there in the dirty bathwater hoping I'd fall asleep and slip down and drown without noticing, and all I could remember of "A Story That Could Be True" was running through me like a river. . . .

If you were exchanged in the cradle and
your real mother died
without ever telling the story
then no one knows your name,
and somewhere in the world
your father is lost and needs you
but you are far away.
He can never find
how true you are, how ready.
When the great wind comes
and the robberies of the rain
you stand on the corner shivering . . .

"Who are you really, wanderer?"
And the answer you have to give
no matter how dark and cold
the world around you is:
"Maybe I'm a king."

fifteen

The guy cooking breakfast was big and fat with a droopy mustache, a shaved head, and a big gold earring. He was working three wide skillets on a wood-fired cookstove. There were lots of people in the room and it smelled great.

"Hello, Henry!" the cook called out. "I'm Dante. I hear you hiked miles and miles just to see *us!*"

"I guess I did," I said. I had slept a lot of hours and felt not great, but better. Felt like talking, too, because these were nice people and I wanted to be distracted.

"And I hear you got hooked and Raven reeled you in."

"Oh I got hooked all right. You know, there's a pot garden up that—"

Dante raised the spatula in his hand, nodding. "We know," he said, "and we feel responsible. Somebody tell Henry the story, or I'll burn the potatoes."

"Hi Henry," said a woman who'd been watching at the near end of the long table. Raven was talking with others down the table.

The woman was older than Raven and was wearing a loose flowery dress. Her hair, which was brown, went way on down her back. "My name's Cecilia," she said. "Would you like something to drink? We've got coffee, tea, cider. . . ."

"Coffee," I said, "I really like coffee. And milk, please."

Cecilia gave a big smile and gestured me to sit down. Most of the others in the room were longhairs too. One man and woman had a lot of gray, a couple of others had some. A few kids were horsing around and jabbering.

Cecelia set a mug and small pitcher of milk in front of me. "What you ran into," she said, pouring my coffee, "we call Neckie's patch." She sat down across from me. She had a wide face, and one of her eyes didn't quite look at you when the other one did. She wasn't pretty, but she seemed made out of warmth. "Neckie was a Vietnam vet. You know about that war, do you?"

I nodded. My dad and I never got that far in American history, but I knew it was the war when he and my mom were kids.

"He came back full of things he couldn't say. He talked to trees and animals, I think, more than he did people."

"Me too," I said. "So he lived here?"

Cecilia shook her head. "He'd come for a meal sometimes," she said with a sad smile. "But even Sweet Grass was too much society for Neckie. He lived in a tent up one of the other creeks. Tended his patch and got along."

The food was coming around now, platters of eggs and fried pota-toes and sausage patties, and toast from homemade bread with homemade butter and homemade jam in jars on the table. I wanted to eat and keep talking too, which resulted in some eggs and sausage falling out of my mouth. "Sorry," I mumbled. Cecilia smiled and I slowed down.

"He hasn't tended it lately," I said.

"This last spring," said Cecilia, "Neckie disappeared. Someone down the road thought she'd seen him hiking into the hills, and that's all we know. There's lots of places to lose yourself in this country, if that's what you want to do." She sipped her coffee, buttered her toast, and watched me eat.

"Yeah," I said. "I found some on my hike."

"Henry?" said Cecilia, leaning forward, "we don't know what load you're carrying, but we'd like to help. Do you have a home to go back to?"

"Not my old one. Two trees fell on our house."

"And your family?"

"My mother died last summer. I . . . I've got to go back and see to my father."

"And you went on your hike because . . . ?"

"Because it's all my fault," I said to my plate. "I made a bad mistake. I'd tell you, but I can't."

Cecilia reached across the table and took my left hand. "Just tell me this, Henry. Are there people you can stay with who will care for you?"

"Yes ma'am," I said. "The people I mean to stay with are my best friends."

"Good," she said. "Now. Could I give you a hug?"

She came around the table, I got up, and we hugged. Then Raven put his hand on my shoulder and said the highway was open, we could go in half an hour.

* * *

Cecilia showed me around Sweet Grass a little, then Raven told me more as he drove us west on a potholed gravel road, then south on a better one. There were ten houses tucked around the Sweetgrass property. Some people lived together, and Raven and two others lived alone. They kept sheep, two milk cows, a few pigs, chickens for laying and eating, and a big year-round garden. Except for the coffee and the flour for the toast, everything I'd eaten at breakfast had come from the farm, right down to the spices in the sausage. I was surprised they ate meat at all, but Raven said, smiling, "There have to be *some* communities for omnivores."

A couple of the guys and one of the women were hunters and usually got a deer apiece, and some years an elk, plus game birds and rabbits. They picked up roadkill, too, if it was fresh and they could get good meat from it. They did for themselves, like the Indians had. They made a lot of their own clothing. Some made quilts or weavings for sale, one made jewelry, and one guy was a wood turner who had invented easy-to-use chopsticks, joined at the top like a very long old-fashioned clothes pin. A couple of people had real jobs, shared their pay, and were excused from some of the chores. The kids were homeschooled, and all the adults took part in the teaching, no exceptions.

"Does everybody get along?" I asked.

Raven didn't answer right away, and I wondered if he'd heard me. "Disagreements come up," he finally said. "We talk them through. People evolve, sometimes they leave. New people come. I think that's healthy."

"Cecilia told me about Neckie," I said, and Raven smiled like a grimace.

"Neckie killed people during the war," he said after a pause. "Two of his best buddies were killed. He saw men with awful wounds, and his countrymen never believed in the war. He probably didn't believe in it himself. It was all too much for him."

I let his words rest in silence as the Jeep truck lurched along the muddy road, passing pastures and now and again a doublewide or small house. I liked it that Raven thought before he spoke. My mother had learned growing up in Chiloquin that Indian people honor silence. White people are always trying to fill it, she said, because we don't get it that silence isn't empty. Raven had the hair of an Indian, but his skin was paler than mine.

"How'd he get that name?" I asked.

This time Raven smiled brightly. "He was a hefty man who could have thrown you ten feet if he wanted to. His neck was as stout as a cedar stump. His football teammates in high school called him Neckmeat, and it stuck through his time in the Army. Hence Neckie, or Neckster. I mean, you can't address a guy as 'Neckmeat' with a straight face, you know?" Raven broke out laughing, and so did I.

"We plan to clean out his patch, by the way," said Raven. "We don't want any more mountain boys to get hung up."

"Too late," I said, "I'm seein' my lawyer tomorrow."

"Henry?" Raven said after a while. "Neckie couldn't talk about his pain. I'm not asking what your pain is about. I just want to say, things will go better for you in the long run if you can talk it over with someone."

I kept quiet a few seconds. "I don't know if I can," I said. "But thank you. I'd talk it over with you if I could."

A few trees had fallen across the road, their tops or middle parts now bucked into firewood rounds and rolled off the road. One low area we came to was nothing but mud and blowdowns. Men with chainsaws just about had it cleared. Raven waved, lifting a hand from the wheel, and detoured through the fields where someone had taken down a section of his fence.

Highway 126 was clear in the same kind of way, a lot of fresh round faces of cut tree trunks looking on from both sides, slash and saw chips all over the road. I opened the window to breathe the sap smell. Little slides had been cleared, and there were detours where the pavement had cracked or slumped. We moved in a long, very slow caravan. I wasn't in a hurry. I dreaded what was waiting.

We listened to the radio for a while. Twenty-six people had died in Lane County. A lot of trees went down on houses, and in the hilly parts a lot of houses went down in earthslides, because the soil was so saturated. The worst single event was the collapsed warming center that killed four. But overall, people were saying it could have been much worse. Two schools took major damage that might have hurt a lot of kids if school had been in session.

"You're really nice to take me home," I said to Raven.

He smiled. "It's a pleasure, Henry. I plan to check on friends in Eugene, too, if I can get there. And you know," he said with a glance, "sometimes things are meant to happen."

"I always wonder about that," I said. "Whether things are meant to happen or if they just happen. Or if there's even a difference. But . . . could I ask your opinion about something?"

"Sure you can."

"If one person did something really bad to another person, and if that other person did something really bad back at the first person, who's more at fault?"

Raven was silent for a long moment, then: "The situation is too vague to say. Can you be more specific?"

"No."

"Well," said Raven, "if the first offender wasn't provoked, he bears blame because he started the trouble. The challenge for the other person is to not retaliate, but he does. He lashes back. So I'd say both are at fault, maybe the first offender more, but what's important is what they do next. They both may be able to improve the situation."

"What if one of them can't?"

Out of the corner of my eye I saw Raven look my way.

After a long pause he said, "The one who does have the chance has to assume responsibility then. He has to act on behalf of both."

"Take that next left turn," I told him.

Shepherd Creek Road looked pretty normal except for one doublewide that had slipped down its hill a few feet and was sagging at one end. The blowdown was small trees, mostly, pecker poles that had been cleared away. On Stamper Road, though, I saw that one of my favorite trees was down, a beautiful white oak that had grown up in the clear by the Long Tom River and had the loveliest balanced crown. Perfectly straight, no lean at all. It had blown flat down in the pasture. The smaller trees nearby still stood.

"Slow down," I said. "My friends' house is on the right, in those trees."

Raven let off the gas pedal and turned into the drive.

I laughed out loud, which must have seemed very odd to Raven. Cart and Josie's house was fine, but a tree had come down directly across the hood of Cart's Toy truck. The trunk had been sawed off it, and now the truck looked like a dog does when he puts his paws forward and his head down to stretch, his rear end sticking up in the air.

Cart answered the door, his hair in Albert Einstein style, and picked me up in a hug. "We were so worried about you, Henry." Then he took me by the shoulders and said, "Where the hell have you *been?*"

Before I could give a non-answer Cart was introducing himself to Raven, thanking him, asking where he had found me.

Raven just smiled and said, "Henry knows much more of the story than I do. I'm glad to see he has a haven."

Then he excused himself to go find his friends in Eugene. "Henry," he said, gazing right into me, "please come see us." He had a warm and quiet way, but something was working at him, too. He wasn't all quiet inside.

"I will," I said. "I'd like to live there. Thanks, thanks for everything."

I'd known Raven and the Sweet Grass Confederacy less than twenty-four hours, and now they were gone.

* * *

Cart was fidgety as a mother hen. "Are you hungry?" he asked. "Thirsty? We don't have power but we do have food. Josie's out in the car trying to buy some more."

I put on a grin. "Awful sorry about your truck, Cart. Are you worried it might be totaled?"

"Ha ha, smartass. But you know, we came through the quake pretty well. The books fell out of the shelves, but only a few broke their backs. Josie lost some glass and frames . . . and Catrick," Cart said, with a sad look. "We let him out when we got home last Wednesday, and he disappeared. A small thing, I know, compared to others—" He stopped his sentence short.

"He knew the quake was coming," I said. "But Cart? My father. . . ."

"Here," he said, "let's sit in the living room."

I sat where he gestured, on the sofa, and he took a rocking chair facing me. He leaned forward, elbows on knees. I felt like a batter with a curveball coming and zero chance in the world of hitting it.

"Henry, I think you must know this, because you tried to save him. . . . I'm afraid your father is dead."

I looked at my lap. Of course he was dead. How could he not be dead?

"I did know," I said. "But I've been alone and I've doubted my own mind."

"He died, then, before you could get to him?"

I nodded, looking down. "I tried. I did try."

"Jonah saw that. He got to your house first and got the debris off your father."

"Thought he might," I said in a whisper.

"It took most of the day for me to get up there," Cart said. "A lot of trees were down on the road. I mean, like pickup sticks. An older couple hailed me—they were okay but their dog was trapped in the basement. We got her out all right. Then a family out on the road with their children—the Morrisons—were concerned about Len Peppers, so I went with the husband—Brad, I think—to check, and Len *was* hurt. He'd gone down in the shaking and broken a leg. He was glad to see us."

I buried my face in my hands. I'd walked right by, in my little old fucked-up bubble.

"He'll be all right, Henry. The Morrisons looked after him, and emergency services flew him to the hospital the day before yesterday."

I just nodded.

"There were a lot of saws going," Cart went on, "a lot of people out in their driveways. You probably know them." He stopped and fixed his eyes on me. "But I'm telling you things you probably saw yourself, Henry. Did you go for help? What happened?"

"Not yet," I said. "Please keep telling your story."

"Well, one man had two big thermoses of coffee he'd made on his woodstove and a lot of paper cups set up on a big round of tree trunk like a coffee stand." Cart chuckled. "'Hope you like it with Irish whiskey,' this fellow said, 'because it's already in there.' I asked him, and others, if they had heard anything about the Fielder place, and nobody had. I kept hearing terrible things about Eugene, most of which turned out to be untrue or greatly exaggerated. You know, the Hilton had fallen, whole houses had been swallowed up by big cracks in the ground with the families inside. Somebody claimed that Spencer Butte had erupted like a volcano. Somebody else talked about weird blue and white lights he'd seen during the quake. He thought aliens might be involved. Imaginations were going off like fireworks."

My own community, I thought. My own people, and I ran away like a thief in the night. Carter Stephens of California is a better member of this community than I am.

"It must have been after four when I made it to your home," Cart went on. "I saw the trees and the caved-in roof and thought the worst. . . . Jonah had come the other way on Stamper, from Duckworth, and got there about an hour before me. He'd been hoping that somebody else would show up. He couldn't lift . . . your dad, and didn't want to drag him. Jonah was pretty broken up, Henry. I wasn't aware he'd known your father that long, all the way back to college."

I felt tears start down my cheeks, and I didn't deserve them.

"Jonah showed me the tools you had used. He thought you'd gone for help, we expected to see you any minute. Jonah had dug around in your room, so we knew you weren't dead." Cart was quiet a few seconds.

"Was he able to speak to you, Henry? When you tried to rescue him?"

I nodded, staring at my boots. "He was calling for me. I was sawing and sawing, both the chainsaws. His voice wasn't strong. I told him to hang on. I got to where I could see the side of his head. He said he loved me and he was sorry and he died right there in his bed."

Cart moved next to me on the sofa and put his arm around my shoulders. "You tried, Henry. You tried to save him."

I shook his arm off. "Didn't try hard enough, did I."

I started crying into one hand. After a few seconds he put his arm back on my shoulders, and I leaned into him and broke down sobbing. Not quite all of me, though. One part of me was just watching, and not with sympathy.

The front door opened then, and Josie walked in. "Henry!" she cried, setting her grocery bag on the floor. "I had the surest feeling you'd be here!"

She and I hugged and the three of us went to the kitchen. It was getting dark, and Josie must have lit thirty candles. We talked quick and giddy, the way people do sometimes when they've had a close call. I asked questions—I wanted to know things, and I didn't want questions from them. Besides my father, they thought three people had died in the Long Tom region. A mother and daughter in the hills south of Daugherty, who lived below a clearcut, had been in their house when the hillside came right down over them. The husband had just left for work. The other person who died, Grover Simpson, lived closer and was a millwright at Siuslaw Pacific. He had hopped into his truck just after the quake to see if he could help somewhere, and a tree came down right on the cab before he'd driven a mile. Perfect timing.

Cart told me my father was at Clarence Funeral Home in west Eugene and asked if I would like to see him tomorrow. I shook my head. "Jonah took him?" I asked.

"He did," said Cart. "We carried him to Jonah's truck. He had a blanket spread out in back, and we wrapped him in it and tucked it under so it wouldn't come loose in the wind. Jonah put some hefty green fir limbs over him, too, just to be sure. It took him most of the night to get to the funeral home. He had to take a lot of detours and talk his way through some road closures, but he got your dad there."

I couldn't speak for a few seconds. Just couldn't see my father *carried* anywhere.

"I need to thank Jonah for that," I said. "When does my dad . . . get buried?" My voice sounded peculiar. I wondered if I'd even heard it before.

"It's all pending," Cart said. "State and county services, the funeral homes, they're jammed. Turns out there's insufficient morgue capacity in Eugene. And I don't think your father's been seen by the medical examiners yet."

"What would they see him for?"

"For cause of death, maybe? I think they do it as a routine thing."

"Cause of death was two trees caved the roof in," I said.

Josie had left the kitchen and now came back with a pan of canned chili and some bread she'd been heating on the woodstove in the living room. I knew she'd been listening, because she shifted the conversation.

"You know, Henry, we wanted to look for you, but we didn't know where to begin. We told the rescue people, and the sheriff's office, but they were overwhelmed, of course."

"I shouldn't've run," I blurted. "I had like a panic attack or something. I was worried what would happen . . . you know, if I'd have to go to an orphanage."

Josie reached and put her hand on mine. "It's perfectly understandable," she said. "I don't pray much, Henry, but I prayed for you. Especially the night before last, the one so bitter cold. I prayed that wherever you were, you had warm shelter."

"Thank you," I said. "Your prayer may have helped."

I'd never seen Josie's graying hair all long and loose before, spread out behind her shoulders like a shawl. She looked like a candlelight angel.

We went on in a silence of spoons clicking on bowls, and then I set my spoon down and started talking. I told them what I've told you. How I got to my dad too late and bolted to the Methuselahs and got my crazy idea to cross the Coast Range. The wet night on Christopher Divide, the wonderful dripping overhang, getting fouled up in the canyons and chased off the ridge by that cold wind and trying to start a fire with money. I tried and tried and it just wouldn't take, I told them, but then, when I'd put in enough dollars, the twigs caught, I got my fire going and it saved my life.

"Maybe that's when your prayer worked, Josie."

I told them I slept by the fire that night and realized the next morning what a stupid expedition I was on. I thought about them, and my other friends, and my poor dead father, and I knew I had to go home. So I hiked down the creek and got hung up in a pot garden—I showed my swollen thumb—and broke out of the woods at the Sweet Grass Confederacy and the good people there took care of me.

Funny thing about telling stories. A lot of what I said was truth, but it wasn't the whole truth, and parts of what I said were out-and-out lies. I lied to them, and I've lied to you too. But as I spun it out in that candlelit room it all *felt* true, even the part about the twigs finally crackling to life, then the bigger sticks I put on to feed the flames, more sticks, big limbs, till I had such a bonfire I worried it would torch the whole forest, even wet as it was, and it got so danged hot I had to move twenty feet away, and even at that my face felt sunburned when I woke the next morning.

It felt true as I told it, Cart and Josie took it as true, and that's the trouble. If they told the story to others it would be true to them too, right on to the end of time, as long as anybody told it and heard it. By then it would have changed a whole lot more, but it would still be true. It would be the best truth anybody had.

sixteen

The next day, Cart and I walked over Boomer Mountain to my old home. Josie had taken their Honda to Duckworth and Long Tom, where she was volunteering at emergency shelters in two local churches. Cloudy Rains was doing the same, and she and Josie were getting to know each other. Stamper Road west of Dismal Acre was open to traffic—Raven had brought me home that way—but the Boomer Mountain stretch had serious cracks and slumps and was closed to vehicles.

It was a day of high cloud cover but dry. The road was littered with wet saw chips and scraps of slash. We stopped in at the Morrisons, who told us that Len Peppers was drugged up and doing all right in the hospital, except that they wouldn't let him play CDs on his boombox. He could listen to Top 40 country on the radio if his roommate didn't mind, but that "whiney pissin' and moanin'" turned Len's stomach. And of course he couldn't drink, either. "He's really ticked off," Bryce Morrison said with a wink. "We think he'll be coming home soon." Several neighbors, Cart was one, had cleaned up Len's house and fixed what needed fixing.

The Morrisons were glad to see me, had heard I was missing. I fudged around trying to explain until Cart moved the conversation on. And of course everybody was sorry as could be about my dad. "Son, you've had a lot of luck this year and it's all been bad," said Sander Feeley, the guy who'd given Cart that cup of spiked coffee. Sander was a solemn man with a face like a basset hound. "Your dad was a mighty good man," he said, and I nodded.

"You know," Cart said as we walked on, "it took an earthquake and a windstorm, but I'm starting to feel part of this community. I was wondering if I ever would."

I never thought I *wouldn't*, I said to myself.

The two Doug firs still lay on the house, wearing their full greenery, as if they'd found home and intended never to leave. The middle of the house was perfectly smooshed, tilting the front end slightly up, as if surprised.

I'd been wondering if I'd want to go in. I decided I would. The front door was jammed shut, so we went around through the back. Somebody had straightened up the kitchen, swept the broken dishes and whatnot into a pile by the door. I didn't feel anything. It didn't seem like my house. It was a cold, rundown relic.

"Those are full of books," Cart said, pointing to a neat stack of cardboard boxes. "I wanted to keep them safe. It's in my DNA."

I started up the hallway while he hung back in the kitchen to let me do whatever I needed to. My bedroom door was shut. My father's, all bashed up, was wide open but I didn't even look. The living room had dust and pieces of plaster all over the carpet and furniture. Two of the windows were cracked, some of the glass fallen out. I picked off the floor a picture of my mom I had always liked. The glass was cracked but the photo was fine.

She was wearing jeans and a blue halter top, her head resting on the sofa back, her black hair spread out a little, and she was smiling as if she'd had a drink or two and had worried about how she looked but had decided she didn't care. I thought of my father coming home from work every night since she died, walking by that picture he had taken and stopping to look—or not stopping, because it hurt too much. Either way, there she was and always would be, smiling, careless, a happy ghost behind glass.

I started back down the hallway with the picture and turned into my father's room. The rubble had been cleared from the bed. The sheets and quilt were all mussed up. I went closer. There were a few spots of blood. The dusty pillow was still there, askew, with a less dusty trough where my father's head had been. I thought I saw a hair on it. I turned away. The chainsaws and other tools were sitting by the door.

Cart was gazing out the kitchen window. I walked right by him and out the back door.

"Henry?" I heard behind me. "Don't you think you should get some clothes? Your toothbrush, things like that?"

I didn't want to, but I trudged up the steps, handed Cart the picture, and got a black plastic trash bag from under the sink. In my room, the bed had been shoved away so the door could open. The beer bottles were there, the rifle gone. I pulled clothing out of dresser drawers and a few things from the closet and stuffed it all into the bag. Cart offered to carry it and slung it over his right shoulder. I carried the picture.

"That place is totaled," I said, once we were out on the road.

"Jonah has the insurance papers," said Cart. "You'll get some kind of settlement."

"There's insurance?"

"You can't buy a home without it. You know, Jonah's an interesting man. I never expected to meet a log truck driver who's also a cellist."

"Oh," I said, "us hicks are full of surprises."

Cart shot me a look to see if I was offended, but I was smiling. He was by far my favorite target for smartassery.

We walked on a while, side by side, just the scuffing of our boots on pavement. I had slept till twelve, and the light was already going out of the gray afternoon.

"Henry?" Cart said, kind of shyly. "Have you thought much about where you'll live, what you'll do?"

"Can't I stay with you?"

"Of course, of course. I'm asking about longer-term. I want you to know that Josie and I—unless there's family somewhere, of course, or Jonah . . . but we would like you to live with us, Henry. Permanently."

I stopped and he did too, awkwardly.

"Serious?" I said.

"I wouldn't say it if I weren't serious."

"Do you know what you'd be gettin' into?"

"Oh, I have some idea. You don't respect Sierra Clubbers. And you're the kid who ripped off our liquor and stash last week."

"Wait. . . . Oh hell."

"Glasses in the sink, ashes on the coffee table. We're old, Henry, but our senses do work."

"Cart, I'm really really sorry. We, we just. . . ."

Cart gave me a pat on the shoulder. "I did worse in my youth," he said. "Just don't do it again. And I'm relieved, actually, to learn you weren't alone."

"I'll pay you back, Cart."

"Stop it," he said. "Now. Do you know what *you'd* be getting into?"

"I'd be getting into a nest of old hippies, and it's better than I deserve."

"We'll expect you to go to school, Henry."

Just then off to our left a light suddenly lit up in the dusky woods. Somebody gave a whoop, and we whooped back. Two other lights were on down the road.

"You know what this means, young man?" Cart had a wild dance in his eyes. "*Hot shower!* You get to go first."

"Nah, you go. I'll smoke some of your weed."

We walked on down Stamper Road, laughing and chattering. Cart was as happy as a shaggy, silver-haired pup. We'd been quiet for a while when he said, "Henry? There's something I have to ask you."

I kept walking.

"When your dad told you that he loved you and he was sorry, what was he sorry about?"

"Oh . . . I don't know. He whipped me pretty hard sometimes. And sometimes I deserved it."

"Jonah found your bedroom door braced shut," Cart said.

"Yeah. We had a big argument. I just didn't want to deal with him anymore."

"Did he hurt you? Because Josie and I have wondered. . . ."

He put his hand on my shoulder as we walked. I felt the weight of my mother's picture in my hand. I held it by the top, between my thumb and fingers.

"Nothing serious," I said.

My ribs are broke, Henry. . . . Pinned flat, in that pain. I stared at the pavement, my face seizing up in a sob that wouldn't sob. "I never should've left him," I whispered. My voice sounded strangled.

"Don't blame yourself, Henry. You did your best—"

"Stop telling me what I did!" I yelled, breaking away. "You weren't there. I should've died in those mountains. I should've fuckin' froze to death."

I took two crow-hops and hurled the picture like a frisbee, hard as I could into the thinned forest. Then I took a few lurching strides back up the hill and sat down, feet in the ditch, forehead on my folded arms, crying my eyes out.

When I looked up, snuffling, I spied a patch of faint green light in the woods, and then the light was coming toward me and it was Cart, holding the picture in one hand and his LED keychain light in the other.

"It's green," I said.

"Go Ducks," said Cart.

"You went to Cal and you know it, you damn outlander."

"I was young," Cart replied. "Don't you accept converts?"

He was wiping moss and woods-crud off the picture, which had somehow not hit anything hard. "I think I'll carry this, Henry. It'll save me steps, because you can't throw the clothes bag nearly as far."

I started to laugh but choked and had a coughing fit. Then I stood and shot a snot-rocket out of each nostril, the habit my mother had hated the most. "Be worse if I did it indoors," I used to tell her.

I swung the bag over my shoulder and we walked the rest of the way to Dismal Acre. The lights were on, but I almost wished they hadn't been. After dusky candlelight and starlight and glowing fire-light, the electrics hurt my eyes and made everything seem so ordinary, so just what it was. We ate spaghetti Josie had made. Then I took the shower Cart had offered and went to bed in the guest room. Not to sleep, though. I sat on the bed and did some carving on my forearms near the elbow, watching the blood come up, watching it start to flow and thicken. You pretty much *will* pay close attention when your body's bleeding, and while it is, your mind is off your troubles. You feel cleaner.

* * *

In my dream it was early evening, and out in the woods behind our house, or kind of our house, my father was a shadow in the trees, moving slowly, pausing now and then as if looking for something. Somewhere beyond him a river was flowing, I could hear its steady wavering chant—a *river*, right there where I lived, and I'd never known! I was in the backyard and couldn't move, heavy as Earth itself, and when I opened my mouth nothing came out. My father stopped, as if maybe he'd heard a voice. Then he reached and picked something off the ground—a tool, maybe—and then he was shifting around in the dim light of the woods again, slowly, deliberately. He had some job to do. Out beyond him the secret river was whispering and calling.

Breakfast was French toast and sausage and Josie's turbo-French roast coffee, which got me nice and buzzed. Josie was pretty wired herself, saying how happy they were that I wanted to live with them, how we'd for sure have to go through some hoops with the state of Oregon but nothing we couldn't deal with. Twice she stopped herself and looked at me solemnly and told me I was absolutely free to change my mind. It was entirely up to me. She'd stayed up late touching up my mother and putting her in a new frame under museum glass, and now she was saying how they wished they'd known her, and how unlucky it was to lose both parents at such a young age. I just smiled as she talked. There was so much they didn't know, but she and Cart too were so full of warmth and love, just pouring it all over me, that I was thinking everything might work out. They didn't need to know anything more. I could just about see myself going to school, getting Cart's help with my writing, learning photography from Josie. . . .

Then Jonah Rutledge came by. He'd heard from Cart that I was back, and he gave me a quick hug first thing. There was a smile between his mustache and goatee, but trouble in his gray eyes. The curly-headed elf had something on his mind. Cart pointed us toward the living room and went to bring coffee.

"You're back from your wanders," Jonah said in a flat voice.

Suddenly I felt like earthquake rubble. "I shouldn't've left him, Jonah. But he was dead, and I guess . . . I guess I panicked."

His eyes narrowed. "I figured you'd gone for help, Henry."

I shook my head. "I sawed my way in there fast as I could. I heard him say he was fading out, so I tried even harder. Broke a chain. I used the other saw, got to where I could see his face, but it was too late."

Cart set a tray on the coffee table and poured three mugs.

Jonah's eyes wouldn't let go. "How could you tell he was dead?"

I felt the back of my neck prickle. "Well, his voice was weak, and when I stopped the saw I could hear him breathe, and it sounded kind of gurgly. Then he just . . . quit breathing."

"Did you check? Did you feel with your hand over his nose and mouth?"

I nodded. "His eyes weren't moving either. They just stared."

Jonah almost scowled. "What did he say before he died, Henry?"

I glanced at Cart, whose hands were wrestling each other. "He said he loved me," I told Jonah. "He said to tell you good-bye, and his mother in Missouri. He told me to be happy. I told him he'd see Mom, but I don't think he believed it."

"Probably didn't." Jonah sipped his coffee. "You know everybody up and down this road, Henry. Did you *think* of going for help?"

"Jonah?" Cart spoke up, "I was out on that road, and yes, there were people up, but they were dealing with their own situations. It's not like he could have just shanghaied someone."

"I realize that," Jonah said. "I'm asking if he tried."

"I told him to hang on, Jonah. But he couldn't."

"So where'd you go?" Jonah asked, settling back in his chair.

"I panicked. I thought the state was gonna take me away to some orphanage. . . . Decided I'd hike to the coast and see how things settled out. It was stupid. I was in shock, probably. . . ."

"Hike to the coast," Jonah repeated with a thin smile. "Did you get there?"

"I spent three nights out, then I got it that I never should've left. Like you said. So I walked south and came out near Cottonwood."

"He got a ride from a fellow on a farm over there," Cart broke in. His hands looked like they were trying to crush his coffee mug. "It was a great relief to see him, Jonah. He's fifteen years old, you know, and he's been through a lot."

"And unlike you," said Jonah, "I've known him for all fifteen." He set his mug down on the wooden table and leveled his eyes on me.

"Let me tell you something, Henry. Your dad didn't die that morning. He didn't die that noon or early afternoon, either."

My gut sank. I had to look down as he went on.

"He didn't die until an hour, tops, before I got to him. His neck was a little warm, on a chilly day. I felt inside his pajama top and his chest was warmer. His belly was warmer yet. So you either mistook him for dead, Henry, or you knew he was alive and walked out on him. Which was it?"

"Jonah—" Cart began, but Jonah cut him off. "Which was it?"

"I made a mistake," I whispered. "A bad, bad mistake."

Jonah nodded slowly, his eyes boring into me. "That's why you keep working till you're sure, Henry. He's your *father*. You don't desert him if there's even a *chance* he's alive. You don't take off on some stupid nature walk—"

"*Jonah!*" Cart hollered, standing up. "He told you, he made a mistake."

Jonah got up and headed for the door, then turned halfway around with his hand on the knob. "There's some more you need to explain, Henry. Meantime, think of him pinned there helpless all those hours, the whole house on him. Broken ribs, bleeding inside. Think about it, Henry."

"Thanks for the coffee," he said to Cart with a grim face and closed the door quietly behind him.

In the loud silence Cart said, "I'm sorry about that, Henry. I had no idea he was so angry . . ."

I wanted to dissolve into the sofa.

"It was an easy mistake to make," Cart went on, sitting down again. "Your father went unconscious, his breathing slowed, it seemed to stop, and . . ."

Mistake, I kept hearing, sick to my stomach. *Mistake. . . .*

"And Henry? Your father had serious injuries. He might well have died even if you'd found help and gotten him free."

Cart was throwing me a lifeline, which I needed more than he knew.

"But it was such a *bad* mistake," I said, weakly. "Jonah's right. . . ."

"Mistakes are human, Henry. Please don't blame yourself."

* * *

I excused myself and took a long walk so I wouldn't have to talk or think about Jonah and my father.

I peeled off Stamper Road through Steve Barton's Christmas tree farm in a spitting rain, weaving through the spared little trees and the sappy stumps of the taken. It's a good kind of farming, Christmas trees, because they don't have to plow the soil and the trees make kids happy all across America—even Japan, where they pay big money for Oregon trees. I climbed up out of the farm into second-growth woods along the side of Brother Jim Butte and around to the south, where the Doug firs give way to a sparser woods with oaks, pines, and a few madrones. Just a dab more sun exposure and you're in a different forest. Our madrones are nothing huge like they can be to the south, but they're beautiful at any size, with their thin red bark peeling in curls off the underbark, which is the exact color of green olives. The dried red curls look like cinnamon sticks and can be smoked, if you're a kid and don't know getting high from getting sick and just crave something rough in your lungs. With those smooth limbs, the sapwood like muscle under that gorgeous skin, madrones look like they wandered from a whole other country into these straight-line, gray-barked woods and forgot to go home.

I settled under an Oregon white oak. They don't spread as majestically as California oaks, or oak trees out East maybe, but they spread the way they can right here. With space and light they'll grow broad with a perfectly proportioned crown; mixed in with quick-growing conifers, they'll go taller and skinnier to fight for their share of sun. They'll do what they need to do. These on Brother

Jim, dressed in their gray-green ghost foliage, were mid-sized and shapely. I leaned against the trunk and listened to the tiny sounds of rain, rain from the sky, rain from those spirits draping the trees. I breathed in the good damp smell of the woods where I was born and brought up, the woods that glowed with rainy light, the country where my mother was buried and my father would be buried and maybe someday I would too.

Maybe, I thought, just maybe, there was ground where I could get my footing and walk ahead. Jonah was angry, his best friend was dead, but maybe he would cool off. I was a kid, I'd screwed up. And Jonah didn't know it, of course, but my father had asked for it by what he'd done to me. Cart and Josie didn't know it either, and that was good. I didn't want anybody to know. That secret had died with my father. Nobody would know the worst he'd done to me, nobody would know the worst I'd done to him, and that was where it could rest. In a way I was looking out for his interest, saving his reputation. I was taking responsibility for both of us, like Raven had said.

Except he wasn't dead. He was alive in his bed with the whole middle of the house on his chest. No one to hear him call for help. His only chance had just walked out the door.

seventeen

My father was buried on Sunday, December 6th. Nobody knew what he would've wanted, so he was cremated and put into the ground next to Leenie. Burned or whole, that was the place he'd want to be for all eternity, next to the only woman he'd ever loved. For the next few billion years, anyway, until the sun becomes a red giant and cremates Earth back into gas and dust, and the gas and dust drift on and by and by start new stars and solar systems. When I could bear to think about his last moments, I wondered if he'd seen something, some glimpse, through the opening doorway that he thought led to nothing. Pinned as he was, he couldn't have reached for it, the way my mother did when her end came, but I wanted to believe—needed to believe, I guess—that he saw something that shocked his materialist mind, some kind of dawn over a landscape he'd never dreamed of.

The medical examiners didn't do a full autopsy. Judging from his wounds, they said, he probably died from a lacerated liver caused by the blunt force of the cave-in. The report was released to Cart and Josie, as my temporary guardians. Jonah was too explosive to talk to, so Josie told Cloudy about it. Later, Cloudy told Josie that Jonah had called the examiners' office himself because he didn't trust anything coming from Dismal Acre. In that conversation, Cloudy said, they'd told Jonah he shouldn't have brought the body in. It's better when we can examine at the site of death, the guy explained. Jonah thanked him for that advice and asked, "Should I have left that ton of rubble on him too? And if rats starting nibbling his toes and buzzards started gathering, should I have called you for instructions?" There was no way, he told the guy, that he'd have left his best friend in the broken mess of his house with the wind and rain coming in and whatever else. If he had it to do over, he said, he'd bust his butt to bring in the body even quicker.

I wasn't brave enough to look at my father in the funeral home, but after he'd been cremated I told them I wanted a handful of ashes for myself. They weren't real keen on it, but they opened the box. The ashes were shades of gray, fine and coarse mixed together, with some bits that had to have been bone. I put my handful in a plastic zip-bag.

The day we buried him was windy, cold, working up toward sleet or snow. Pastor Rogers had to hold down the gold-edged pages of his Bible with his gloved fingers as he read from Ecclesiastes, and he kept it short. He'd spoken in the church service, earlier, but the best words came from Jonah and Cloudy and Wendell Truckner from Siuslaw Pacific, the guy who'd hired my dad twice. Len Peppers was there, in a wheelchair, looking like a prophet fallen on hard times. He tried to say a few things about my dad, but he was pretty loopy from painkillers, probably whiskey too, and it didn't go well.

We sang a few hymns in the service and Jonah played his cello, solo. With his eyes closed, like always. Whoever wrote that music, it was beautiful to hear. It kind of rose and fell in slow surges and never settled down till the very end. As Jonah drew his bow across the strings it felt like he was drawing the feeling up inside me, letting it ease back a little, then raising it again as if he and the music had no choice, they couldn't help themselves and neither could we. Some people were crying, and I was one.

After the service everyone tried to comfort me. That was the hardest part, people hugging me up with sympathy I didn't deserve. I just nodded and smiled a little and acted numb. Didn't have to act, really. Everything was suddenly hitting me and I just kind of shut down. Jonah didn't talk to me, but I felt his eyes on me.

Len called my name and came weaving his wheels through the people. He looked like hell, his face pale and blotchy, and he was really working to breathe. "I wanted to tell you, Henry. . . . Your daddy and I were fishin' a river once . . . you were three, maybe . . . and he had a piece of clothesline, you know, and he'd . . . he'd tie you around your middle and tether you to a tree, when he stopped to fish a new hole. . . . You never whined once," Len said, "just sat there watchin' your daddy fish . . . and you poked around on your leash, you found a flower or an ant lion pit or. . . . Your dad, what I wanna say, he watched you with the most dee-lighted look on his face. He just *beamed*, Henry. An' I said . . . 'George,' I said, 'that child'll grow to a smart man. He's curious, he looks at things. . . . He takes it all in.'"

A little cluster had gathered around me and Len. "You can't rope a kid anymore," an S.P. worker said. "That's child abuse."

Everybody laughed, and I did too, though I was also crying.

"When you gettin' out of that chair, Len?" somebody asked.

"Where's the pastor?" Len said, peering left and right. "I'll be leavin' this chair when . . . when Christ walks barefoot over Fern Ridge Lake . . . or when I'm good and ready."

My grandmother from Missouri was there with her husband. Zelda stood tall, her white hair—which had once been dark red, like her son's—pulled under her black hat and veil, and of course she was really hurting. A mother isn't supposed to outlive her grown son. I didn't know what to say, and she didn't either, so we just hugged and cried and held hands for a while. She had a calm spirit. Georgie, his mother kept calling him, her little boy. I told my grandmother he'd said to say good-bye to her and that he loved her, which made her cry but I think she was glad to know it. Sometimes telling a lie is the truest thing to do. All I could think was, *I am so glad you will never know more than you know right now.*

Cart and Josie had taxied Zelda and Hubert from the airport to their motel, trying to make a good impression, and the day after the funeral Cart fetched them out to the house for tea. He'd drugged his hair with something to make it behave. I was worried they'd want to take me to Missouri, but they didn't. They were glad I had a nice home and good people to live with. We sat in the living room. I talked a little, but mainly—I hope she didn't think it was rude—mainly I couldn't stop staring at Zelda's face. It was my dad's face, George Fielder's. And it was little Georgie's face too.

* * *

Jonah had said there was more I needed to explain, so Josie met with Cloudy the day after the burial. When she came back she talked to Cart and then called me into the kitchen.

Jonah had found some disturbing things in the house, Josie said, picking her words like placing her feet on a narrow mountain trail. "He found many beer bottles, for one thing. Empty and full." She paused, looking at me. "And, he found your father's rifle by your bed, loaded, with one spent bullet on the floor."

"One empty shell," I murmured. "Didn't you see all that yourself, Cart?"

He shook his head. "I didn't go into your room, once Jonah told me you weren't under the rubble."

"Did Jonah find anything else while he was snooping?"

Josie nodded. "He found two pieces of paper you had written on. One sentence said, 'You son of a bitch I wish you were DEAD DEAD DEAD.' And some others were about shooting him and hauling him out back and leaving him for the buzzards, except he wasn't good enough for the buzzards. . . ."

"You're just telling the nice parts," I said. "I wrote that I'd like to ram a twisted fir branch up his ass. Let's see. . . . Maggots eating his eyeballs . . . oh, and an Indian coming along, cutting off his balls and dick and stuffing 'em into his mouth, like they did to Custer's men at Little Big Horn. That was the day before the quake. I was half crazy."

"And half drunk?" Cart asked.

"Not till later," I said, and told them about slipping out that night and the crazy birds and the blue light shimmering around Brother Jim Butte and feeling like a lunatic and grabbing the half-rack and drinking as fast as I could in my bedroom, then my father coming to the window.

"Did you shoot at him?" Cart asked.

"I sighted him up and told him to get away from the window, then squeezed the trigger quicker than I meant to and shot the window out. Scared him, I think."

"I can imagine," said Cart.

"Henry?" Josie gazed at me in the eyes a few seconds over her glasses. "You barricaded your door, you wrote those things, you got drunk, you shot the rifle . . . *near* your father. That's extreme behavior. What brought it on?"

"We had a big argument. I wanted to go back to high school, and he said no, and I said I was gonna live with Abner or somebody and have real teachers again. He got mad and whapped me around some, and I decided I'd had enough of that."

"He had whipped you before, yes?"

"He'd whip me with a willow stick or smack me in the face sometimes."

"But you never reacted this way before. What was different this time?"

I shrugged. "Older and bolder, I guess. And those days before the quake, didn't you feel it? The birds and animals were acting crazy, and I was too."

"Henry," said Josie, "I need you to be completely honest. Did your father ever touch you inappropriately? In a sexual way?"

"What? Hell no. Why would he do that?"

"It happens, Henry. And if it happened to you, it would in no way be your fault." She kept her eyes on me. "Have you told us everything?"

I nodded.

"Henry," Cart said, "there's something else. Your father didn't leave a will, but he had two life insurance policies—one through Siuslaw Pacific, and a private policy on top of that. They were both payable to your mother, and after she died he made them payable to you. He appointed a custodian, though, to be in charge of the funds if he should die before you were twenty-one. You can guess who he appointed."

"I don't care about any money," I said.

"You have to care, Henry. He never missed a payment. I don't know how much, but it's probably several hundred thousand dollars."

"I don't deserve it, don't you *get* that?"

"Henry," said Josie, "however cruel your father may have been, he did this for you. It could put you through college. But to have it before you're twenty-one, we need to patch things up with Jonah."

"Won't happen," I said. "His best friend's dead and I'm the reason."

* * *

While we were talking it had started to snow, big heavy flakes sifting down and beginning to stick to the rhododendrons. Normally it would've thrilled me—western Oregon at our elevation doesn't get a lot of snow—but all I could think about, watching through the bedroom window, was the one time I'd been in lots of snow, enough snow to get buried in, on a ranch in eastern Oregon where we'd been invited to spend a weekend. The people there had made a course down a long hillside for sledding on big inner tubes for truck tires. The sky was a blizzard of cold light like I had never seen, an open range of stars with the Milky Way clouding through the middle. I was six, too little to sled by myself, so my dad laid himself across a big tube and held me in his arms, looking up, as we went shooting down the course among the junipers, riding high on the banked turns one side to the other, the stars twirling as we spun on the tube, starlight flashing on the snow. Near the bottom we were going so fast we flew off the last turn—I launched out of my father's arms and for a moment I was flying in the stars, alive and wild. It happened too fast to get scared. My dad pawed me out of the snowdrift, apologizing, but I was laughing like crazy as we traipsed back up the hill, my hand in his, and found my mother by the fire at the top of the run with hot chocolate.

Now it was coming down harder and I wanted to be in it. I got my gear together, told Cart I'd be camping out—"In the *snow?*" he said—and hiked north up Schuyler Creek, the nearest little tributary to the Long Tom, to a flat spot maybe half a mile from the road. The snow was sticking, three inches already, and coming down thick. I set up Cart's tent—he'd tossed out my tube-tent and given me his old two-man—then set to work breaking dead branches off the trees and made a big heap, then piled another heap for extra fuel.

As dark settled in, I lit the fire with my new Bic and pretty soon eager flames were climbing the pile and merging into one great flame, and the heat forced me back, sweating on one side and goose-bumped on the other. I started turning like a chicken on a skewer to even out the heat, then I stripped down to my boots and danced. Didn't know any Indian dances, any dances at all, so I invented my personal snow dance round and round the fire, yipping and wailing like a coyote, screeching like a Steller jay, honking like a goose in flight, my shadow dancing on the snowy ground and the circling trees. I tossed more wood on, sparks billowing up, and danced and danced and danced, rolling in the snow now and then to cool off. When I got tired, I opened the zip-bag and tossed some pinches of my father's ashes into the fire. *Earth to earth, dust to dust, ashes to ashes.* . . . I danced slowly then, asking the fire demon what wanted to be born in his glowing red heart, and then I got too cold and grabbed my clothes and pad and ran to the tent and shivered to sleep in my dry sleeping bag to the tiny sounds of snowfall beginning to bury me.

* * *

Josie corralled me the next afternoon to help take a load to the dump in their new rig. They'd spent the morning in Eugene and came home with a new charcoal-gray Toy truck. "Pretty handsome," I'd allowed.

"And four-wheel drive," Cart crowed.

"Thank god," I said. "This one won't be so embarrassing to ride in."

Stamper Road was only a little slushy over Boomer Mountain and Brautigan Ridge. Cracks in the pavement and stair-step breaks had been filled and graded with gravel for the time being. The speed limit was 10. Spots where the pavement had sagged from little earthslides were marked with signs that said "Sunken Grade," whatever good that was supposed to do.

Down on the flat, Josie braked to a stop when I spotted a gray tabby crouching in the ditch, but it wasn't Catrick. "We do miss that creature," she said with a sigh.

She was still doing disaster relief, but it wasn't needed so much now. The dead were dead, the injured were cared for, and those that couldn't return to their homes had found other quarters. Most people had their power back. The Army Corps of Engineers had found that Fern Ridge Dam was probably okay, but they wouldn't let the lake fill again until they could take a longer look. The weather was cooperating—just the snow and a few little rains since the quake. No big wind, either.

In Eugene another body had been found, but there'd been a mir-
acle story, too. Seems like there always is. A guy had survived for a
week under rubble in a downtown basement, living off water dripping slowly from a pipeline above him. He'd used a piece of
foil-backed insulation to channel the drops to his mouth. There was
a lot of insulation in the jumble above him, and that had kept him
from hypothermia. It was a public building, and he'd been sneaking
into the basement to sleep every night, it turned out. Nobody expected anyone there. He'd lost his voice hollering for help, so the
next time he heard human noises above he'd started whistling "My
Country, 'Tis of Thee" and they'd heard him.

A newspaper story had just cleared up one earthquake mystery, or
at least made it a different kind of mystery. I wasn't the only one who
had seen strange lights around the time of the quake. Most people
said they were blue or blueish-white, like I'd seen, and a couple of
others said greenish. A *Register-Guard* staff writer did some research
and found that weird lights had been reported on every continent,
before, during, or after nighttime quakes. Blue and white were the
most common colors. Nobody had an explanation, but some scientists thought the grinding of rock against rock is so powerful, it releases a charge that electrifies the air.

That could have made me zingy, I figured. And the animals. And
maybe my father, too.

Driving through Duckworth Josie and I saw a cattywampus house
here and there, several collapsed carports, broken windows sheeted
over with clear plastic, a lot of slash and sawdust and tree-parts everywhere. One sweet little yellow-sided home had been totally stove
in by a big white oak that no one had gotten around to sawing off yet.
Just like the Fielder place. Not a hurry in the world.

The county transfer station was mobbed with a great democracy
of citizens with wreckage. The trucks and cars were lined up, people
standing outside their rigs to talk, jumping in to pull forward when

the line moved. It was a happy scene, the energy revved me, but I stayed in the truck so I wouldn't have to talk to people I knew.

While we waited, Josie told me that she'd called the Department of Human Services, and somebody would come out soon to assess our living situation. For now, they just wanted to see that I had a safe place to live while she and Cart filed to become foster parents.

"They can't make me move, can they?"

"Technically they can," said Josie. "They consider your preference but aren't bound by it. They'll be interviewing you, your living relatives, and me and Cart. Unless one of your grandmothers decides she wants you, our chances are good."

"I'm staying," I said. "Does Cart know he needs to hide his stash in the freezer and spray his room with deodorant?"

Josie smiled. "He's already buried it. And the smell you may have noticed is him burning beeswax candles in his study. He might even wash his walls."

"He should wash his books too," I said.

They had talked with Duckworth High School, and everybody agreed there was no point in me coming back until after New Year's. I'd been half-hoping to start right away, but I was dreading it too, the crowd at lunchtime, the talk talk talk, in class and out. The administrators weren't very impressed by my father's teaching records, but it didn't matter. They had to take me.

Abner Truitt had heard about my father in the local news, and then a rumor that I had gone missing. He got Cart and Josie's number— remembered their name from our little party there—and called when phone service came back on. "Tracker, I was *worried*," he told me. "You couldn't read my smoke signals?" I cracked, but I was touched. Abner knew me, so he didn't think it so strange that I'd gone on a three-day Coast Range walkabout. "Dude," he said, "your dad just died, you had no parents, your house was totaled, your world was one big cluster-fuck. You had to wander the wilderness and find yourself.

Anybody would've needed it, but only you would've actually *done* it."
I told him I'd be in high school again and he shouted "Yass! Yass!"
We'd both read *On the Road* that fall, and Dean Moriarty was Abner's
new hero.

Ten minutes after we'd hung up, the phone rang again and it was
Tess Bailey. Our conversation went better this time. She'd been worried about me too, and was so sorry about my father, and so right
away I played her. I spoke mysteriously about my three days in the
wilderness, told her I couldn't convey the experience over the phone.
We agreed to get together soon, some afternoon when she got out of
school. My world was looking a little less cluster-fucked.

When Josie and I finally got our junk dumped, we drove back to
town and pulled in behind Big's Hi-Yu-He-He to give a garbage bag
of deposit cans and bottles to the homeless people who hung out
there. No homeless were home, so we left the bag. To the side of the
building I showed Josie the faded red paint splotches and told her the
story, which gave her a kick, then we did the grocery shopping across
the road at Foodland. As we walked the aisles, I remembered shopping with my mother, riding in the cart or later walking behind or
ahead, nagging for a box of Cheez-Its. As an experiment I nagged
Josie for a box, and she caved right away. An excellent omen.

Later that day I layered up, got on my bike, and pedaled over
Boomer Mountain to my old house. My father's beat-up brown pickup
was right where he had left it. He'd only driven it to work once after
he'd put silicone powder in the gas tank and oil case, ten miles total.
The engine might still be okay. I got the socket set from the tool bench
and a grubby plastic basin and slid under the truck and opened the oil
drain plug. The oil was fairly new, not yet black, so I could see the black
grit. The system would have to be flushed. I needed advice on that, but
this was a start. The dozer wouldn't be so easy, but I didn't care as
much about it. That machine probably *should* die, I figured. They'd
used it to scare peaceful people, and now they'd use it to carve up a
piece of land so they could strip it.

In my father's bedroom, I looked at the bed again, the pillow. I had come to forgive him and ask him to forgive me, but nothing came out of my mouth. How could he forgive me? He couldn't hear me. So I tried to pray instead. I dropped to my knees and started, but it sounded hollow because I didn't know who or what I was praying to. Who did I have the *right* to pray to? I wasn't Indian, I wasn't Christian. And what exactly was I praying for?

So I knelt there with my hands together, snuffling, my spirit all bound up. And then my vision opened inside. I saw my mother as I had watched her often, pulling the brush down through her straight black hair, down and down again, the brush lifting the hair just a little, pulling it straight and letting it go with a little bounce, and I remembered her saying that my truest prayers came when I was in my gift, when I wasn't asking for anything but was just *aware*, open to the living spirit. I felt my breathing even out like a slow stream, a little riffle flowing into a pool, the pool flowing out in a riffle again, the given received and given again. . . .

When I came back to myself, a breath of spirit turned my head. There, perched in the busted-out frame of my father's bedroom window, was a rufous-sided towhee, head cocked to one side, checking me out. Came a freshet of old joy. I slowly turned on my knees to face the window and bowed my head to the floor. I knew, as I lifted my head, that the bird would be gone.

I took the gift with me.

eighteen

Jonah was surprised to see it was me who'd rung his doorbell.

"Could we talk, Jonah?"

"About what?"

"I didn't *want* him to die, Jonah. I was mad at him when I wrote that stuff. We'd had a fight, he'd been whipping me for this and that. I didn't try to shoot him, either. I shot the window out to scare him, that's all. I—"

Jonah raised a hand to stop me. "Come in," he said.

We sat in the gray light of his kitchen, him expressionless across the table, his arms folded. He looked tired. "Your father worried about you, Henry. You weren't doing chores or lessons, you were getting loaded all the time, you were lying to him, taking money—he didn't know what to do with you."

"He knew what to do with a willow stick," I said.

"Well, what'd you expect? Ice cream? What was the big fight about?"

"I wanted to go back to high school. He said I couldn't."

Jonah's face twisted, unelf-like. "*That's* why you barred your door and shot at him and wrote that hateful stuff? Come on, Henry."

"It was the build-up to the earthquake too, Jonah. You must have felt it. The animals were acting crazy. *I* was half-nuts when I wrote that stuff."

Jonah tapped his fingers on the table. "Let me get this straight. You're blaming an earthquake that hadn't happened yet for writing awful things and just about shooting your father and leaving him helpless? That's pathetic, Henry."

I flared a little. "He did something else, too, but you wouldn't believe me. Sorry I bothered you. Guess I'll just have to live with you hating me."

"I don't hate you, Henry. But all I hear from you is lies and excuses."

"My father did something really wrong, okay? Then I did something wrong, and I guess we evened out."

"What did he do, Henry?" Jonah spread his arms to show he was all ears.

I shook my head. "You'd just call me a liar." I stood up and walked out.

I biked to the old homeplace and sat in my mother's white Dodge, breathing its familiar smell. Her silver-netted dreamcatcher hung from the mirror. I had a question for it, but the answer came before I could speak. When she came to me as that beautiful black bird in a white sky, when she sank me with a stabbing pain back into my cold body, she did it for a purpose.

I'd have to tell the truth, and the truth was something in the dark, something you pretend's not happening, then pretend it didn't. You never asked for it but it comes to you in the night with whiskey breath and there you are, on your belly with the feel of slick sweat and skin against skin and the pain of a surging power you can't stop, like the weight of stormwind in the trees when something has to give way, has to give way, and the only thing there to give way is you.

And that would be the easier part of the truth to tell. I had lied to Cart and Josie, I had lied to Jonah, and I've lied to you too, reader. I've lied about something important. I did it because I couldn't make myself write what really happened, just as I couldn't believe at the time that it really was happening. Lynn called me on it. Lynn's good at that.

"But you told me this isn't journalism or history," I said. "You said it didn't have to be exactly true like that. . . ."

Lynn's head was shaking, black hair shifting side to side, no trace of a smile. "This is crucial, Henry. This is the heart of the story. There's no point writing the book if you fabricate this."

"Oh hell," I said, drowning in my own lameness. "So much for memory and imagination being all one."

"Contrivance isn't memory *or* imagination," Lynn said. "It's covering your ass."

"All right," I sighed. "I'll go back and change it."

"Don't," said Lynn, now with a very cute hint of a smile. "Just go ahead with the story. You'll tell the truth before long, because the story will force you to."

* * *

We sat in the living room that evening, and I told Cart and Josie I was thankful that they wanted to be my foster parents, that I would always obey their rules, and I knew there'd be no drinking, but that just this once, to talk the way I needed to talk, it would help to have black rum. They looked at each other and Cart brought me some in a small glass.

So I took a sip, looked at the floor, and started with what they already knew. Waking to the quake, the roof caving in. My dad answering when I called. Getting the tools, tunneling in, gagging on the fumes, clearing debris till I could see his head on the pillow, his matted red hair and stubbled cheek. He could talk, and he was pissed.

"'Can't you fuckin' *hurry*?' he said.

"And I said, 'I don't want the load to shift and make it worse.'

"'Couldn't *be* any worse. I can't move here, can't you see?'

"I cranked the saw but it wouldn't catch, cranked it again, him ragging at me to hurry the hell up. And then I just rested the saw on the floor."

Cart and Josie were huddled on the couch like little kids watching a scary movie. I wanted to bolt the whole small glass of rum but took only a sip. The next thing I told them felt like stepping off a cliff.

"I said to my dad, 'I'll get you out of here, but you have to do something. You have to tell me you're sorry for what you did.'

"'Did what?' he said.

"'You know what I mean,' I said."

Josie started to interrupt, but I held my palm out toward her.

"I heard him breathing in the silence," I went on, "kind of gravelly."

"'All right,' he said after a while. 'I'm sorry. Now would you get the fuck back to work?'

"And that's what I should have done," I told Cart and Josie. "I should have started the saw and finished the job. But I asked another question.

"'Why'd you do it, Dad?'

"Maybe he was in shock, maybe he had a screw loose from the pain, maybe he couldn't face up to it, I don't know, but he went off. He blew up and said he'd worked hard for me and done everything for me and my mother and I had no right to be grillin' him when he was pinned helpless in a wrecked house. And he was right, he was totally right, but I couldn't let it go.

"'Tell me why you did it, Dad.'

"'Because you wouldn't mind me, Henry. You forced me to it. You had it comin' and you know it.'

"'I didn't have it coming, you pervert.'

"'Yeah you did. And I bet you even liked it.'

"I'd been looking at him through the opening, but now I looked down at my hands. I heard the wind whining through the busted roof, and suddenly I felt cold and sure. I left the saw where it was and crawled backward out of the tunnel I'd made and went to get my gear together.

"He called my name a few times, but I just kept packing.

"'Henry,' I heard him call. 'Are you there, Henry?'

"'Used to be,' I said, and I walked out the back door."

"Oh, Henry," said Josie, tears on her cheeks.

I went on. "For the next three days I thought about finding my route, the weather, the windfalls and mudslides and a poem I couldn't remember. I was hiking to the sea. If I felt him sneak close there was this door I could shut on him, made of heavy wood planks with black iron straps like the entrance to a castle. But then on the third night my mother came to me, and the door cracked open. I knew I had to come home. I hoped he was still alive, that Jonah or somebody had come along and got him out. . . ."

Josie wanted to hug me. Cart wanted to raise my father from the dead and strangle him. "Henry," he said, "if you just could have *told* us—"

Josie elbowed him in the ribs. "It took a lot of courage to tell us what happened, Henry. Thank you for trusting us. What your father did to you is not your fault, and neither is what you did to him."

"Tell Jonah if you want," I said. "But he won't believe you."

"Of course he'll believe us," Cart said. "It explains everything."

* * *

That night I had the dream again, the shadow of my father working in the woods behind the old house. I couldn't see the river but it was a joy to hear, that river I'd never known was there. This time, my father seemed to know I was watching. He paused his work and turned his head toward me, but under the bill of his cap his face was just a dark smudge. I was frozen there in the backyard. He had some kind of tool in his hand—a hammer? chisel?—and then he shifted slowly back to work. There was something he was making, I couldn't see what. Everything was shades of darkness, like Hades when Odysseus went there. I thought maybe I heard my father whistling, but it might have been a bird, it might have been a sound of the river, that crazy surprise river flowing easy and unseen.

* * *

This time Cart and Josie both went to talk with Jonah and Cloudy. They came back with the news I'd expected. Jonah had told them there was no way George Fielder would or *could* have done such a thing. Whippings with a willow stick, a hand across the face, sure, but not that.

You're here from California not even a year, he'd said, you hardly knew George and obviously didn't like him, and you come to me with this awful story? Him with no chance to speak for himself? From a kid who was always partial to his mother, and strange in the head, and tried to shoot his father?

And this was the reason he acted as he did, Cart had said back. Why do you think he barricaded his door?

I have no idea, Jonah had yelled. Why did he write those disgusting things? He's always had a screw loose. Sorry, I'm not drinking your Kool-Aid.

Cloudy had tried to calm Jonah down, but he wasn't having it. Why did that boy Kip Kinkel shoot his mom and dad and those kids at Thurston High? Because his head was twisted, that's why.

If Henry were lying, Josie had said, why would he invent a story so personally painful and degrading?

To hook gullible people, Jonah came back. Listen, he lied to my face in your living room. He was lying to his father right and left, George told me so. And he's lying to you.

I have to say, Cloudy put in, I find this very, very hard to believe. George had a temper, certainly. But rape, Josie? His own son?

It shocked us too, Josie said. He'd been drinking heavily, Henry told us. For weeks and months.

Jonah snorted at that. Yeah, he was drinking, but I'll tell you what. If the night 'it happened' was the night you say, it was Henry Fielder that was drunk and stoned half out of his head. I found him and his buddy falling off their bikes on Boomer Mountain. Doubt they'd've made it home if I hadn't picked 'em up.

Jonah stared at them. He lied then too, by the way. Any idea where he found the booze and pot?

Jonah said he absolutely would not release the life insurance money and even talked about going to the sheriff to see if charges could be brought, at which Cart blew a fuse and the visit was over. As they left, Josie pleaded with Jonah to hold off, but he made no promises. She and Cart came home with their tails dragging.

"Cloudy is uncertain," Josie said to me, "but she accepts the *possibility* that you're telling the truth. Jonah might move her way."

"I doubt it," said Cart. "I bet we're looking at a legal fight to get that money. Could take years. And the whole story would go public."

"Hey," I said, "no public, all right? And no money. I just wanna go to school and hike and read books and not bother anybody."

Cart slumped back on the sofa. "I hope you'll be able to, Henry. You didn't ask for any of this."

"No, but I guess I earned it," I said. "I'll stop going to church. That way I won't have to see Jonah."

We were quiet a while. Then Josie said, "It might be better if you did go to church, Henry. It might be the only way to regain their trust. You'll show Jonah you're the same boy he's known and loved for fifteen years."

"I don't know," I said. "I don't know if I am the same boy."

part three

That loneliness, that needing, and that wanting,
they're all part of longing, they're your saving grace . . .

—Kenny Loggins and Scotty Emerick,
from "Love's the One and Only Thing"

nineteen

In January I began the middle of my sophomore year at Duckworth High, and I didn't take well to being cooped up. It wasn't torture, exactly—it was winter, and a cold one—but I did find myself staring out the window a lot, watching clouds, birds, trees, scraps of paper in the wind. The freedom of things the way they are. In the breaks between classes I wanted to bolt, to leave behind the talk and shouts and giggles, and head for the woods. My hoodie said, "Preserve the Right to Arm Bears." I put the hood up, put my head down, and got through the day. I felt zombied, on mute, not really there.

The other thing I didn't like was undressing and showering at PE. I knew better, but I worried that other kids could see what my dad had done to me, that it had marked me some way. I took little looks and noticed that some boys had more hair down there than I did, and some had pretty big dicks, too, bigger than mine. I had no idea what that meant. I showered and got dressed quick as I could and pressed through the crowd to my next class.

I did like the normalness of classrooms and textbooks and teachers, everything in order—rows of desks, raising your hand to ask a question, even the pledge of allegiance—and I especially liked the quiet when we were reading or taking a test, just the sounds of pens moving and pages turning and the occasional sigh or groan or yawn. It was a comfortable routine, like the smell of Josie's turbo-roast coffee in the morning and *All Things Considered* on the radio in the early evening. I got into the English class I wanted, with Mr. Sterry, and my other classes were all right—World Civilizations, Biology, and beginning Spanish. In math I struggled with geometry, as I had with my father, but my teacher, Mr. Spindor, took pity and spent extra time with me, and as the weeks went along I got to understanding it better and even began to see some beauty in it. It was much cleaner than the rest of my world.

To the kids that knew me a little and some who didn't, I was the guy who had lost his mother to cancer and his father in the Thanksgiving Quake. Some came up and told me how sorry they were, and I got used to just mumbling thanks and moving along, the ridiculously unlucky kid who was too awkward to speak to. I felt like a secret agent from my old life on a mission into the future, but I didn't know what the mission was.

Abner and I hung out in the woods after school sometimes, breathing a hit or two of bud if he had some. At school he was the center of a social solar system, as always, which he liked but got weary of too. It seemed to me that he enjoyed it when it was just us, and he didn't have to hold court and talk a lot. I liked being able to do that for him. We'd always been easy with each other.

Tess Bailey and I sat together at lunch, and she was just as pretty and friendly as she'd been that day on Hammerstone Mountain, but lunch was loud and I was self-conscious and couldn't think of things to say. Probably runs in the family, I brooded. My mother had told me how she and my dad first met. In her sophomore year at Oregon State she was sitting in the student union reading and drinking coffee one night when a tall, red-headed guy in jeans and old sneakers walked by to put a cup into the trash can. A little later he came back and tossed something else, and this time he stood looking around—kind of brushed her with his eyes—before going back to his table. His eyes were hazel green, he was cute, and she decided to leave and see what he would do. She was out the door into the night, disappointment growing, when she heard footsteps running up behind her. Nobody else was around, it was a little creepy, but she trusted her feelings and she wasn't afraid.

"Hey," he called. His first word to her. She turned around.

Once he caught up to her, "Hey" was his second word, too.

"Hello," she said.

"Hey . . . I saw you in there and was wonderin' maybe if I could, uh, buy you a cup of coffee?" She remembered him shifting his weight from foot to foot as he talked, in his OSU hoodie with a ferocious beaver on the front.

She liked the soft Missouri music in his voice and thought he was handsome. "I've had enough coffee," she said. "Would you like to take a walk?"

So they walked the campus and the streets of Corvallis for probably two hours, she told me, talking a little. He had trouble picking his words. He walked her to her dorm when she was ready, then tied himself in knots trying to ask if he could see her again.

Finally she laughed and said, "Yes. I would like to walk with you again. And have a cup of coffee."

They took more walks and went on dates in his white Dodge. He stayed in Oregon that summer, they had fun, and he asked her to marry him, but she said she needed more time. She understood, she told me, that she would never be able to discuss books with him, and other things, but she decided she could do that with friends. He was smart enough, in his way, and he seemed more of a man than the other guys she met, including the ones who could talk about books. He didn't drink a lot, and she was sure in her heart that he would be faithful and a good provider. She hadn't been around many faithful men growing up, including the father she never knew. She was pretty keen on George Fielder's build and hazel eyes and auburn hair, too. What really got her, though, she told me with a giggle, was his Hey-Hey-Hey approach. "It worked," she said, "but Henry, I think you can do better than the triple-hey strategy."

Or not, as it turned out. Remembering the story, I realized that when my mom and father met on that spring night, they were not much older than I was now—she was eighteen, he was twenty. They both must have said stupid things and been unsure of themselves. My dad must have worried that his shoes were dirty. I smiled inside to think of them and felt a strange pang—as though somehow they were the kids and I was the adult, watching them play and laugh in a front yard somewhere. I wanted to talk, to get to know them, but if I stopped on the sidewalk and said hi they wouldn't answer me, they'd go silent and fearful. To them I'd just be some random stranger.

* * *

Things improved when I bet Tess that I could find a back way to her house in Long Tom if she'd walk with me, so she wore hiking boots to school the next day and after final class we hit the woods. It was messy. We had to slog through a mucky swale and got ourselves scratched up bushwhacking a few thickets. "Just what you were hoping for, huh," I said to her with a grin, but she was a good sport about it and I was stoked. Finding our way on an expedition made talking not nearly so hard.

When I'd twice led her out of the woods nowhere near her home, I turned to her in a soggy meadow and said, "I forgot to warn you. Wilderness guides are wrong a lot." Tess, in a red rain parka, came up to me, pulled a couple of twigs out of my hair, and kissed me on my lips. "You may be wrong," she said, her brown eyes warm and bright, "but you also seem quite right."

"Whoa," I said. "Not meaning *stop*, of course. . . ." and she laughed, and I laughed with her.

My next attempt led us to the back side of a dirty singlewide with blue tarps on the roof and a lot of junk strewn around. In the Northwest a place like that screams meth kitchen, active or abandoned, bad news either way. We backtracked fast, and just as it was getting too dark to see we broke out of the woods a couple of blocks from Tess's house.

After that adventure I sometimes rode the bus home with her and we messed around in her basement, talking, listening to music—she was definitely *not* into country—or playing board games. We tried Scrabble, but Tess could win only if I let her, which was against my principles. One day I had some vodka miniatures I'd bought from a guy at school, so we made cranberry juice cocktails and Tess asked about my three days in the wilderness. I nodded my head somberly.

"Well," I began, "I dug into the rubble to free my father, but he died just as I got to him. I was afraid they'd put me in an orphanage, so I built a little sweatlodge, purified myself, and hiked up into the mountains on a vision quest. I camped that night on a ridgetop and drew blood from my forearms, like the Plains Indians do, crying to the Great Spirit for a vision." I pulled up one of my sleeves. Tess flinched when she saw the scars, then traced the lines softly with her forefinger.

"But I wasn't given a vision," I went on, "so I hiked on west to another mountaintop the next day, feeling kind of crazy—I'd been fasting the whole time, of course—and it got so cold that night I had to stuff myself into a hollow log, which I'd lined with grasses and Doug fir boughs. It was that super-cold night, two days after the quake. I didn't know if I was gonna live or die, but I got my vision. My parents came to me as a pair of ravens and said they'd hated to leave me, but it was for the best and someday I would understand why. For now, they said, I should get myself together and go home. They promised they'd be with me always.

"Next morning I hiked downstream and came face to face with a cougar not twenty feet away, hissing and growling." Tess looked horrified. "I calmed myself and that calmed him. I asked him if I could pass through his kingdom, doing no harm, and he turned away. Then I came out at a commune near Cottonwood, where the leader told me he'd had a feeling for three days that somebody would come down out of the hills. I broke my fast there, and the next morning the highway opened and one of them drove me home."

There was more to the story I spun for her, but that's the gist.

"Henry, my God," said Tess. "That's amazing."

I nodded. I got away with it only because she was a city girl. "I might go and live at that commune," I said. "I'd learn more there than I'm learning in school."

We had another drink and Tess decided it was time for Kissing 201, with the possibility of advanced studies. I'm not sure I was a good student but she definitely was a good teacher, and pretty soon we were rubbing together and I was getting good and stirred up right where I was supposed to and developing grand ideas about taking the final right then and there—and we heard the front door open. "Tess dear," her mother called down the stairs, "are you home?"

"Cool down, tiger," my girlfriend whispered, and we pulled ourselves together. Mrs. Bailey was very nice, I liked her right away. Her only flaw was her timing.

* * *

That was a happy day, but I still felt flat, not really in my life. I was drinking and smoking every day that there was something to drink or smoke. I stole from the liquor cabinet, carefully this time, mostly from bottles way in the back. Nasty stuff, some of it, but I wasn't drinking for flavor. I felt guilty doing it, but not guilty enough. I was glad not to be crying anymore but sometimes wished I would, just to be feeling *something*.

Abner caught me after school the next day and said he'd heard a strange rumor that I had tried to shoot my father, because he had—Abner didn't often struggle for words—"abused" me "in a real wrong way, you know."

"Are you kidding me?" I said. "My father's dead in his grave and somebody's tellin' lies like that?"

"Exactly what I told him," said Abner. "I said he was full of shit to his eyeballs. You're in enough pain without people spreading evil gossip."

"They just do it 'cause I'm different," I said. "Who was it?"

Abner put a hand on my shoulder. "You don't need to get involved, Tracker. I'll deal with the dickhead personally, and with anybody else if I hear it again."

That was worrisome. Jonah or Cloudy must have talked—Jonah, probably—and it'd found its way to school. Numbed-out as I was, though, I didn't worry too hard. Abner would deal with it, and Abner was my medicine man. He scored a vial of crystal meth and we spent a weekend snorting through it, fooling around on our bikes and talking nonstop—he did, anyway—as we got even more wired on coffee at Lily's Lift. Most people don't know how godly meth makes you feel—you delight in every little thing you see, from a flattened Coors Light can on the pavement to a passing crow to the humongous American flag rippling in the breeze over the parking lot at Foodland. Trouble is, though, sooner and sooner after every snort, worry sets in like a thin cloud beneath the sun—doubts and fears eating at my high, and I'd want another hit but it was Abner's stuff, and he was fair with it but wasn't ready for another hit himself, and I couldn't just up and ask for it. Abner didn't get snarled up that way. He played with drugs like a toy, the way you can when they're something you don't really have to have.

At Dismal Acre, on the other hand, things had never been better. Cart and Josie were so eager to please I had to tell them to relax, they'd already passed the test, I had no plans to trade them in for a new pair. I knew how lucky I was to be with them. The interviews had gone well. I told the lady from Human Services that I wanted to stay right where I was, and the living situation at Cart and Josie's probably looked like heaven, Josie figured, compared to a lot of homes those people must visit. No drugs had been discovered other than alcohol—that one never seems to count—and it wouldn't be a problem that both Cart and Josie had been arrested a few times back in the 1960s and '70s for protesting the Vietnam War. Turned out that being a foster family would make us rich, too. Cart and Josie would get a monthly check for my room and board, and I would get great health insurance and financial aid if I went to college. I could also get Social Security, the lady said, and she told us how to apply.

The church had taken up a collection, which I wanted to give back—nobody in that congregation was wealthy—but Pastor Rogers said, "It was given in love, Henry. You are obliged to accept it." Siuslaw Pacific had paid the funeral expenses—we never saw a bill—and sent me a check for a thousand dollars "to help you through this hard time," said the note from Wendell Truckner.

For all my good fortune, though, I didn't feel so lucky. As the weeks went by I wasn't real sad, wasn't real angry, I just wasn't *real*. At school I only paid attention in Mr. Sterry's English class. In the others I did just enough work to get by. Tess wondered about my mood but I couldn't really talk about it. I started cutting afternoon classes to walk in the woods and find my joy again, but the critters picked up my zombie vibe and shunned me. If I saw a deer it was her white rump, hightailing into the woods. Squirrels denounced me from trees, chanting their hostile gibberish like mini-machine guns. Birds flew away as if I'd just ruined their neighborhood. The only animals that could tolerate me were hawks and vultures drifting high, and as I watched a red-tail one afternoon I imagined it screaming out of the sky and driving its talons into my chest, then a vulture picking my innards after the hawk had stripped my flesh. It felt kind of inviting, to die in the grasp of an innocent god and move on, my spirit lifting clear, in slow circles, of the lame story my life had become. I wanted to go where my mother had gone. It was crazy, but I felt *old*, as if I had used up my life. I'd been born into a handsome world, well made. Nothing was wrong with the world, but somehow I was wrong for it.

What I really yearned for was to *make* something—a pottery bowl, or carve something from wood or stone, or hammer red-hot iron. I looked at Josie's photos and wished I could make something that beautiful. I wished I could play Beethoven's Seventh Symphony in an orchestra—Cart was tutoring me in classical music—or at least steel guitar in a country band. I pulled books off the shelves, neat and fine in their jackets and nice bindings, fat ones and thin, tall and short, every one of them good enough to get published and sell for money.

I felt eons away from doing something like that, but here I am, actually getting after it. Only took me twenty years to get started. This morning I printed out what I've got so far, and it's a pretty fair sheaf of pages—193, to be exact, a stack an inch and a quarter high. It was satisfying to see, but then I started reading it and the bottom fell out of my mood. I wrote hostile comments in the margins, crossed out sentences and whole passages, wrote in new language that wasn't any better, and just about lost faith in the whole project.

"Calm down," came Lynn's stern but reassuring voice over the phone, "and quit rewriting. Get the whole story down in a nice, messy draft. Get all the clay on the table, and *then* you can shape it and smooth it. I'll work with you, and I'm sure Cart will too. Write page 194."

* * *

It was the frogs and Len Peppers that got me through late winter.

One night during a pineapple express, a warm storm out of Hawaii that drops a lot of rain and raises the temperature ten degrees, I hiked by headlamp to the little marsh behind my old house to hear the Pacific chorus frogs in their favorite weather. Only an inch or two long, they have an expando-throat that blows up bigger than their body and puts out a shrieky holler with beads of percussion rattling in it, and all those hollers pulsing together can be loud enough to seriously disturb the sleep of bears in their dens and tree roots in the ground. The big rolling wave of the chorus drops off suddenly now and then—a critter passing, or maybe just to rest—and then a few frogs start back in, then more, and more, and a new wave is rolling through the night.

I wasn't disappointed. The congregation was fully assembled and going at it like I'd never heard, the shrill calls mixing and tangling so loud their mortal disharmony hurt my ears, like ten thousand manic meth-heads out-shrieking each other in the dark. It's all about males calling for a mate, they say, but if that's so the females might like different music, because every night, all through the rest of winter and most of the spring, lots of the boys—fewer, but plenty— would still be calling, almost as noisily as they did now in February. Losers, maybe, but optimists. And who's to say, maybe those balloon-throated believers just consider it their sacred duty to light up the wet winter woods with a holy racket. I stood in the dark listening, smiling, imagining Pastor Rogers or Jonah Rutledge with me to hear their witness, though I doubted either man was ready to consider amphibians his spiritual brethren.

* * *

Early in March Bryce Morrison called. Len Peppers hadn't been able to stay on his feet for long, so they'd taken him to get checked out and brought him home with bad news—news for Bryce and us, because it turned out Len already knew his heart was failing. That's why he'd been short of breath. They'd started him on some drugs when he was first diagnosed, but now the drugs weren't working. He had cardiomyopathy, which I couldn't pronounce but Len could. "It's called alcoholic *car-dee-Oh, my-ol'-path-ee*," he told me. "My ol' pathee's led me to ruin, Henry. . . . As Mr. Bojangles says, 'I drinks a bit.' . . . Thought it'd be my liver, but that's . . . that's workin' fine, wouldn't you know it . . . though I seen a picture of it, an' it looks . . . like some old shoe on a riverbank."

Len was propped up in a bed on wheels—white hair spilling down over the pillows and his pajama collar, eyebrows bushy as briar thickets, his stained beard laid out on his upper chest. He wanted to die at home, and Deanna, his daughter who lived down the Willamette in Canby, had just moved in to help him do it. I'd met her once before. She had blond hair with a curl, spoke clearly and calmly, and seemed always to know what to do. "He'll be *so* glad to see you," she said to me at the door.

Len was in a talky mood, seemed open to anything, so I asked if he was afraid.

"Well," he said, "a man's not a man if he ain't a *little* scared. . . . But I've faced up with an angry bear and . . . firestorm in thick forest and a capsized boat in . . . in the worst of Hells Canyon . . . I reckon I can deal with this." His chest shook a little with silent laughter. "And what am I gonna do, old son? Turn tail and out*run* it?"

My eyes were tearing up and I didn't care. "I'm gonna miss you, Len. A lot of people are."

"I know it," he said. "I've always preferred makin' friends . . . to losin' 'em."

"Is there anything you haven't done that you wish you had?"

Len chuckled. "Oh, I helped myself, pretty much. . . . I do wish I'd been more faithful to Bess. . . . I had the love of a good woman, Henry. . . hope you will too. Had the joy of lovin' music. . . . Let's see . . . oh, my. This child never had to work indoors one day of his life— how 'bout that? Breathed . . . breathed good mountain air, worked with good men, spirited men . . . and they *paid* me for it." He smiled, his chest shaking again. He paused, eyes closed, for so long I thought he'd fallen asleep. But then his eyes opened.

"You see," he said, "my generation had the privilege, Henry Fielder . . . downright *honor*, really, of loggin' the last great timberlands. . . .

Ran the high-lead shows that got them granddaddy logs up the hill. . . . Ain't rocket science, sure, but . . . see here, you got you a redcedar butt-cut twelve feet through . . . and it's all jammed up 'gainst a couple of big stumps. I'd like . . . like to see the rocket man wrap the chokers on that fat boy just right . . . to roll it clear of those stumps and . . . and send it up to the landin', the mainline jumpin' and singin', ohhh, that butt-cut pitchin', rollin' . . . scatterin' chunks and logs like a *whale*, Henry, like a . . . a lee-viathan of the Earth. . . ."

Then he did fall asleep, and I felt guilty for wearing him out. But Deanna had been listening in the doorway, and she was beaming. "Pop never lied to my mom about his women," she said. "I've always respected him for that. He was a happy drunk, too. He never once mistreated Mom or us kids. As a little girl, I couldn't have asked for a sweeter father. His stories were as funny the tenth time as the first, he was that good a teller. And oh, but he could cuss a silver stream. He was one of the last great loggers who turned profanity into an art."

When Len woke half an hour later, he asked me to deejay for him. He had a crazy-good collection of country music on phonograph records, cassette tapes, and CDs, but his storage system was a lot like the system a hay heap has for organizing hay. He wanted to hear gospel standards, mostly—"Peace in the Valley," or Johnny Cash singing Kris Kristofferson's song, "Why Me, Lord?" or Willie Nelson doing "Nobody's Fault But Mine," and that great old standard, "The Far Side Bank of Jordan." Len wasn't confident that Bess, who'd died of a stroke six years before, would be waiting on that far bank and would come splashing through the shallow waters reaching for his hand. "She'd have every right not to," he said, "but I'll keep my eyes peeled. . . . She was a fine woman, lot finer than I deserved. . . . And if she ain't there . . . well, it's still an awful good song, ain't it, Henry. A *fine* song."

I cried all the way home on my bike, and it felt like a good rain.

twenty

Three pointed white petals, each angling over a broad green leaf, on a six- or eight-inch stem barely stout enough to support it all. That year, like most years, I came upon the first open trillium in late March, the first wildflower of spring (except for a little one with blue-violet bells I never could identify). I sat cross-legged facing the trillium, as always. Usually a wildflower surprised me for a split second, as if I'd never seen it before. The trillium I saw as if I had known it before I was born.

But it wasn't the same. Three white petals, three broad leaves, but I saw just the shapes and colors, where before I'd get all caught up in wonder about how it comes out of the ground every early spring so faithfully, in small clumps and singletons scattered through the shaded woods, and nobody ever planned it or asked for it. It just *happens*, a gift of the ground. And other flowers, the apple trees by the old house—how can a gnarly little twig sprout a white blossom with a faint sweet smell, and along about the end of August it's all weighed down with a red-and-green-streaked apple? How do you get a whole new body of being—an apple, a fawn, a me or a you—coming out of where, out of what?

I sat, I looked, but it was no good. I remembered the wonder, but the wonder itself had seeped away.

* * *

I started going to church again that spring. I'd ride my bike if the weather wasn't too leaky, and when it was, Cart or Josie would take me and somebody from the congregation would drive me home. I felt beholden to the church people for the money they'd given me, and I missed the singing and the general mood of happy humility and praisefulness. Josie's advice had stuck with me, too. I missed Jonah, especially talking religion with him. We had different notions of God, but we both believed. Cart and Josie weren't much interested in belief. And Jonah, of course, had been my father's best friend, the one I'd let down the worst. My foster parents kept telling me I wasn't responsible. My father had raped me, raping a kid was unpardonable, and he had no right to expect mercy from me, whatever the circumstances.

I didn't use the word "rape" myself, and winced when Cart or Josie said it, probably because it made me sound like I was a woman. I really wanted to see it their way, though. I was still telling myself that my father had done something awful to me and I had done something awful to him, so we were even—except that he was ashes in the ground up on cemetery hill, and I was still upright with the rest of my life ahead of me. I didn't deserve getting off the hook because I was a kid, either. I wasn't any kid, I was me, old enough to think about my actions and able enough to have gotten him clear if I'd kept trying. My father had been helpless and talking crazy. I'd let him get to me, and I shouldn't have.

Why did he do it? I kept wondering. And why did he do *that?* He'd never seemed gay or anything. I talked about it with Josie a little, and she told me that rape isn't so much about sex, it's about power and domination. That seemed to fit as far as it went. I'd been taunting him, blowing him off, doing whatever I wanted. . . . *You gonna mind me now?* I wondered if he'd planned it, but my hunch was it had just flared up in him. I was out of it, he was angrier than I'd ever seen him. Josie said I'd never know for sure. She kept urging me to go to a therapist, and I kept saying no. Just as before he'd died, it was our little mess, his and mine, and I was the one who needed to work it out.

In church I snuck peeks at Jonah, and he probably did the same at me. We caught eyes once and both looked away quick. Cloudy wasn't there the first Sunday I went, but next time she was, and she smiled at me and I smiled back. The Sunday after that, she gave me a quick hug as church was letting out and told me she was praying for me. I was so grateful for that. Jonah stood off a ways waiting for her.

On Saturdays I went with Cart to cut firewood for the occupiers in Chelamela Village. They had come through the earthquake fine, as I'd figured. Three of them had hiked out for news and met supporters chainsawing their way in as fast as they could. There wasn't terrible news for any of them. A few left the village to deal with damage to their homes; a few supporters, including Cart, spent shifts in the village to replace them. "What's retirement for?" he said. It was a happy little community of tents and Coleman stoves and a fire pit and a rented porta-potty and a little sweatlodge built pretty much the Indian way, a low dome of green branches covered with a tarp plus dirt and clay from digging the fire pit. For their meetings and meals and general hanging out, they'd made a big teepee out of long poles covered with brown and green tarps and called it their tarpee. They'd installed a woodstove but weren't about to cut firewood illegally on federal land.

I knew the dead but still-sound Doug firs and white firs my father had meant to take next, and from working with him I knew enough about felling trees to not get killed, if I stuck to the ones with a natural lean and a clear landing. Cart was a little shy about the chainsaw—a healthy instinct—but he got halfway comfortable after a while and felt more countrified than ever. His Euramericano was the shaggiest I'd seen it, and looked especially wild spraying out from underneath his Wilderness Society ball cap. He said it expressed his inner soulfulness. I didn't know if the Kalapuya had taken scalps or not, but I told Cart that no Indian anywhere could have resisted taking his.

My hair was getting long too, straight and black like my mother's. My dad and I had gotten our haircuts at Mac Johnson's barber shop every six weeks or so. Mac always had the scoop on what was going on in the community, and I enjoyed listening to my father jaw and joke with other men. I'd never minded my buzz-cut at all, but now my hair was getting down over my ears, and I liked it. I felt like a hippie crow. Or a young brave, except for the brave part.

Up at Karen Creek, Cart and I passed stove wood by the armload over the gate to a villager who carried it a little ways and handed it to another, and on up the slope that way like a bucket brigade to the fire pit and tarpee. We delivered a load one clear and cold early evening and were invited to stay for a sweat. The rocks were heating in the fire pit already. Seven of us, four guys and three women, undressed in the tarpee, quickstepped through the dusk to the sweatlodge, crouched to slip in through the entrance covers, and sat in a circle on mats around the shallow pit in the middle. Two rocks were already in place, glowing red in the dark. A big guy with a mustache knew from Cart that I was into the Chelamela and asked if I knew how they did their sweat ceremony. I didn't, but my mother had taken a few sweats when she was a girl at the river camp of Edison Chiloquin, a Klamath Indian elder who'd refused a quarter of a million dollars from the federal government for title to his share of ancestral land. Indians came to his camp from all around the West, and my mother told me that they shouted a blessing when they entered and when they opened the doorway for more rocks. It wasn't Klamath, it was Lakota: "Mi - *tak* - wi - *AH* - sin!" Which means, "*Alllll* our relations!"

So we called it, all together, in Lakota then English. Then the helper outside handed in three glowing red rocks one at a time on a deer antler prong, and the mustached guy took each rock on his antler prong and laid it in the pit. It didn't feel all that hot until the guy poured a coffee can of water on the rocks, and what a blast of steam! I couldn't breathe, then I could, and all of us were instantly sweaty and high. Somebody suggested that we meditate in silence about the Methuselah forest and the greater Coast Range, so we did. In the next round of glowing rocks we meditated on people we knew who needed prayers (I prayed that Len Peppers really was feeling ready to die), and for the last round we asked for strength from all our relations—the four-leggeds, the winged beings, the crawlers and swimmers and sliders, the invisible tribes of the very small, and the humans who had lived here so much longer than we had and would always belong to the land.

We poured out of the sweatlodge yipping and howling in the night like coyotes. There wasn't a river to jump into, but the villagers had a cold water shower near the tarpee—they collected rainwater for it. I let out an insane yell when the water hit me and rejoiced that it didn't kill me. After everybody who wanted to had been doused, we huddled in blankets around the woodstove in the tarpee. I felt right at home.

The cops and the loggers would probably show up soon, the villagers told us, when the ground had dried a little. They'd gotten no help from the courts. Tree sitters were setting up their high perches, barricaders were trying on the armor and chains. The ones who had spent all winter there said they felt different now. They had come to the forest and now they had joined it. They were confident and they would be ready.

I'd seen the bulldozer as we drove in, and I saw its hulk in the headlights as we drove out. I was happy and didn't give a damn about it.

* * *

Cart and I started a pretty good argument on the way home. He was explaining that the insurance on my old home hadn't paid yet because the company was trying to decide if the trees that killed the house had been felled by wind or by earthquake. Wind they would pay for, quake they wouldn't.

"The wind was blowing trees down before the quake ever hit," I said.

"But those two fell right after the quake, didn't they?" said Cart.

"Yeah, but don't they know it was rain, too? If the soil hadn't been so wet, wind or quake or both of 'em might not've been enough."

"Might not have," Cart said. "You're right, it was a rare coincidence."

"Well," I said, "we'd have to know the whole history of Earth to know if it was rare."

"It only makes sense, Henry, that rain, wind, and quake together is less likely than any of the three by itself."

"Probably so, but I'm beginning to think everything's a coincidence. This science writer I like says if the force of gravity had been the tiniest speck weaker there'd only be gas and dust and darkness. No stars, no planets, no life. Gravity and a zillion other things were set just exactly right."

"Well sure they were," Cart said with a shrug. "We're here, so that's a given."

"Something else could've been given, Cart. All the ways it could have gone, there was almost zero chance it would go like this. 'It's almost as if the Universe knew we were coming,' this guy wrote. Gives me goose bumps."

"You're attributing purpose to the universe, Henry. What's your evidence?"

"You are," I said. "I am. The universe made us, and we're sitting here talking about it. We're the universe talking about itself."

"But that's circular reasoning—"

"What's wrong with a circle? I can't explain it, Cart, but I think it *means* something that we're here. Chance is part of it but not all of it. Yeah. I do think there's a purpose to it all."

* * *

There was a full moon that night, I wasn't sleepy, so I took a midnight stroll in Jimmy Hepworth's pasture. The night air was cold, my breath clouded in front of me. The moon was so bright that I walked in the shade of trees along the fence so I wouldn't get a moonburn. Jimmy's few head of cattle were off a ways ripping grass, and his horses were snorting and nickering, having a lively talk. It was nice living with farm animals near, drifting by as a day went along, and double-nice that somebody else was doing all the upkeep. I walked easy, breathing the night, glad to be alive, and with the word "glad" I thought of sadness and gladness, the sister twins. I felt my mother close by.

But suddenly I sensed another spirit, smaller, in a body. I stopped. A tiny squeak came from the trees and a little animal stepped toward me in the moonlight.

"Catrick!" I said. "Long time, dude. Where'd you go, home to Ireland?"

He let me pick him up, and he was just about lighter than air. "You need back on the gravy train," I murmured. "I know two people you're gonna make very happy."

He warmed my hands and started to purr as I walked home.

"I took a long walk too, you know. Met your great uncle."

In the kitchen I gave him a saucer of milk and some leftover chicken. He ate fiercely, smacking his chops. I reminded him where his box was—right where it'd always been—then very quietly cracked open Cart and Josie's bedroom door. I slipped Catrick inside and eased the door shut. He'd go straight to the warm bed.

twenty-one

Tess came over to our house for dinner a couple of times—Cart and Josie liked her fine—and we hung out at her house after school, but we couldn't be alone for long in either house. I wanted to advance our studies. Abner had been having sex for at least a year, other guys too. I felt like a slowpoke, a retard. Tess seemed happy to oblige, so we schemed a way we could go on a date.

On a Saturday afternoon around Eastertime, I walked out the back door of Dismal Acre with my backpack on. I'd told my foster-folks that I'd be camping out that night. Instead, I hiked the back way to my old homeplace, started the trusty white Dodge, and picked up Tess at the Long Tom skate park. She had told her mother she'd be staying over with her best friend. We headed for Eugene and the Bijou Theater, giddy with our conspiracy and scared half spitless that we'd be spotted.

The weather had warmed. Tess was wearing jeans and sandals with a white top, and a leather thong necklace with some silvery charms. I tried to talk with her, but I was trying to drive carefully, too. I hadn't practiced on the highway. By Fern Ridge Lake I checked the rearview mirror and saw a car riding our bumper and about eight cars and two big trucks stacked up behind him—I was going 40 on a straight-ahead state highway. Gassing it up to 55 felt like going a hundred. In Eugene, then, I missed a turn and couldn't remember where the Bijou theater was. My cool was totally blown. Finally Tess put a hand on my shoulder and said, "It's different when you're the one driving, isn't it. Go two blocks and take a right."

The movie was foreign, with subtitles. A loner kid with long blond hair who gets picked on by bullies makes friends with the new girl in his apartment building. She can do things like scurry up tall buildings and climb in through any window. He asks if she's a vampire, and she just says she's been alive for a very long time. His mother makes him break it off, and then the kid seriously pisses off the bullies. It all comes down to an indoor swimming pool, where the alpha-bully, at the edge of the pool, holds the kid's head down trying to drown him. You see it from underwater—he's thrashing, bubbling from his mouth, he might really die, but then something falls into the water trailing a dark cloud and it's a hand, then something bigger falls in and it's an arm, and the blond kid comes up gasping and there leaning over the water is his girlfriend, her eyes burning with love, her mouth all bloody. The boy smiles, lazing in the water, grinning up at his sweetheart savior.

During the whole movie I'd been debating when to put my arm around Tess's shoulders. She might not like it, I worried, but then why the hell *wouldn't* she like it, but then again. . . . Finally, when the bloody hand hit the water I just gritted my teeth and did it. Tess leaned into me as if I knew what I was doing.

At Denny's, afterward, I didn't know how to talk.

"Henry, you seem kind of out of it," Tess said. "Are you okay?"

"Well," I said, "I guess I miss my mom and dad."

I said it to melt her and it did. She reached a hand across the table, I reached out mine for her to take.

I took the back way home, north of Fern Ridge Lake. Much mellower driving—dark now, few cars, Tess snuggled up close, and just to make it perfect, Patsy Cline came on the radio singing *"Crazy for cryin', crazy for tryin', I'm crazy for lovv-in' you. . . ."* That's a song you have to love, even if you don't love country. I suggested we pull off on a gravel road and park for a while, and Tess was all for it. While she fussed with something in the dark, I fetched a liter of Coke and a pint of whiskey from my pack, poured half the Coke out the window, poured the bottle full again with whiskey. We sat in the dark trading swigs, my hand on her thigh and hers on mine. When I guessed it was time for two hands, I fumbled the cap onto the bottle and reached for her, but she said, "Wait, Henry. First turn on the light so I can look into your eyes." She leaned close, I flicked on the interior light and lurched back with a scream—her eyes were burning into me, her mouth smeared with blood. It was ketchup from packets she'd lifted from the restaurant, but who knew that?

"You scared the *snot* out of me!" I said, slumping in the seat.

"I couldn't resist," said Tess, still laughing. Now she pulled me close again and looked me in the eyes for real. "Henry, please turn out that light and kiss the blood off my mouth."

Things warmed up in a hurry. My hands got under her top and didn't like her bra very much and pretty much pulled it apart at the clasp. *That* was an improvement, smoothest skin ever, new place to kiss as I fumbled at her jeans.

"Slow down," Tess whispered. "It's not a race, Henry."

She took my head between her hands and kissed me long and slow, her tongue tip moving between my lips, and I followed along, and pretty soon my dick was about to bust through my zipper if *something* didn't happen, so I was yanking at her jeans and got mine down and was all over her clawing at her underwear and feeling the nice wet target and only then did I hear her shouting and feel her hitting me and trying to push me away.

I stopped, breathing hard.

"Get *off*," she sobbed.

"Tess, I'm sorry, I thought. . . ."

"You thought you'd tear my clothes off?"

"Tess—"

"Please get out of the car. Now."

I opened the door and got myself out, holding my pants up with one hand and the Coke bottle with the other. Buckled my pants and sat down on a stump. Turned out we'd parked by a clearcut, which seemed perfect. I took a pull from the bottle and had taken a few more by the time Tess thumped on her closed window.

I got in the driver's side, slowly.

"Please take me home," she said.

"Okay," I said, "I will, but Tess, I didn't mean. . . ."

"You scared me, Henry. It felt like you were trying to rape me."

Now I just shut up and drove. *Call it what you want,* I said inside. We were on pavement now, and I took the curves with little squeals from the tires.

"Henry," Tess said, "first of all, slow down. Let's not get killed. Second, I know you didn't mean any harm, but lovemaking is all about how you do it."

"Whatever," I said, ripping through a curve to the right—and there was a buck in the road, bolting left as I swerved hard right to miss him. The skidding rear of the car caught him a glancing shot and kept on skidding to 180 degrees, tail-first into the ditch with a *clunk* as the car high-centered on the shoulder, the headlight beams slanting up into the trees.

"Tess, you okay?"

"No worse than before. What's our next adventure, Henry?"

She got out of the car. I left the lights on and got out too. No sign of the buck. He'd have a sore left haunch and ribcage tomorrow, nothing worse. I, on the other hand, was completely doomed and it pissed me off. *Would you like to know who taught me "lovemaking?"* I was thinking, and might have said, but a pair of headlights rounded the bend from the direction we'd been coming. The SUV slowed and stopped, the passenger window sliding down. An older woman behind the wheel leaned over. "Looks like trouble," she said.

"Do you think you could you take us to Long Tom?" Tess asked.

"Surely," she said. "But what about the car?"

"I'll take care of that," I said. I went to turn off the headlights, got into the back seat of the SUV, and we rode the twenty minutes to Long Tom. The woman was nice enough not to ask any questions.

I called Cart from the pay phone outside Foodland. It was a short conversation. They both came, in the Honda. I slunk into the back seat and tried to disappear as we headed to meet the tow truck he'd called, Cart firing questions over his right shoulder. Whose car was it, why the hell had I been driving it, why had I lied to them, what in the world had I been thinking. . . .

The tow truck got there just after we did, and in ten minutes the Dodge was back on the road. The left rear side was a little flattened from the deer, but the car wasn't hurt. Cart took the wheel, me beside him, as Josie followed in the Honda.

"Were you drinking?"

"No," I said.

"Then why do I smell it on your breath and all over this car?"

I shrugged and slid down in the seat.

"Have you been drinking at home?"

I shook my head.

"Was anyone with you in the car?"

I said no.

Dismal Acre was dismal for the first time. Josie made a pot of coffee, poured two mugs, and sat across from me at the kitchen table. She held out two fists, cocked upward, and opened and closed her hands a few times. "What are these?" she asked.

I just stared at her. She kept doing it.

"These are warning lights, Henry, and they're telling you this could have been awful."

"It wasn't that bad, Josie. There was a deer and I just skidded."

"Stop," she said. She looked me dead in the face and did the lights again. "Wake up, Henry. Denial goes nowhere. The car could have rolled or hit a tree. That deer could have come through the windshield."

"Not really," I said. "But okay." I could hear bottles clink as Cart went through the liquor cabinet.

"You lied to us, you were driving underage, using a car we didn't know about, and you were drinking. That's a path to nothing but trouble, Henry."

Cart came over with a couple of dusty bottles showing finger marks. "You've been into these too, haven't you."

I nodded.

"Yet another lie," said Cart.

I put my head down on my hands. "Can I just go to bed?" I whispered.

"Not yet," said Josie. As I stared at the table top, arms folded, she told me that I'd been traumatized, I was in pain from it, and that was why I was drinking. I didn't deserve the pain but it was real, it was dangerous, and it wouldn't heal until I recognized it and could talk about it. As soon as she could arrange it, I'd be going to a therapist. Then she did the warning lights again, which completely annoyed me, and let me go.

But Cart was in my bedroom, finishing up a search. He'd found the baggie of mummified bud I'd collected at Neckie's patch.

"That's not even smokable," I blurted. "It's from my time in the mountains. You can't just go through my stuff like that—"

"I can and I have," Cart interrupted. "No drink. No drugs. You come directly home from school every day. Understand?"

I nodded. "Now could you leave me alone?"

He softened a little. "Listen, Henry. All we want is to keep you alive and healthy so you can be an old man someday."

"Yeah? You're an old man, and you've been drinkin' and tokin' your whole life."

"Most of it. But I've always had a rough sense of how much is enough and when I shouldn't at all. That's what you need to learn. For now, any is too much."

All I'd wanted was to sleep, but I couldn't. I stuffed my head under a pillow and lay there sputtering inside like water drops hitting a hot stove. I knew Cart and Josie were just being good parents. I knew I'd been stupidly polluting myself, too. But what really worried me was tomorrow, when Mrs. Bailey would call with some twisted news about their foster son, the sexual assaulter. Wouldn't matter that it was only attempted rape. Even doing it all wrong, I hadn't got it done.

I threw the pillow across the room, got up and sat at my desk. I took my pocketknife out of the drawer and sharpened both blades on the little whetstone, taking my time. When I was ready I slowly, slowly, made a new cut along the inside of my right wrist, watching the blood come up like a welling spring. The pain and the rich blood calmed me. I felt alert, like in the woods when an animal was near. I made another cut, parallel, and studied the two incisions. Then I made a third cut. I sat for a while, satisfied with my work, then went to the bathroom and washed off the dribbled blood. In my room I tied a dark bandanna around my wrist and fell asleep.

I dreamed of my father again. It felt like prison, waking inside the same dream. *Why am I still here?* I asked. He was in the woods near the river like before, but he wasn't working or pacing around but just standing, looking at me, and now he sat and leaned against a tree. He had his ball cap on. Beyond him in the shadows I could see the vague form of whatever he'd been working on. *Are . . . you . . . finished?* I called, each word an awful effort to pronounce. The river was out there, I hungered for it. He tilted his head back as if laughing. Then he slowly pulled the bill of his cap down over the dark hollows of his eyes and crossed his arms and settled a little lower against the tree.

* * *

I didn't like the therapist. He had a fringe of gray hair around his bald head and wore loud Hawaiian shirts just to show how loose and cool he was. I probably knew better, since Josie had prepped me, but I didn't like how he worked, either. I thought he'd just tell me about how I'd been hurt and how I could heal, but instead, he asked me questions and expected me to do the talking—like I was the one getting paid—him just sitting there staring me down through his gold-rimmed glasses. We had some long silences, and they weren't the calm and filled-with-spirit kind. I was sick to dying of my story anyway, all the versions, the true parts and the stretchers and the outright lies. I pleaded with Josie till she let me quit the gray-bald shrink while she looked for another.

My days were divided between Dismal Acre Penal Colony and Duckworth High School Forced Learning Center. I was sulky at first. Didn't enjoy my food—they did feed me, at both institutions—hardly talked, kept to myself. At the Learning Center I put up my hood and weaved through the between-class traffic in my own world. Tess and I avoided each other. I glimpsed here time to time in the cafeteria, or out front around the buses, and imagined her talking about me with her friends. Abner offered his good offices to heal the split, but I told him not to bother. Tess told him the same, I think. He and I talked a little, but I didn't have much to say. He wore a mournful look around me, as if his little brother had met with tragedy and he couldn't save him.

At the Penal Colony I was expected to work two hours outdoors after school, then eat my gruel and pursue the penance of my homework until bedtime. Outdoors I worked alone or with one parent or both. We weeded and got the tree-trash out of the flower beds, mulched, mowed, raked, built a burn pile, and got a little trail laid down through the middle-aged Doug firs that covered half the acre. Cart and Josie wanted some sword ferns to pretty up that tiny woods, and talked about paying a fee and getting a permit from the BLM to gather a few. I just about threw up at their feet. "You don't need a permit from the Bureau of Little Men," I said—my father's name for the agency—"you need a pickup and some shovels." We hit the gravel roads and gathered a load of nice ferns and some salal too, and in this way the inmate lured his captors into his world of crime. And lost some of his sulkiness.

Cart and I went after dead limbs on the Doug firs that could become widowmakers, widowermakers, cat-flatteners, felon-slayers, roof-punchers, or rhododendron- or rosebush-abusers at the very least, if allowed to fall on their own schedule. Knowing how common coincidence is, I took satisfaction in reducing the chances. Up in a tree using Cart's climbing gear, I'd hang in my harness, tie a rope to a limb for him to pull on, and then saw the limb off, Cart yanking it toward a safe landing not on himself. We did squash a fern or two. Len Peppers would have laughed his head off to see us.

My jailers allowed me visitations with Len now and then, warning me not to accept whiskey. It was easy to keep my word on that, because Len had quit himself. Deanna said he was sleeping more and having some trouble breathing, so the doctor had upped his medication. He still seemed pretty easy in the face of his mortality. We listened to Garth Brooks, trying to decide if he was the real thing. I thought yes, Len thought no, though he did like the song "I Got Friends in Low Places." We argued about it like two low-place friends.

Mrs. Bailey, it turned out, never called, which made me respect Tess even more than I already did. Gave me hope, too. I could have talked to her any day at school, but I knew I'd probably bungle the words. Email felt all wrong, too cold, so I started a letter. Worked on it for days, changing this, changing that. In one version I told her what my father had done to me, but I never got close to sending that one. Too embarrassing, but it felt lame, too, like making an excuse. The letter I finally sent was pretty short and simple. I just apologized for my boorish roughness and for getting us into an accident, told her I totally understood why she was breaking up with me, and said I really cared about her and admired her as a person anyway.

A few days later, Josie told me when I got home from school that there was a letter for me on my desk. Hope and dread turned to bafflement when I saw the return address—Cottonwood, Oregon, which didn't register till I opened the envelope. The letter was written in real ink, not a ballpoint, on heavy paper with a lot of grain. I'd never touched paper like that. Raven wrote a lot like he spoke, thoughtful in not many words. He just wondered how I was doing, since it seemed that the earthquake had been a time of big change for me. *If you only knew*, I thought. He said that he and Cecelia and Dante, and others there too, had been remembering me and wishing me well, and they all hoped I would visit. "Our doors are open," Raven wrote, "and whatever your story, we admire the way you arrived." At the end he wrote, "I hope you've been staying at the other end of the line from any fishhooks."

I wondered for a moment how Raven knew my address, then remembered that he'd delivered me here to Dismal Acre, and would have seen the address on the emergency signpost. I'd thought about him, too—the way he paused before he spoke, the feeling of deep calm I got from him. His green, green eyes.

Now that I was condemned to prison, I decided to devote my life to correspondence. I imagined exchanging letters with fifty friends, which meant they'd be coming and going all the time. I would write in real ink on heavy-grained paper, using well-chosen words—from my mother's dictionary, when necessary—right there in my lonely cell. Tess had been first of the fifty, and Raven would be second. I thanked him for his letter and told him I would love to visit but wasn't quite old enough to legally drive, and that I lived under the thumb of dictatorial foster parents, enslaved to hard labor at home and in school. There was a glimmer of hope for future freedom, I wrote. I told him that our conversation as he drove me home had helped me understand what I needed to do. I thanked him for his kindness and hoped he was having a good spring in the Sweet Grass Confederacy, which in my opinion was Paradise.

There were times that spring when I craved getting high—or low, or sideways, to poke *something* into the spokes of the normal—but the normal all in all was feeling better. I could have scored weed or pills any day at school, but I didn't, and I didn't toke up with Abner. I stayed sober, got over being sullen, and my keepers rewarded me by relaxing their tough-cop routine. It'd never really suited them. It was clear as day that I answered a whole lot of longing in them, a kid and grandkid all in one, but I was only beginning to see what that implied. Their weakness meant I had to be stronger.

* * *

Josie told me one afternoon that Cloudy Rains had asked if she could come over the next day and speak with me. "She wants to ask a few questions, Henry. She's asking for Jonah, I think, maybe more than herself. You'd do well to talk with her."

"I'll talk with Cloudy anytime," I said.

She pulled in a few minutes after I got home from school, and we went for a slow walk on a rough track up Schuyler Creek, where I'd done my winter snow dance. The dogwoods were out, dreaming their white dreams, and swamp lantern was lighting up yellow in the creek.

I'd never been alone with Cloudy before, and the sweet pudgy face I'd always seen laughing now was somber. She didn't waste words.

"Henry," she said, "it's very hard for Jonah to accept what you've told us. If George did . . . what you say, wasn't there any sign of it before?"

"Uh-uh," I said. "He used the willow stick and hit me sometimes, but I started standing up to him and said some really mean things, too. . . ."

"Things like . . . ?"

"Like he was a bad father. Cart and Josie were smarter and better. I wished I lived with them. I was gonna join the protest at Karen

Creek. Then I came home loaded that night, he was loaded too, and I think he just snapped. Josie told me rape isn't really about sex."

"He felt humiliated, so he humiliated you?"

"Yeah, like that. I'm sure he didn't plan it."

"Did you try to fight him off, Henry?"

"I was drunk and stoned, I'd been asleep, I thought it was a dream. By the time I came to. . . *then* I struggled, you bet, but he had me pinned. I'm eye-level with you, Cloudy. You think I could've bucked him off?"

"No," Cloudy said, almost under her breath. "But why didn't you go to the sheriff, Henry? Or to somebody?"

I halfway laughed. "Well, the earthquake happened. But I'm embarrassed talking about it with you. Are you sure you'd've called somebody? As a kid?"

Cloudy shook her head. "A lot of women don't."

We walked on a ways. A robin was singing somewhere by the creek. They always sound bold, like they mean every syllable.

"I knew he'd have to go to jail, too, and I was runnin' low on parents."

"Did you mean to kill him, when you shot?"

"No. I told him to get the hell out of my sight, twice. Then pulled the trigger when I didn't mean to."

"And if he hadn't moved . . . ?

"If he hadn't moved, he would've taken it in the face. I'm glad he moved. Though he ended up just as dead."

"And that morning?"

"That morning he was yellin' at me to hurry up and get him out of there. I got mad and said, tell me why you did it. He said I'd forced him to, nothing else worked. 'You had it comin',' he said. And then . . . that's when I walked out."

Cloudy didn't speak.

"Look, Cloudy, it was wrong. He didn't know what he was saying. I left him helpless. I'll regret it till the day I die."

She stopped and turned to face me. Her lovely amber eyes were glistening with tears. "You didn't make up a word of this, did you, Henry."

"I'm good at making stuff up," I said. "I do it too much, but not this. This is the sorry truth, Cloudy."

She hugged me close. "I'm so sorry, Henry. We've only made more pain for you."

"Do you think Jonah will believe me now?"

"I hope so," Cloudy said. "Be patient."

Walking back I saw a trillium I'd missed walking in. The petals had a purple blush, which I've always considered a lucky sign. I would have picked it for Cloudy, but I never pick a trillium.

twenty-two

"Henry," I heard behind me on the walkway. I turned around and there was Tess. I don't know what my face did, but she smiled, which touched me like a sweet spring breeze. She was wearing jeans and a brown-and-white sweater.

"Hey," I said (and groaned to myself).

"Hi Henry. I got your letter. Thank you for writing it." Her short brown hair shook just a little as she spoke.

"Tess, I'm sorry, I really am. I was an idiot."

"Your letter goes a long way," she said. "Let's talk sometime."

"Yeah? Soon?"

"I need to get to class now," she said, smiling again.

"Okay. . . ." I watched her go and couldn't help thinking she was gone for good. As the weeks went by we did speak a little, and I could see she still liked me, at least, but she was going out with another guy now, and all I could do was try to smile. I hung out as much as I could stand in Abner's social safari. He and I didn't spend much time just the two of us, mostly because he was ridiculously in love with a new girl at school, or in lust anyway, and I wasn't into talking.

I didn't drink or drug, but I cut myself sometimes. Watching in a mirror one night, I cut beside both nipples. As the blood dribbled down my chest, I imagined myself a real Indian, a Lakota warrior hanging pierced through the breast, crying for a vision—but I knew how bad that bullshit smelled. In my short life I'd been granted visions and waking-life miracles both, as real as rock and water, and I'd pissed those blessings away.

Truth be told, I wasn't made for school. Duckworth isn't even a big high school, but for me there was too much going on, like a rough patch of river full of suckholes and deadmen and rocks gnashing their teeth. Most kids seem to like it fine. I wondered now and then if I might be an Aspie or something, but it didn't matter. I was what I was. My dad had the right idea, in his wrong way. I'd have done better with old-fashioned tutors—one for reading and writing, one (with great patience) for math, and a few more for biologycosmologyphilosophyreligion, my favorite subject.

What happened next wasn't school's fault, though. I left one afternoon, glad as always for the fresh air, and headed behind school toward the hiking-way home. In the first trees there were three guys sneaking cigarettes, laughing and talking. I knew them only by their faces.

"Hey Fielder," one called out. He had short blond hair, a nice smile. "C'mere and have a smoke."

The smoke did smell good, and technically maybe it wasn't a drug. The guy tapped a Marlboro out of his pack and lit me up with his Bic. "Hey," I said to the other guys.

The blond guy took a drag and leaned back against a tree. "Fielder," he said, "I'm curious about something. What's it like gettin' banged in the ass by your old man?"

Snickers from the other two.

"What are you talkin' about?" Everything but my mouth was frozen.

He pulled another long drag and let it go with a little shake of his head.

"Dude, I'm just asking if the story's true. He banged you, and you either shot him or left him for dead in the earthquake."

I threw my smoke at him and lunged, but the others got arms in front of me. I spat at the guy, but it didn't reach him. "Stop tellin' lies about me, moron."

"Easy, easy," the blond boy said, holding his hands out palms down like a peacemaker. "I just wanted to get the story straight."

I remember the rest like frames in a film. I swing my elbows and hit somebody hard and break loose. I rush the blond guy. He drops his cigarette. My right fist glances off his cheek. His right catches the side of my head and he shoves me to the ground. I'm up again. *"Settle down,"* he says. Hands are pulling me back but I scream and throw elbows again. The guy's eyes are blue. *"Dude, chill!"* he says. His eyes are blue and his eyes are scared. I run into his fist with my left eye, but instead of going down I surge. Somebody's hollering. I punch the wind out of his gut and he doubles toward me. I come up with a fist to his face and he goes down. A girl screams. Blood on his face, a smear of it in his pretty blond hair, and I taste either my blood or his as I'm down on him yelling, *"Anything else, shit-for-brains? Any more questions?"* I spit in his face and somebody's pulling me off as if I weigh nothing, and it's Mr. Spindor, my math teacher.

Sitting in the school office with the vice-principal I'm wired, zingy, a humming force field. My head hurts, my left eye can't see, I don't care. I feel like never before, better than meth. *I kicked his ass!* Through the window to the hallway I see they're helping him in, he's holding a towel to his face, blood on his light blue Duke University sweatshirt. He's not big enough. Talking his shit he'd looked big, but he's not much taller than me. The vice-principal is bald and heavy beside me and he's asking who started the fight, but I'm not talking. Do I know that I opened a big gash on Josh's face? I'm not talking.

Let Josh talk, let everybody talk their tongues off. Expect to be suspended at the very least, the VP says, and I grin. I'm in my force field, my humming aura, and it's all good. "What's this?" I say to the bald VP, a finger to my left eye. "What's this, a kiss?"

Cart was over at Karen Creek, taking a shift at the gate, but Josie was home and came to get me. She and the vice-principal talked a while and then we drove home.

"Henry Henry," she said like a sigh. "Tell me what happened?"

"The whole school knows about me. The whole fucking school."

"So this Josh kid knew?"

"Duh."

Josie flashed me a look. "I know you're upset," she said. "But you will speak politely."

I calmed down a notch and told her what'd happened, but not the exact words of blond-haired Josh. Those words made me crawl with rage. Those words would never appear in my voice.

Josie reached over and patted my knee. "Fighting will only make it worse, Henry. You have to be stronger than the kids who taunt you."

"Easy to say," I told her. "Doesn't matter, though, 'cause I'm through with that fuckin' school."

"Right now, let's just get you home and see to that eye."

In the house she wrapped a freezer pack in a towel and had me lie down holding it on my eye. The side of my head throbbed too, where Josh had landed a lucky punch, so Josie brought another pack and tied a towel around my head to hold everything in place. I lay back like a triumphant sultan. Josie debated whether to take me to the emergency room, but I said no, I didn't need it, and Josh might be there. "Hope they've got plenty of blood for him. I gashed his face."

"And what exactly have you gained by it, Henry?"

"He was bigger and I kicked his ass."

Josie was shaking her head. "Whoop-de-doo," she said. "Just what the world needs, another fighter boy. Violent behavior is nothing to be proud of."

"He'll lie," I told her. "He'll whine and say I beat him up for no reason. If I get kicked out of school, he should too."

"Get some sleep, Henry. Tomorrow you'll see the doctor."

"Now my knuckles hurt," I groaned. "A bowl of ice, please."

"Let your knuckles and your head counsel you not to be a knucklehead," she said, and left my room.

Sleep was a good idea, but sleep was nowhere near. I tried reading with my right eye, but that just made my headache worse. I put Waylon and Willie on my music machine and lay down again. *"Cowboys ain't easy to love and they're harder to hold, he'll prob'ly just ride away. . . ."* I tried to get Josie to listen with me but for some reason she wouldn't. I listened to the whole CD, and then to the great Merle Haggard—*"You're walkin' on the fightin' side of me . . ."*—and I still wasn't sleepy, so I found Josie and begged for a sleeping pill. I knew they had some because I'd stolen a few in my drug-fiend days. "All right," she said. "But only if you stop that god-awful music."

Pretty soon the pill kicked in and I was gliding on a warm wind. *I won the fight,* I kept thinking. But then every lousy word that Josh had spoken came back to me, each one slow and sure, that little smirk on his face, and my anger boiled again. I heard the air go out of him as I rammed his gut. God I hit him hard. But now a crow was flying over, again and again, calling *Naw, naw. . . . Naw, naw, naw. . . .* My victory glow went cold.

Okay, I said inside me. *This isn't what you meant. This isn't Eagle Boy. . . .*

* * *

Dr. Steck, my pediatrician, said mine was one of the top-five shiners she'd ever seen. She'd heard about the fight and told me that Josh'd had to have a lot of stitches to close his wound.

"Well, he shouldn't have messed with me. Fuck with the bull, you get the horn."

"Let's see, have you been reading Hemingway?"

"Nope, that's totally original. With somebody."

Dr. Steck said my eye and head would be fine. I wasn't even hurting much, but I talked her into a prescription for pain pills. She had no idea I'd been a recreational user. My suspension from school was for five days, the maximum. I looked forward to a lazy vacation of Vicodin and music and enjoying my black eye.

But that afternoon a call came. The hammer had come down at Karen Creek.

A horde of state troopers had swarmed in that morning, cut the seven blockaders out of their armor—Cart had been one—and cuffed their hands behind their backs. Most of the other Methuselans sat down in the road in solidarity, so they too were arrested, and the whole crew was loaded into a school bus and shipped to the Lane County Jail. Ones who weren't arrested were told to break camp, fill in the fire pit, clean up all trash, and get off the property. A squad of BLM rangers had gone up the road to deal with the tree sitters, on federal land. Arresting them might take days if they didn't come down on command. They weren't likely to.

Josie and I drove to Eugene to see if we could spring Cart from jail, but they told us the arrestees wouldn't be released until they were arraigned, which wouldn't happen before tomorrow. No visiting. No injuries had been reported.

"Good thing he likes a firm bed," Josie said. "He's probably having a great time telling the youngsters arrest stories from the sixties."

From town we drove out to Karen Creek to see if we could help, but the troopers in charge turned us away. The law enforcement operation was ongoing, they told us. I thought I saw the yellow Cat up the road in the woods, beyond the open gate.

On the front page of the *Register-Guard* next morning was a picture of the blockaders before they were removed from the gate, Carter P. Stephens at the center looking resolute. Josie clipped the photo and story. "This is the way to protest, Henry. Slugging somebody only incites more violence."

"But they're losing," I said. "The trees are gonna get cut."

"Probably so," she said. "Justice is a long haul." She tapped her finger on the picture. "But this registers in the public mind. Courage. Dignity. It was this, not guns or rioting, that brought the civil rights movement as far as it's come."

Cart and the others ended up spending three nights in the slammer. He came out officially charged with second-degree criminal trespass and higher than the Three Sisters. "I feel twenty years younger!" he exulted as we drove home.

"Well you don't look it," I said from the back seat. "How come they didn't shave your head? I thought they did that to criminals."

"I was treated with great deference," Cart replied. "They offered me a rollaway bed on account of my age, but I told them I wanted the standard bunk my comrades had. And—oh, did I tell you about the guy who arrested me? They took us to the bus one by one. Some of us chose to walk, some didn't. When a cop came for me, I told him I wouldn't walk but wouldn't resist, either. He said, 'That's cool.' Ha! He and another fellow dragged me slowly by my shoulders, and he said, 'Let me know if this is too hard on your butt, Gramps.'"

A couple of days later, we argued at dinner. I was due back at school on Monday. Cart and Josie said they knew it would be embarrassing, some Josh-like kids might be cruel, but I had to go and I had to stay out of trouble.

"Easy for you," I said. "Do you even *remember* high school?"

Josie said I was underestimating my classmates. There would be a lot of sympathy for me, and the teachers and staff would be looking out for me. "*If* you don't get in more fights," she said.

I scoffed. "You two just don't get it."

"And you need to get this," said Cart. "Kids your age go to school. Period."

"Not if you homeschooled me, I wouldn't have to."

There was a silence, then Josie said, "We love you, Henry. It's a privilege to be your foster parents. But we do have our own lives, our vocations, our habits of many years. To be your teachers as well as your parents would be . . . would be a little more than we're ready to take on."

"Yeah? Well, my father was a millworker, and he found a way."

I got up and left the table.

* * *

The weather was clear on Monday morning, so I said I'd ride my bike to school. Out on Stamper Road, I put on the pack I'd stashed overnight and was on my way. The day was bright and I was stoked. Cruising down Shepherd Creek Road I thought about the note I'd left on my bed:

Dear Cart and Josie,

I can't go to school because I can't breathe there.
I need to get away for a while. Please don't
worry about me and please don't call anybody.
I'll be safe. Just to be sure of that, I'm not
taking the car. (Ha ha.) I'm not walking
to the coast, either. And I don't know when,
but I will come back. I feel crummy about
leaving like this, and I wouldn't do it if I didn't
have to. Bye for now. I really will be all right.

Much love, Henry

P.S. Tell school I have head lice, and they're inside my head too.

I decided it wasn't the best thing I'd ever written but good enough.

I took the turn onto the Florence highway, which only gets heavy traffic on weekends. Most of it has a few feet of paved shoulder, too. I had a long ride ahead of me and I didn't plan to hurry. It would be after midnight before I arrived, but my bike had a headlight, and reflectors front and back.

A couple miles along, passing a lush empty meadow on my right, the color of the grass seemed off somehow. I braked to a stop. The moment had snuck up and just about snuck by me. The greenest green of April grass looked different because it was all shot through with the bluish haze of a gazillion camas flowers just opening.

I didn't linger, worried somebody I knew might see me, but as I rode on I was visualizing the harvest. It must have been the prettiest sight of spring for the Chelamela, those flowers rising in the prairies they'd burned in the fall. Camas was their staple. Women and kids picked new shoots to eat raw, or boiled them up like spinach. Later, when the plants were full-grown, the shaman of the band—who could be a man or a woman—would dig up the first bulbs with an antler-handled stick of yew wood, just enough for everyone to taste, and then the women would take to the fields with their digging sticks and the harvest was on. It would continue through the summer. They roasted the bulbs in pit-ovens lined with stones—got the stones hot with a big fire, layered on leaves of swamp lantern, filled the oven with camas, sealed it off with more leaves and then dirt. The bulbs roasted and steamed for a day or two. They ate some of them when they opened the oven, sun-dried the rest and ground a lot of them into camas meal, which they worked and pressed into fat cakes for the winter.

I remembered the time my mother slow-roasted some camas bulbs in the oven. We weren't blown away with the taste—starchy like potato, with some onion flavor—but agreed it probably tasted pretty good to the Indians after the Hunger Moon at the end of winter, their supplies dwindling. Camas kept the people going, the thousand or so Chelamela who lived in the Long Tom watershed, through the year and through the centuries. Archaeologists know the age of their pit-ovens from the charcoal—eight thousand years, some of them, maybe older. Kalapuyas up and down the Willamette Valley harvested camas every one of those years and never used it up. It isn't food anymore for most of us, but for anyone who wants to think about living in the land, the blue haze of April is a reminder that human beings once made a life from it here, and if we did it once we could probably do it again.

* * *

Each car that passed from behind slapped me with a wave of wind. When I heard an eighteen-wheeler coming up, I hunched down and gripped the bars hard to stay upright. The noise-blast hit like an army attacking. Still, I was glad to be on the move, and a long ride, day into night, gave me time to think.

The people passing in cars and trucks. . . . Each one had a purpose, a destination. Pastor Rogers often preached that God has a plan for every human life, and for a while I had believed it. Then my mother got sick, and once I understood cancer, I asked myself, who put *that* in her plan? What kind of God would watch those malignant cells dividing in her belly and just let it happen? A God like that is worse than a boy pulling the legs off bugs, because the boy might not know any better. I talked to Pastor Rogers about it, and he said, "He works in mysterious ways, Henry. Sometimes He's testing us. He wants to see how we deal with things, the good and the bad, and later we might understand why they happened."

That didn't satisfy me, but the part about understanding later made sense, and a vague notion I'd had for a long time came into focus. Maybe it's not just that God's ways are mysterious to people— of course they are—but they're mysterious to God too, to God his very self. Maybe he's just finding his way like we are, like Douglas firs and elephants and every creature on Earth. Maybe that's why species evolve from what they were into what they are and will be. God doesn't plan it and he doesn't sit somewhere watching it, he *is* it. He gave himself into matter and over the billions of years he's discovering—remembering, maybe—who he is, and he can only find his way as every life in the universe finds its.

Evening came, the traffic sparser. As a car drove up from behind I heard it a long way back, the engine and tire noise growing as one, the beam of its headlights brighter and deeper on the roadway ahead and it passed, the sound trailing away, a pair of taillights glowing smaller and fainter before me. Cars coming the other way were just headlights, their high beams blinding me as they drew near with their own less-loud roar of motor and wheels—then darkness again, the sudden relief, the noise easing away behind. A moment came when I felt a strange sensation of pedaling in place, somehow at the center of things as the happenings of life rushed toward me and passed. Maybe that's what eternity is, I thought. Everything's going, coming, always leaving and never arriving, everything right where it was and is and will be. The thought floated just out of reach, but I knew that I would always remember this moment, and that when I remembered it would *be* this moment, and that someday I would write about it and for the reader it would be this moment too—the great night, me with my little light proceeding, receding, the air cold on my face, my body warm, ready, alive with the journey.

I guessed at the turnoff north, but the gravel road felt wrong and I turned around. Another mile along the highway the right one appeared. A bumpy hour north, I knew I was due for a right turn onto a lousier road. I stopped at a junction, unsure, and was about to pass it up when something touched my spirit from the side road and my headlight caught the eyes of a coyote watching me. I took the turn, and the coyote was gone. "Thank you, grandfather," I said to the night. The road was as rocky and potholed as I remembered, jolty as all hell, and several times I almost dumped the bike. Another hour, maybe, and then a rutted road split off to the right and I thought I saw a building and a house or two. No one was up. A dog barked a few times but didn't mean it. I pedaled over the grass to the last little cottage, laid my bike down—would've fed it oats if it could've eaten—took the three steps up to the tiny porch and knocked. Several small sounds later the door opened and there, wrapped in a blanket, blinking at whatever his eyes were seeing, was Raven.

"It's Henry Fielder," I said. "Sorry to wake you, but you did say come visit."

"I'm delighted to see you," said Raven.

twenty-three

We drank tea, me on the small sofa, Raven in a rocking chair. "You're taller," he said.

"Really?"

"An inch at least. Your hair's grown too. It looks good."

"I may not grow it as long as yours," I said. "So . . . I was thinking on the way, I hardly told you anything about me, right? And you were too polite to ask."

Raven just smiled. There was the same deep calm about him.

"It's long, people have grown old and died listening to it, but would you like to hear my story?"

Raven leaned back in his rocking chair. "I'll cancel my appointments," he said.

So I took my boots off, poured some tea, scrunched myself up at the far end of the sofa, and said, "Just to prove it does have an end, here's the last line of the story: 'And that's why I'm skipping school today.'"

"And will it tell me why you have a black eye?"

"Yep. That too."

I gave him the most complete version I'd given anyone. The only version more complete is the one I'm giving you, reader.

Raven listened carefully, wrapped in his blanket in his rocking chair, putting up a finger to ask for a pause when he wanted to pour more tea. He asked no questions. At times he laughed. When I told of my mother's death he got tears in his eyes. When my father did what he did to me, Raven looked shocked, and he seemed stunned, and tearful again, at the story of quake-day morning. He listened with a look of awe to my account of the foxfire tree and my mother coming out of a white sky and the visitant who got me through the night. I had never told that part and worried that Raven wouldn't believe it, wouldn't believe in my gift—but I paused, and looked, and I could see he did.

When I was done, he looked a while at the candle flame on the small table between us. Finally he said, "I knew you had a serious backstory, Henry. I had no idea it was this heavy. Thank you for telling me. Thank you for surviving it."

"I've told it before, but you're the first person I've *wanted* to tell."

"I'm honored." He put his palms together and made a little bow in his chair. "So you must feel, what . . . grief, anger, uncertainty?"

"More just numb, spaced out. I don't like school, that's all I'm sure of. I'd like to live here and learn some useful things."

Raven was silent. Maybe it was more waiting than thinking, it occurred to me, waiting for the pool to fill. "I followed that longing," he finally said, "but I was older, Henry. I was twenty."

"Damn. I thought you'd be on my side."

"I am," he said with a smile. "Maybe we'll find an idea you can take home to your parents."

I nodded, my head suddenly heavy as a watermelon.

"Before you sleep," said Raven, "I want you to go with me to Commons and phone or email Cart and Josie. They're worried."

"How 'bout after sleep," I said.

Raven shook his head. "They're worried right now, Henry. You owe it to them. You've been through a lot, but you're putting them through a lot, too." He popped up from his chair. "I'll get some clothes on."

I unscrunched myself from the end of the couch and pulled my boots on. When Raven came out of his bedroom he put his arms around me, and I hugged back.

The sky was opening with dawnlight and the air smelled clean and grassy.

At Commons Raven collected some leftovers from the kitchen while I emailed. I told my fosters that I'd arrived at Sweet Grass and was staying with Raven and was breathing easy and would write again. And that I loved them.

Back at Raven's cottage I was too sleepy to eat, but too hungry to sleep. I wolfed some lasagna.

"You know where the bed is," Raven said. "I made it for you. And don't protest, because out here I would just have to tiptoe around you."

I slept till midafternoon and felt guilty that a lot of the day was gone, but Raven silently shushed me and made an afternoon breakfast.

I stopped shoveling French toast into my mouth long enough to ask what he had done with his day. "I meditated," he said, "as I always do. I had a small breakfast and worked in the group garden for a while—I owed a few hours there. Weeding, mending frost covers, planting seedlings. Then I came back here and wrote in my journal, as I also do every day. I cleaned the kitchen and straightened up the house and wondered if Henry would wake up soon, and you did."

"See," I said, "that's what I wanna learn—gardening, pigs and chickens, all that stuff."

"Sweet Grass will be here, Henry. For now let's get you through high school, okay?"

"Why the hell should I wait?" I said. "My English teacher told us, don't be that guy who looks up at the stars twenty-five years from now and hungers for when his life was more authentic."

"Good advice," said Raven. "Feel like a hike? I've got something to show you."

He led me up Stranger Creek, the one I had followed down from the mountains in November, but he knew a deer trail that made for easier going through the brush. None of it looked familiar, but going up any stream course is different from going down. You're moving slower, you don't see as far, you notice things close to the ground. In a gravel bar I found a piece of green chert that might have been flaked off an arrowhead or spear point, and then I found another one. Siuslaw Indians, this far west. Raven was interested, wanted to know all about knapping, so I told him what I knew.

As the streamside on the right flattened out in a shelf, I saw a girdled alder. "Wow," I said, "you guys really cleaned this up."

"We found fifty-one punji sticks like the one you stepped on, Henry. You're lucky you didn't trip and fall. Neckie told us that the Viet Cong set them out by the hundreds in fields and also in pit traps, pointed straight up on the bottom of the pit and angled down on the sides. Your leg goes into that, it's not coming out without tearing a lot of flesh." He gave a little shudder.

"Hey," I said. "Check out the little pot plants! Volunteers?"

Raven chuckled. "No," he said, "we planted these. In memory of Neckie."

It was a nice clump of six plants, growing in a dug-up area going back to grass. A thin black plastic line was delivering a seep of water from upstream.

"From his seeds?"

"We found him, Henry. A Sweet Grasser went into the mountains to seek a vision, and looking down from the brink of a small cliff he saw a boot. He scrambled around and down to the base of the cliff and there was Neckie, worked over by the creatures but the skeleton intact, some skin and sinew and hair in place."

"Wow. So he jumped?"

"We don't think so. It looked like he'd just leaned back at the base of the rock wall and never got up. Took something, maybe. Three of us gathered him up in a tarp and carried him down the mountain."

"What'd you do with him?"

Raven smiled, his green eyes bright. His hair was as black and straight as mine but finer.

"Ohhhh my god. He's right here!"

"The roots are down inside his ribs now, around his wizened heart."

"So cool! You honored him perfectly."

"The Marines never leave a comrade behind. We thought we shouldn't either. I played 'Taps' on my flute as we buried him."

"You know what Willie Nelson says, don't you?"

Raven shook his head.

"'Roll me up and smoke me when I die.'"

We poked around Neckie's patch for a while—I found one last punji stick—and started back, but we had taken our time and twilight caught us short of home. The sky had clouded, no moon or starlight. Neither of us geniuses had brought a headlamp, so after losing the deer trail we had to thrash through endless willow thickets, laughing and babbling like drunken fools. The good part was, when we stumbled and fell the willows cushioned us. I thought of *Catcher in the Rye*, how Holden dreamed of protecting kids playing in the tall ryegrass who came too close to a cliff. The willows were catchers, Raven and I were catchers, hauling each other up when we fell, and there wasn't any cliff, at least none I could imagine.

Close to home, Raven leading, I thought I saw a faint light coming from an old stream channel, so I went over and looked down on the near bank. "Raven," I called. "Come back."

"Hel-*loh*!" he said. "Starry night!"

The whole mossy bank was flecked with faint points of light, concentrated in clusters here and there. "It's the way the universe looks," I said. "Clusters of stars, clusters of galaxies."

"Is this the stuff you spent that night in?" Raven asked.

"Nah. These are glowworms."

"Glowworms?" he just about shouted. "Living breathing glowworms? I know glowworms only in English poetry."

"They're beetle grubs," I informed him. "Does the poetry tell you that?"

"I didn't know we *had* glowworms here. . . ."

"Most people don't, 'cause they don't tramp the woods at night. And all the light pollution spoils the dark."

I felt Raven's hand slide across my back and settle on my left shoulder. I froze. Then I put my arm across his shoulders.

It was too late for dinner with the confederates, but Raven had some cold salmon and cheese and his homemade whole-wheat bread and butter, and he chopped up carrots and turnips and peppery mustard greens for a salad. For dessert we had more bread and butter with plum jam he'd made last summer.

After supper Raven read me a poem by an Englishman a few centuries ago, bidding his lover goodnight:

> Her eyes the glow-worm lend thee;
> The shooting stars attend thee;
> And the elves also,
> Whose little eyes glow
> Like the sparks of fire, befriend thee. . . .

We talked, he read some other poems, and we were quiet for a while.

"Henry?" Raven said at last. "If you don't mind me asking, in all that's happened to you, what is the hardest memory to bear?"

I started to speak, then stopped and let the pool fill.

"He called my name a few times and I didn't answer. Then he said, 'Henry, please.' Like a little boy would, Raven. And I walked out."

* * *

I wanted to spend a few days at Sweet Grass, but Raven said I owed it to Cart and Josie to settle the school issue, so I compromised and emailed that I'd spend one more night away. Josie had emailed back to my first message, not angry, just thanking me for checking in. And sending their love.

At breakfast in Commons I saw Dante and sweet Cecilia, who were just as warm as they'd been the first time, and met a few other confederates too. Then Raven and I worked in the garden, which was huge, deer-fenced, and had some empty beds but also cabbages big as soccer balls, whole fountains of collards and mustard greens, and row after row of beets and carrots and rutabagas in the ground. (I claimed it was pronounced and spelled "rootabeggars," but Raven later proved me wrong.) As he showed me the pigs and chickens and the two dairy cows, I thought of my father, tending livestock when he was Georgie and young George. I could only picture him as I'd known him at home, doing what needed doing, not happy, not sad, just getting it done, usually without my help. There were a lot more things I could have learned from him.

The happiest I saw him was on road trips with Mom and me, and just about always when he and I went fishing. I need to catch a fish to keep my spirit up, but Dad seemed content just casting, working the hole. It settled him. I think it settles a lot of men. He was probably happy at work, too. He was a good lumber grader, and the work was challenging enough to pass the time. Obviously he was happy with Leenie, and even though he didn't always show it, I think he was happy with me.

It came to me after a while that I was seeing George Fielder from a little ways off, not so totally caught up in the storm of the last year.

Later that afternoon, while Raven was writing in his journal, I watched a confederate named Spencer dress out a rabbit, one of two he'd caught in snares. He made it look easy, like my father did on a deer. Spencer cut off the feet and head, slit the skin up the belly to the neck, and peeled the hide back from the slit, loosening it with quick flicks of his very sharp knife. The exposed muscle was pink, not a drop of blood anywhere. He peeled the hide off the legs and then off the carcass entirely. Now he cut into the flesh around the genital area and carefully straight up the belly to expose the innards, which he lifted out in one train and dropped in a bucket.

Spencer was a man of few words. He put the clean carcass in a kettle of brine, rolled up the hide for brining later, cleaned and steeled his knife again and beckoned me over, nodding at the second rabbit. I got the jitters, of course, and needed his prompts, and everything took me twice as long.

"Loosen up," he told me, grinning through his bushy black beard. "The patient's already dead." Laughing helped, and I managed to do a tolerable job.

"Come out with me sometime," said Spencer. "I'll show you how to snare 'em."

"I sure will," I said.

Spencer told me where to take the gut bucket, to a little meadow in the woods as far as possible from the pasture where the sheep grazed with their guard llama. Made for a nice walk, just me and the dry gray sky and a piece of country as quiet and lonesome and pretty as any in the world. I thought of my father again. *First time on your own, Henry, that's pretty good work.* . . . I was nine, the first time he took me hunting. We were on Steens Mountain in the High Desert, holed up behind a lava crop as sunrise, over the mountain to the east, cast the pebbly clouds overhead with rosy orange light. We were looking down in the stillness across the cheatgrass slope toward the trees along a stream, where my dad thought a buck might show. It felt like the beginning of the world.

"Dad," I whispered.

He turned his head. He was wearing a billed cap with red flannel earflaps.

"Can the deer hear me when I whisper like this?"

"No," he whispered back. "You're all right."

"Well, what if I have to . . . what if . . . oh *no!*" and I ducked my face into my lap with my arms tight over my head and sneezed. When I unrolled myself, my dad was shaking with silent laughter. "Good job with that," he managed to whisper, as I wiped my nose on my jacket sleeve.

Now he tilted his head toward the trees. "Keep a lookout down there, Henry. You might see him before I do."

And oh, did I look. I burned holes in those trees. After a while my dad turned toward me with his biggest smile, the crow lines from his bright hazel eyes down over his cheeks all contributing. "I think we might get ourselves a deer today, Henry, but you know what? This right here is the best part." He reached over and rubbed my shoulders.

The memory ached. *On your own . . .* kept sounding silently as I walked toward Raven's cottage. At the doorway I wondered if I should knock, then just walked in. "Mmm," I said, "smells good in here. Somebody comin' for dinner?"

"He just arrived," said Raven.

I washed up, got the rabbit off my hands, and when I came out, Raven had candles burning and places set at the little kitchen table with glasses of wine and a salad in a wooden bowl. He brought plates of whatever he'd been cooking, then sat and reached across the table with both hands. "I like a moment of silence before each meal," he said. I took his hands, closed my eyes, and felt it even stronger now, his stillness of being. Not quite sharing spirit, but touching. It felt like aspen leaves barely moving.

"Whoa," I said, chewing a first bite. "What is this?"

"Chicken marsala," he told me, "with rice pilaf. You like?"

"Are you kidding? I feel like I should've dressed up."

"Oh, you're much better dressed than last time. Cleaner, too."

"I didn't know you were a big-league chef," I said. "This wine is really good too. I haven't had anything to drink for a month."

"That's good. Sounds like you were drinking and drugging a lot."

"Yep. Tried to drown my sorrows. Failed."

"This kind of drinking brings warmth to human company, Henry. If it leads you to drink too much, though, you'll probably have to give it up entirely. Some people can deal with Uncle Al and some can't."

"Uncle Al," I chuckled. "My foster parents tell me the same thing."

"Your elders aren't inevitably wrong, you know."

"Oh, and how old are you, Mr. Wise Old Elder?"

"I'm twenty-two, sonny."

We finished the wine and chicken and then the salad—first time I'd been served the salad last—and I told the chef to kick back while I cleaned up. I faked shock that there was no dishwasher and had him going for a second, then I poured hot water from the kettle on the woodstove, pushed up the sleeves of my hoodie, and went to work the old-fashioned way.

I had just dried my hands on a towel and was reaching to take a book Raven had found for me when his face went white. "Your arms!" he said.

"Oh hell, you weren't supposed to see that."

"Henry, you didn't tell me you've been cutting yourself. . . ."

"So? It's not your business, is it."

"I'm sorry, Henry. It's just—"

"It's just that you're gay and you're attracted to me, isn't it."

He looked down with a kind of sour chuckle in his throat. "That isn't all it is, but yes. It certainly is that."

"Well, my father went gay on me, and that didn't work out real well."

Raven nodded. "None of this is fair to you, Henry. You're sixteen, you've been through hell, you don't need more pressure. If I . . . restrain my feelings for you, can you allow us to be friends?"

His voice and face were filled with sincere appeal. "You're a totally good man," I said. "I want to be your friend always."

I took the book from his hands and set it on the counter and hugged him. I felt the relief in his hug back. I felt the love, too. He took a long breath and let it go.

We talked for a couple of hours after that. Raven opened another bottle of wine and told me that he'd grown up in Yakima, over in central Washington, knowing he was gay and hating himself for it. His schoolmates smelled his difference and pushed him around. He was lonely, the smartest kid in class, a pussy on the playground. His mother figured it out when he was a high-school freshman and supported him. His father, who ran a hardware business, couldn't deal with it then and couldn't now. That must be hard, I said, and he said yes it was, it made him sad and angry, but he and his mom had stayed close and they hoped his dad would come around to acceptance. Raven had picked UO over UW or Wazzou because changing states felt like getting farther from his home town. He majored in English with a Music minor, visited Sweet Grass with a friend who knew somebody there, and decided he'd like to live there while he figured out *what to do / how to live / who to be*, as he put it.

We talked on a while, then Raven turned in. I went to the kitchen for a glass of water and saw the book he'd found for me, a collection of William Stafford's poetry. I took it to the couch and started leafing through the pages. Sometimes a book comes your way exactly when you need it. I turned a page to a poem I'd read before—"The Farm on the Great Plains"—and hadn't connected with. Now it felt so spooky it gave me chills.

It's winter, there's a farm out in Kansas somewhere and a phone line to it, where birds perch. The guy who's speaking the poem grew up there, and every year he calls and gets only a hum. But he has faith that some year he'll pick the right night and catch somebody home—"the tenant who waits, the last one left at the place"—and he imagines the conversation like this:

> "Hello, is Mother at home?"
> *No one is home today.*
> "But Father—he should be there."
> *No one—no one is here.*

"But you—are you the one . . . ?" the guy asks, and that's the moment. It's not about his mom and dad. He himself is the last one there, the one he's been trying to find all along:

> Then the line will be gone
> because both ends will be home:
> no space, no birds, no farm.
>
> My self will be the plain,
> wise as winter is gray,
> pure as cold posts go
> pacing toward what I know.

Not that this solves all his problems. "Wise as winter is gray" doesn't sound like total enlightenment—more like an Oregon winter—but as I read and read that poem on Raven's couch that night, I believed in it. To be wise has to be gray, because black and white aren't true enough. And like those telephone poles across the plains, the guy paces *toward* what he knows. Could take a lifetime, might never get there, but it's him, his journey.

That poem felt like ground to stand on, like the sun just coming up.

* * *

We went to breakfast at Commons, then I packed and rigged up my bike while Raven fixed me sandwiches for the road. He'd offered to drive me, but I wanted to go as I'd come. "They'll probably ground me again," I said.

"You handled this in a pretty mature way, Henry. I predict they'll just be very glad to have you home. I, on the other hand, am going to piss you off all over again."

He took my shoulders in his hands and brought his face just inches from mine. "Promise me you won't cut yourself again, Henry. Promise your mother. Think of her anguish watching you cut your arms."

He was gripping my shoulders hard enough to hurt.

"You obviously won't let me go until I do. So okay."

"Say it out loud, Henry."

"Mom, Raven the Fierce, I promise I won't cut myself anymore."

"You'll feel the urge, Henry. How will you stop?"

"I'll imagine you crushing my bones with your bare hands."

"Good. Now don't be alarmed, but I'm about to kiss you on your cheek."

His kiss felt good. I put my hand on his shoulder. "Thanks for talking, thanks for listening. Thanks for being here."

"Always, Henry. And would you mind if I visited you?"

"'Course not. Just don't arrive in the middle of the night with a lot of problems, okay?

"So long, Green Eyes," I hollered as I pedaled away.

twenty-four

I remember how subtly spring creeps up in those Coast Range hills. All through gray winter there's the steady green of conifers, ferns, mosses, grass. Buds appear on the wild hazelnuts before all the old leaves have fallen, swelling through January and February as tiny violets bloom in the yard—white ones, purple—and the chorus frogs chant, and robins swarm the wet pastures. In March the tempo quickens—Indian plum puts out its hanging greeny-white clusters, trillium spears up, the hazelnut buds pop open their sheaths. And then, in April, spring comes like a rising river: the yellows of swamp lantern and the first Oregon grape, dogwoods blooming like sparse white clouds in the woods, fruit trees blossoming in yards and orchards, blue camas taking over whole meadows and pastures. A song sparrow sings, a rosy finch, bees get to stirring in the cleft Douglas fir, the hazelnuts show little paired leaves like wings, the vine maples' more like paired mittens. Fiddleheads push up unfurling amid the flattened fronds of sword ferns, blue-violet clumps of wild iris seem to appear overnight along roadsides, and as April swings into May, the rhodies put on gaudy shows, armies of Scotch broom muster along roads and in unsprayed clearcuts, hummingbirds buzz each other like duelists, and gangs of goldfinches swarm the feeders and flit and swirl their yellow and black among the bright mossy oaks, whose twigs are greening, beginning to obscure the ghost foliage of winter.

The first time my mother took me to the Eugene Symphony, I liked the music fine, Beethoven's Seventh Symphony especially, but we got there early and I really loved the warming up, too—on the rumbly sea of trombones and tuba and pounding kettledrums, gusts of violins and their kin blew every which way with trumpets and high flutes piercing through, bassoons and clarinets not quite drowned in the riot, all the noises carousing, running up and down scales and everywhere with their wild tones and rhythms, like some kind of large, loud, and very confused family. That's what the spring speed-up felt like, the deciduous trees leafing out in their countless textures and shades of green among the darker, consistent conifers, sun and rain switching off and playing together and sometimes throwing a rainbow, the birds going at it, the frogs still trying, all of it razzing and popping and tumbling together as the moist earth sings, *Don't know what it means, but we're doin' it again!*

* * *

I'd read that bracken ferns can shoot up three or four inches every day in the spring, so one May afternoon I decided to watch one grow. I found an upcoming bracken behind the house, about eighteen inches high, and planted a yardstick in the soft ground right behind the growing stem, and lay down on the grass with my chin propped on my hands, eyes up close at stem-tip level. It was hard to concentrate. After a while the stem-tip moved—or was it my head? I resettled my chin in my hands and a minute later the tip moved again. But maybe my breath had done it, so I breathed at different strengths to see what it took to move the tip, and after that the tip looked different and I couldn't remember if it had always leaned to the right at that same angle, and my neck was sore from arching it and my eyes weren't focusing well and I was getting some pretty bad itches, so I noted where the bracken tip measured and laid my head down on my arms.

A little shivery in the wan sunlight, I imagined the roots of Douglas firs in the soil beneath me, the cells of their tips dividing, feeling their way with strands of fungus connecting them, and the green pitchy tops where the old Doug firs were still children, and the oaks and Oregon ashes, the fruit trees, the flowers and grass, all of it stretching and growing—*and me too*, it suddenly came to me. My cells were dividing. I'd probably put on eensy dabs of bone and flesh and gained a hundredth of an inch just in the time I'd been lying there. Inside the Henry who looked the same in the mirror each day, inside everything alive, Nature was working in the dark like a wise old woman never seen, casting her spells and humming her charms, weaving the possibilities, and I fell asleep in a dream of an underground stream whispering deep below.

When I woke I checked on the bracken tip but couldn't remember where it'd measured before, so I declared defeat and put the yardstick back in the garage. It felt more like a victory.

I had time to do that experiment because I wasn't in school. Raven had suggested that what I'd done—leave home to make a point—was an act of nonviolent disobedience, in the tradition of responsible protest that my foster parents believed in. I hadn't thought of it like that, but I framed it that way to Cart and Josie, without puffing it up as some kind of courageous act. Josie nodded but pointed out that leaving on a forty-mile bike ride, much of it in the dark, raised real safety issues, and I said yes it did, just as Carter Stephens had raised real safety issues when he chained himself to a gate with heavy machinery rolling his way.

"We don't disagree," Cart said, Catrick the Voyager comfortable in his lap, "and Henry, we want you to breathe. Here at home, everywhere."

I mentioned a private school in Eugene I'd heard of, but Josie stopped me.

"We have our own proposal, Henry. Cart and I have decided that we were too hasty in dismissing the homeschooling idea."

"Serious?" I said.

"Serious*ly*, please, but yes. There are two of us to share the load, it wouldn't take all our time, and it would be something new for us. A fresh challenge."

"Whatever you've been smoking," I said, "sign me up."

"Hang on," said Cart. "We have two conditions. Number two, we want you to teach us, too. Take us places, show us what you know. Number one is harder. You need to be around other kids—not just Abner—and homeschooling doesn't get you that."

"What if I don't want that?"

"The fancy word is 'socialization,'" said Josie, "and it matters. So be thinking about how we can make it happen."

"Well, hot damn," I said. "Who gets stuck with teaching Math?"

"I do," said Josie, "and I have high standards. Make no mistake, Henry, we'll expect you to work hard and take your lessons seriously."

"I've never done that," I said, "but I bet I could learn."

* * *

Jonah came to me at church on Sunday and asked if he could drive me home.

We didn't say anything until he asked if I'd be willing to stop a while and talk. He looked grayer, both his goatee and his curly hair.

He drove us up Stamper Road and turned in at my old house. The Fielder place. He turned off the ignition and shifted on the seat to face me, his left shoulder against the door.

"Henry," he said, "you know I've been wrestling. I can't believe your father did what you say he did. But Cloudy came home saying she couldn't *not* believe you. So that's the fix I'm in."

He paused, keeping his eyes on me.

"I couldn't believe it either, Jonah. Not then, not after, not even now sometimes. But it happened."

"The Fifth Commandment says, 'Honor your father and your mother.' I know you honored your mother. Did you—do you—honor your father?"

I thought of Raven and let the pool fill. "I didn't, not nearly enough," I said. "I disobeyed him, I lied to him, I was mean to him. He hurt me but I hurt him too, some things I said. And I abandoned him."

"The Sixth Commandment, 'You shall not murder.' Did you break that commandment?"

Again, I took a while. "I never meant to kill him, but I did fire a shot that might've grazed his left ear. And I did leave him helpless. I don't know if that's murder, but he's dead, and I had a lot to do with it."

"The Ninth Commandment. 'You shall not bear false witness.' Are you keeping that commandment right now?"

"Not when I lied to you, but I am now."

"Come with me," said Jonah, opening his door. I followed him around the side of the house and in through the back door. The place smelled sour with mold and rotting carpet. Jonah walked through the kitchen into the hallway and then into my bedroom. He turned to face me, came close, put his right hand on my left shoulder.

"Henry," he said, his gray eyes bright, pain all over his face, "I don't think you and I worship the same God, so I'll invoke yours. Do you swear, by nature's god, by everything you hold sacred, do you *swear* to me, that George Fielder came into this room and this bed, on Monday night before Thanksgiving, and did to you what you've said he did?"

I waited, keeping my eyes on his. "I swear, Jonah. By Nature's god, by everything I hold sacred. I swear."

He held my eyes a few seconds, then he nodded his head slightly a few times and said, "I see what Cloudy saw. I apologize, Henry. I've done you wrong. You didn't need any more pain and I sure gave you some. I hope you can forgive me."

"You were just being fierce, Jonah. Nobody loved my dad more than you. I forgive you right now."

"No one's more disappointed in him, either," said Jonah, quietly. He gave my shoulder a squeeze and let go. "I'm disappointed in myself too, Henry. The day after that night, your dad came by the house. He was hungover, dull in the eyes. He had some trouble on his mind. All he said was, 'I may have gone too far, Jonah.' I couldn't get any more out of him. I figured he'd whipped you and drawn blood or something."

"Thanks for telling me," I said, my voice breaking. "I'm glad to know it bothered him."

I put out my hand and we shook.

Jonah looked at his watch. "We better git," he said, turning, then stopped. "When did you barricade your door, Henry?"

"That same day you talked. That night."

A look of wonderment lit Jonah's face. "Think of it," he said. "If he hadn't done you that evil, and if you hadn't defended yourself, you would've been sleeping right there in that corner and I'd've found you crushed flat on Thanksgiving morning."

"He and I both would've died," I said. "Sometimes I've wished we did."

"Never wish that, Henry. God was looking after you."

"Well," I said. It wasn't a smart time to argue, but I couldn't help it. "I'm grateful if he was, but if he was, why wasn't he looking out for my father or my mother? Or that mother and child that got buried in mud?"

Jonah shook his head, smiling. "I don't know, Henry. 'We'll understand it all by and by,' that's what the song says."

"If we understand it, maybe God will too. 'Cause I don't think he understands it now."

Jonah squinted. "He's the God who created heaven and earth, Henry. I reckon He understands everything."

"But he created heaven and earth to *change*, Jonah. The universe has been evolving for fourteen billion years, and God's not up there directing it, he *is* it. He's got this fierce desire to become. There's blood and cruelty, there's beauty, there's love, and God's as lost in it as we are."

"Oh dear me," sighed Jonah. "You've always had a wonderful imagination, Henry Fielder. Let's keep talking in the truck."

"If God's as confused as humans are, who's to say what's right and what's wrong?" Jonah asked, raising his voice over the engine noise as we climbed Boomer Mountain.

"We are," I said. "And doin' a poor job of it. But maybe we're learning."

Jonah frowned at the windshield. "How's it possible to have faith in a God like that, Henry? What's there to believe in?"

"Well," I said, "we're here and we know we're here, that's two things. I don't mean to be disrespectful, but I think God is born in you and me right now. I have faith in that. I don't know the beginning or the end, so I guess I have faith in the journey."

As we pulled in to Dismal Acre, I told Jonah that I'd been remembering a lot of good about my father, things we did, things he taught me, things that showed that he loved me and reminded me that I loved him. Jonah was pleased to hear it.

* * *

The next day there was a letter for me, posted in Long Tom. Josh, was my first thought. His parents were suing me and my foster parents and he had a pistol and if he saw me again he'd put holes in me. But it was from Tess, handwritten in neat cursive. She had heard my story, like everybody at school, and she was writing to tell me how terrible she felt about it. She had no idea I'd been through something like that. It explained a lot, she said. She had never liked Josh because he was a loudmouth jerk. She wondered when I was coming back to school and hoped I would call her if I felt like talking.

I did call her, and a few days later, about four in the afternoon, I knocked on her door. She was wearing a turquoise blouse, brown corduroy pants, and a smile. We hugged and sat on her living room couch and talked a while. She was curious what my father had been like as a dad and husband, not just as an abuser. She wanted to know about my mother, too. I appreciated that and found it easy to tell her things.

We'd been eating some chips and dip, and now Tess came out of the kitchen with a bottle of cranberry juice and a fifth of vodka.

"Um," I said, "won't your mother be here soon?"

Tess smiled and shook her head. "She's in Portland, overnight. That's why I asked you to come today."

"Does this mean I get another lesson?"

"Only if you want one," she said.

I raised my hand. "Yes, please. But what about that guy you're dating?"

"Oh, we're not that serious. And you know what, Henry? I think I overreacted a little on our first date."

"No you didn't. I was a dumbshit."

"Well, we'd be fools to argue about it." She ran her fingers through my hair. "Fix us a drink, Tracker."

The red spirit juice did its thing, and we did ours. I told Tess to lead the way, so I wouldn't mess up like before. She smiled and whispered, "Just enjoy this."

She leaned me back in the sofa and unbuttoned my shirt (I had dressed up for the occasion), then she kissed me from my mouth right down to my bellybutton and then through my jeans. I was starting to sweat. She unbuckled my belt and helped me out of my pants, then she kissed me through my briefs. "Something wants out of here," she murmured. I was breathing ragged as a thief with the cops closing in. She slid the briefs down off my legs, knelt in front of me, and kissed her way up my thighs, side to side. Then it was all warm mouth and lively tongue and I wanted it to last forever, but in just a few seconds—my bad!—I exploded. As Tess coaxed a little more out of me I lay there gasping, like a distance runner who'd just crossed the finish line. There wasn't a doubt in the universe that I was the winner.

"Holy cats, Tess. . . ."

She chuckled, kissed me on my lips, got up and came back with a quilt and snuggled under it with me. "I'm glad you liked it, Henry."

"Oh, I sure liked it. Does it . . . taste all right?"

"It's sweet," she whispered, "like you. If you can stay a while, we could explore further. . . ."

So I called home and explained to Josie that Tess and I were figuring out our relationship and I might be late. She said that was fine, but added, "If your figuring involves sex, Henry, promise me you will use protection."

"What?" I said. "Okay . . . whatever." It was no use trying to fool Josie.

Tess microwaved some burritos and we had a nice romantic dinner in the kitchen with more spirit juice, me still bundled in the quilt. We didn't really have much to talk about, but it didn't matter. We laughed a lot. She was beautiful with her short brown hair. I felt manly and lighter than air.

In her bedroom Tess turned on one lamp and got some easy-listen rock going. I waited in the cozy darkness under my quilt, peeking out at the doorway while she was in the bathroom. She came in wearing a blue robe and slid in next to me. "Ooh," she said, "there's a boy in my bed."

"Hope he gets a good grade," I said.

"Just do what you were doing in the car, Henry, five times slower and gentler. I've saved you the trouble of tearing my clothes off."

We kissed, and her lips taught a trick or two to mine, and before long I kissed my way down to her breasts and roamed that sleek country for a time, slowly, hands and mouth. She was making some sounds that encouraged me. Now the robe was getting in the way so I asked her to sit up and helped her out of the sleeves and we went back to kissing again, and I slid my hand down over her belly to the wilderness below. My gear had been ready the whole time, so "Tess?" I whispered, "would right now be too soon?" She laughed softly and opened a condom from the nightstand and handed it to me, but I fumbled with it and worried it would tear so she got it done and opened her legs and gave a little gasp as I slid in and there we were, riding the waves, the swells rolling easy and then rolling faster and rolling us all the way home.

* * *

There was good news at Dismal Acre the next evening.

Cart had been in Eugene all afternoon with his fellow occupiers and their lawyers. I was reading in the living room and Josie was in her darkroom when he flung open the front door and shouted, "Now hear this! We got a court order that stops the logging cold!"

I gave him a double high-five, Josie came out of her room and hugged him. Cart paced the living room and kitchen, hooting and clapping his hands.

"Does this stop it for keeps?" I asked.

"No," he said, "but the judge found errors in BLM's assessment of potential environmental impacts, so now it goes back to the agency, and then back to the court, and that process will take many months. But during that time," he just about sang, waving a finger, "not a single tree will fall. Not one. *And,* if we drag it out long enough, they just might get tired of fighting."

"How much have they cut so far?" I asked.

"Very little. They wanted to blade a few spurs off the main road for access, but the big bulldozer wasn't running right—and today, we heard, it shut down completely." Cart chuckled gleefully. "They had to load it onto a lowboy trailer and haul it away."

I heard myself ask, "Is that the same Cat they brought up there last fall?"

"The same machine, Henry. Maybe it got radicalized, wearing all that beautiful greenery."

twenty-five

I'd heard from Deanna that Len Peppers had taken a downturn, and now she called again to say I might want to be there. Len recognized me with a smile when I took his calloused hand, but didn't speak. He looked like an exhausted Santa Claus out of uniform, but he looked pretty easy, too. Deanna explained that the heart muscle, from decades of drinking, just gets weaker and weaker till it quits. Breathing gets very uncomfortable toward the end, but morphine eases that, and Deanna had seen to it that Len was getting plenty. I asked if I could stay a while and she said, "You can stay all night, Henry. Pop loves it when you're here." Then she went and brought me a mug of coffee.

I wanted to say goodbye to my friend, if this was it. By his own account Len was ready, or at least not too afraid, and he knew that he'd done his part to earn what he was getting. Len Peppers was hiking the great divide, that ridge we've all got breath to climb, and I wanted to walk him up. I started talking a little, saying how lucky I was to know him, how he'd been a great friend and a great help to me, like a grandfather or the coolest uncle in the world, how his advice had always been good and how *he'd* always been good, just being who he was. I wasn't getting it said the way I meant it and trailed off after a while. I held his hand and shared spirit in silence. His body was dying and all drugged up, but his spirit was alive in there, slowly stirring. I could touch it.

When he spoke I thought the voice was inside me, but he was whispering aloud. He said, "I'll be lookin' for you, Henry. . . ."

"Where, Len?"

"Oh, you know . . . down there . . . down where the river bends."

"I'll hold you to it, Len. I'll take it personal if you don't."

He gave my fingers just the slightest squeeze. "But damn sure . . ." he whispered, "you take your time, old son. . . ." I heard a soft rumble in his throat that might have been a laugh.

A while later somebody knocked and it was the Morrisons, the ones who had looked after Len so well. They'd brought their kids, and I moved from the bedside to give them room. Over the evening others came, and eventually Jonah Rutledge walked in with his cello in its case, a man and woman with guitars right behind him. They got themselves set up in a corner and tuned up and then they were playing, not loud, Jonah taking the melody with his bow or finger-plucking a bass line, the guitar players strumming, picking a little, and then the three of them were quietly singing, harmonizing, and soon the rest of us were singing along, Deanna too, when we knew the words. The musicians led, we gladly followed, and Len was right there with us. I'm pretty sure I saw him smile, or maybe I felt his smile inside, when they led us into one we all knew the chorus to, that fine old song made of questions:

> *Will the circle be unbroken*
> *By and by, Lord, by and by?*
> *Is a better home a-waitin'*
> *In the sky, Lord, in the sky?*

As I sang I imagined Len's answer to the second question: *I've worked and loved and known some music of THIS home, right here on this good ground. If what's waitin' in the sky is better—it'll have to be pretty damned good.* He might have believed, as I do, and was starting to believe even then, that when we die and shed the body and the burden of being the person we were, there's some kind of reunion with those we've loved and who have loved us, and we know them and they know us in a wholer light. I don't think we shed our sorrows, but maybe we understand why we had to have those sorrows, why we had to be torn and tested the way we were.

Nobody wanted to stop singing that song, so we just rolled right ahead, repeating the verses, and those like me who didn't know all the verses learned them that night. The last one puts it simplest:

> *One by one their seats were emptied,*
> *One by one they went away.*
> *Now the family is parted,*
> *Will it be complete one day?*

As the music played, new visitors arrived as others left. Len Peppers lay there, magnificent, a simple light around him, his chest rising and falling unevenly. My breathing rose and fell with his. I felt the waning warmth of his spirit.

When Jonah and the guitar players packed up to go, I thanked them for their gift to Len. The woman smiled and said, "It's a gift for us too. We're just grateful we can make a little music."

"I'm grateful you can too," I said.

I stayed on as their seats were emptied, as they went away. I asked Deanna if she really didn't mind me being there, and she said she was glad for my company. Then she heated some macaroni and cheese for a late supper, followed by warm strawberry-rhubarb pie and ice cream. I liked Deanna a lot. She was, and is, like quite a few women who grow up living in the country—plainspoken, warm, spirited in a quiet way, capable of doing the work of living. More capable than the men, really, stronger in the ways that require more than muscle.

The moment came at daybreak. Deanna woke me from napping on the couch. Len's breaths were slowing and coming rough from his throat. They sounded like work, like each one was the most his body could do. I wondered how many breaths he'd breathed in his lifetime, how many heartbeats he'd had, how many mornings he'd waked to meet the day. One of the windows in the room looked out to the southeast, where traces of pink and gold were gathering in a few flat clouds. The color was on Deanna's cheeks and forehead and in her eyes as she sat calmly watching her father. His breaths came farther apart, and then he gathered a little extra wind, it seemed, and let it go one last time. It sounded for all the world like he had just set down a heavy load and now could rest.

Or maybe that was me. I felt weightless, like a balloon must feel tugging gently at its string. Deanna had tears running down her cheeks but she was smiling, and the smile was true. She had the sunrise on her face, on her blond curls and glistening eyes, and she was beautiful. So was the mighty truth of Len Peppers, his white hair strewn across his pillow, head leaning slightly to the left, eyes closed. The three of us kept still for a long time.

I witnessed my first good death that morning, Lynn commented after reading this. Len wasn't in a nursing home that smelled of antiseptic, and he wasn't pinned in pain under a collapsed house with me walking out the door. As Len died I felt things I can express a little better now than I could then. Sunrise and sunset are made of the same light, and, like gladness and sadness, you can't have one without the other. Sunshine on a cloudless day is how some people think of heaven—fine enough if all you want is to snooze and lie around forever, but there's no mortal beauty in it, no exploring, no creating, no loving, no winning or losing. In that heaven William Shakespeare wouldn't have written about yellow leaves and twilight and dying fires, how they "make thy love more strong, to love that well which thou must leave ere long." Beethoven and Willie Nelson wouldn't have made music, William Stafford and Walt Whitman wouldn't have lifted a pen, and I wouldn't be writing this book.

*   *   *

At home I slept all day, and there he was in my dream again—seemed more like *his* dream now—back at work on his project, moving slow but sure in the shadows among ghostly trees, whistling. He must have felt me watching him, because he put down his tool, which looked like a saw, and lifted his cap by its bill and beckoned with a long sweep of his arm, the way I'd known him to do sometimes when he was happy. A warm shimmer went through me. I wasn't frozen anymore, I took a few steps, stiff as limbwood, but I still couldn't see his face, couldn't be sure what he had back there. I heard the whispery voice of the river and felt it flowing slow and deep, sending up small swirls to its surface, near-silent licks and murmurings. I longed for it, but there *he* was, standing, bending to his work again, shifting away and shifting back. He waved me over with his cap again, and I didn't know if I couldn't go or just wouldn't. It seemed to matter. I watched, listened. I stood my ground.

It was pretty much the same in my waking life. I wasn't sure if I couldn't be happy or was just refusing. I'd gotten what I wanted, no more school. My two favorite people in the world were my teachers. I'd had a great time with a great friend at Sweet Grass, I had done the deed with my girlfriend, but none of the good feeling seemed to carry far. I was sad that Len was gone, but that sadness I cherished because I knew where it came from and what it was worth. My problem was the part of me that couldn't feel sadness or gladness, or could but wouldn't, whatever. That was it—the *whatever* part, the me with *Shit Happens* bumper-stickers all over his car, himself the best example of his lame philosophy. Sometimes I even felt bored, and that drove me crazy, because for all my short life I'd had nothing but scorn for people or characters in books or movies who said they were bored. To be bored is to disrespect the gift of life.

The only living feeling that came to me was anger, and it blew up in sudden storms. One night as I lugged the trash and recycling out for the morning pickup, I tripped on my own loose shoelace and let the garbage can tip over. Suddenly I was kicking it as hard as I could until garbage had spilled all over and I had to pick it up and got grease and tomato sauce and whatever else all over my hands. Cart heard the ruckus and opened the front door. I told him I'd just run off a black bear.

I argued with Tess about nothing. I yelled at the computer when the satellite wouldn't let me online. *Goddamn son of a bitch!* I screamed when I couldn't find something in the mess of my room, or when the Mariners lost a close game I was listening to, or when I was trying to split a knotty round of firewood and kept missing the center and not getting it done, swing after swing, just butchering the fucker and swinging so wild I almost planted the six-pound maul in my right foot.

Josie found me another shrink, and I liked her better than the first one but still didn't feel like talking. The person I needed to talk to, I kept telling her, was my father. What would you say to him? she asked. Right, I said, that's the problem. . . .

A few days after my birthday I got my license and became a legal driver. It didn't feel all that special. On the back roads in my mom's boxy white Dodge I felt cut off, like a critter in a big metal crate. On a bike you've got wind in your face, like a happy dog, and you smell the news—mown grass, horse apples in a pasture, stream dank, quick clouds of lilac or rose, a waft of cannabis through somebody's hedge—and you're going slow enough to see things, too, like the first wild iris of spring, or a little cloth bag of weed someone must have tossed in a panic, or the little homemade shrines where someone had died, or a sign I liked under one guy's front-yard American flag: BURN THIS FLAG AND I'LL BURN YOUR ASS.

Driving my mom's car all I really saw was the road, and to make things worse I ran over a squirrel, squished half of him flat. I had officially joined the society of American Killers by Car. All I could do was peel the poor critter off the pavement and lay him in the grasses while the car purred like a well-fed cat.

My fosters had cleared me to drive short distances only, but Abner had his license now and wasn't restricted, so in the first hot weather of June we drove to a swimming hole on the Nesqualla River, near where my dad and I had fished for steelhead. I hadn't seen Abner and his fine blue eyes since leaving high school. He had braided his brown hair into dreadlocks, which he shook liberally as he gripped the wheel.

"Dude," he said, "you *raked* on Josh Jameson. If I'd known you were a UFC champ, I'd've been scared of you."

"Yeah, I was gonna take his scalp but I decided blood was enough."

"So that thing with your father, it really happened, huh?"

"Yeah. It was that night when you and I got so plastered at Cart and Josie's. I passed out in bed and he was on me before I even woke up."

Abner shook his head mournfully and squeezed my knee. "That's so twisted, man. But you could have *told* me, okay? You're my best friend. You didn't shoot him, did you?"

"No, but be probably felt the breeze. I was that mad at him."

"Of course you were, Tracker. But good thing you missed. That could haunt a guy."

"Yeah," I said. "It could haunt a guy."

We walked a ways through woods to the swimming hole, and we had it to ourselves, a little falls feeding a nice pool you can dive into without rocks to worry about. We stripped and skinny-dipped till we were good and cold, then hauled out on the water-smoothed rock slabs and let the sun settle our shivers. Abner had a bota bag of tequila and, as usual, some good bud. I had a Vicodin for each of us, the last ones from my black-eye period. We got into a conversation about careers. Abner wanted to study in France and become a chef, but first he wanted to travel the West as a ski bum and be a smoke-jumper, maybe. I wanted to be a major league second baseman but allowed that I'd settle for being a kingfisher, like the one we could see darting around downstream, rattling out his call. If those jobs were taken, maybe I'd write books.

"You totally *could* do that," said Abner. "Serious." He was lounging on his back. I was sitting up with my arms around my knees. I had almost never felt as relaxed around people as Abner seemed every minute.

"You've been drinking," I said.

"I mean it, Tracker. You think deeper than the rest of us. We're like the riffle down there, babbling in the shallows. You're like this pool."

"The riffle looks like fun," I said. "How do you riffle?"

Abner laughed, tossing his dreads. "Hasn't Tess been showing you?"

"She's showing me a lot. All good."

Abner kept looking at me. "You deserve all good luck for the rest of your life, Tracker. That business with your dad. . . . And I can't feature having even one parent die. Does it just hurt all the time?"

"Not really," I said. "More like I'm still waiting to feel it. Is that stupid or what?"

Abner sat up and gave my shoulder a shake. "Not stupid, Tracker. When I was in that car crash, with my brother? Got my leg gashed, arm broken? I didn't feel *anything*, man, not till the hospital. Your brain and nervous system protect you that way. Same with you, different kind of pain. You will heal, my brother. You know that, don't you?"

He pulled me closer and looked me straight in the eyes. "You . . . will . . ."—his blue eyes rolled up now, showing the whites—"*heeaalll*, I say, in the name of the Holy Badass Honcho of us All, you will *HEEEAAALLL!*"—and he got to his feet lifting me by my armpits and shoved me into the river.

We horsed around trying to drown each other, raging and hollering, then we stretched out on the rocks again, toked a little more and
finished the tequila, getting drowsy in the sun. Riversound took me
in and carried me along, swirling warm and fluent, sliding and sidling along like one great story of stories, whispering, chanting,
laughing, sobbing, because life is what it is and has to be. . . . My
mother was near, I felt her warm hand on my chest, and as I eased
up out of my drowse to the warm rock where we lay, I lifted my right
hand and laid the back of it on Abner's belly.

He didn't respond, so I moved it just a little. Then his hand pushed
mine away. "What are you *doing?*"

"Huh?" I said, as if just waking. "Oh shit, Abner, I'm sorry. I
didn't know what I was doin'. . . ."

"That shit's not for me, Fielder." He got up and started to get
dressed. I did the same. "I was still asleep, Abs, I really didn't
know. . . ."

We talked some on the way home, but it was Abner with a lid on,
hardly Abner at all. I kept thinking, *Now I've wrecked it with my best
friend.*

I went to my room early that night, sat at my desk and sharpened
my knife. I stared at the blade as I touched its point to the skin of my
wrist, touched and pressed, touched and pressed. Then I saw the pain
in Raven's face, I saw my mother crying, I saw Len Peppers remembering his life with joy. I pressed the point hard enough to draw one
tiny bead of blood, then folded the knife and put it away.

* * *

Josie had been working for months on something she said I had in-
spired, a series of photographs of well-thinned forests. "You see lots
of images of old growth," she said, "and you see photos of clearcuts,
but nothing in between."

I thought she caught the beauty of the thinned woods pretty well—the openness, the mix of sun and shade, the look of a forest you'd like to walk through. In some of the pictures small stumps were showing, which would help people get the idea, I said.

Josie sighed. "Yes, they tell a story, of sorts. But old growth and clearcuts *are* stories. Visual drama. It's hard to make much of these young, straight-line Oregon conifers, one so much like the others."

"Well, when I hear of a woods that's gonna be thinned, I'll tell you. You could do before and after."

"I suppose. But pictures of thickets would be even less dramatic. . . ."

"Well, *I* like these," I said. "Can I hang one in my room?"

I had a visual drama running in my head involving a certain yellow machine. I saw it clanking and blapping up the gravel road, pouring black smoke, aimed dead-on at Cart Stephens and his friends. I saw it blading the forest floor, scraping up moss and duff and black humus that had taken years and years to form, right down to the yellow clay. I saw it dragging a turn of logs behind it on a choker, planting its tread marks deep in the mud. The story in the *Register-Guard* said the engine had been ruined, clearly by sabotage, and repairs would cost thousands of dollars. I didn't feel bad about that, because I couldn't think of anything positive that yellow machine would have accomplished in the Methuselah forest. Work for a few men, a little timber for the mills, nothing more. An investigation was under way, the article said.

I'd only seen two cars that night, but still I worried that someone might have spotted me driving into Karen Creek or driving out. And what about tire tracks—could they match tracks to my tire tread? Or what if I'd dropped something. . . . I knew I was just being paranoid, that I'd pulled off the operation flawlessly, but wasn't that how every criminal feels, before the bust comes down?

Cart had a long phone conversation one afternoon and came to dinner looking grim. "The sheriff is calling us all to be interviewed," he said. "The entire collective."

"Why?" I asked. "They know you're nonviolent. That's the last thing any of you would have done."

Cart sighed. "There were arguments about it early on," he said. "The authorities will want the names of those who were for action against property. I'm afraid it will turn us each against the other."

"It's a shame," said Josie. "A great success in court, now this."

"I still don't get it," I said. "Why are they accusing *you* guys? You're not Earth First. You're not the Earth Liberation Front. . . ."

Cart shrugged. "One, we're against the logging. Two, we're the only people known to have been in that area all winter. It's all circumstantial, of course. To prosecute they would need direct evidence. But it casts suspicion over everything we did. Eco-terrorism, they're calling it."

"Do they have any clues?" I asked. My voice sounded hollow.

Cart looked at me. "Do you think they'd tell us if they did? We're suspects, Henry. All of us."

twenty-six

Tess was on vacation all of July with her father and step-mom in the Idaho Sawtooths. She sent me a couple of postcards. Abner was away with his family too, on the California coast and Baja. Just as well, after the disaster at the river. I played summer baseball, which pleased Cart and Josie because I was with other kids. A little over a year ago they'd been settling into an Oregon retirement; now they were cheering on a kid—*their* kid—at baseball games. I worked hard at making myself a better second baseman—improved my flip to shortstop, got to more grounders up the middle, learned to shade my eyes with my glove as I tracked a pop-up.

I still struggled with the bat, but I got some help on that from an unexpected source. Raven called and drove over to visit, and he came to a game with my fosters. I handled all my chances at second but went 0 for 4, and afterward Raven asked politely if I would be receptive to some coaching on my left-handed swing.

"From you?" I said.

"You're a natural slap-hitter trying to be a slugger," he said. "Don't try to pull it, don't try to kill it, just go with the pitch. If it comes in on the outer half of the plate, lead with your hands, meet the ball with the barrel of the bat, and rap it to left field. If you try to pull that pitch, you'll miss it or foul it or hit a weak tapper. As in your"—he cleared his throat—"first two at-bats."

I stared at him. "That's what my father used to say. How do you know all that?"

Raven laughed. "You can be gay and enjoy athletics, Henry. It's not against nature."

"You played?"

"Summer ball, like you. I wanted to play in high school, but a few of the players had figured me out and were nasty about it. I've watched a lot of baseball. It's a beautiful game."

"Well I'll be go to hell," I said, mimicking Len Peppers. "You surely are a wonder, Green Eyes."

He had arrived at noon with a gift of Sweet Grass smoked sausage and spiced pear jam. Cart and Josie found him delightful, asked him questions about the Confederacy and talked about their experiences in communities back in the Stoned Age. Raven talked art and politics with them too, disagreeing now and then, with an ease I didn't have and doubted I ever would. He had been in their Bay Area bookstore once, it turned out, and he wanted to know all about the book business. I got a little grumpy, the odd boy out. What was I supposed to do, go play with my toys? But I watched Raven with admiration. He was so comfortable, here in my home world. He seemed older, more adult—not so many years my senior, and so much more knowledgeable. He was wearing jeans and a faded blue work shirt and a pair of brown hiking boots.

Raven stayed over on a cot in Cart's study, and after breakfast I took him to some of the points of my compass—Brother Jim Butte, Noble Dog Ridge, and the cool and leafy stretches of Evelyn's Run and the Long Tom River, where we spied on little cutthroat trout and crawdads going about their day. At the edge of an alder woods we came on a doe with twin spotted fawns. I gestured for Raven to hold up and stepped slowly ahead. The doe and fawns fixed me in their eyes. Our spirits touched, like trembling soap bubbles meeting in air, but *pop*—the mother turned and high-stepped away, tail in the air, the fawns right behind her on their legs too long for their bodies.

"That's what I get for trying to show off," I said. "But my gift's gotten really sketchy, too."

"Is it any wonder, Henry? You're like that bobcat. Your spirit's been knocked for a loop. . . ."

"I guess," I said. We started walking again.

"It'll come back, Henry. Don't lose faith."

"I don't know," I said. "I keep thinking my bad luck is over, and right away there's trouble again."

Raven raised his eyebrows.

"Well, it won't be big trouble. Did you hear about that bulldozer that got sabotaged over at Karen Creek?"

Raven nodded.

"Well," I said, "I did it."

He burst out laughing. "Sure you did."

"No. I really did. I poured the engine oil and diesel full of grit."

Raven stopped. "Henry. . . . My God, you mean it."

So I told him about my two secret missions that rainy, blowy night, which I'd left out of the story I'd told him at Sweet Grass. We talked about it as we hiked an old logging road toward Dismal Acre.

I explained that I didn't regret monkeywrenching the Cat, because they meant to do damage to the forest with it.

Raven said nothing. We kept walking. Then: "But is that really why you did it, Henry?"

"Well sure it was."

"It wasn't that you'd just been raped and were consumed with anger at your father?"

"Yeah, that too. . . ."

"Would you have done it if you hadn't been raped?"

"Please stop using that word. Are you a lawyer or something?"

Raven paid no attention. "Does it bother you that Cart and the others are under suspicion?"

"Are you on my side or what, Raven? They can't prove it on 'em. Nobody's goin' to jail."

We kept on walking. The grassy logging road was thick with daisies in the sunny stretches. Bees were working the last white blooms of the blackberry patches. Somewhere off to our right a nuthatch gave its small, lonesome call.

"I can't believe they left it there all winter," I said. "It's like they were daring somebody to mess with it."

* * *

After church on Sunday I talked with Jonah and Pastor Rogers about an idea for a kids' group. The pastor had doubts about my name for it, the Holy Handymen, but he did like the idea—a squad of teenagers committed to a few hours every month mowing lawns, trimming bushes, painting walls, or whatever needed doing for the elderly in our congregation. Jonah and the pastor said they'd help out when we needed some guidance. Cart had said he would too, though not with Jonah. Josie had forgiven him, but not Cart. I told Jonah and the pastor that Cart thought the group should be called the Secular Humanist Handymen, which made Pastor Rogers a little happier with my choice.

Jonah drove me home with his elbow out the open window. "I've been thinking about our last talk," he said. "Have you heard of 'projection,' Henry? It's when a guy sees aspects of his own character in others. No offense, now, but don't you think the God you're imagining is a teenage God? You know, an immature God trying to find himself?"

"Could be. So what are you projecting, a grownup God? Why's that truer than mine?"

"Well, for two thousand years a whole lot of people've been projecting the same picture. Kind of validates it, don't you think?"

"Yeah, except for everyone who's been projecting Allah, or the Great Spirit, or Nature with a capital N. . . ."

"Well, they're missing the full truth in my opinion, but even those are long traditions."

"Hey, traditions start somewhere. And the universe could *be* a teenager, Jonah. Fourteen billion sounds old, but maybe in universe-years it's only fourteen. Might not even be old enough to drive."

Jonah chuckled. "Good thing God's there to steer, then."

"I don't think it's steering, but I agree it's not just 'Stuff Happens.' There's something urging it along, giving it room for mistakes and accidents. Something wants it to succeed. Wants *us* to succeed . . . but it's up to us to get there."

"Hmm," said Jonah. "And 'there' might be something like the Kingdom of God?"

"I've always liked that name," I said.

"But the Kingdom is right here, Henry, for all who open their hearts."

"Yep. Right here, back there, still ahead. There's no end to it."

* * *

At Sweet Grass, Raven had told me about taking psychedelic mushrooms. It was unlike anything else, he said, not a drug for fun—though some fun was likely—but a medicine for consciousness. "Mushrooms woke my being," he said. "It's as though I hadn't been all the way alive." I was interested, Raven said he'd think about giving me some, and when he came for his visit he brought a few spindly gray-brown mushrooms in a zip-up plastic bag. "Most kids your age wouldn't be ready for this," he told me, "but I think you are, Henry. You've got the sense of self and the spiritual imagination to handle it. It might help you clarify things."

Be alone, he said. Be outdoors in a place you love with nothing else to do for a whole day and evening. Bring a notebook. Eat the mushrooms. Meditate, clear your mind. Expect nothing.

I'd been pretty responsible since the disastrous date and the fight at school, so my fosters smiled and said okay when I asked if I could camp alone at the coast for a couple of nights. A friend at Oregon State had showed my father an almost-secret spot on the central coast where it looked impossible to get down the rock bluff but you could, down to a tiny beach you can't see from the highway. My dad had taken me there a few times. I parked and locked the white Dodge up a gravel road east of U.S. 101, got into my pack straps, hiked north a quarter-mile on the highway shoulder pretending to be a hitchhiker who wasn't even trying, then waited for a break in the traffic and bolted across the road, vaulted the guard rail, and slipped down into a slot between slabs of basalt. The slot turned into a chimney, easy down-climbing, which led to another slab that angled down to the beach. The last part had sketchy footing, but someone had bolted a nylon rope to the rock face for a handrail.

I set up camp in a sandy-floored cave that went way back under the bluff, above the high-tide line, where you see nothing but sky and the great river with one bank, as the coastal Indians called it. Cars and trucks pass above on 101 but you'd never know it, their noise drowned in the tireless boom and rumble of surf. I spent the evening walking the little beach, breathing salt air and wondering where the waves were born and how long ago. A bright half-moon came over the rocky brink, turning the breakers silvery as they crested and collapsed in sliding sheets of foam. I woke now and then that night to the pound and spew of high-tide breakers, the spent waters hissing as they withdrew over sand and pebbles into the next wave.

In the morning I made tea and oatmeal on Cart's backpacking stove, then ate the mushrooms and sat down trying to expect nothing. Half an hour later I was expecting nothing with a headache, a little sick in my stomach. I lay down for a while and just got grumpier, so I gave up on getting high and left the cave. Wind on my face, bare feet in the sand . . . nothing was different but everything was. The air was charged with light. My mind had melted into my body. I knew who I was, and who I was opened out into everything there. Two seagulls veering and crying overhead were such . . . *seagulls*, the sea such a bright roiling cauldron, and suddenly I was crying in helpless wonderment.

I tried to say in words how amazing it was, how beautiful, but the words kept tangling—*because I'm trying to say what I already know*, it came to me, and I laughed out loud.

Time expanded, one ongoing moment. I gazed into tide pools at anemones and sea stars and tiny crabs scuttling sideways. I stood singing long low tones that mingled, perfectly it seemed, with the infinitely variable voice of the sea. I took off my clothes, rolled and crawled and half-buried myself in warm sand. The light darkened—sudden fear!—but it was only a cloud passing under the sun, and soon I was laved in light again. I sprinted down over wet sand and plowed through the shallows and dove headlong into a wave. Came up sputtering, bellowing, burning with cold, and dashed out to the warm sand again.

Later I sat looking out to sea on a rock shelf, and every person I cared about came to me, one at a time, their faces forming and fading. I greeted each one. My mother came first, my father came last, and for him I felt love and sadness—but a streak of joy, too. I was on my own, just setting out, my life ahead like a range of mountains, forest and rivers and peaks unknown. I noticed the scars on my arms, and the awareness that was me and more than me felt sorrow for the boy who had cut his skin. But I knew for truth that the scars were mere scratches on the surface of what I was.

At dusk I drank tea in the cave, sitting in the dark with a flooding desire there was nothing I could do with. I yearned for Tess, for *someone*. . . . It felt better to move, so I went out and walked the short beach back and forth. The moon was a blurred luster through clouds. The trouble and cares of my regular life were returning, gaining weight like snowfall, and it felt a lot like coming out of my gift with an animal. A letdown, a pang. I learned that day that only when I was in my gift had I ever been alive to the present moment. What we call the present is actually the flickering film of what just was, not the moment itself. Not the treasure.

I walked back and forth with my troubles and the joy of the afternoon came again, the enveloping warmth, and I remembered—of all things—my father, five or six years before, showing me the green chain at Siuslaw Pacific. "Watch how they do it," he said, shouting over the din. There were two workers on each side of the wide conveyor belt that carried heavy green planks and timbers out of the mill. Each guy was looking for lumber of a certain dimension, and when a piece came along he tugged it partway off the belt and at just the right moment shoved the end down, levering the plank off the belt onto rollers lining the sides, and let it slide through his gloved hands along his leather-aproned hip, guiding it neatly into place on the stack. They weren't burly guys, my father pointed out. A plank might weigh fifty pounds, but the mill hands had learned to work with the belt. "You channel its power right through you," my dad said. "Fight the belt, get your ass kicked. Work with it, you get paid."

Now, walking the beach, I saw my father's red hair, his hazel eyes full of light, and I heard his patient way of speaking, his freckled hands pointing and guiding, when he tried to teach me what he thought I should know.

I probably spent half the night on that beach, feelings drifting through me like mist. I felt the seething greatness of the sea that gave me birth, its moist breath, the firm wet sand beneath me. *I can handle it*, I understood. *I can bear this load.* I walked and walked, going nowhere because I was already there. I walked not wise as winter is gray, not wise by any reckoning, but alive to the journey, pacing toward what I know.

part four

Morning is when I am awake and there is a dawn in me.

—Henry Thoreau, from *Walden*

twenty-seven

Cart and Josie took the news pretty well, shocked more than anything. Josie was compassionate, said it was understandable under the circumstances. Cart just grimaced and said, with a wry smile, "You've evolved as an activist further than I'd imagined, Henry." Then they started talking about how we should handle it.

I felt a lot better after confessing and started thinking about what books I'd take with me to prison, how many pens and pads of paper. I'd have plenty of time. Maybe I'd write a book. I hoped I'd have a window. I might have to work, I realized vaguely, and I really hoped they wouldn't put me in one of those gangs clearing weeds and litter on the roadside, on display in a day-glow orange jumpsuit.

Cart consulted the enviro-lawyers who were carrying the legal fight on Karen Creek, and they recommended James Rodnips, a respected defense attorney who had represented many juveniles (a word I would hear a lot and get very sick of). Cart and Josie met with him and told him about my mother dying and my father's abuse. Then the three of us met with Mr. Rodnips at his office in downtown Eugene. He had thinning dark hair, a silvering black beard, and he looked like he'd been doing a lot of reading. He was wearing a white dress shirt and slacks.

"Well, Henry," he said when we'd got settled, "here it is in a nutshell. You're probably looking at a charge of criminal mischief."

"Mischief?" I said. "That doesn't sound serious."

"Not serious in the least. For Criminal Mischief in the First Degree, they can only lock you up for five years."

"Whoa."

"Mmm-hmm. Breaking the law has consequences, Henry. Even if you did it for a good cause, even if you've suffered abuse, even if your mother died recently, even if you're sorry you did it, even if you turn yourself in."

I felt heavy in my chair. "I don't know what to say."

"Good," said Mr. Rodnips. "Means you heard me."

He smiled, which proved that he could, and leaned forward, elbows on his desk. "Now, your record is clean, you've had the courage to admit to the crime, and I think any judge will agree you've had a pretty terrible year. All that will be taken into consideration. I'm confident you won't get five years, but you should expect to do a little time."

"How much time? Where?"

"Best case, just a couple of days in the Juvie lockup here in town. Now here's the plan. No guarantees, but I will seek a plea agreement with the D.A.'s office that's called a diversion. You plead guilty to Criminal Mischief in the First Degree, and the court grants you a one-year diversion with four conditions. You will make full restitution for the damage you caused, you will get psychological counseling for the trauma you've experienced, you will report regularly to your caseworker as instructed, and you will obey all laws.

"Bottom line? Satisfy all conditions for one year, and the charge will be dismissed. It never happened. Fail on any of the four conditions, though, and you could do some serious time."

"How much is the rest . . . restitution?" I asked.

"We don't know yet, but certainly upwards of ten thousand dollars. Your foster parents tell me you have a life insurance settlement."

I nodded, relieved to be reminded, but cringing at the thought of telling Jonah Rutledge why I needed him to write a very very large check.

"Must he be locked up at all?" Josie asked.

"It's standard in cases like this. The soup is pretty bad. If you make the delinquent take a spoonful or two, he'll be less likely to order it again."

Mr. Rodnips leaned back in his chair, hands clasped behind his head. "I'll work hard for this agreement, Henry, but I need you to do your part. Will you work with me?"

"I will, sir."

"Have you been in any other trouble I should know about?"

I froze.

"He was in a fight at school this spring," Josie said. "Henry was considered the aggressor, but the other boy taunted him about him and his father."

I looked at my feet, my face hot.

"That won't help," Mr. Rodnips said. He asked a few questions, then instructed the three of us to write a detailed account of the fight. "If the D.A. digs it up," he said, "we'll deal with it best we can."

"Mr. Rodnips?" I said. "Can we go and do it right now?"

"Do what?"

"Turn myself in."

He laughed. "Never on a Friday, Henry. When we do that, they'll probably release you back to your foster parents pending arraignment, but somebody might be having a bad day, or the planets might be lined up wrong, and they might take you into custody and you'd be stuck there all weekend.

"What are you doing Wednesday morning next week?" he asked with a chuckle. "Are you free?"

* * *

Wednesday morning came warm and muggy, after one of those rare summer nights in Oregon that don't cool down much after a hot day. In the distance as we drove to town, haze was blurring the Cascade foothills. In the flats past Fern Ridge Dam it wasn't hard to imagine the land as it might have looked to the Chelamela—roads and cars and houses gone, powerlines and fences too, just a broad prairie, the tall grass green with silvery sheens in a breeze, bounded only by the mountains and a forest of oak and cottonwood along the great Willamette. Most Chelamelas would be away in the hills this time of year, hunting and fishing and gathering, but there might be smoke from a cooking fire, a few low wooden lodges, a few human figures moving in the grass under the hazy blue sky—ordinary creatures going about their lives, like the hawks and deer and the fish in the river.

If only we could start again, I thought. Maybe we could do better.

James Rodnips was waiting for us, in a light-colored suit and tie, in front of the Juvenile Justice Center in Eugene. It's a serious-looking building—a lot of brick and metal, tall concrete columns around the entrance. I had on my best blue dress shirt and khaki pants and some brown leather shoes Josie had bought me, which were stiff and made my toes hurt. Cart and Josie were spiffed up too. The four of us looked fine enough to take a limo up I-5 to the fanciest restaurant in Portland.

"Well, Henry, you ready?" asked Mr. Rodnips.

I had flutters inside, my mouth was dry, I just hoped I'd be able to speak. I nodded, and we walked in. Right away we had to unload our pockets and go through a metal detector. I'd been imagining this moment and had worked up a dramatic statement: "I believe you've been looking for the criminal who sabotaged that bulldozer up at Karen Creek? Well, my name is Henry Fielder and I'm your guy." I didn't get to say it, of course, because Mr. Rodnips had been talking with Juvie and they knew all about me and were expecting us. A caseworker Mr. Rodnips had worked with before, Ms. Matheson, came out and introduced herself and led me down a hallway to an interview room, Mr. Rodnips at my side with a hand on my shoulder. It all felt unreal. All I could think was, *What beautiful red hair. . . .* Cart and Josie had to wait in the lobby.

Ms. Matheson was serious but not mean as she explained what we'd be doing. At Mr. Rodnips's request she turned on an electronic recorder, and she also took notes as we talked. She asked what had led me to commit the crime, how I had learned how to do it, every detail of what I'd done and my thoughts and feelings as I did it and afterward. Afterward was all about the earthquake and my father, I said. I told her what she had heard from Mr. Rodnips, which was what he had been told by Cart and Josie, which was what they had been told by me when I first arrived back at Dismal Acre I'd tried to save my father, but he died before I could reach him. It wasn't the truth, but even Lynn agrees that sometimes you have to lie.

I lied some more when Ms. Matheson asked if I had regretted my crime in the weeks and months that followed. I nodded, said I'd regretted it a lot, but I was grieving for my parents and worried what would happen to me and still angry at my father, and my regret kind of got lost in all that. Ms. Matheson of the glorious red hair didn't exactly melt. She said she was aware of the trauma I'd experienced, but that eight months was a long time to wait, and if I had turned myself in earlier the damage to the bulldozer could have been avoided.

I wish I'd done that, I said. Now that I have more perspective, I told her, I regret with all my heart that I didn't speak up sooner. I bowed my head. For once in the past year I *wanted* to cry, but I couldn't. My dry eyes spoke truer than the words from my mouth.

Afterward, Mr. Rodnips told me I'd done fine. He and Ms. Matheson spoke privately for a while, and when he came out to the lobby he was smiling.

"You'll be arraigned a week from today, Henry. They're preparing the citation now, and once you have it you can go home. I'll be working toward the plea deal. Just don't be late for arraignment, all right? Judges frown on that."

He reached out his hand and we shook.

* * *

A few days later I took Tess for a hike around Brother Jim Butte, to show her how the second-growth Doug-fir forest gives way as you circle south to oaks and pines and a few madrones. It was a muggy gray day and pretty soon it was barely raining, just enough to wet the brush we were whacking through and raise its gorgeous scent.

My misadventure with the law had upset Tess—because she was concerned for me, but also, I was picking up, because this new dimension of delinquency was stretching her comfort zone. She wondered why *I* wasn't upset. "It's out of my hands," I said. "Whatever happens, happens."

"I doubt your foster parents are so easy with it," she said.

"They're not. But they're not in my hands either, right?"

"They love you, Henry. I'm sure they're worried sick."

I turned around—I'd been breaking trail—and opened my arms. "You'll come see me when I'm locked up, won't you? You won't be too embarrassed?"

She pushed me away. "It's not all a joke, Henry. People worry about you, and you don't care."

She kept up a game face as we walked, and we talked a little, but her pants and socks were wet from bushwhacking, she had bits of brush all over her, and the vibe was not positive. She liked the madrones, which were the biggest she'd seen, but the oaks and pines, she said, were like trees she saw every day.

I went to her and started picking bits out of her hair. "I'm sorry, Tess. I know I'm different."

"I love your difference, Henry. But you keep yourself inside so much. You're hard to know. . . ."

"Well, how's this," I said, and tried to kiss her. She pushed me away again, gently.

"Well hell," I said. "First I'm too enclosed and then I'm too close. And I'm too easy-going, too. I'm just *me*, Tess. Isn't that all right?"

Her lips tightened, her eyes shining with tears.

"I'm sorry I dragged you up here," I said. "I thought it would be fun."

"It is, Henry. It's Henry-fun. But I like to do other things too, things in town, with other people. Would that be so hard?"

I shrugged. "We can start back now."

I led us overtop the butte, which isn't that much of a climb, through maturing forest and then a replanted clearcut, the new trees about twelve feet tall.

We were watching our feet, navigating the slash and broken ground. I headed us toward a big blackberry patch in an open area on the far side of the cut. As we got close, I felt uneasy. Then my spirit warped and shrieked and a black bear reared up tall behind the patch. I heard rustling in the replant trees to our right.

"She's got cubs," I said, grabbing Tess's arm. "Don't run. We're gonna back up slowly. Now."

"*SORRY, BEAR, WE MEAN NO HARM. . . ,*" I chanted. "Say it with me, Tess, loud. *SORRY, BEAR, WE MEAN NO HARM. . . .*" Her trembling voice joined my trembling voice. Suddenly I caught a boot and fell hard on my back. The bear dropped to all fours and charged out beside the bramble patch. She slapped the ground with a paw, and Tess gave a little cry.

"All she wants is for us to leave," I said. "Keep backin' off. *WE ARE SMALL, BEAR, YOU ARE GREAT . . . WE ARE SMALL, BEAR, YOU ARE GREAT. . . .*"

One cub, then another, scurried out of hiding toward their mother. We kept backing till we lost sight of them through the replant trees, and soon we were in standing forest again.

"She won't follow us, will she?"

"No. We startled her, that's all. Everything she did was defensive."

"My God, Henry. She stood so *tall*."

"She wanted a better view. Bears have bad eyes."

"I've never been so scared in my life."

"That means her plan worked perfectly. Wait a second." I put my hands together, went to my shaky knees, and bowed my head to the ground in the bear family's direction. Then I took Tess's hand and we hopped and laughed ourselves down the mountainside the way we had come.

When we got to the big madrones, Tess stopped and pulled my face to hers. She was beautiful, her brown eyes just a shade darker than her hair, the misting rain glazing her face like an apple on the branch. We kissed, a long one, lips parted. I stroked her sides, her thighs, and soon we were down on the moss and sticks and grass, two ordinary creatures getting after it.

* * *

In the courtroom we sat in the spectator seats with Mr. Rodnips, waiting for my case to be called. It was a busy day in Juvenile Court, a lot of arraignments and pleadings and other business. When I heard my name, Mr. Rodnips led us forward through the gate and to the left. We stood behind a table facing the judge. A deputy district attorney was sitting at a table to our right, and my caseworker, Ms. Matheson, joined him there. The judge looked to be sixty or so, with a gray buzz-cut and a not-very-Oregonian tanned face. He summoned Mr. Rodnips to the bench—that's what they call it, but it's high and handsome and more like a throne, or at least a pulpit—to give him the statement of charges against me. Mr. Rodnips and I read along on his copy as the judge read it out loud in a stern voice—Criminal Mischief in the First Degree, up to five years in custody. . . . The judge then asked if I understood the charge and the possible penalties, and I said I did. "Very well, then, Mr. Fielder, how do you plead?"

"Uh . . . not guilty, your honor."

The judge looked at Mr. Rodnips with raised eyebrows, and Mr. Rodnips explained that he, the caseworker, and the prosecution had begun a plea negotiation and were confident that an agreement could soon be reached. The judge turned his head toward the other table, where the deputy D.A. rose and concurred.

"Get it done, gentlemen," said the judge. He set a date, asked the deputy if the state had any objection to me remaining out of custody in the meantime, the deputy said he didn't, and we were done.

"The deal is coming along," Mr. Rodnips told us, out in the hall. "But I have to warn you, Henry. This judge is kind of a hard-ass. I think he'll accept our agreement, but he doesn't have to. He can give you anything, right up to the maximum. Now, before he pronounces sentence he'll direct you to talk about what you did, and why. What you tell him, and how you tell it, will be crucial. Be ready."

"And will they haul me off to Juvie right from court?"

Mr. Rodnips smiled. "I'll warn you if that's their intent, but my experience tells me they'll give you a date to report."

He gave me a pat on the shoulder and we said good-bye.

Cart and Josie and I went to lunch at Fifth Street Market, then walked around Eugene for a couple of hours. The town looked pretty well healed from the Thanksgiving Quake. Some buildings had fresh, repaired faces. Several had been rebuilt or reinforced, including the old churches used as winter warming centers. The one that had collapsed and killed four people was now a vacant lot. The city was thinking about buying the land and putting up some kind of monument to honor the dead and injured, and to remind everyone that we had experienced only a wake-up shake. The Big One is still coming, tomorrow, next year, next decade.

The city and county had waked up to the embarrassing fact that there wasn't enough morgue space even for the casualties of the Little One—they'd actually had to borrow a refrigerated meat wagon from Portland to hold a few bodies for a while. People in the South Hills, in some of the nicest neighborhoods, had learned the risk of building on hillsides in a wet climate where hills occasionally rumble, and out our way, where some streams were still running muddy, I hoped we were getting it that too much clearcutting and road cutting is a good way to lose mountainsides and human lives too. People kept saying what a perfect storm it had been, rain and wind and quake all together, and *that* surely wouldn't happen again. But it will, of course. Coincidence is a specialty of this universe, and it always happens when it does.

We walked, we stopped for coffee at an outdoor espresso place, we went into a bike shop, a gallery, J. Michaels Books. The afternoon was warm but with a breath of wind. Now and then I took glances at the man and woman I was walking with. Carter Stephens, he of the careless Euramericano, had changed in the parking garage into shorts and his green Chelamela Village t-shirt. He had slimmed considerably from his hours on a bicycle, indoors and out, and though his saggy eyes and lined face made him look a little tired, he walked with a saunter, as though he intended to live long. And Josie Stephens, lithe and light on her sneakered feet, her long graying brown hair gathered in a girlish ponytail, looked around constantly as she walked, shooting a picture now and then with the small camera she always had with her. When she wasn't smiling, her lined face promised it was just about to.

How did I get so lucky? I wondered. I'm in a *family*. I felt my mother there, a brief warm shiver on my right shoulder.

We had started our homeschool sessions. Cart and Josie had me reading some challenging books, had me thinking and writing and doing geometry problems. Cart, sometimes Josie too, critiqued my writing and gave it back to me for revision. I studied in the darkroom, too, and in the kitchen. Cooking, to me, had meant dropping bread into the toaster or roasting hotdogs *a la* Len Peppers. Now I was learning how to make meals. I was tutoring Cart in country music, but it was a hard sell. He was having better luck tutoring me in classical.

It wasn't fair to compare my new schooling with what my father had tried to give me, so I didn't. He'd had the right idea but was the wrong teacher. Mostly I just felt sorry that he'd never had anyone in his life, apart from my mother, to open his mind and imagination. He never developed all the branches and leaves he could have. Some of it was his own fault, for sure—aside from meeting Eileen Durham, he'd more or less wasted his time at OSU, and he just wasn't very curious about anything other than hunting, fishing, sports, work, and his family. He'd had to work hard and grow up fast, from the day his father died beneath his tractor in that Missouri ditch. Maybe that had hardened him somehow. I didn't know then and don't know now.

At the old house, earlier in the summer, I'd found a snapshot of my dad fishing, from around the time I was born. He was skinnier then, his hair almost to his shoulders, a mustache down the sides of his mouth. He was smiling, a sharp glitter in his eyes. It wasn't hard to feel what my mother had felt. He was a very attractive man, and in that moment a happy man. And now he was nowhere, except in my dreams where I didn't want him. I'd stopped talking about him with Cart and Josie, with Tess too, because they always told me not to feel bad, he probably would have died anyway, and what he'd done to me was so awful, so terrible, *of course* I'd walked out on him. . . . Bullshit. I did him far worse than he'd done me. It stuck in my throat like a bone I couldn't cough up.

I'd been biking over to the old place every now and again, to look for any last things I wanted to keep. The two trees that had crushed the middle of the house had been bucked and hauled to the mill, the rootwads and slash piled for burning when the rains arrived. Jonah and his friend Chris, a builder and the most skilled jack-of-all-trades in the Long Tom region, did the bucking and trimming, the loading and hauling, and I told them to keep the cash they got paid at the mill. Jonah had done a lot for me and my dad, and he had gone through his own hell as surely as I had through mine. Besides, I was getting richer all the time. The home insurance company had come through in the end—out of pity, probably—and wrote a big enough check to pay off the mortgage with a few thousand left over.

The day after the arraignment, I went to the house one more time and realized I had everything. My mother's books were on shelves that Cart and I had built against my bedroom walls. The tools, which Dismal Acre much needed, were stowed in the garage and shed. And I had the things I treasured most—small things of my mother's that my father had saved in his top dresser drawer. When I touched those, I touched him touching her. The silver chain she liked to wear, with a turquoise set in silver. Their wedding rings, hers of worked silver, his a plain gold band which Jonah had slipped off his finger and stashed in the drawer. And of course I had the dreamcatcher from my mother's white Dodge. It was hanging from the lamp on my desk, with me as I wrote my essays and letters and pieces I hoped were poems or stories, and it's been with me all the years since. That woven willow hoop hangs in my Southeast Portland apartment, next to me at this kitchen table where I eat and write. For some reason I'd left it in a drawer, and when I started this book and language wasn't exactly rushing onto the page, Lynn came over, asked where it was, and hung it from my work lamp.

I got off my bike, stared at that rotting, back-broken house, and didn't even go in. I sat in the backyard and remembered, daydreamed. The house was dead as a home could be, but it was my whole life, too.

It was me and my mother and father, my strange little cockeyed family. Suddenly I knew what to do. "You're gonna be beautiful," I said to the house and biked home happy, the wind fresh on my face.

In my bedroom I wrote a long letter to Raven. I thanked him for steering me with questions and eloquent silence toward taking responsibility for sabotaging the Cat. I told him I was lucky to know him, lucky to have hiked out of the mountains right down Stranger Creek to his porch, right to someone who cared for me and helped me back into my life and could talk with me about chance and destiny and God and time and all the mysteries that stir my spirit. How does luck happen? I asked. How is it that my father abuses me and I move my bed to keep him away and two nights later that saves my life? How does it happen that I hole up in a hollow log on the coldest night of winter and by all rights should freeze to death, but my mother in spirit and a visitant in warm flesh come in the night and keep me alive? How is it that wild creatures sometimes aren't scared of me and we can touch in a way I don't understand, yet it's as real as rain? How does it happen that Nature grows a plain little fungus that just happens to be a sacrament that opens the human heart and spirit to the nature of Nature itself?

I went on and on, writing on nice heavy paper I'd bought at a stationery store. I wrote with a pencil, so that I could make changes without making a mess, but I didn't erase that much. What the pencil wrote felt right and so I followed its lead, and when I was ready to send the letter I had to use a ten-by-thirteen brown envelope and spend three dollars at the post office to mail it.

twenty-eight

I was at my bedroom desk, doing homework, when a motion caught my eye in the light-spill outside the window. An orb-weaver spider was doing her thing. I turned off the lamp and watched with a flashlight to see it better. She had already made a few anchor lines between two big rhododendrons, and one or two going down to a fern, and she had made an outside circle and the spokes. Now she was laying down her sticky web—the anchors and spokes are different silk, not sticky—circling it spoke to spoke from the outside in, spiraling toward the center. She needed all her legs, because two or three of them would be moving her from one spoke to the next while another leg or two guided the silk from her belly and a couple of others took the strand and stuck it to the spoke while those first two or three were already moving to the next one. That sounds slow, but she was *fast*—a nimble dancer homing in, and when she was done she rested, smack-dab in the middle of what she had made.

I don't know what those spiders do the rest of the year, but early fall is when I used to see their webwork strung like dreamcatchers between tree branches and under the eaves of houses and sheds and out in the bushy clearcuts and thin woods where sun gets in and careless insects fly. In daylight the spider tucks behind a leaf, connected to the web with a strand of silk, and when she feels motion she's instantly traveling the spokes to the fly or moth that's having the worst and last few seconds of its life. She's blind, completely blind, but she goes right to the spot. She sees with her legs, with her whole being. She knows where she is. She knows what to do.

When this spider had finished and was resting I went to bed, wishing I'd noticed her sooner. How did she make that first connection, from a twig on one rhododendron to a twig on the other? You see those support lines strung sometimes across four, five, six feet of space. I vaguely remembered reading that she gets to a high perch and spins out a long line and lets it drift in the wind until it catches somewhere. From the middle of that line she drops a new one down to an anchor below, then adds other anchors and she's in business. But that first one, what if there's no wind? She couldn't drop down and walk the line over, she'd get it fouled. . . . And then, as I was melting into the great river, I remembered being out in the autumn night watching those tiny specks of mist swirl through the flashlight beam, never still, spirited by a silent breeze my skin couldn't feel.

* * *

The first rains came in late September, heavy, and people were saying oh no, not again, but the wet fronts eased off in October, some rain some sun, the sunshine coming down on the yellowing leaves of alders and big-leaf maples with a hint of that slanted light that Emily wrote her poem about, wind stirring the tops of the tall Douglas firs with the rising and falling sealike murmur from far away that made me sad and happy at the same time. Whole armies of crows set down in Jimmy Hepworth's pasture, yakking raucously in their crow tongue like a festival of young lords shouting jeers and challenges. We cut firewood from dead limbs on Dismal Acre and dead trees I felled on the ten acres that now belonged to me. We picked chanterelle mushrooms, too, and relieved the two old trees by the house of several bushels of apples, which Josie and I turned into applesauce and apple butter and apple crisp and apple pies.

I fretted about Abner a lot. He hadn't called or emailed since our time at the river, and of course I hadn't either. Tess told me he was obsessed with his girlfriend. I asked if he had said anything about me—she said no, and wondered why I was asking. Then, in Dairy Queen one afternoon, there he was in a very full booth. He saw me before I could turn away. "Fielder!" he called, shaking his brown dreadlocks, "get over here, man!" I mumbled that I couldn't, I was late, and peeled off for the men's room as if that had been my mission. Abner hollered again when I came out. I just waved and looked down and got out of there.

Tess and I were doing fine. She ate with us at Dismal Acre now and again, and she and her mom and her mom's guy-friend had hosted me at her home. I met some of her friends and went to a party or two with her, too many people at a time for me but tolerable if we didn't stay too long. I was trying not to drink. Tess and I and a few of my Holy Handymen had a blast painting an old couple's house in one day. She appreciated my willingness to give Tess-fun a try, and we found time for some Henry-fun too.

I'd been expecting a letter from Raven, and didn't get one, and worried that the huge sheaf I'd sent him had been total garbage and he didn't know how to politely respond. Then I answered a knock on the door one afternoon, and it was Raven himself in jeans and a UO hoodie.

"Hey!" I said.

He smiled, but there was no calm in his emerald eyes. "Could we talk, Henry? Not in the house?"

I took him around back to the little woods. We sat on the ground, Raven with his arms around his knees.

"First," he said, "thank you for *all* you wrote me. You really opened yourself, Henry. It was a beautiful gift."

"Glad to hear it. I worried it might've. . . ."

Raven shook his head, smiling. Then he closed his eyes, took a deep breath, and let it go.

"I wanted to respond in kind, but my feelings are just too wild. I tried not to come here. And right now I'm trying not to say what I came to say, though you already know it anyway, so I'll say it. . . . I'm in love with you, Henry. There's no other word. And I shouldn't be telling you that, it's entirely unfair—"

"What's unfair? You're just being honest."

Raven took and released another breath. When he spoke his pale face was childlike, his voice timid. "Henry, do you feel anything like that for me?"

I was quiet a long time. "I think I love you like a best friend," I finally said. "Or like . . . like the best big brother in the world."

Raven looked down, nodding his head. "I thought so," he said. "And it's probably for the best. If you did love me the way I love you, it would be complicated."

"Why?"

"Because you're too young."

"Says who?" I scoffed. "That's my business."

"The state makes it its business, Henry, and there's reason for it. You're sixteen, you've had the most awful year, you're vulnerable, you've got a girlfriend, and here I am dumping my feelings all over you. Just what I pledged to myself I *wouldn't* do."

"Hey," I whispered, crawling over to him. He hugged my head to his chest. I could hear his heart. "You're not hurting me, Raven. You're the last guy in the world who would. I'm just sorry *you* hurt so much."

He kissed the top of my head then held me away hands-on-shoulders, his ridiculously beautiful eyes glistening with tears. His spirit was pouring in a flood.

"Someday, Henry Fielder, you will hurt like this."

"Gosh, thanks," I laughed. "Do I have to?"

"If Fate is at all fair, yes, you'll have to."

"You know," I said as we walked to his truck, "my mother told me that I'd know it when I fell in love. 'How?' I asked. 'You just will,' she said. Trouble is, I'm not the smartest critter in the woods. I don't always know what I'm feeling."

Raven put his arm across my shoulders. "You and many other young men, Henry. But you're doing a great job of being yourself."

I slung my arm over his.

"Hey," I said through the open window when he started the engine. "Can you come back in two weeks? I'm throwin' a party."

* * *

I'd always thought of libraries as something our country does right, public places where people go for private reasons, respecting everybody's right to do the same. Same with voting, and maybe courts belong on that list too, I thought to myself as I sat with Mr. Rodnips and Cart and Josie waiting to be sentenced. Nobody has a gun, nobody cusses or swings a fist. People dress up—a little, at least—to show respect, everyone has rights, the stories get told and the lawyers argue and we all say "your honor" to a guy in a black robe who's no better or worse than anybody else. He gets to decide things, or twelve ordinary people do, because one way or another we've chosen them to do that. It's not perfect, but what is?

When I stood with Mr. Rodnips before the judge with the gray buzz-cut, the deputy district attorney read out loud the terms of the negotiation. I would plead guilty to Criminal Mischief in the First Degree. I would be sentenced to pay restitution in the amount of

22,174 dollars for damage to the bulldozer; to receive therapy for my trauma; to report regularly to my caseworker as instructed; and to obey all laws. I would also serve five days in the custody of the Department of Youth Services. Mr. Rodnips had proposed two days, but the deputy D.A. had wanted more. That shocked me a bit, but not the restitution bill. Mr. Rodnips had told us, and Jonah, with a grimace and a few choice words, had already written the check.

The judge asked in a flat voice if I understood the charge to which I would be pleading guilty. I said I did. He asked if I understood that the maximum penalty under the law was not five days but five years in custody, and that he, the judge, was free to impose any penalty allowed by law. "I understand," I said, queasy in my gut. It was one thing to have Mr. Rodnips explain it in his office. It was another to hear it from a guy on a throne in a black robe who sounded like an Army general about to sentence a soldier to the firing squad.

"Mr. Fielder," he said, staring me down over his black-framed reading glasses, "tell me exactly what you did to that bulldozer."

My mouth was dry as feathers. I couldn't speak. Josie handed me a glass of water from the table and I could talk then, but with a lot of stammers and stumbles. I told the judge everything I'd told Ms. Matheson—getting the know-how on the computer, driving in the night to Karen Creek, finding the oil and gas intakes, pouring in the grit, making my getaway. I even told him about my panic when I thought I'd left the diagrams behind. The judge probably had Ms. Matheson's report right in front of him, or had read it at least, but he wanted me to have to say it out loud in public—to own it, I guess, to take responsibility with my own mouth. It made sense.

When I'd dwindled to an embarrassed silence, the judge asked when my intention to commit the crime had formed. That same day, I told him, in the afternoon, biking by the S.P. mill.

"And why, Mr. Fielder? Why did you decide to do it?"

I let the pool fill. "Well, I'd like to say I did it to protect the Methuselah forest, which is true, but really it was to get back at my father. I think you know what that was about. Another reason, too. A year ago when the protest started, they used that Cat to intentionally scare seven peaceful people chained in a roadway. My foster father was one of them. I didn't appreciate that."

"At what point did you come to regret what you had done?"

I took another sip of water. "To be honest? Not till summer, when they started suspecting the protesters. Before that, I had a lot of other things on my mind."

"The court is aware of those things." The judge paused. "Tell me, Mr. Fielder. Would you have come forward if your foster father and his group had not come under suspicion?"

I took a few seconds. "I hope so, your honor."

"In a similar situation in the future, Mr. Fielder, would you damage property again?"

"No sir, I would not. If I want to protest again I'll do it the way my foster father did at Karen Creek. Out in the open, in daylight, in peace. And take the consequences."

"Very well, Mr. Fielder. I appreciate your candor. How do you plead to the charge of Criminal Mischief in the First Degree?"

"I plead guilty, your honor."

The judge nodded and looked down to read.

"This court sentences you according to the terms negotiated by counsel, with one exception," he said, looking directly at me again. "Due to the extraordinary circumstances that contributed to your criminal behavior, and provided you strictly adhere to the provisions of this agreement for one full year, you will not be required to spend time in custody."

The judge took off his reading glasses and leaned back in his chair. Amazing how quickly a hanging judge can turn into the best, kindest uncle you never had.

"Mr. Fielder," he said, "I understand you're an avid reader."

"Yes sir, I am."

"Our laws are made of language. Do you know the derivation of the word 'mischief'?"

"No sir."

"The root is from Old French, and it means 'to end badly.'" He paused a moment. "Many young people who've made one poor decision—like you, Mr. Fielder—have passed through this court. In some cases the family was in poverty, in some there was no family, in many the defendant was involved with drugs. Years later, some of those young persons are still shuttling in and out of the legal system. Some are serving prison sentences for a more serious crime. A few I know to be dead, not from natural causes."

Now the judge leaned forward and just about lasered me with his eyes. "You've been through great trials, Mr. Fielder, great trials, but your advantages are great as well, compared to many others. My advice to you is simple. The year ahead is your story to write. Take it to a good ending, Mr. Fielder. I'm glad to have met you, and I hope never to see you again."

"Thank you, your honor."

"Good luck, Mr. Fielder."

He rapped his gavel and we were free to go.

In the hallway Mr. Rodnips was wearing a big grin. "Damn, Henry, I worried you might be blowing it, but you were the best lawyer in court today. Now keep your word, and everybody wins." He shook hands with the three of us and headed off in his rumpled suit, briefcase in hand, to meet with another young client.

* * *

I burned the old house in the first week of November, on a drippy day that dried out toward evening. The volunteer fire department had wanted to start it that morning, but I didn't want the entire glory of my fire diminished by daylight. "You need to practice at night too, don't you?" I asked, and they agreed to late afternoon. The situation was safe enough. There'd been plenty of rain, there weren't any near neighbors, and the place was crawling with firefighters and firetrucks. They wrapped the garage and shed and well house in fireproof space blankets, the apple trees too, and got the blaze started, using lots of gas or whatever it was because the house was so damp. Flames were soon cracking the glass out of the windows that still had any and licking up over the eaves. The volunteers ran their drills, laying out hoses, bashing in doors, talking over how they would respond if a life was at stake in a certain room.

Neighbors and a few strangers showed up like moths as twilight came on, yakking happily and going *ooh* when a part of the roof fell in and sent up huge whirls of sparks. The heat got a little less ferocious after the house had mostly collapsed and slower yellow flames had settled into the small jobs they hadn't cared about when they were young and out of control.

Fierce and fine as the fire was, though, I felt let down. I'd thought it would charge me like a big hit of meth, or hitting a home run, to watch my past pour up into the black hole of night, but all I felt was a dull sadness. Not because I was losing the ruined house, not about anything in particular, just a blue and somber mood as I walked circles around the burning house, somehow not all there like the fire was.

Tess came by for a while, but I was keyed on the fire and didn't feel much like talking. I apologized, but she said she totally understood, I should do what I needed to do and follow my feelings. We hugged, made a plan to see each other soon, and she took off. I'd worked up my courage and invited Abner, too, and looked around for him as the evening went on and the visitors thinned out.

I squatted to watch as the last pieces of inner wall fell, raising brief flurries of new flames, the house reducing to a cellar-full of brilliant red coals drifted in dunes, with jutting pipes and two or three standing timbers. I settled in the backyard, the yard where I used to feed the chickadees from my hand, where the owl and other birds had thrashed out of the trees on quake-day eve, where my father and I had played catch and thrown a football and shot beer cans with the .22, where I had played in the sandbox and the towhee came like a friend who knew me, and where my mother had carried me in her arms on cloudy days and sunny, on moonlit nights and starlit nights and even on gently raining nights, she told me, letting the rain come to my face, so that I would know this place even before I knew myself. *This is the world we are given, that we may give ourselves to it.*

Raven came out of the darkness after a while and sat next to me. He had arrived that afternoon and hung out with Cart and Josie, knowing that what I needed most right then was space. Now we sat in silence until I heard myself start talking. "I think what I'll do is, in a few days I'll clean up the pipes and other junk, and spread the ashes around. Maybe I'll sheetrock the garage and install one of the woodstoves from the house, you know, so I'll have a little place to come to. . . . Or maybe I'll sell the land and . . . ohit, what the hell do I know? I'll be the last one to know. . . ."

Raven let the night absorb my ramble. After a while he said, "You'll know when you have to know, Henry. There's no need to have a plan."

"I thought I'd feel really high," I said, "but all I feel is sad."

"Sadness is rich soil," said Raven. "Henry Thoreau called his sadness 'fertile.' He said it saved his life from being trivial."

"My soil just grows weeds. Why do I feel so *old?*"

"Maybe because you've scarcely had a chance to feel like a kid," Raven said. "I'd like to help, Henry. Any way I can."

I reached and touched his shoulder. He put his hand on mine, then kissed my hand and gave it back.

A car slowed on Stamper Road, turned into the driveway, and pulled up next to the white Dodge. I could hear reggae pounding through the closed windows and knew it was Abner.

"Tracker, what up?" he called, heading our way with a bottle in his hand.

"You are, dude. It's great to see you." We linked hands and gave each other a quick hug. I introduced him to Raven and we all sat down.

"Tracker, this is brilliant," said Abner, firelight all over his exultant face. "Let's roast fifty pigs! Feed the hungry! Here," he said, "drink and be saved."

I hadn't had drink or drug in four months, since my day at the beach with mushrooms. Tonight I'd given myself permission. I took a pull of tequila and so did Raven, who then excused himself to take a leak. He always knew the right thing to do.

"This is what a volcano looks like inside," said Abner. "This is the cauldron of possibility."

"Let's hope so."

"Dude, any chance you'll come back to school?"

I shook my head. "I don't mix well, Abs. But you know what? You're my best old friend and I wanna keep it that way."

"Yass!" said Abner, and we stood up and sealed the pact with tequila. "Make it gurgle, Tracker," he said, shaking his hair as I took my gulp. We both made it gurgle.

"Come on," I said, "let's take a turn around Krakatoa."

We took several, laughing, jostling, Abner bitching about his moody girlfriend, me reminding him he always had six more standing in line, all puckered up. We remembered funny stuff that had happened in my house and yard. We picked up lengths of water pipe that the firemen had pulled clear and whacked and jabbed at the coals, sending up blizzards of sparks, singeing our eyebrows, and Abner started a long riff on Pele, the Hawaiian fire goddess who longs for her lover but also kills her lovers. . . . "So you see, Tracker," he wound up, "she totally covers the whole expanse of human experience, see?"

"Does she cover this?" I said, and shoved him sprawling into a big rhododendron. Then I hauled him out and both of us took a drink and wore ourselves out howling into a drizzling rain.

There was only a slosh left in the bottle Abner handed me as we lurched toward his car. "All yours, Fire Dog. I'd help, but I never drink just before driving. . . ."

Raven was sitting shotgun in the white Dodge, reading with a headlamp.

"Tracker?" Abner said, with drunken earnestness. "Listen. Any way you turn—I mean, *whatever way,* man—we are friends forever. You hear me?"

"I hear you, Abs." We gave each other a full, hard, wrap-around hug.

"And you really, really shouldn't drive right now," I said, "but you will, so go with God, old son."

"Thanks for sharing your inferno!" he hollered from his car as he drove away, blasting reggae with the windows down.

I dumped myself into the back seat of the Dodge and handed the keys forward. "Home, Raven Bird. I'm a danger to society *and* the natural order."

He laughed and slid over to the driver's side. "You have a wild friend, Henry."

"Abner? Hellfire, I'm wilder'n him. I'm God's own fool."

Cart and Josie were still up and weren't upset that I was drunk. They'd given their okay. We had mulled cider and Raven played his flute for us—slow passages of something classical, mostly in rich lower tones that trembled all through me. Suddenly I was seized with envy that he could make beautiful music and all I could make was a big fire. Pretty soon I fell asleep on the sofa.

At breakfast, Cart talked with Raven about buying some pork the next time Sweet Grass slaughtered a pig. He and Josie had questions about the confederacy, wanted to visit. They went on talking as if

they'd known each other for years. I was hung over and had a hella-
cious headache and smelled of smoke and didn't get into the conversation. I got up, leaving half a waffle on my plate, and said goodbye
to Raven. I took Alka-Seltzer and two aspirin in the bathroom and
went back to bed.

twenty-nine

The weather was cold and clear, then warmed with a two-day rain. On my mom's birthday I drove my father's pickup to the graveyard. I'd found out how to flush the crankcase, done it twice, and the engine was running fine. It was a good old truck, a Ford, and I regretted trying to murder it. I'd been in it for thousands of miles with my dad. It kind of smelled like him. Lately I had started to smile when I thought of him, but something always choked it off, something that felt like a piece of barbwire hooked inside me. I'd been feeling pretty cheap since the judge had sentenced me. He thought monkeywrenching the bulldozer was the worst thing I'd done. If he'd known more, he would have been a lot harder on me. I halfway wished I'd confessed it to him, to Mr. Rodnips, to Ms. Matheson, to everyone. But this particular case was in the court of Henry Fielder—defendant, prosecutor, defense attorney, judge.

I hadn't been to the cemetery since I'd laid my father's ashes in the ground next to Leenie's, almost a year ago, so now I saw the two simple gravestones side by side for the first time. Same shape, same style of lettering, hers just a shade darker from taking half a year more weather. There lay their material remains in little boxes underground, their birth and death dates cut cold and final into rock.

I walked the woods looking for something to leave for my mother. I'd been so distracted, so unsettled, in the two weeks since burning the house that I asked Cart and Josie for an early Thanksgiving vacation to sort myself out. The big fire hadn't helped. Tess was on my mind, Raven was on my mind, and my mother and my father, of course, all pulling at me. *Why don't I know what I want?* I kept asking.

When I was little I'd sometimes wake to dawnlight in the window and the first birdsong—the first I was awake to hear—and I'd feel hungry for something I couldn't name. I'd go through lists in my mind of things I liked to eat or drink, but what I wanted wasn't anything I could name. By the time I gave up thinking, morning would be pouring through the window, the birds would be going it, and I'd be distracted and wouldn't feel the hunger anymore. Not till the next time I woke early, wondering how much earlier the first bird had sounded its first note while I was sleeping.

That hunger had felt pure, as if a single thing could answer it. My desire now felt much more complicated, yet I sensed that whatever it was that I wanted wasn't far away. I remembered what my mother had said when I told her, ten years old, about my dawnlight hunger. "*Longing* is a name for it," she told me. "It's a good path, Henry, a holy path. And longing is the path itself, not where the path leads."

As I remembered her words I saw what I hadn't known I'd been looking for—a leaf, recently fallen from a small oak, with two speckled brown galls the size of ping-pong balls on its underside. Galls are eggs, in a way. In the spring, a little wasp lays eggs in a green twig or leaf, and over the summer the oak forms a growing shell around the growing larva. By fall the larva is a young wasp eating the inside of his chamber, and one day he chews a hole clear through and flies away. Change of worlds! The gall dries from green to brown and stays on the leaf or twig. Some oaks grow those things like fruit, and they're more handsome than any crabapple.

My mom and I used to wonder, how did the tree come to make this deal with the wasp? Why a deal at all, since the oak gets nothing from it? The little wasp gets a condo with food and moisture, and one day it meets the air and never looks back. The scientific name for the wasp is *Besbicus mirabilis.* My mother found nothing about the first word, but she tracked down "mirabilis"—it means "miraculous." Felt that way to us. From the oak, we decided, it must be just a favor, a gift. When you have plenty of life you give some away. One more way the universe has found to be beautiful. One more verse in the greatest story never told.

I laid the galled oak leaf on her headstone, then stood facing my father's. Suddenly the barbwire yanked inside me and I found myself on my knees. "Dad," I said out loud, "you were wrong but you should still be here. I love you. I miss you. I'm sorry." I knelt a long while, then placed three things on his stone. A black-and-gold Roostertail, one of his favorite fishing lures. A thirty-ought-six cartridge, the kind his deer rifle took. And a yellow Bic lighter—the white man's fire drill. *Good idea to carry an extra. They're cheap and they don't weigh nothin'. . . .*

* * *

Back at Dismal Acre, I stoked the woodstove and set a mug of coffee on it to reheat. Josie appeared after a while, fresh from her darkroom.

"Thought I heard you," she said. "Come, I've got something to show you."

In the sour chemical smell of the darkroom, two of the prints hanging to dry were of me. In one I was sprawled on the backyard grass reading a book. The other, the one I liked, was a close-up—head turned, surprised maybe, my mouth slightly open with just a hint of a smile. "It doesn't look like me," I said.

"You look older," said Josie. "Your eyes especially. It's Henry moving on, able and ready."

"Or Henry ever-clueless in the one moment he looked almost smart."

I enjoyed Josie's laugh. "Are you feeling any more settled?" she asked.

"Maybe. But mainly clueless."

"I don't mean to pry, Henry. But if you feel like talking, I'd like to listen."

"I know," I said. "Maybe sometime. . . ."

We left the darkroom. I turned toward my bedroom, Josie toward the kitchen. Then I stopped.

"Josie?"

She turned, eyebrows lifted.

"How do you know if you're in love?"

She smiled and stepped toward me.

"If you're asking the question, Henry, you may be in love. For Cart it was sudden, but I didn't feel it right away. For me it was a close friendship that deepened. One day I realized, I've never felt this way before about anyone."

"But what if you think you love someone and it turns out you don't?"

"Then there's pain," Josie said. "For the other, if that person loves you, and for you too, because you at least *like* that person very much. Love is risk, Henry. Each person, each couple, lives it their own way, but to love is to open yourself to hurt."

"Okay," I said, "but what if the person you love is. . . ."

"Is what?"

I shook my head. "Never mind, but thanks."

Josie gave a sly smile. "Would you like to share anything more?"

"No I wouldn't, Ms. Nosey. But thank you. What you've told me helps."

* * *

A lot of Indians don't care for Thanksgiving any more than turkeys do, and why should they, but they have their own ways of expressing thanks. All people do. I don't know what religion is if it isn't giving thanks, kneeling to the greater power you belong to. Most people call it God, and that's a word I still use, but Nature is a better name. People speak of Nature as if it's something they don't live in, aren't part of, but we are *made* of Nature, body and mind, and the spirited body of the universe has been seeking forms and seeking life for billions of years, and I doubt it'll quit any time soon. "Nature," the word, goes back to a Latin verb meaning "to be born." The verb doesn't say what it is that's born or what gave birth to it or how the birth happened or why or when. Nature means that which is born, from the Big Bang to you and me and whatever's to come. Religion and science and philosophy all tell stories of it, and no story has all the truth but every good story has some. The one thing no story can deny is that there *is* a birth, and all things including us and our stories have come of that birth and belong to it, like a child belongs to its mother's breast. That, to me, is the mightiest truth of all. That's why I write Nature with a capital N.

Twenty years ago at Thanksgiving dinner, though, I was thinking of more specific things I was thankful for. The dinner was at Jonah and Cloudy's home. (She had moved in with him, an unprecedented development in their on-and-off romantic history.) Cart had finally warmed up to Jonah—time and a few beers at the Sam and Max Saloon had done it—and brought him a set of CDs by the cellist Pablo Casals, and Jonah was way, way touched. Josie brought him a handsome portrait of his log truck, all muddy and noble. Pastor Rogers, a widower, was at the dinner table, and Jonah's musician friends who'd played at Len Peppers's bedside, too. As usual, Jonah's barbequed turkey was moist and smoky, the rest of the food was fine and the conversation lively. Cloudy fed tidbits to Miss Clover from the table, at which Jonah berated himself for not yet accidentally stepping on Miss Clover's neck. He and Cloudy talked about my father, how much they missed him, and so I told about deer hunting on Steens Mountain when I was nine, the dawn that felt like the beginning of the world, when he'd said that I might see the buck before he did. I also told Len Peppers's story about my father tethering me to a tree to keep me out of trouble while they were fishing. I was talky from the wine with dinner, so I kept right on about Len—his music collection (which he had bequeathed to me, to Cart and Josie's horror), the dinner of hot dogs he roasted on a gas stove burner, his stories of the glory days of high-lead logging, and the way he'd had of advising me without ever once telling me outright what to do.

I shut up then so other people could testify.

Jonah and his friends played music after dinner, and then Cart and Josie brought out the dessert they had made, a plum pudding served warm with something called hard sauce, which is made of butter, sugar, and brandy. Not a hard sauce to like. With the pudding Cart served a special spiced coffee topped with blue-flaming brandy that he lit and spooned into each cup. The flame lasted a few seconds in the cups and was beautiful in the candle-lit room.

I'm in a new world, I thought, lying in bed that night, a world I might never have known. I thought again how lucky I was—for my mother, for the country and the state I was born to, for the gift that I might still have, for Cart and Josie and all the good people I knew. It was a treasure, a mother lode of good fortune, but something inside me kept saying no, no—some cramp, some cloud beneath the sun, some word spelled wrong that could never be right because I refused to see what it meant.

I know I slept because I know I woke. I made myself wake, I hauled myself right out of a dream that wasn't a dream at all. It started like the others but in color this time, in cold morning light, out behind the house again, but this time I don't see my father in the woods. I'm stiff, I'm clumsy, but I'm walking now, my footsteps crunching the frosted grass. I'm looking but can't spot him or what he's been working on. In the trees now, dappled shade and sun, I hear the river, and the joy that I might see it shivers me, but where is *he*? Standing straight like the tree trunks, grinning in the boughs? In the ground, ready to reach up like a root and trip me? Hunched in the open like a riverside boulder? But he's not, he's not here, and I break from the woods running through tall frosted grass for the river, I hear it, I'll see it any second, but suddenly a smell stops me—the grass is strewn with sawdust, sawn-off boards, curls of planed wood, and my knees buckle to the frozen ground as I breathe the good smell of the S.P. mill and stare disbelieving at a long imprint in the stiff grasses, square at one end, pointed at the other, and fresh boot prints where he leaned down and hefted the boat to his strong shoulders and walked it to the river.

The river! The river at last, only and always the river, the curling, sidling, rushing and whispering full-throated river, its numberless currents weaving as one and all of it slow-swirling from its depths in shadows blended with amber light, all of it eacing and riffling and rushing and gliding downstream, downstream, and away. The cry I've been hoarding so close for so long rips out of me—*Father!* He was here, right here, building his boat with the same hands that pulled me from the snowdrift and high-fived me at ballgames and lifted my quivering fish from the water and rubbed my shoulders as we lay watching for deer at the dawn of time. I look downstream where the river bends but there is only the river, only and always the river, flowing through and around me now, but I'm rising out of its lit and shadowed current because now is not my time. I must return, I must come back to the boy now crouched on his bed heaving with sobs and lit with a glimmering new joy.

The bedroom door flies open, Josie flips on the light with Cart behind her but I wave them off—"It's good," I manage to say, "it's something good"—and I get a pencil and pad from my desk and go back to my bed, the tears running, and sit and begin to write this down exactly the way it happened.

* * *

I slept again, deep, dreamless. When I woke, I knew. My compass had been set, like waking in the Methuselahs knowing I would walk to the coast, like waking in the foxfire tree knowing I must go home.

Cart and Josie looked anxious when I appeared in the living room, but I had showered and put on clean clothes and had a smile on my face from deep inside.

"Didn't mean to alarm you," I said, "but it's all good, it really is. I heard from my father. And now I have to make a little journey, and I have to drive, and I'll be gone overnight. Will you trust me?"

Josie spoke. "We do trust you, Henry, but we want to be sure you're as settled as you seem. . . ."

I walked over and took her head in my hands and kissed her forehead. "How's that?" I said. I did the same with Cart, then stood back and shrugged at them. "You knew this would be weird, right?" And I was out the door, Cart opening it behind me to holler "Call us, Henry. Be sure to call us." I waved my agreement.

It was late morning by then, I'd slept in. The day was bright and cool. I took my time, almost obeying the speed limit. Stopped at the coffee stand near Walton—it was open, amazingly—to fuel up with a triple short latte, then, a few miles later, pulled off on a gravel road to get out of the truck and make sure. I was nervous, fretting, but somewhere I was calm. I took some slow, deep breaths and pledged allegiance to my heart. My mother was beside me, riding shotgun, as I drove on and made the turn north, watching Eagle Boy throw Thunder into the water and walk away with his people. My father had thrown himself, he had done me that kindness, but I had been wrestling. Maybe I had even been fierce, though I wouldn't have guessed that fierceness would involve so much confusion and tear-fall. I was crying again when I made the next turn—and there, across the road in an open field, in daylight this time, was the coyote.

I got out of the truck and approached him slowly with my wet face and the open palms of my hands. He didn't run. I was broken wide open, and he knew it. He stepped toward me a little. I crossed the shallow ditch and stepped into the field. He came a few more steps, a few more, then sat on his haunches twenty feet away. I sat too. I looked into his yellow eyes and felt us merging like two sure streams. He wasn't pouring as full as I was—in his calm there was wariness, barbs of fear, the animal sense that had kept him and his ancestors from leg-hold traps and bullets and cyanide baits. He was sharing what he rightly could. It felt like a sunrise inside me, and in that new light a promise formed. In years to come I would struggle to keep it, betray it even, but I wouldn't give it up. I spread my arms and spoke within—to the coyote, to the visitant who'd saved my life, to my mother and my father, and to great Nature itself: *I will not waste it*, I said. *I will not waste this life.*

I felt the promise settle inside me and into the ground beneath.

I heard a car coming, so I slowly stood and bowed to the coyote. He kept sitting. I walked back to the truck, turned to look, and he was loping toward the woods. The car passed noisily on the gravel road.

At Sweet Grass I drove slowly past Commons, parked on the grass, and walked. A couple of confederates were out and waved. Raven must have seen me through the window, or maybe he just knew, but he was out the door before I got to the porch. I didn't say hi or ask if he was busy, I went up the steps and hugged him. I felt his sure hands, the firm warmth of his back and shoulders.

"I almost went home for the holiday," he said, "but something told me to stay."

I smiled. "You always know the right thing. My father came to me, Raven. One last time."

As I told him about it in the cottage, the words came out lame and stumbly, didn't do justice, but maybe I felt it so intensely the words didn't matter. I was shivering when I quit talking. We were quiet a while.

"He came to forgive you, Henry. I think you've forgiven him. Can you forgive yourself now?"

"I don't know," I said. "All I want now is to mourn him. The pain of it just ripped up inside me, Raven. We loved each other and he ruined that and I ruined him. It'll always hurt."

He came to the couch and held me, stroking my back as I cried. "Maybe now," he said, "you hurt enough to heal."

I nodded against his shoulder, got my breath back, and worked on my sniffles while he got up to bring the tea he'd set steeping.

"You know something?" I said. "You didn't even know what the trouble was, and you helped me. You said, if two people do awful things to each other and only one of them is left, it's up to him to make it better. I took that to heart."

"And he's helping too. He's taken his leave."

"Hey," I said, "remember that story I told you? Eagle Boy? At the end he throws Thunder into the lake and could totally destroy him, but he doesn't. 'You will never hurt me or my people again,' he says, 'but you will always live, muttering in the mountains and along the lakes and rivers.' That's my father."

We drank tea and after a while we took a ramble around the more-or-less boundaries of the Sweet Grass Confederacy, loose and free, talking about the coyote I'd shared spirit with, and a dream Raven'd had about me, and the house burning, and the glowworms, and Neckie. . . . "And the river!" I said. "Raven, I wish I could describe the river. . . ."

"You did a pretty good job. And I'm envious. Not all of us have numinous dreams."

"And not all of us know what 'numinous' means, Professor Bird."

He laughed. "You do know. You lived it last night."

I fell silent for a while, squirming inside with what I needed to say, wondering if I would, if I could. Raven felt my unrest and asked if something was wrong.

"Well, there's something else to tell you, and I don't know how to do it."

I saw his face freeze.

"No," I said, "I didn't mean. . . . I just mean, I can't believe I'm saying it. I hardly know you, Raven . . . but I think I'm in love with you."

He made a sound like a sigh and a groan together.

I put my palms to his chest and felt him, his flanks, his hips. He put his arms around me and we swayed together, side to side. He smelled musky, good, like old sweat. He kissed my neck, then let go and ran his right hand through my hair, then both hands. His face was pale and beautiful in the twilight, his eyes swimming with tears.

"I've loved you from the day I met you, Henry."

"I know," I said.

"Let the evening sky and first stars be my witness," he said, looking straight into me. "Henry Fielder, I will love you and honor you and care for you as long as you will let me."

We walked home in the dusk, holding hands.

"So," I said in the cottage, "I don't know what we do now. . . ." It felt like rafting toward Rainie Falls that first time, like setting out west from an earthquake toward the Pacific Ocean.

"I do." Raven smiled like a kid, raised a finger, went to the cupboard and poured two glasses of black rum. We clinked glasses, then I started laughing and he did too.

Raven asked me to stoke the woodstove while he put some music on—Patsy Cline, in my honor—and tooled around the kitchen pulling some supper together, sandwiches, beet and carrot sticks, a bottle of red wine, and one candle on the table between us.

"I don't know how to tell Cart and Josie," I said.

Raven reached across the little table and took my hand.

"They already know, Henry. I mean, they don't know what you've told me today, but that first time I came over, to watch you play ball?

I told them my feelings for you. They had every right to know. I told them I would never pressure you into anything. That I would pull back at your first sign of discomfort."

"And they said . . . ?"

"They said, *'Get out of here, you fucking faggot!'*"

When we were done laughing, Raven went on. "They told me how much you mean to them, told me about Tess, and said they understood my feelings. They had no objection, they said, but they would hold me to my word."

"Wow," I said, shaking my head. "Those two just keep amazing me. You know, I said I'd call them tonight, and I was dreading it, but you just made it a whole lot easier."

When I came back from Commons, Raven had some different music on—a piano concerto by Rachmaninoff, he told me—and we sat on the couch and drank wine and smoked some weed grown straight out of Neckie's heart. We told stories of growing up and dealing with school and feeling puny and having fathers we loved who didn't get us. I talked about my mother and he talked about his. We decided we'd go to Yakima sometime so I could meet his mom. Eventually I fell asleep and woke, slowly, with my head on his lap, his left arm on my side and hand on my chest.

"Mmm," I said. "Can we go to bed now?"

"Yes," murmured Raven. "And I'll hold you all night if you'll let me, Henry, but that's all. If we have sex I'm raping you, by law."

"Hey. What I do is up to *me*."

He gave a mirthless chuckle. "In some states the age of consent is sixteen, which makes more sense, but I don't feel like driving."

"That's fucked up," I said.

"I owe it to your parents, Henry. And to you. You're on probation, remember?"

In bed we talked some more, laughed a lot. Drowsy again, I stroked his hair and asked, "Is this why you named yourself Raven?"

"And because the raven has many voices," he said. "I'm a poet and writer. Or I hope to be."

"So what's the name your parents gave you?"

He groaned. "I suffered from that name. It's Lynn. Lynn Sorenson."

epilogue

Who are you really, wanderer?

—William Stafford,
from "A Story That Could Be True"

I probably should apologize for tricking you like that—if I did—but I refuse. You made your own assumption. Chalk it up as a cheap stunt by a guy who's never written a book before.

Raven and I courted for the better part of a year. To use his word, it was lovely. We went on dates, we hiked and camped in the mountains, on the coast, but well before my 18th birthday it just got too silly. Raven was iron-willed to the end, so I took it upon myself to seduce him into seducing me to put both of us out of our misery. It wasn't hard to do. When we entered into sexual love it felt as entirely right and natural and beautifully pleasurable as anything Tess Bailey and I had done together.

It taught me something painful, too. I knew I would never entirely know what drove my father to rape me. He had lost Leenie, he was losing me, he expressed his pain as anger, I resisted him, mocked him, and a moment came when I was vulnerable and he was drunk enough to let himself do it. It was a moment of wildness, when Nature boiled up unrestrained. And, though it was painful and humiliating and felt all wrong, not every part of me may have agreed. The cruelest aspect of sexual abuse, a therapist helped me see, is that the victim sometimes feels a degree of pleasure and hates himself for it. On quake-day morning, it was only when my father said I'd probably enjoyed it that the cold fury came over me and I walked out and shut him and the memory behind a door. He'd violated me. It was terribly wrong. But as I explored with Raven the terrain of physical love, I came to see that I had left my father to die because I couldn't accept an aspect of my own being I thought forbidden.

We lived at Sweet Grass in the little cottage for almost a year—I got my wish—then migrated north so that Raven could do graduate work in English at Portland State. I worked as a waiter in a few restaurants and took some writing and literature courses at Portland Community College. We lived in Southeast, the Hawthorne district—it was less trendy then—and from there I walked all over the City of Roses and got to like it very much, especially the river and the coffee houses and the bookstores. I naturalized to Portland as easily as the raccoons have. Raven and I cheered on the now-extinct Triple-A Portland Beavers at Civic Stadium, played softball in a league, and when we could afford it ate out and went to the symphony, the opera, and every Willie Nelson, Merle Haggard, Garth Brooks, and Emmy Lou Harris concert that Raven could tolerate.

So what happened? Lynn—he'd switched to his birth name by then—was writing poetry and creative nonfiction, got some published, and was accepted into an MFA program out East. I had started going on solo backpacks and climbing some Cascade peaks, and I balked at leaving Oregon. I took an airplane to see Lynn once and came home on the train, resolved never to fly again. We talked on the phone and wrote letters for a while and never officially broke up, we just kind of drifted into separate lives. I was sad about it, he was too, but it didn't feel tragic. It felt like a season had turned.

I wandered the West in my father's truck for a few years and came to love dry landscapes—southeast Utah, northern New Mexico, Baja

California. I fished, hunted a little, lived cheap, slept in the truck a lot, drank in dives with good jukeboxes. I didn't work a job very often. When I'd hit twenty-one and Jonah signed over my full fortune, I'd been smart enough to sock three quarters of it away in safe investments with Cart and Josie in charge. Uncle Sam was still sending me Social Security, and I lived mainly on his kindness. I kept a journal, and every once in a while I scratched out what I hoped might be a story or a poem. I hooked up now and then but found I don't care much for casual sex. Call me old-fashioned, but I believe sex is a wildness best contained in a vessel of monogamous love.

I kept returning to Oregon, checking in on Cart and Josie and my home country, and when I was twenty-seven I went to a Duckworth High School reunion to see Abner Truitt, who had made good on his ambition to be first a ski bum and then a chef and a ski bum. Tess Bailey was there. We had parted on fairly good terms, though she had been shocked that I was breaking up with her for a man. Now she was coming off a brief bad marriage to a guy she'd met at UO. We dated for a while, were smitten again, and ended up living together in Portland for a couple of years. If we weren't in love we were at least deeply in like, and we were happy. Her clock was ticking, though, she wanted kids, and though she was too kind ever to say it directly, she didn't see a lot of future with a bisexual vagabond who was almost thirty, had vague ambitions to be a literary writer, and was taking the slow scenic route from boy to man.

So I resumed my drifty ways. I worked on a ranch in eastern Oregon and another in Nevada. I tended bar in a small-town tavern or two, and never stayed away very long from my old compadre Uncle Al. In the spirit of the times, I resumed and advanced one of the bad habits of my teenage years—Vicodin or oxycodone plus beer or whiskey. When you get the balance right, every moment plays in the key of Warm Delight Major, and it's not a rough landing the next morning.

I knew perfectly well I was failing the fierceness test. I knew I was breaking my promise to the coyote, to the visitant, to my mother and father, and to Nature itself. I didn't feel worthy of the sixteen-year-old who had made that promise. Then, one evening at Big Sur, on my way to Mexico, I watched the sun go down, and right below me a gray whale spyhopped in the calm swell. Seemed to be looking right at me. My mother's long black hair trailed through my sleep that night, and in the morning I turned the truck around and drove back to Portland. To keep away from the pills and hooch I started doing long hikes and summit scrambles again. I met some serious rock climbers on Mt. Washington and developed my skills at Smith Rock, Yosemite, the High Sierra. I was not a gifted climber but became a capable one. It felt like something real, a solid foothold, to be pretty good at something I loved to do.

My occasional dabbling on the page became a nightly session, and I brought to the work a new grittiness and patience. Writing is a lot like climbing—the route isn't entirely clear at the start, each move makes possible the next, and when you finish you've worked hard and you see a little more than you saw before. I didn't dare call myself a writer, but I had taken up the work. That's where I was when he of the green eyes re-entered my life, asked the inevitable question, and nudged and cajoled and practically whipped me into writing this book. Lynn and I hung out and slept together and for a while I thought I was in love with him again. I wasn't, and he wasn't in love with me. We were both in love with the way we had been in love those years ago. We will always be friends.

Writing my story seemed to put me back into my life again, and somewhere along the way I decided I would move back home when the book was finished. Two months ago I unpacked in my old bedroom at Dismal Acre. ("When we need a full-time nurse you're out the door," Cart warned.) I'll be moving again soon, but not far. I cleared the Scotch broom and blackberry brambles off the old homeplace, and before winter, I hope, I'll be done converting the garage into a little home. I think it'll be a good place to write. My vegetable garden is prospering in the big raised bed of the old house foundation. I'm getting my stove wood in, thinning dead and live pecker poles in the parts of the woods that need it.

I intend to meet the neighbors, if they'll have me. My gift has flickered now and again in the last twenty years. There was a particular pigeon in Waterfront Park, a bobcat in the Escalante country of southern Utah, here and there a deer or crow. Mostly I've ignored it, so mostly it's gone to sleep. Lynn always said that my gift is a sport, a genetic mutation, and I owe it to Nature to have kids and pass it on. Maybe. I think it's a potential in all of us that we'd do well to develop. We write and make movies about meeting extra-terrestrial beings, but we've scarcely gotten to know our evolutionary home-folk here on Earth.

Speaking of which, Cart Stephens and company couldn't, in the end, stop the logging at Karen Creek. But they did win stricter limits, and the thinned areas of the greater Methuselah forest have healed over, though some sizeable ghost stumps haunt the woods. Timber communities are still hurting in western Oregon, and the federal money they've been getting to replace public timber revenues is dwindling. Siuslaw Pacific is still in business, though, and another mill south of Daugherty is set to reopen next year. Timber will never be king again, but Jonah Rutledge does as well now in his specialty tree service as he used to driving his log truck. (And by the way, he and Cloudy married and had a boy, now fifteen, and I'm his godfather). The Rutledges and Stephenses and I belong to the Long Tom Watershed Council, along with woodlot owners and environmentalists, ranchers and farmers, city dwellers in south Eugene, and a lot of others who care about where they live. A watershed gathers everything it touches, humans included. As I told Tess Bailey twenty years ago, the wildness is still in the land and always will be. Wolves are coming west from the Snake River country. They're in the Cascades now. Some night I hope to hear one howling right here in my hard-worked Coast Range hills.

Cart and Josie are in their early eighties and doing pretty well. Cart has had three joints replaced and hopes to live long enough, he likes to say, to complete the set. Josie is white-haired, unslowed, lighter than air. They want to stay on at Dismal Acre as long as they can, and I aim to help. Don't think you have to, they keep saying, you don't owe us a thing, you should live your life. I'm living it, I tell them. And to myself I say: I keep my own accounts.

I pretty much ignored my mother during my rambling years, but now she's coming around again, an easy breeze, a warmth like a hand on the back of my neck. She's here and gone before I know it, leaving me with a pang and a smile.

I think of my father often and mostly with pleasure. I remember him teaching me how to fish and swing a maul, how to move my feet as a second baseman. I often wonder what would have happened if he had held on and Jonah had rescued him and he had recovered from his wounds. I know I wouldn't have shunned him. I wouldn't have turned him in to the law, either, or allowed Cart and Josie to. I forgave him many years ago for raping me. I like to think he wouldn't have forgiven himself, but I hope it wouldn't have crippled him, either. It didn't cripple me. If he had lived, it would have taken time to know each other in a new way. We would always be father and son. Maybe we could have been friends.

When the afternoon darkens and I hear him grumbling and muttering in the hills, I smile, I breathe the good air freshening with rain. He's that close, and closer yet. I'm thirty-five years old. He's in the reflection I see in the window every night when I sit down to my desk. He's in the way I make biscuits and gravy, the way I steer the truck with my left hand, the way I brood sometimes when the wrong team wins. If my father had lived, I hope he'd have forgiven me for walking out on him; but he didn't live, and for that

I will never forgive myself. The memory is like a limp that pains me with every step, but the pain also reminds me that I am alive, that the journey goes on, and that maybe I'm a better man now than either of us was when each of us did the unforgiveable. I like to think so. And I like to think, if he had lived, my father might even have been proud of me.

acknowledgments

This novel had a long coming of age involving much help from others. I am particularly indebted to my editor, Jack Shoemaker, who responded with considerable patience, forbearance, and loyalty as the manuscript evolved, and to Tracy Daugherty, without whose insights and encouraging interest I might have abandoned the effort. Jim Hepworth read early and late drafts and saved this newbie novelist from several embarrassments. Rick Sterry read multiple drafts and gave valuable criticism practically every step of the way.

Marilyn Daniel, Morgan Smith, Jane Vandenburgh, and Susan Bobst read the novel at one stage or another and gave helpful feedback. I'm particularly grateful to Morgan for her steady encouragement.

For sharing her expertise in local natural history I thank fellow writer Evelyn Hess. Jim Spindor gave knowledgeable advice on legal affairs. Old friend Dan Patel, M.D., had answers when I had medical questions. Any inaccuracies reflect my own confusion, not theirs.

The following people too were helpful informants or advisers as I researched and wrote the book: Andre Lee Call, Marilyn Daniel, Mike Davitt, Jon Derby, Mick Garvin, Schuyler Hamilton, Stephen Hamilton, Sally Kirkpatrick, Josh Laughlin, Chris Spindor, Jon Spindor, John Stacey, Norm Vidoni, and Ray Weldon. My sincere thanks to all.

John Laursen gave invaluable advice on the design of the book.

ACKNOWLEDGMENTS

I am also grateful to these businesses, institutions, and agencies:

Applegate Pioneer Museum, Veneta (Special thanks to Violet
    Shafer, Manager)

Elmira High School, Elmira (Special thanks to Shannon Hart,
    English teacher)

Hull-Oakes Lumber Company, Monroe (Special thanks to
    Nathan Nystrom)

Lane County Juvenile Justice Center, Eugene

Lane County Sheriff's Office (Special thanks to Linda Cook,
    Emergency Program Manager)

Lane County District Attorney's Office, Medical Examiner
    Division (Special thanks to Kathleen Korth)

Papé Machinery, Eugene

Swanson Brothers Lumber Company,
    Noti (Special thanks to Ronda Shankle and Cliff Thorne)

Two books were crucial to the American Indian presence in this
book. Great thanks to Judy Rycraft Juntunen, May D. Lasch, and
Ann Bennett Rogers, authors of *The World of the Kalapuya* (Benton
County Historical Society and Museum, 2005), without which I
would still be scrabbling for information, and to Jarold Ramsey, editor of the indispensable *Coyote Was Going There: Indian Literature of
the Oregon Country* (University of Washington, 1980). And my deepest thanks to the Kalapuya peoples and the Klamath and Modoc
peoples whose oral literature I have made use of.

ACKNOWLEDGMENTS

Like most of my books, this one was written mainly at home, but I did significant work on it during these residencies elsewhere:

The Grass Mountain Residency at Cascade Head, Oregon,
a program of the Sitka Center for Art and Ecology, founded by Frank and Jane Boyden. Summer 2011.

The spirited retreat called Playa, on Summer Lake, Oregon,
founded by Julie Bryant and Bill Roach. Fall 2012.

The bayside home of David and Marge Steward, Baranof Island,
Alaska, arranged through the Island Institute in Sitka.
Fall 2013.

Ocean Haven, best writing hole-up on the Oregon Coast,
owned and managed by Christie DeMoll with the spirit of Bill James. Numerous stays, 2006 to 2016.

A place known simply as "the ranch," my dryside home away
from home, Roger and Karen Hamilton, proprietors.
Numerous stays, 2008 to 2016.

Last and first, I thank my wife, Marilyn Matheson Daniel, whose love has held steady as a rock amid the torrents of wealth and glamor my writing career has brought us.